Palms and Minarets

SELECTED STORIES

Vincent O'Sullivan

VICTORIA UNIVERSITY PRESS

VICTORIA UNIVERSITY PRESS
Victoria University of Wellington
PO Box 600 Wellington

© Vincent O'Sullivan 1992

ISBN 0 86473 230 9

First published 1992

This book is copyright. Apart from
any fair dealing for the purpose of private study,
research, criticism or review, as permitted under the
Copyright Act, no part may be reproduced by any
process without the permission of
the publishers

Published with the assistance of
a grant from the Literature Committee of the
Queen Elizabeth II Arts Council
of New Zealand

ACKNOWLEDGEMENTS

'Grove', 'The Boy, The Bridge, The River', 'Palms and Minarets' have appeared previously in *The Boy, The Bridge, The River* (John McIndoe Ltd/Reed, 1978); 'The Corner', 'That's the Apple for You', 'The Witness Man', 'The Professional', 'Dandy Edison for Lunch' in *Dandy Edison for Lunch* (John McIndoe Ltd, 1981); 'The Club', 'The Last of Freddie', 'Good Heads', 'Survivals' in *Survivals* (Allen & Unwin, 1985); 'Billy Joel Her Bird', 'Putting Bob Down', 'the snow in spain', 'Testing, Testing . . .', 'Terminus' in *the snow in spain* (Allen & Unwin, 1990); 'Coasting' in *Landfall* 181, 1992, 'Hims Ancient and Modern' in *Metro*, June 1992.

Printed by GP Print, Wellington

Contents

7	Grove
18	The Boy, The Bridge, The River
63	Palms and Minarets
81	The Corner
87	That's the Apple for You
93	The Witness Man
110	The Professional
114	Dandy Edison for Lunch
132	The Club
144	The Last of Freddie
156	Good Heads
162	Survivals
183	Billy Joel Her Bird
187	Putting Bob Down
199	the snow in spain
209	Testing, Testing . . .
215	Terminus
222	Hims Ancient and Modern
235	Coasting
252	Taking in the East

for Deirdre and Dominic
arohanui

Grove

Grove's face wasn't injured, as far as you could tell, but it curved in on one side, so that his left temple and jaw were at least an inch further out than his left cheek. Whether he talked or smiled, his lips on that side stayed straight and together, and the right side of his face moved by itself. And there were two deep lines that ran from beside his nostrils almost to the end of his chin. He wasn't scarred or hideous or funny. You didn't want to laugh at his face and you didn't want to say you felt sorry for him. But I can't remember being in any company with him when people didn't tend to look at him rather than at anyone else. They wouldn't let on, but they were absorbed by his dent.

'You can't take your eyes off it can you?' Mary said. She was McCaffrey's daughter, and used to come round to the flat on Wednesday nights, on her way home from CYM or whatever she called it. She'd come in on Saturdays to get my lunch, and of course I'd have to go to her place whenever I took her out. Her father insisted on the old niceties, sitting there with his scotch in his hand in front of one of his own latest TVs. He'd led his wife a dance with his drinking but he never offered me one because of his daughter.

'Well you can't either,' I told her. Grove had been in the flat two months, and Mary was still as fascinated by his face as when she'd first seen it. We'd asked him to share that weekly dinner on Sundays, but he ate with us only twice. Then he told us a lie and said there was a small group he blew with at one o'clock. I found out later that the group met at three, yet he left shortly after midday, and must have bought a hamburger in town. When I told Mary this she told her mother and her mother said that it showed how delicate he was. I didn't think the word gelled with the bent face and the long awkward silences and I said, 'I think he's scared of women, that's the real reason.'

'No fear he isn't,' she said.

We seemed to talk about him a lot, about what we didn't know more than what we did. 'He likes music, all right?' Mary said, ticking off the little finger of one hand with the forefinger of the other.

'Right,' I said.

'He's polite, and he's clean.'

'Right again.'

'He's always punctual.'

'And that's about it.'

'It *can't* be,' Mary said.

'What else is there?'

'What else should there be?'

I said, 'If there's nothing else why do we think there is?' Mary laughed and said, 'As long as he keeps playing wherever he is for the next hour, anyway.' We'd been lying on my bed talking about him and I began unbuttoning her blouse. We always seemed to have our eye on the clock.

'Just a minute,' she said. She took a chain with a medal on it from round her neck. She leaned across me with it closed in her fist, and put it beside the alarm clock on the chair by my bed.

'Think it's not so bad if you take that armour off?' I asked her.

'Never you mind why I do it,' she told me. Sometimes I thought of old McCaffrey when she looked sly like that, her lips slightly apart, her hair brushing my face as she came back from depositing her medal. I thought how he'd need more than his bottle of scotch a day if he knew how his little lady ended her Wednesday nights and Saturday afternoons.

One day I said to him, 'Why do people always call you Grove?'

'They always have,' he said.

I was rinsing a shirt in the bath while he stood before the mirror, shaving the straight side of his face. 'I didn't mean that,' I explained to him. 'I mean why don't you get called Graham like your parents called you?'

'They've always called me Grove too,' he said. 'It's no problem.'

It was like that when you spoke to him. He gave you the feeling that it wouldn't matter what you asked him, or that it made any difference to him whether you liked his answer or thought it was nonsense.

'It's like he can't imagine needing to stress anything that's the truth,' Mary said. This was another time, when she asked him one afternoon if he ever danced himself at the places he played at, and he said, No, that if he liked a girl it was better to talk to her than dance, and that if a girl didn't like him it wasn't fair to bail her up, she might say yes she'd dance with him because she felt sorry for him, or because he was in the band and some girls liked the band to make a fuss of them. 'So there's no point is there?' he'd said.

When Mary said the bit about truth I said, 'That's all very well but he lies about Saturday afternoons doesn't he?'

'That kind of excuse's got nothing to do with it,' she insisted. 'It's not the same thing at all.'

I hardly saw Grove except at weekends and breakfast. Mostly in the mornings he'd be finishing in the kitchen when I came in. If we were there at the same time he'd chat about the band, or occasionally about work, where he'd just been put on some union committee, I think he said. On Sundays he would do his washing and read. He had no preferences when it came to reading. He'd pick up any kind of book and seem to enjoy it. Mary brought him a couple of novels once that he said he liked, but he said the same about some Plymouth Brethren thing a fellow at the milk factory had given him, and about a book he'd found in the bus shelter. It was a study of Mexico and must have been left there by a student.

'But you can't like *everything* you read,' I said to him. I'd looked at the Mexican book, and it wasn't accounts of battles and peaces that didn't last but about growth rates and projected development and there were pages of graphs and figures.

'I don't read so very much,' he said.

'But what you do read.'

'There's reasons for books,' he said. 'Even not very good ones.'

'What's that got to do with it?'

'I mean the reasons are always interesting,' he said. 'The reasons why they write them.'

He had his hollow side towards me and I thought for a minute is he having me on? But Grove didn't ever joke, so there was no point thinking he didn't mean what he said. A couple of times he had seen me with electrical books, and he stood perhaps two or three minutes looking at the one diagram, although he didn't ask what it meant. One time the diagram was of a radar system that theoretically dispensed with antennae. The other was in a fifty-year-old book that I'd picked up for curiosity, and it explained positive and negative charges in a way a child could understand. He looked at both of them carefully then put the books down and began on something else.

I'm certain McCaffrey thought his daughter could do better for herself than take up with me. He was hardly in a position to say it, seeing the maintenance work depended mostly on my efforts, so he just said to Mary had she ever thought of a trip overseas? He'd give her half the fare if she saved the other half. And he never mentioned her to me at work. He was out half the day, at golf if the weather was all right or along at the Commercial, in the private bar where he had his own private tankard on a peg near the Johnnie Walker ad. A couple of afternoons he might sit in his swivel-chair going through orders and catalogues that sooner or later he'd pass on to me.

I was glad often that it was his daughter I was having a go at. It kind of evened things, although that had nothing to do with my liking her, I mean, that was an extra. I'd seen her in the workshop several times and was thinking how to speak to her before I even knew who she was. She was about an inch taller than I was, and if she wore her hair up she could look unapproachable. Then once I was meeting her after work we'd go for a drink before walking over the bridge. I'd leave her at the corner of the park beside the river and keep on, up past the ugly grey church and the statue with its arms raised as though it were in a line-out. The old man wouldn't let her out more than two nights a week, and as often as not if we went to the movies her younger sister would come too.

'You're nearly twenty,' I said. 'Tell him to get lost.'

'That wouldn't help,' Mary said. She looked at me as she did when she wanted to tease me and said, 'It'd scare you like hell, wouldn't it, if I left home to live with you?'

'That wouldn't be fair on Grove,' I said, to make a joke of it. 'Ladies' things in the bathroom and all.' And then I said, 'You know, I wouldn't mind going down to the Arcadia one night.'

'To listen to him?'

'And watch him,' I said. 'I can't imagine what he'd be like when he's playing and in public and that can you?'

'Wait until he asks us,' Mary said.

'God,' I said. 'Imagine old Grove with strobes on!' Suddenly I could see him there after all, with his bell-bottoms and the medallion he carried in his pocket until he was in the hall and the light sliding up and down his trombone and his head like a dented kettle.

'Don't be at him all the time,' she said.

'Rather stay home for a treat then?' I asked her.

'That'd be nicer.'

When we did get home that Saturday, after an afternoon up at the park, Grove was sitting on the sofa with a woman who must have been pushing thirty-five. He stood up and said very formally, 'This is my friend Ruth.'

'Hello.' She smiled and I could tell her teeth weren't her own. Her breasts were huge inside a pink blouse and silly pale blond curls were licked down over her forehead. Her skirt was short although Mary said that length had been out for months now.

'Hello,' Mary said. Grove asked her would she like to sit next to Ruth?

'No, you stay there Grove,' she told him. She sat in the armchair near the window. She looked very good like that, the pale curtain just stirring behind her dark hair.

Grove was dressed up in his suit and glitter shirt and string tie. I thought how ridiculous he looked next to that tart, his jaw longer than ever in the way the late light glanced over it. I could tell he was pleased that we'd come in time to meet her.

'Ruth works in the TAB,' Grove said. 'Her husband grows strawberries along the Cambridge Road.'

'That's when I'm there, that is,' Ruth said. She smiled knowingly at Mary and Grove smiled quietly on the other side, pleased to see the two women taking to each other.

'She doesn't get on with her husband,' Grove explained.

'The other way round, more likely,' Ruth said. Her tongue came out and ran along her lips, making the pale lipstick like a wet lolly. I thought for God's sake Grove haven't you any idea at all? Mary said she would make a cup of tea and Ruth said yes, that'd be lovely, she was dry as a sandpit at the moment. I followed Mary about thirty seconds later. I went up close to her but she put her finger on my lips and said in a loud voice that was meant to sound ordinary, 'You can rinse the teapot if you want to help.' I tipped the old leaves out beneath a scraggy hydrangea and stood in the back porch. Mary kept making signs to me from where she leaned against the bench. She said later that she thought I'd break out laughing or say something Grove would hear and be hurt by.

From the kitchen I could see through the door crack into the sitting room. Ruth had opened a metal powder compact and was rapt in the little mirror. Grove touched very lightly the hair that curled above her pink collar. It was a shy sort of touch, as though he were brushing the skin of a baby. He didn't speak and she smiled at him before she clicked the compact shut. Mary had told me once that compacts like that look like the things priests take with them to accidents.

Mary became impatient with my prying at them. 'You can take the tea things in,' she told me. 'Then you can put some biscuits on a plate for us.' As I took a cup and saucer in each hand she added in a whisper, 'Don't stay in there longer than you have to. We'll go round home for tea.'

We sat in the room with them for ten minutes. It was long enough for me to have a quick second cup, and for Ruth to tell us what must have been half her life story. The climax was that old pig who was the father of her two children, who was becoming more objectionable all the time. 'You wouldn't believe what he says in front of those kids.' She clicked her tongue, to give us some idea of how vile he was.

'How old are they?' Mary asked.

'Peter's eight and Bronwyn's six,' Ruth said. And then, carefully, 'We've been married just over nine years.'

'That's where the children are now,' Grove told us. 'Their father's looking after them.'

'Not for much longer, he isn't. Not if I can help it.' I poured more tea rather than say anything. It amazed me that Grove just didn't see what was obvious as the day. I mean, she only had to hitch at her bra strap through her blouse, or uncross her legs so that she could ease down the heel of one shoe with the toe of the other, for you to tell what a bag she was. You didn't need to get as far as her teeth or her gritty hair or the ladder that began in a small hole behind the crossed knee and disappeared somewhere in the lump of her thigh.

Grove actually spoke to her as he'd once spoken to Mary's mother, when she had called in to say Mary had flu coming on and would I like a lift round to see her? She had tried not to stare at Grove and I think he knew this, yet he asked her to sit down, and in a few minutes he had old lady McCaffrey telling him about the time she'd lived in Eltham, years before Grove's family had settled there. Her eyebrows were cocked as much as to say you wouldn't think me that old, would you?

Even now Grove looked solemn. He sat with an elbow on the arm of the settee, his fist knuckled into the hollow side of his head. I made the usual allowances for women not being as affected by looks as men are, but he still struck me as pretty near impossible. I said this to Mary later in the evening and she said, 'You're getting obsessed with him. You should look for a new flat if he's getting on your nerves.'

'He's all right to flat with,' I said.

'Then the rest is his business, isn't it?' She had to agree though that

Ruth was a bit rough round the edges. When I'd almost finished my second cup that afternoon and Mary was waiting for me, standing in the doorway with her suede jacket already pulled up at the collar, Ruth had said, 'You'd think he'd make more effort with the children though, wouldn't you?'

'Won't he let you have them?' Mary asked.

'Oh, I haven't left him. I mean, when you've got a young family well you've got a young family, haven't you? But I feel like a few nights off *sometimes*,' she said. Her appeal was very simply to reason.

'He doesn't even cook for them properly when she's not there,' Grove added. He was looking at her although he spoke to us.

'Cook?' she said. '*Cook*? That's not half of it.' She leaned towards Grove, her hand resting on his knee. Her cigarette was burned down almost level with her stained fingers. 'You mightn't believe this,' she said. 'The kids' own father. But the other morning I went in about breakfast time. I'd been at my girlfriend's for the night, and I can't ring him to let him know because he's too stubborn to have the phone reconnected. So I walked in just as they were all sitting at the table, no cloth or anything, just their plates of Kornies, and he said right across the kids as if they weren't even there, "Been out rooting again, have you?" Can you imagine that in front of kids? "Been out *rooting*?"'

I looked to see how Mary took it. I was always careful what I said in front of her and I felt embarrassed, but she simply said, 'I suppose he was worried about where you were.'

Except for a few pale spots where a camellia tree stood, it was dark at the side of the house when we came back from Mary's. We'd told her parents we were going on to a dance. It was only nine o'clock. I held Mary's hand until I'd crossed the kitchen and felt above the fridge for the light cord.

'We've got four hours,' I said.

'At least four.' Mary kicked her shoes off and moved her feet backwards and forwards over the lino the way a bull paws. We'd been impatient to get away and back to the flat, only it was the one Saturday in a dozen when her father had come in early. He'd had more than his share, Mary's mother said, which meant he kept pouring himself a third of a glass of scotch and sloshing water on it while he kept up this spiel about the shop and the retailers and the rest of it. He had taken me into the lounge, to talk in his uneven slurred voice about the business in Frankton he was going to take over. 'He's had the place for two years and hasn't made a cracker out of it. He thinks there's no money in TVs! I thought haven't you heard of colour, mate, but if he wants his funeral in black and white we won't be the ones to stop him, eh?' Mary came and put her bare feet on my shoes and her arms round my neck and said, 'Get along then.' Her weight pressed where the laces of one shoe went crooked into my foot and I wanted to tell her to get to hell off, it was hurting me. I was halfway across the sitting room, my hands holding the tops of her legs under her dress to balance her, when she brought her arm around and spread the palm of her hand flat across my mouth. I licked her palm but she said 'Shhh!' against my ear and nodded her head at the sofa. Ruth's purse and her scuffed white shoes were lying on it.

'What're they there for?' I said.

'They can't have gone out. They must be in Grove's room.' I let her down from my shoes and swore. 'And what are we supposed to do?'

'Just keep quiet,' Mary said. She took my hand now, and led me on tiptoe to the open door of my room. Grove's door was closed. It seemed ridiculous to think of him tucked away in there with a woman.

Inside my bedroom I said, 'Well there's no need for us to go sneaking about. They must have heard us come in.'

'Be nice to them,' Mary said. She wouldn't let me put the light on, then told me not to let my shoes drop to the floor. To make sure, she knelt down and took them off for me. I'd already unzipped her dress and I unhooked her as she squatted in front of me. With only the street light from up the road her breasts were like two pale bowls.

'Hurry up,' I said. I wanted her to think I was on edge to get to bed but I disliked her in front of me like that. Her shoulders looked rounded like an old lady's and she had forgotten for once about the chain and medal around her neck. Later on when I lit a cigarette her fingers were moving round her throat and touching it, although she said nothing.

She took my shoes and put them at the end of the bed. We made sure the bed didn't creak in one corner as it usually did by putting a pillow between the wirewove and the wooden beam you get in those old-fashioned beds. Mary already had my cigarettes in her hand when I went to lean across her, in case I tipped something off the dresser. I lay propped against the top of the bed, with one arm under her head. Suddenly she raised her head and pressed my hand. There was an odd sound from the other side of the wall. I wasn't sure at first if it was an animal or what it was.

'What is it?' I whispered to her. We lay without moving and I could hear the blood threading through my ears.

'Grove's singing to her,' she said.

The sound was more distinct. He must have been moving within four or five notes, yet it wasn't a song, or like anything I'd heard him trying around the flat. Only those few notes, a kind of deep soft swell, but so little difference between crest and fall that it was there, but hardly there. It was a sound that wrapped round and touched softly and was never meant to be overheard.

At first I wanted to laugh—Grove with his thirty-five-year-old mother of two curled in his arm as Mary was in mine, Ruth's dyed hair brushing his dented side as though the hollow was there deliberately for her to nuzzle into. And to think he'd thrown away his evening with the band, and very likely his job as well, to catch what was probably the easiest lay around even for a man ten years older than he was. I tried to think of them only a foot or two from where we were, but it was too much, Grove and his naked woman! For a second I thought what if she sings back? She didn't though, and I'd left it too long to laugh. I could tell Mary was serious by the way her fingers lay against my cheek when she meant to be keeping them over my mouth. Sometimes it was like a hive of bees behind the wall, on one note. Then he would run notes together, quickly, for maybe thirty seconds, before the humming sound again, and I thought we can't listen to this any more, it's like being a peeping Tom. Then Mary surprised me for the second time that night, and more than the first. She had gripped my arm tightly then thrown the blankets back and her tongue was working over my chest and down to my stomach. It seemed that Grove was holding that sound of bees in a box at my head, until I didn't notice exactly when the sound stopped, only that it was silent again when Mary came back to lay her head on my arm.

'He's stopped singing anyway, thank Christ,' I said.

'I know,' Mary said. 'They've just left.'

McCaffrey sent me to Wellington for a month when a branch manager had peritonitis. This was the Thursday after Grove first brought his lady home, and a fortnight, exactly, before he died in a car crash on the way back from playing at Ohaupo. The band had left the hall at two o'clock and Grove had sat next to the driver. Mary said Ruth must have had a crisis of conscience, because she was usually with Grove, but that night she was home again next to her strawberry-grower, ready to give the children the breakfast they deserved.

Mary put through a toll call the next morning. At first I took it for granted that he must have died of head injuries. It seemed the obvious way for him to die, as only his head ever occurred to you when you thought of him. But then later that week I heard how his chest had been broken up, that he had died in the narrow speeding confines of the ambulance, minutes away from the hospital. At first he was conscious and when the St John's man asked him did he want anyone he said, 'No, it'll be all right, thank you.' I could see him very easily like that, not letting on much as the ambulance sped back between the hedges and through the country, the red light flashing and even the lean of trees and sheds and the front porches of houses lit for a second as though a fire was moving past them. And Grove there silent and polite and his head caught too in the red flare and then in the darkness and the siren growing thin as a thread as Hamilton came up from the right, but too late.

I wrote a letter to Grove's sister in Eltham and to his brother in Gisborne. Only the sister replied. She said she hadn't seen much of Grove over recent years, and if there was anything in the way of records or books I'd like for mementoes, to take them by all means before his gear was packed off to her place. I passed that message on to Mary, but as far as I know she did nothing about it. Then, no more than three weeks after, she wrote to say that seeing her father was leaving me in charge of the Wellington shop, perhaps we would be wiser to let things cool for a while? She'd see me at Christmas when we'd both know how she felt. Of course by then she was in England as she must have known all the time.

When I did drive through Hamilton soon after New Year I wanted to talk about Grove. (He had been cremated so there wasn't even a bit of ground I could look at.) But Mary wasn't there and no one else I knew had known him. So I went to the TAB beside the Riverina and asked for Ruth. A neat man spoke to me through the grille.

'She left a couple of months ago,' he informed me.

'You don't know where she's gone?'

The man looked at me more attentively and said, 'She wasn't here that long you know.'

'I wanted to see her for family reasons,' I told him. 'Could you tell me where her husband lives then?'

He called a woman from another window and spoke to her. Then she came to the grille where I was waiting and said, 'She didn't have one.'

'I thought he grew strawberries or something. A kind of gardener.'
'She lived in a flat off Hood Street somewhere,' the woman said. 'You're welcome to any gardeners you find up that way.' The neat man smiled over her shoulder and held up his palms as he must have seen in movies. 'If we could help,' he said.

I thought if I could track down his band that might throw up something, at least someone who could say a few sentences about him, but only the bass player was with them from Grove's time, and he was away on holiday. I spoke about Ruth again, on the off chance. The pianist I spoke to tried to think of her, but then he said, 'That's not enough to go on, is it, thirty-odd, randy, falling apart a bit? There's quite a few like her round.'

I'd tried to do something for Grove and I left it at that. The notes of his Ruth song have almost come back to me once or twice, although it's a good thing they haven't. All that does come back is a blonde with plastic teeth who thought she had to lie to him. And a siren that grows thin as the city lights lift above the swamp.

The Boy,
The Bridge,
The River

1

  It was four kilometres along a straight road from the village to the barns, and six kilometres coming back, if one took the looping road that diverged to run beside the river. The poplars were high on one side of the road and the movement of their leaves, even on a night so still as this, sounded more like a river than the river itself, that sluggish expanse of water turning slowly with the sandy road. The cart held to the centre of the road and its rubber-rimmed wheels kept up a steady soft pouring between the muted stepping of the horse. There were several bags of grain in the cart and a six-year-old boy sat on top of one of them, and leaned back against the others. The boy watched his uncle's back, so dark and unmoving except when one of the arms would rise a little to flick at the reins. The boy wore a black sailor's cap with a stiff peak which he believed made it the captain's, and when light from a farmhouse touched the river or the cart moved over the bridge as they came near the village, it was for him the sea that glimmered and passed beneath their deck.
  'Shall we get to land soon?' the boy asked.
  'Soon enough,' his uncle told him. They drew onto the bridge and the sudden clopping after the padded stepping on the road slowed and slowed until the cart jolted slightly and was still. The river slid between the supports of the wooden bridge and a continual broad hissing rose up from beneath them. The few lights from the village were a thin string to their left. There was nothing in the darkness to tell where, between that house beside the church and here on the bridge, the land might begin and the water end. You knew of course that even a boy could almost throw a stone from where they were stopped to the other bank, but that was not now, there was water and water the child thought until those lights beside the church could be the wharf. The horse and the man and the boy were silent above the slow push of the river, its thick sibilant washing against the piers. Then one of the

lights from the village winked out as a window was closed or a lamp extinguished.

'All right?' the man asked quietly, without turning his head. 'Yes,' the boy said. He turned one of the lugs on the sack he sat against and adjusted his captain's cap. 'I'm just fixing this lever here,' he told his uncle, and the man said, 'Tell me when we're ready to cast off then.' There was another moment while they heard the sea curling against the bows, the gushing pliancy of the sea which was three days travelling at least from the village and which the boy could see stretching, widening until there was nothing and nothing for half a year, and then America that would lift up very slowly and would look from the distance like the thin row of lights he could see across there now, while he tugged again at the sack and tapped against the side of the cart with a stick to let the engine-room know. 'Yes,' he told the man, 'You can go full ahead now.' The horse's stepping was again very loud on the wooden bridge, then the soft pouring of the wheels against the sandy road. The man turned and saw his nephew's small shape against the pale sacks, the stick still tapping against the side of the cart, the face he imagined absorbed with the business of berthing as the hooves suddenly rang on the stones of the small square. When they turned into their own street the light from the house at the corner moved right along the tackle, down from the glint of brass at the horse's mouth until all the light seemed to push along into the man's fists and snapped there for a second on the plain ring on one of his hands.

'Those are bright lights from the wharf,' the boy said. He was glad those sacks were there behind him; he was tired now that they had arrived.

'They have to be,' his uncle said, 'or we wouldn't know where to tie up, would we?' And when they had driven into the small yard behind the house his uncle hooked his hands under the boy's armpits and swung him high over the side, so high that the boy could look down on his uncle's head and along the horse's back that shone like it was polished when his mother opened the door and the light spilled over them.

'The captain brought us back safely,' his uncle called out and laughed, and so did his mother, who took the boy and pressed his face against her own and said, 'It must have been cold out there. Are your hands cold too?' She put both of his hands inside her own and closed her fingers round them and then blew down between her thumbs.

'We stopped on the bridge, you know,' the boy told her. Then his father came out but he was not smiling. He ran his hand along the horse's neck while his uncle bent underneath the animal to unbuckle a strap. His father took the gear from the horse's head and said while he was doing it, 'The news

has just come through. They have reached the capital already. They will be here in a couple of days.' Then his father went to the cart and carried two sacks at once, one resting across each shoulder, and took them into the house. His uncle carried another in front of him like carrying a calf, the sick calf they had inside for the worst part of the winter and his uncle used to pick it up like that. You could tell by feeling it and then watching it when you put it back on its legs how it was getting better. And one day he had taken the boy's small hand and made him press where the bones were bumps stretching the skin and said, *'See how she's getting fatter every day?'* And then for a joke his uncle had made him put his hand inside his own shirt and tell him which of them was growing faster, because those bumps were there under his own skin as well.

'He's asleep is he?' his father said. Then they had stood in the yard together before they went inside, and the man had looked at his nephew and his sister and his brother-in-law's long tired face against the light thrown up from the lantern. He could smell the urinous reek from the stable. He had taken the cap from his nephew's head as it tilted up when the boy sank against his mother, and noticed the red line where the brim had pressed into his forehead. He had touched the line with his thumb.

2

He waited for the bus at the small collection of shops at the end of the street. It was almost seven o'clock and the morning was cold and bright, the grass verge at the edge of the road stiff with frost. The regular passengers nodded to each other or if they spoke their voices were unexpectedly clear in the freezing air. A girl stood by herself in the doorway of the dairy, beside the stacked crates of milk, a cigarette in her black-gloved hand. Latty watched her stamp on her cigarette butt and pull her coat higher round her ears, her blonde hair billowing into a puff above the collar. When the bus approached she picked up a pair of white boots from beside the crates, and stepped ahead of the men. One of the men put his tongue into his cheek and looked across at the friend he was standing with. 'Not too cold to think of it though,' the other one said.

Latty waited until the rest had boarded the bus. He answered the driver's greeting and smiled at one of the other men who winked as he moved to the seat he always took, beside the middle door. Whenever the bus stopped and the folding doors hushed back, the early morning air would flood into him, the cold air of frost on a morning like this, or the smell of hay in January, or depending on the stop, the scents from the Dutchman's orchards or the drifting pungency of pig-shit from the long low grey sties. Latty liked to sit where the differences of air and temperature and smell would most easily reach him, a few feet above the road, behind the curved tubular railing at the middle door. A simple young man with a narrow pale head always sat on the other side of the aisle. He watched Latty with open-mouthed surveillance, or would swivel to gape at the girl who sat behind them, who this morning carried her marching boots and kept her collar high about her ears. Latty knew she marched in the team that his friend Len sometimes mentioned to him. She was one of the girls who on summer evenings manoeuvred and wheeled and marked time so precisely and pointlessly in the park beside the cenotaph. But it was autumn now, Latty thought, they had disappeared like birds who sought some kinder climate until the frosts and rains and winds of the next few months had iced or fallen or blown themselves out. Another season, he thought, until the smoothed and rollered lawn received again those children at their strange rite of obedience and drill and swishing skirts, the accurate falling of their boots.

After it crossed the high bridge that spanned the river, the bus stopped first at the post office, and again at the corner where the white wooden church sat handsomely among the splendid oaks. The sun splintered through their branches. There were few other stops for this early bus. The cold fields, some of them recently harvested of their maize crops, flowed past the window. Several brown hawks drifted low above the sliced stalks of the maize. Latty surmised they were after mice. The hawthorn hedges were whiskered with the greyness of the cold, and he noticed before the outskirts of the city how the puddles were frozen beneath the blue strutting birds with their bright beaks. Then the bus no longer moved between paddocks and sheds and milkstands, for the houses were closer now, long low bungalows or peaked beamed structures with careful gardens and curved drives, the ten-acre people he heard Dryford talk about at work. These were the dentists and accountants and land speculators who had made havens of ease on land that should be worked and laboured at. Latty was amused at how he always thought it, *I am a peasant still,* but land should bear crops or support cattle, it ought not be given to these ornamental shrubs, not the weak-boughed acacias and clumped camellias, the children's pampered horses behind whitewashed fences. After the dip with its last lovely crowding of willows and poplars along the edges of a creek, the bus rose to the neatness and the pastels of the suburbs, not country and not town, the ugliness of local brick and dull slatted wood. Latty wondered at how much could be spent on what looked so drear, these houses which *again to my peasant mind* he thought did not seem like homes, which had coiled electric tubes instead of open fires, where kitchens were for eating as quickly as possible and lounges for television, where there was no one space where young and old might come together for food or talk or singing or grief, for the closeness that was life. *Yet this is not my country, I do not understand.* He thought of the toss of chance or history or design that had set these quiet deliberate people in a place so fine, and then as if with malice had deprived them of so much that he remembered from home, where the land was dull and hard and the winter enough to kill, and sufficient to eat had been the constant goal. Yet here whatever fate you liked to call it had taken joy and exuberance and the delight a people should come to in the simple fact that they were born to this one place, together. Then as frequently, once he had thought such things, Latty was ashamed. How many of these people here, he asked himself, had betrayed a neighbour in the way the river engineer had betrayed the owner of the bookshop, that mild man with his rows of faded volumes who married a girl the engineer had once pursued? And twenty years later to the day, the father of four children, he had faced rifles at the side of the church because an old rival had lied of his sedition. How many, like his own cousin, would permit their daughter to leave each night at nine to go to the barracks of invaders? To stay until dawn with the tall captain who later sent off to camps the women who at last and in exasperation had taken the girl as she left her home, scarred her and shaved her and thrown her back at the barracks' gate? Latty looked at the dull houses and the undemonstrative people taking in their morning papers or their milk bottles from their gates, or walking on the clean deep pavements. He thought of those he worked with at the office, and grew confused. He had been here now for nearly half a lifetime and there was no answer to these things.

Dryford was the boss. He paused for a moment at the side of the desk, the shadow from his thick body falling and covering the papers in front of this foreigner whose job was to check the figures and the returns from the buses, to set these against the sheets the drivers handed in.

'Forget your English numbers or something, did you?' Latty took the sheaf held out to him. He saw that a circle had been scored in red biro around a figure on the top page. The error was no more than a slip of the pen, a three where a two should have been entered.

'I'm sorry,' Latty said. 'It is of no consequence.' He took up his pen and leaned forward to correct the figure.

'Oh?' Dryford lifted his head and looked vaguely ahead of him, like a beast that has detected what it cannot yet define. 'Of no consequence?' he repeated, as though the words were a novelty to him. He turned to the woman at the next desk, a widow who checked the catering accounts. Dryford spoke to her in a quiet, reasonable voice.

'Would you say, Mrs Cleary, that it's of no consequence that a two is mistaken for a three?'

The woman pressed one dimpled fist with the pencil she held in her other hand, so that a little circle of white shone round the point. She knew too much of Mr Dryford's oblique humour to offer her opinion. 'Well you, Shirley,' he asked the girl who was passing through to the ticket counter. 'As your elders who work so much with figures are reluctant to commit themselves, would you mind telling me? The difference between three and two. Would that be of no consequence, would you say?'

The others in the office had stopped working now; they were prepared for the entertainment that made their boss the almost single topic of conversation which they shared. Shirley looked at the broad shoulders, the close-cropped hair. 'Depends,' she said carefully.

'Depends, does it then? Whether you get a two or three bus home, for example? Have two meals a day instead of three? No difference to speak of?' Mrs Cleary felt how the voice was rising. She watched the thick forefinger, hardly longer than the curiously elongated thumb, tapping on the edge of her own desk to the rhythm of his words.

'Two or three children or wives? Or arms or legs?' The girl herself and Mrs Cleary and the two other men in the office were smiling, the boss was in full spate now, there was no spin-off likely in their direction. He had taken the papers with the mistake in order to fan them out, to shake them, in front of the foreigner's nose. '*You* might come from two or three countries and *that's* of no consequence, you can put your money on that,' Dryford said. He thrust the papers on Latty's desk and ran his square thick thumbnail along the lines scored with his pen. 'That mightn't be,' he repeated, 'but this bloody is!' He knocked his closed fist on the papers and passed through to his own desk behind the panelling and the frosted glass. He knew the performance had gone well, that the rest of them were looking to their own business and that Shirley would let them know at the counter, they'd all know within minutes that he was on form. He had left the desk and the knuckled papers without so much as looking at the man he was putting down. He knew that those eyes with their brownish lids like some kind of suede would be looking back at him, no sign of fear, and none of insolence, but looking as though at something on a screen. The others would know that too, that was the trouble. Later he would say, 'The bugger's too thick-skinned for anything to get through,' as he had said it at least once a week for a couple of years. He would say it as he stood at the lowered tray of the cocktail cabinet, beneath the large reproduction of Tretchikoff's swan, that dying erotic slab of colour which he had bought his wife for their twelfth anniversary. And he would say again, 'I'm damned if I know where this stuff goes to, people seem to forget it doesn't come cheap as water.' His hand would move down among the bottles for the almost emptied quart of gin, a reflection of his hand lowering in the greenish-tinged glass panel behind the bottles. And as for the sticky rings on the lowered tray, even a slattern, he had remarked two nights ago, would keep things a little more agreeable and hygienic than that.

'You're the only one who uses there,' his wife said.

'The only one when I'm at home,' he corrected her. He took his gin and tonic and handed his wife a sherry as he crossed to his armchair. From the landscape window he looked down on the streaming traffic along the Drive, beneath the glare of orange lights that made his wife think of aquariums, of orderly deadly rows of metallic fish. She knew she saw too often the threat of daily things, the reflections in firetongs as suddenly intense and sinister, a cutlery drawer too like a tray of dubious instruments. The fear would brush her mind for no more than seconds, as though this other world, this domain of secret threat, withdrew as soon as it was observed. She knew too that it would need to last so very little more than those few seconds for panic to direct her, for perhaps the innocence of curtains and sofa and the cold sides of the tea-service to cross that line as well, to join the other world. Yet to talk of it was nonsense, it was to invite from her mother the advice to take a holiday, from her doctor another note for the masking veil of valium.

Dryford took a large mouthful of his drink, washed the soft fizzing against his tongue and throat. 'That's better,' he said. There was a respite in the traffic he overlooked, no sound in the room they sat in.

'He's at it again,' he announced to his wife. 'That bugger in the office.'

'Yes?' she said.

'He's got just that knack for getting under my skin.' His wife waited while he drew again at his glass, made the smacking sound of satisfaction after he swallowed. 'There's one of the drivers, see, a half-caste or something,' he began to tell her. It was a story like many she had heard before. She thought of her boy who this evening was down at the gym, whose father forced him she was sure against his natural grain so that he might do the things that must be done, grow to the pattern that was already set. She also heard how dollars were missing, how ticket numbers failed to tally.

'Was he taking it?' she asked, and, 'Very good,' Dryford commended her, inflecting his voice like a teacher's. 'Mind like a razor sitting over there.' He finished his drink and rose to mix another, taking his wife's glass with a kind of swoop as he returned to the cabinet. She heard the soft splashing behind his voice, as he poured and kept on speaking. 'The old case of tickling the peter, as you might well think,' he went on. 'Old Hori salting a bit away for next pork and puha day. The figures come in each morning after our Polack checks them and three days on end there's this gap—tickets say one thing, money another.' There was a heavy chink as the sherry decanter knocked against its neighbours. 'Take it,' Dryford said, returning his wife's glass. There was a long pause while he crossed to his chair, eased himself into its comfort with exaggerated pleasure.

'Where was I?' he asked. He watched his wife as she said simply, 'They didn't match.'

'Very good again,' he told her. Then he said to cut it short, anyway, he had called the driver in. 'I was just on the verge of scaring the living shit out of him when he says oh didn't Latty pass it on? Didn't he tell you about old Gray's eggs?' Dryford's wife remembered the elderly man whom she hadn't seen for years, the owner of the company who had no interest in buses apart from what profits they brought him, who spent his declining years breeding siamese cats. 'This driver see had run into him and he said how he kept his own chooks out there near the pa where a bloody hen'd have the time of its life, it's all one great fowlyard. So he drops these bloody eggs off each week at Gray's driveway out past Te Rapa and he just takes the money from the fares. And I'm supposed to run a business like that.'

Dryford's wife thought of the lean pampered creatures the old man drove about with him in his car and carried at least one of wherever he went, their vile frank eyes staring at you, she remembered. She had said to Gray—was it five years ago?—'Those awful eyes!' and the old man had pressed his fingers close against the animal's neck so that its purr must have vibrated against his own flesh and he answered, 'Ah, they know everything.' He had offered her one hadn't he, said he would be delighted to give his manager's wife one from the next litter? And she had told him, No, she couldn't think of taking one, they were worth a small fortune. And she thought now of the seething newborn kittens, blind and indecent, butting against their slack-bellied mother. Her husband had stopped talking and she knew that it was her cue.

'And where's your foreigner come in?' she said.

'Him, for Christ's sake,' Dryford said. 'He comes in because he knew all the time, that's all. Would you credit that? The driver had told him and instead of passing it on like any normal person, not on your life. He just keeps putting in the takings and the ticket numbers and I'm supposed to find out by clairvoyance or something!' Dryford tilted his glass and jogged it, the drink lapping towards the rim. He forgot his irritation for the moment and thought of Shirley's arse when it moved against the side of the chair this morning and he had touched it, surprised himself that he was doing it, and she had turned and looked at him without amazement or concern and held his eye, simply waiting until he had taken his hand away. He would play his cards pretty carefully there, he thought. He saw his hand against the denim of her skirt and remembered looking up at the swelling of her tits and her hair falling to one side as her head tilted to look down at him, by God that was lovely.

'So you spoke to him?'

'What?' Dryford turned from the window to look at his wife. He took in her careful perm and her small upraised face, the boy's mother all right, there was so much more of her came out in him. He was a good kid and he was keen but he didn't have the build, that was the trouble, Dryford couldn't imagine him making the first team in anything. His wife spoke again but he left her question unanswered, he made a grating noise with his sinuses and stood facing the motorway, the streaming lines taking the broad curve of the gully. He thought again of Shirley and then of the club, of how much time he put into it and how you had to keep yourself in the clear, you couldn't afford a wrong move there any more than you could at work, not if you wanted to keep up with the play. His wife watched him stand there against the night and the reflected glow from the Drive. She thought what she had never said, that her husband was dominated by this man at the office for a reason so obvious and so sad, that it was the foreigner's last care in the world whether his boss smiled at him or raged, favoured or reviled him. And mustn't a man who could go untouched by her husband's selective spite hold some centre of balance, some certainty in himself, which was a simple richness she could scarcely put a name to?

3

In his lunch hours Latty liked to visit the public library. There were several magazines which he looked at, like the illustrated French monthly which he read no more for its articles on expensive furniture and art and elaborate dwellings than for its stories of the rich and the beautiful, their world of reflected profiles and Mediterranean coastline. He read it for the sake of the language, which he knew imperfectly yet better than he suspected, the language of a country he had marched into in the grey uniform of the Germans and where he stayed on, once he had deserted, in the blue overalls of a labourer. Often, in these past few months, he found himself going over those years, recalling some isolated event which until now had lain embedded in that block of his life which for the greater part had been fear and hunger and cold. And between the fear which a dozen times had turned his guts to water, and the hunger which he had carried like a heavy dead unappeasable child month after month, were those acts which had lifted him it seemed on a crest. After decades of remoteness they now came into his mind when he did not expect them, and he felt in them neither pride nor shame.

Before he walked down to the library, Latty would eat in the lunchroom the small stack of sandwiches he prepared for himself each morning. Sometimes there was a slight exchange with the others at work, a rare attempt to draw him into chat, but there was no expectation that he would take up their offer, no belief for a moment that there would be anything more than the customary polite murmur, the mild withdrawal which was decisive as a grille lowered between them. He once heard Mrs Cleary declaim as she scoured her cup at the lunchroom sink, her back towards him as he entered, 'It's not as if he can't talk English properly, is it? It's as if he just doesn't *want* to be sociable.' And the girl standing beside her, a slight angular child who had left to marry a Mormon, said in a way which had touched him, 'He must have his own things to think about anyway, mustn't he? Everybody has but you don't have to go on about it.' Then Mrs Cleary, who thought the girl an upstart quite apart from who she was going to marry, said, 'I wouldn't know about that. I believe in being open myself.'

'Well I'd rather have him than anyone else here,' the girl persisted. 'He's not always trying to be smart and that, you can tell he likes people.' Latty stepped back quickly along the corridor so that they would not observe him. He knew the girl would be embarrassed, and Mrs Cleary angry. She had told him before, a couple of years ago when he began at the office, that he should have been a burglar the way he moved so quietly between the desks or came into the room. 'You're like a cat,' she said, and he had looked back from his eyes which never seemed properly open. She watched his face which she thought was like off-white putty, and that stupid little black beret thing which was what really drove Mr Dryford mad. He looked and smiled and said nothing, of course.

'You've pissed him off now,' one of the others had said.

'I wouldn't say so,' she answered, and that skinny thing who wouldn't drink tea any longer because of her boyfriend said, 'He wouldn't give twopence what any of you thought, anyway.' Mr Dryford was in the office for the last bit of it and he had put her in her place nicely, he said, 'Probably he's a religious nut too, then,' and young Miss Bones as they called her had gone red as a beetroot.

Latty would take his magazines and mount the stairs to the second floor, to a gallery where he could sit at a small desk and look down into the life of the library. Sometimes he would place his hands side by side on the smooth opened pages and simply look at the activity on the floor beneath, at the figures moving between the steel shelves, at the librarians in their odd frocks which made them look pregnant. Or as he read, the French words would rise to him from the page, words which he believed he had forgotten and which did not so much invite as force him back to the grey towns which he remembered almost always as under drizzling or snowing skies, although he had spent two summers there as well. The grey sky and the line of trees like pencil strokes against it. He thought of the farm kitchens and the small apartments where how many times, he wondered, he had sat opposite a man dressed usually like himself, whose real name he was never to learn and who addressed to him a few words which at first he scarcely understood.

*

There was no light when they had left the farmhouse in their peasant clothes and their thin canvas shoes. The cold, not long before dawn, was intense. The stars were chinks of ice turning and glittering. His companion he sensed rather than saw in front of him, he followed him along a ditch and then passed through a wire barrier which accomplices a few minutes before had severed. At the edge of the village where two sentries stood guard at opposing corners (or so he had been told and must believe) he had left the other man and moved against the roughcast walls, towards the soldier who stood invisible a few yards ahead of him. He pressed against the wall until he heard the light fall of a stone which he awaited, and the sudden alerted attention of the guards. A voice now only feet away spoke in German, and was answered from the opposite corner. The guards relaxed and exchanged a few words, there was the stamp as the one so close to him moved his booted feet against the frost. And Latty was filled he remembered with his own ice-cold concentration. He drew out the thin piano wire coiled in his sleeve and tugged briefly at the wooden peg on either end of its short span. The wire gave its odd almost living vibration as he drew it taut. His hands rose like a priest's he had thought at the elevation, delicate and confident, and fell over the helmeted head, the crossed pegs biting against his straining fingers.

Latty looked down at the moving figures in the library, the young girls and the aging men, the women with pushchairs and the students taking notes at one of the tables. Those human lives whose names he did not know, which passed as did his own in the endless indecipherable web of drawing breath, of breeding, of hope and distress, and for all of them that moment waited for and yet denied, the weakening of some artery wall, some ravenous cell, *the hands falling and crossing, the single width of wire.*

For twenty years those memories had not touched him, and now they returned to him almost every week. They were more clear to his mind than the events of a month ago. And more often too he experienced those dreams which had come to him intermittently for years. Dreams of the flowing river on the last night of which he had any memory from home, the lights when they had halted on the bridge and the boy was sitting behind him, commanding from the high deck of the grain sacks. And as he woke, as he saw the lightening sky through the squares of his window, he would sometimes find himself calling out, or beginning to raise his arms to swing the tired child from the back of the cart.

*

Latty's bach was a converted toolshed, with a small kitchen added at one end and a bathroom at the other. The room was carpeted and lined with hardboard, and a double-bar heater made it cosy in the winter months. There was a window above the heater, and another had been fitted at the side of the door. The furniture was a large bed and two armchairs, a table covered by a plastic cloth patterned to look like lace, and a bookcase which for the most part carried folded newspapers and a few books drawn from the library. There was nothing, not so much as a folded shirt or a pair of shoes, which lay casually out of place. The room's one brilliant feature was a red and white Greek rug, which lay over the bed as a cover. The landlady's niece had sent it to her as a gift, and the woman had passed it on, believing that as a foreigner Latty would appreciate what she thought garish and crude. Those thick double threads of wool could have been worked, she said, by a child. And there were two preserving jars which served as vases, one on a shelf behind the door, the other on a carefully folded square of paper in the middle of the table. Both jars were filled with clumps of holly from the hedge in front of the house. The small sharp leaves glistened as though oiled. His landlady had seen them and said, 'Might as well put weeds there,' and was glad to return to the taste of her own front room.

Once a month Latty went across to the house with his rent book. She took his notes and counted them, and on the large oval table she opened a book and entered the amount in one column, the date in another. 'Thank you,' she would say. Light slid across her spectacles as she raised her head, and Latty looked into her unwell eyes, their scaled pinkish rims and the mucus in their corners. At the last payment before Christmas and once or twice through the year, on some day perhaps whose significance she chose to keep to herself, she would offer Latty a glass of blackberry nip. They sat on opposite sides of the table with its white bowl and the clump of plastic flowers, large yellow-centred pieces with inflamed lashes, and raised their glasses. 'Season's greetings,' she would say to him at Christmas, and at other times, 'Your good health.' Latty thanked her, and his heavy pale face smiled towards her. Her hand with discoloured tan spots trembled very slightly until the glass touched her lips. Neither she nor her brother had married.

'Likes her drop, I'll tell you that,' Len said. He was a shortish man who had spent a lifetime with the local borough council, and now in retirement lived with his one sister. He would walk beside Latty with the slightest depression of his left foot. It was injured by a baler when he was in his early twenties, a few years before the War. 'That's luck for you,' he told Latty. 'I'd have been up and off and out of this lot with the first volunteers if it hadn't been for the old leg. Two toes, that's all, but it put paid to any gallivanting I might have got up to.' He moved his hand towards the town, to the unspecified lucky ones who had got away. 'All those other buggers over Italy and Greece and what have you.' Or he would laugh another time when his injury was raised, and the War he was deprived of. 'Probably wouldn't be here now anyway, so what's the odds?'

At the weekends the two men frequently shared their walks. Their walking together had begun by chance, after Latty had rented the bach for the best part of a year. His landlady's brother had nodded to him whenever they passed in the street. Then one weekend they met, by taking different routes from the house, at the corner of the bridge. Together, they had begun to cross the high span over the dark heavy flowing of the river.

'My old man remembered the day this thing was opened,' Len offered. 'That's going back a bit for you.' They had stopped when they were at the middle of the bridge. The river was almost black as they gazed straight down on it. Thirty yards upstream a thick column of water fell and broke against the current. 'Seepage,' Len said. He leaned against the metal railing. 'The odd kid still walks across this ledge for a dare, they reckon.' Latty stood beside him with his hands in the pockets of his gaberdine coat. He watched the stream of water from the bank impacting on the moving surface of the river. Two large fern trees projected from the damp tangle of the bank, two green wheels with drooping spokes. In places the clay of the bank showed through like a wet heavy skin.

'You never get tired of this view, you know,' Len said. 'Like looking straight back there, between those banks where you can't see any houses and that. Must have been like that for hundreds of years, except the water's a darn sight dirtier now.' He pointed to several clots of brownish foam, some of them strung out over several yards, that moved downstream with the current. 'Top-dressing or factory stuff or something,' he said. He leaned forward so that his heels were off the ground and his chest rested on the railing like a schoolboy's as he peered down into the river, at the slight lifting and crosshatching of the surface where wind moved across. After that first meeting they always stopped on the bridge, and Len's remarks were very often the same. He liked to say how this view of the banks, the stretch where houses were hidden, had been like this before any of them came, before the land was cut up into farms and the farms cut up into sections, maybe even before the Maoris had slipped down through the bush to the level of the river.

Their weekend walk became as certain as the weekend itself. In the summer they would stand on the embankment where the road divided, and look down on a swimming pool and its throng of splashing, shouting young bodies. 'Does you good to see them enjoying life like that,' Len said. Or if they came across a wedding party at one of the churches further up the street, where the grand spread of the oaks and chestnuts gave the wooden buildings an air of charm, Len's view of things would again come out.

'Wonder how much of this they'll remember in thirty years?' he had said one morning. They were watching a heavy, solemn girl standing for her photograph. Her husband of a few minutes ran one finger down the sides of his moustache, his other hand signalling to a cluster of his mates. 'If only they all got what they were hoping for, eh?' and he had sighed rather like his sister, Latty thought, when she set down her glass on one of those rare occasions, and said as she carefully refilled first his and then her own, 'It's like a key, of course, we all know that, don't we?' meaning the sweetish liquor, the flood of memory rising with it. Latty smiled slightly. He watched his friend's absorbed interest in the young couple and thought how lucky perhaps a man might be to have lived so simply. Len's life had been spent only in this town, his schooldays and his working life, the death of his parents, the long closeness with his sister. That, and maybe a hundred or so friends and acquaintances who were the full range of his life. He had once told Latty, 'There's not much happens anywhere mind that you couldn't see here if you kept your eyes peeled.' At times they walked in silence, Len's slight limp and Latty's soft stepping beside him. Except in the warmest days of summer Latty wore his gaberdine, his hands deep in its pockets, his black beret set above his round face.

'You look foreign, you know that, Latty? You can tell by just a look I mean that you're not one of the locals. Not one of us.' Then he had said, 'I don't mean any offence by that.' Latty had smiled at him, looking down at the reddish grey hair which was level with his own shoulder. There was a saddle of freckles across Len's nose that made his face seem boyish and pryingly eager, although the men were much the same age. At times they covered miles in silence, at others Len would talk as if taking breath were something of a luxury. Usually he would be unwinding an intricate account of some gossip or event which that year or twenty years before had stirred the town. One morning he pointed out a man who had killed his wife with an axe because she had left their canary out in the porch during a frost. The man had done fifteen years and had come back to the very same house, where he now had what you might as well call an aviary, finches and budgies and Indian whatever they were, brown birds anyway with a red tuft like a little crown. 'We don't have too many to match him mind you,' Len said. Another morning he touched Latty's arm as they passed the broad doorway of the post office. He edged his head discreetly to a woman in front of the wall where the private boxes were like small cells in numbered rows.

'You won't believe this one Latty but get a load of her when she comes out to her flash car over there.' The men stopped a few yards further on, supposedly engaged in the land agent's display of houses and properties, sections and farms. Latty looked at the meaningless figures written below the photographs, sums as remote to him as the prices that might have been asked for palaces. Then as Len directed, he turned to see a handsome middle-aged woman step briskly across the pavement to a sleek emerald-coloured car. Her large breasts stirred at each step and two teenagers riding their bicycles on the pavement yelped at each other at their sudden luck. One of them held huge imaginary globes in front of his jersey while his mate doubled between his tall handlebars with delight.

'Well her,' Len said. He watched the woman ease the car from the kerb and as she drove past them Latty saw the diamantes on her watchstrap shiver against her arm. 'She used to be married to a bloke who managed the dairy factory on the road out to the hydro, the road up from us. Her old man was away quite often and the whole town knew she was a player, but this time it came out in the maddest way. No one ever worked out quite what she was at, mind you, but she was actually taken off to hospital—ambulance and the whole works—with a french letter, you know, a frog, stuck in her throat like a fishbone or something. It as good as choked her.' Len's own face showed surprise as he told the story, a boy's face amazed at what adults can bring themselves to do. And his eyes followed the car while he was talking, it was not a dirty story he was giving his friend but yet another segment of what made life rich and various and endlessly of interest, and the car turning there now at the cenotaph, drawing over and pulling up at the wine shop, was freighted with glamour. 'She's got a nerve living here after that,' Len said.

They paused again at the nursery shop and examined the plants that were in the window. Len had known the chap who ran it when he didn't have a penny to his name; now he had this shop and another two in Hamilton. He spoke of him while they walked on up the town's main street. Then suddenly 'Look,' Len said. He held his friend's eye and said, 'You just tell me if I ramble on a bit won't you? You will, now?' Latty touched Len on the sleeve. 'I like this walking with you,' he said. 'I like you to tell me things.'

'Well I mean I can listen too,' Len said. 'You don't seem to need to say much Latty but don't forget, if you do.' Latty's hand still shook as they waited for the stream of traffic near the park. The football season had begun and several games were now under way on the large square with its rim of trees. He did not understand why he was so affected, why a life which had given so much of itself to control and dissimulation, to discipline and will, should at this very moment, this late in the day, reveal something new. He was glad that his strange talkative friend had gone on ahead, and was now stepping up the slope to watch the game. Latty's eyes were confused. He saw the branches of the tree immediately in front of him run together in an unexpected blur. *This is the first time*, Latty thought, *this is the first time in this country where I have been for half a lifetime, when I have touched another person not by necessity or politeness or accident, but as a friend. I have touched him as a friend because words were not enough.* Len already was rapt in the game, in the player who ran the ball over half the length of the field before he passed it across in a deft confident lift. 'He's got the makings all right,' his friend was saying, 'he's a cut above the others.'

4

There was half a year of which he remembered nothing. There was the journey with the cart, the darkness and his talk with the boy, and what the boy's father had said when they were back home, unbuckling the horse while his sister carried out the lantern and placed it between the men on the cobbled yard. He thought of before that, of waking in the morning, waking and walking to the kitchen, to the long broad table and the barrels in the corner and the open fireplace which had warmed them since his childhood. Waking to his brother-in-law silently gazing from the window, across to their farm which was the first on the edge of the village, while he plucked at the large chunk of bread he broke each morning from the loaves in one of the barrels. Woke to his sister who sometimes sang, who so deserved, he thought, the man she had and the child at the table with two fat books on a chair to raise him high enough to eat. Mostly he remembered his sister in the kitchen and in winter, the reflection from the broad flat expanses of snow thrown up on the beams and ceiling at that hour of morning. In his memory Latty himself was mostly sitting at the table across from the boy, his sister moving from the hearth to the table, a bowl steaming in her hands, and the light lifting always from the snow, the cold pure radiance that seemed without source, the very quality and permeation of the air itself. The light showed against her face, lightening the firm handsome line of her jaw, and the scar which he noticed especially at that time. And further back they were children on the riverbank, it was spring. Their father managed an orchard whose owner not only they but their father too had never seen. There was row upon row of pink blossoming trees. To walk along the spaces between the rows at that time of year, to walk there when the wind stirred, was to be in the constant slow flicker of falling and turning petals.

The children played in the orchard as in the middle of a story, his sister saying once she was the queen, her bare arms held out before her and the trees spreading and packed behind her, a hall of spring and colour. And she had said that day the forbidden thought, 'Let's climb the tree, let's shake the blossom down like a real storm.' The boy was younger than his sister and afraid. Their father had thrashed a visiting cousin for so much as shaking a branch. 'You are killing fruit each single petal you make fall,' he had told them. 'Whatever you touch this time of year, you kill.' But she had climbed the tree and sat in its gorgeous branches, her navy smock showing between the mass of delicate flares. She had braced her feet on one branch and taken hold of another, slightly above her head. He remembered standing in the tall grass as he watched her grey serious eyes looking directly at his, implicating him while his own hands were limp beside him, and she began to shake the tree. A thin shower of blossom, so much paler when it was falling than when it was on the tree, began to descend on him. And then what seemed a smother, a thickness of the drifting weightless fragments until his own call, surging in his ears before he realised he had called it, 'Father! Father!' Latty recalled nothing of his father's approach, of the shouting or the anger which must have followed. The memory finished with his sister's falling, the attempt to leap from the tree and her foot catching in the notch of a branch. She fell into the grass beside him, and lay for a moment so still that he had grown afraid. And when she had raised her head her hair was stuck across her mouth. A stone had opened a gash along her chin, the blood coursing down her throat, and small petals from the blossom adhered to her skin, some of them curled and drenched in the flow, like the thin papers he *had seen men use on their chins while shaving. It was that scar from the orchard he saw whenever his sister's throat and jaw took the reflection from the snow, the thin line he had seen for the last time when she raised her head in the yard, raising it to rest the tired boy against her shoulder.*

Of that half year which he had lost as permanently as an amputated limb, Latty learned and pieced together that he had crossed three borders and been recruited for an army before he woke on a striped filthy mattress in a basement not only in a town, but in a country, he did not know the name of. His head was bandaged and for a month he could not see from his left eye. The uniform he wore was Russian and the officers were Russian, but at least half of the men he saw, the other wounded and those who cared for them, spoke his own language. They said his village was no longer there, that it had been won and lost and won again, although neither victors nor losers were the people who had lived there. They said there was nothing left, there were craters formed on top of craters, only the levels of bombardment. The journey which had led him from the yard and the family, from the child and the cart, to his waking on the sodden mattress and his wounded head, was a dark corridor which was never to lighten. It was one life ended as it seemed simply by a blink, another begun with the opening of his eyes. He was a man with not one continuous life, but lives that were like the broken tracks of a railway, lines that ran towards each other until where they met was in fact where they did not meet at all. The fracture gaped irrevocably in those images of his hand last seen raised in the soft light to touch the sleeping boy, that same hand next seen lying across the canvas mattress in a country he did not know. Armies had merged and pressed against each other like a matted entanglement of maggots, one filling the space where another had been, wavering across a map which covered a third of Europe. The undulation moved above him as he lay in the basement, while this town like his own slipped beneath alternate armies. Latty had lain there in a fever while the man on the mattress beside him died, and men in other uniforms came and dragged away the body. He remembered that the man was gross and that the two uniformed boys were incapable of lifting him. Latty's mind had gone back to the farm, to a beast which had fallen into a canal. 'Drag him,' he said. Each soldier had taken a leg and hooked it at the knee beneath his arm, then lurched the weight across the concrete floor. Briefly, the body wedged in the doorway. One of the soldiers forced it through with his boot, like shoving at a sack of grain that had stuck. Then there had come the steady thump, seven times he had counted as the man was dragged up the seven steps and his head jarred against the ascent. He looked at the broad slur the body had scoured across the filthy floor. Then he had slept until the soldiers returned and he was carried to a clean bed, his head freshly dressed by a doctor whose hands were soft as gauze. He was interrogated, cured, assigned to a division of men who like himself were the derelicts of war, the sweepings of smaller nations. They were the salvageable flesh from the writhing lines of combat.

And now as autumn sank into winter, as the frosts gave way to winds and days of rain, Latty thought about the War. He walked as usual each weekend with Len, and one night a week his friend came to the room in the converted toolshed. Together they would share a bottle of sherry which at first Len had offered shyly, and which then they took it turn about to buy. Len would talk on, of the town and its people, his parents, what he had heard and half believed of his great-grandfather, the Maoris, the whores from Auckland who were supposed to have come down this far for the regiments stationed at Alexandra. Latty sat on a wooden kitchen chair and insisted that his friend take the cane basket one which he had found at the Shakespeare Street dump, and carried home through the streets.

'You just lugged it along in the open?' Len had asked.

'Of course,' Latty told him. 'Like this.' He mimed his carrying the chair by its two arms, the seat above his head and the back falling behind his shoulders like a stiff cape.

'No wonder they think you're an oddball,' Len laughed. He liked looking at Latty's face. It hardly changed its expression no matter what he was listening to or talking about. You could only just see his puckered eyes as they looked from above his broad cheeks. It wasn't still so much either, it was—Len felt about for the word he wanted, and found one which he had never used he supposed in his life before. It was *repose* in his friend's face, that was it. It would take a lot to change it, Len thought, that was what he really meant.

The two men would sit and sip slowly at their sherry. One man who had killed and killed and crossed the world, who had not known friendship for over twenty years, whose mind returned to a road at night and a small boy in the cart behind him; another who several times had travelled the hundred miles to Auckland and twice the three hundred-odd to Wellington, who as a young man had caught his foot in a machine and then worked in one job all his life, who lived as though his small town and all that took place in it were extensions of himself.

'And why Latty anyway? Why that name?' Len had asked him one night.

'When I first come,' Latty said. 'First come soon after the War, I mean, and I am working in the timber camp where I stay as a logger and when I am too old for that, in the office, right until I come here. And in those days I did not know much English and they say "He's from Latvia or somewhere," and so they call me that.'

'And you don't mind?' Len said. 'Don't mind not having your real name?'

Latty stood to refill his friend's glass for him. He looked down at the freckles, at the forehead that stored like the files of a newspaper the lives and deaths of the town. And now Len had asked not as anyone else would *where were you from then?* but *don't you mind?* instead. He said 'All right?' when the glass was almost full and Len told him 'Lovely, that'll be lovely.'

I am learning all the time, Latty thought. *There is nothing which is what one expects, nothing I have the right to predict.*

5

It's not as though marching were only a pastime, Shirley thought. It was that of course, but it was posture as well, it was discipline and rhythm and team spirit, it was as she remembered from the Governor General's speech both aesthetically rewarding and physically fulfilling. She remembered too the phrases from the last social night of the season and the way her cheeks had burned when her own name was called out. She had pushed past Gary and Lynaire and the others and gone up on the stage to receive her trophy, the most improved girl of the year. Her face had felt as though there were hot cloths laid across it. And as well as the cup the club president had pinned the badge shaped like a small shield on to her blazer and put his hand on her shoulder and kissed her on the cheek! She could have died, she admitted later. When she came back down the hall Lynaire had said, 'He's a bit keen on you, Shirl,' and Gary got that mad! He had sulked the rest of the night. Then afterwards they sat in the car down near the swimming pool. It must have been two o'clock and she was worried about her mother carrying on if she was back as late as that. He had just sat there, his hands opening and closing on the steering wheel until she had said for goodness sake, Gary, and touched his trousers until he let go of the wheel and held her and started unbuttoning her, and then it was OK again. Mum had said a couple of years ago, when she first went out with boys, there's one thing you don't want Shirl and that's a boy who's jealous, and she knew now from Gary what that meant, didn't she just.

'It wouldn't have been so bad if it was just the presentation,' Lynaire said later. 'It was all that laughing at supper that did it.' There was a lot of fooling round and no one was quite sober and Shirley had been talking to the president's wife. She was a sort of sad woman who just smiled when her husband said those embarrassing things about Shirl being the best looker in the team. Lynaire said, 'She looks a bloody hundred years older than him anyway.' But she was nice though, nice in the way she listened when you talked to her and covered up for her husband when some kid in the juniors with braces on her teeth and flat as an ironing board came up and looked at Shirley's medal and then spoke to the president, and it was Mrs Dryford who remembered the kid's name. But even when Shirley was talking to the older woman Gary had been surly. He had gone off when she spoke to him without hardly answering. Then later in the car he had kept on sulking, even when she was moving her hand on him and he was lying back with his eyes closed, when she was moving him like that and she leaned forward and kissed his neck and his throat and told him, 'You know there's no one else I give a stuff about,' he hadn't answered her like she wanted him to. As soon as it was over and they had made themselves look respectable he had said they should be getting back, he didn't want to be too late. He had told the boys he'd be out at the lake by nine, it was no good getting up on the skis if you felt poked. She had been pretty hurt at that, he must have known she would be in for it with Mum, yet she hadn't gone on about it had she? He hadn't even passed her his hanky after she had done it for him.

'You're well rid of that one,' her mother said when Gary was transferred down to Palmerston North. 'Anyway you're only eighteen, there'll be plenty more.' That hadn't been much consolation, not for the first few months. Gary had come up and she had gone down a few times, and once she had said she was going to Taupo with Lynaire but in fact she was meeting Gary, they were going to have the weekend together at a motel. She must have been a child, Shirley thought. She had taken the Road Services bus on the Friday after work and when she arrived there was Gary sure enough, he was waiting and grinning and he waved as the bus drew round into the depot. She was carrying the white imitation leather overnight bag she had bought just for this. The bag had a mirror in the lid when you opened it and there were compartments for cosmetics, and gathering and tucking round the inside so it all looked like a piece of lingerie. Shirley had thought about their meeting on the way down through the open country that the moon had made look so gentle and smooth it could have been moulded, and then through the long road with the pine forest on either side. The moon kept appearing and disappearing between the whisk and blur of the trees like something that was keeping pace with them. It would be like being married in a way, she had thought, as she sat with the square leather case on her knees and her hands folded over the handle on the top. Inside was the nightie she had bought yesterday at lunchtime in Garden Place, and the face cream she hadn't touched yet, a kind she knew nothing about but smelled divine, fitted into one of the compartments. She stepped from the bus and Gary had kissed her. She tasted the rum on his breath and laughed when he told her, 'Can't wait to start feeding you a length, Shirl.' He led her through the depot to the street where she could see the stretch of the lake.

'There was a moon all the way down,' she said.

They walked to the hotel on the corner. 'I've booked here instead of a motel,' he said. He opened the door to a house bar and Shirley squinted her eyes against the pall of cigarette smoke. He took her to the bar with its line of leather stools and to a man she had never seen, several years older than Gary. 'This is Jay,' he said. 'He drove up with me for the weekend. We're all booked in together.' Gary laughed as he said this and Jay smiled without laughing. His eyes looked directly into hers and Gary stood back a little, watching them and laughing still and saying, 'Here, Jay's got you a Kahlua.' As she placed her heel on the chrome rung of the stool and then lowered herself to the seat she felt Gary's hand beneath her, his middle finger raised, and the man she had just met smiled jointly, it seemed, at Gary and herself. He leaned forward and slapped Gary's hand. 'Here,' he said, 'we won't have any of that thank you,' and both watched Shirley as they laughed. Much later they had all gone to bed together drunk and before the men had woken Shirley took the overnight bag she had not opened and walked out into the empty road. She saw the lake there under a dull sky, the water lying like a broad sheet of perfectly rolled lead. She had looked at it for a moment, at the dark blue line of hills, or mountains they might even be, right across on the far side of the water, then stepped to the edge of the footpath, her thumb extended, to the first car that approached her, and hitched back home.

After that she had moped for a couple of months. Her mother had come to her one morning, one Saturday when the rest of the family was out and Shirley sat in her dressing gown on the back porch, in the sun. Mum brought her a cup of tea and carried a cup for herself as well. 'That's nice,' she said as she took the cup and held it carefully between her two palms almost as though she expected it to break and the pressure of her hands was holding it together. Then, 'Listen,' Mum had said, so matter of fact that Shirley had nearly died when the rest came. 'You're not in trouble or anything are you?' She felt herself going red and put her face closer to the steaming tea. As far as her mother knew she mightn't even have kissed a boy properly. She felt awful when it came out like that. 'What on earth are you on about?' she asked, and Mum had asked it again. 'Well are you?' she said. Her mother leaned across and opened her hand and for a few seconds let it lie on the quilted dressing gown. There was no weight as it lay there and then the hand was taken away, as though her mother too was embarrassed by what she had asked. There was a silence and Shirley said with her head only inches from the cup and the steam wisping in front of her, its little particles visible in the sunlight, 'You needn't worry about me, you should know that, Mum.'

'Then you need a tonic,' her mother said. 'You've been so down to it lately.'

'I'm just tired from work I think,' Shirley said. She thought how her mother was sharper than she realised. Since that awful time at Taupo she had hardly spoken to the family, or she was scrapping with her brother. Then as if her mother was thinking about that too she said, 'I know Wayne can be a little bugger but he's at that age. He'll be all right in a year or two.' 'Oh, it's not Wayne, Mum,' Shirley said. 'I think I need a change or something.'

Then everything came right without her having to try. She had been up at the clubrooms as they were called, that old cricket pavilion which was going to be pulled down until someone said why not get it for the girls, why not let them get changed there or meet in there if it rains during practice. It was only a few days after Mum had raised that business about thinking she was in trouble.

'It's no good trying to get a new job out here,' Lynaire was saying. 'You have to go into Hamilton whether you like it or not.' Her friend was a tall girl with thin legs, and was always a problem in the team. No matter where you put her she seemed out of place. Shirley liked her because she knew she looked a fright and didn't make a thing of it. She was always the last to get a boy when they were away with the team and she would sit next to Shirley on the bus coming home and say, 'I'll tell you this, Shirl, if I had looks like yours you wouldn't get me going back to a dump like this.' She meant the town they were born in and had gone to school in and would probably marry in as well. 'No way,' Lynaire said. 'I'd be off like a shot up to Auckland, the Pink Pussy Cat or somewhere and I'd be shaking them in their faces every night. I'd make ten times the money I get in this hole and I'd get a few decent bites as well.' She couldn't care less what she said, Lynaire. The chaperones told her to go easy sometimes, they said she had a mouth like a freezing worker, but even that wouldn't stop her. 'Freezing worker my arse,' she had said. The chaperone for that weekend was furious with her, and the team had been in an uproar. They all knew the old bag was a wowser anyway and watched the girls like a hawk. 'Still thinks you get pregnant from rubbing noses,' Lynaire said, and when she christened her the Nun the name had stuck.

'Well I'm sick of working in that bloody garage out here anyway,' Shirley said. 'It's just a matter of finding one in town that pays you something reasonable.'

Mr Dryford had come in and was pinning notices about fixtures and so on to the board. The girls hadn't known he was listening. He was often in the clubrooms, he or his wife, and he was so easy to get on with they more or less forgot he was there some of the time. 'If it wasn't for his whistling you'd be dropping your daks before you knew he was in here,' Lynaire said once. Now he asked her, 'Ever thought of the Bus Company, Shirley?' and it was as simple as that. She was taken on as a kind of office girl, but she did a lot of messages and driving about in Mr Dryford's car for him. Then in the summer she found that half her time at work just about seemed to be spent on marching business, or things to do with one of the half dozen other clubs Mr Dryford was tied up with. Of course he had a sharp tongue at work that you would never have suspected if you only met him with the team, he was more like a good-tempered father with all the girls. But Shirley grew used to that, it was never at her expense so it wasn't for her to worry, was it? And as Dad used to say, no one ever thought work was supposed to be fun anyway.

Shirley caught the bus at the same stop each morning as the foreigner. She had noticed him before, walking about the town with old Len who did odd jobs round the clubrooms, but it was at the office she first took any notice of him. Or rather, the new job made her see two things at much the same time. One was that he was quiet and polite and a bit pathetic, with his large face and little beret affair and his eyes squeezed into the folds of skin so you hardly saw them. The other was that Mr Dryford hated his guts. On her first day for instance her new boss had taken her and introduced her to the staff in both offices and in the garage and the cafeteria as well. The dream girl from the marching team he had called her when he took her into the lunchroom for the first time. He had been very kind and repeated everyone's name except for the large quiet man's who was putting on a raincoat in the alcove near the lockers. Mr Dryford led her past without saying a word, and she had asked, 'Who's that?' and he had turned to her and said loud enough for the man to hear, 'That? He works here too but there's no need for that to worry you. Not like it worries me but then I'm the one who pays him.' Shirley had seen the man looking back towards them as he buttoned his coat. Well there must be a reason for it, Shirley thought, Mr Dryford wouldn't have it in for him unless he asked for it. That used to be another of Dad's favourite sayings, that it took two to make a quarrel. Though after she had been there for a few weeks she couldn't very well imagine Latty making one, he was about as argumentative as a pudding. She had never known anyone who minded his business quite the way Latty did.

'Look,' Mr Dryford said one evening. He had to drive out to a meeting with some of the club officials and he was giving her a lift home. She mentioned how she and Latty caught the same bus in the mornings and Mr Dryford asked her if they ever talked together. Not talk, she said, they nodded though after a couple of weeks but Latty sat in the same seat every morning, the one near the middle doors, and she always sat in the high seat at the back. Shirley said, 'We're not bosom pals, you know.' She had laughed at that but Mr Dryford hadn't. It was then he said, 'Look, you can't give them an inch, Shirley. I've been round longer than you have and I've seen them all, Dutchies, Eyeties, you name them. And there's not one of them you'll ever get the length of. They mightn't all be no-hopers but they're different to us, you can't get past that one.'

'I think he's pretty harmless,' Shirley said, and Mr Dryford had snorted at that, he said, 'We'll see how harmless he is one of these days.' He let his hand fall on her knee then, just for a moment. 'Still, he needn't be your problem,' he said. 'Need he?'

Later when she told Lynaire she said, 'It could have been like an uncle or something, his hand just touching me for a minute.'

'Only uncles don't as a rule, that's the difference,' Lynaire said. Well she didn't mind that much anyway, Shirley thought to herself. And one day when she saw the old bloke walking up past the war memorial with Len the caretaker, she pointed him out.

'That's him, that nice old foreign joker at work.'

'Probably plays stink finger with little boys if you ask me,' Lynaire said.

'Oh, stink finger yourself!' Shirley had said, and Lynaire opened her eyes very wide, like a comedian on TV or something, and said 'Wouldn't be the first time would it?' They were still cracking up at that one when they arrived back home. Mum was in one of her moods and she said to them, 'You've got about as much sense now the pair of you as when you were fourteen.'

'We're laughing about that foreigner Shirl works with, that's all,' Lynaire said.

'I've got enough to think of here without foreigners,' Mum had snapped.

6

Latty and Len sat on one of the wooden benches above the lake. A little in front of them the ground dipped then fell sharply in a steep bank. Through the branches which carried the fresh leaves of early spring they could see a distant corner of the lake, the greyish water, the massing of clumped reeds. Latty had been off work for a fortnight, and now it was Friday morning. They were the only people in sight.

Latty looked up to the clear sky through the newly living trees. 'I have not missed my work before, not one day since I come to this country.'

Len smiled as he sat with his hands, palm downwards, tucked between his legs and the bench. 'You're not letting that upset you?' he asked. 'I mean, you're not one of those roosters who thinks it's a black mark to be off crook?'

The two men had walked slowly from the house down to the bridge, over the high spanning of the dull sliding river, and up through the town. 'It is quite different you know,' Latty had said, 'out here on a workday.' He had never thought of it before now, the women with their parcels and cartons, pushing their prams or crossing the pavement to the cars parked slantingly towards the kerb. It was good to see the women, the colours of their clothes, on these early days of sun. He had been in his room for almost ten days, with Len or Len's sister bringing him his meals, the dull pain the size of a tennis ball behind his ribs receding until now there was no sign of it left. The doctor twice came to the bach, and this morning in his surgery, had said, 'An x-ray and a few tests, I think, just to be on the safe side.' Latty had come from the doctor's surprisingly cold hands and the neatly trimmed head caught against the sharp light of the window, and his friend was sitting in the waiting room, cross-legged and leaning forward like a boy, a magazine opened on his knee. He felt a tenderness for the row of waiting people, not only for Len his friend, as their eyes raised and looked at his own while his hand moved to his pocket for the black beret. His friend stood up and as they stepped from the waiting room to the concrete path, into the warming sun of a new season, he said, 'I am quite well, Len.' Without surprise his friend answered him, 'Of course you are, Latty, you're right as rain.'

They had walked at an easy pace among the mothers and the shoppers, past the butchers and drapers and grocers Latty had not seen at their work until this morning, but knew only by the words painted on the windows and that dullish empty reflection, the hollow shine that shops give back at weekends when they are closed. Latty wondered as he always did at the children, the firmness of their limbs, the clear simplicities of food and peace. Ah, to be sick, even with this mild brief indisposition of his own, and then to walk out on a day when there is sun and moving drifts of cloud and wind that stirs against the new leaves, against your own face as you sit here above the grey ruffling lake . . . What was it, a kind of lightness, an uncomplicated pleasure in looking and breathing and sitting for long spells of silence beside his friend? It was as though the clarity of the day, the muted light from the lake and the constant papery shiver of the leaves against each other, had entered into him. Then his mind was taken by a strange image. He saw the bright streaming of the day between the banks of his own life. What he had lost was on one side and what he now made do with was on the other, and yet he stood contentedly enough above it, as though on a bridge, a man he imagined above pellucid water on a day sharp and bright as this, watching his own shadow thrown out across the stream.

'I don't need to see him again, I think,' Latty said. He spoke of the doctor, of the fact that these last weeks had been the only time in his life he had needed one, apart from the examination when he came here not long after the war. *(He did not count the injury to his head which somehow had taken him from the yard at home and woken him in the cellar that stank of decay and urine. That was not true sickness, not something within himself. It had been a fragment of that large dark force which destroys and erases, eliminates and forgets. It was like a roller, like a tank. A man's own illness, even his own death should it come naturally, come suppose as that warm pain the size of a tennis ball inside his chest—that is something very different,* Latty thought. *That is the second and enduring obsession one has with one's own body. That is the successor of love, which is the first.)* Latty looked ahead of him, between the branches of a tree whose emerging leaves reminded him of gas flares, pale against the sun. There was gaslight still in France, he remembered. *A night in France and he was very drunk, he had not cared for that night whether he was taken or not. He was dressed as a farm labourer and had ridden in a high creaking wagon into a village of grey-walled, stiffly angular buildings. The driver slowed without speaking to him and he had dropped quietly to the unpaved road. He walked to where he had been directed, to the two-storey house which was unlocked and empty. Whoever lived there, whoever had sat at the long refectory table and last lit the fire which held some remnant of heat as he scraped and prodded the pile of grey ash, had run. He was to wait there until he heard, that was all he knew. Wait until a tap upon the window or a soft scrabbling at the door would signal him and take him as it had before then and would a dozen times more, lead him from a kitchen or the sacristy of a church or the cellars of a chateau, and deposit him again where his hatred and his gifts would ensure as much protection as could be offered. His hatred which came to him so oddly when he thought of it now, above the slightly shifting water, like the sound of a far-off cry hardly recognisable as his own. And the gift, his curious deadly knack, for which men and women risked their lives in order to move it wherever it might work to its fullest. His hands, the soft priestlike fingers, dedicated and deadly, resting now in the mottled light upon his gaberdine as innocently as those of his friend, the man whose world was a few miles any side from where they now sat. That night he had drunk two bottles of wine he discovered hidden behind a stack of empty crates. He drank the bland red liquor then shattered the bottles against the wooden door, and laid his head against the long table, shouting and weeping for his own village that was a pocked scrap of mud. When he woke to the two men pouring water on him, he had seen the gas flare one of them lit rise delicately and transparent against the window behind it, against the first greyness of the morning. The light came through the pale flare,* as now through pale leaves. Len was speaking, Latty realised, his friend was looking at him and waiting for him to answer.

'I am a long way away,' Latty said. 'You must say it to me again.'

'It's just that blazer business,' Len said. 'Remember I mentioned it a while ago, right back near the end of last season?' Yes, he remembered that. It was the day they had watched a football match, when the skies had opened in the second half and they huddled beneath the huge naked trees. Len had pointed at the shed-like building with the small pillared verandah, and told him yet again about the marching teams. He had said what a good lot of kids they were, how he enjoyed the odd jobs he had done on the clubrooms for them. It wasn't something he was paid for, he wouldn't have taken money if they had asked him to, just to see the kids happy with his bits of painting, with his putting together the odd bench and a row of lockers, that made it worth doing. He had knocked up a sink affair for them even, they could make themselves a cup of tea if the weather turned ugly on them. And now he was glad that Latty mentioned the things he had told him so many months before. He said, 'Well you might remember too how Mr Dryford said after I'd done that bench job that he'd have to get me a club blazer like him and the others wear? Remember I said that to you and how I'd just laughed at it? Well anyway he was dinkum about it all right. He told me a couple of nights ago when I was up there putting the second coat on the new lockers. He came in and he said what's your chest measurement, Len?' He was smiling quietly while he told his friend, he was like a boy talking of something he had wanted and now knew for certain he was going to get. 'I thought what's he on about, I didn't click for a minute. And then I saw he was really waiting for me to tell him. He said, "Look, it came up at the committee meeting about all you've been doing for the club and I said how chaperones and managers wore club blazers and you've done a bloody sight more than some of those bludgers." That's exactly how he put it.' Len paused again and looked down through the trees, at the line of shadow gradually receding from the water. He had joined his hands between his knees and was leaning forward, one thumb slowly stroking across the other. 'I wouldn't have hoped in a hundred years for something like that, Latty.' As he leaned forward his head had moved into a spot of direct sunlight, his hair for a moment was red as it must have been years ago, an aura that blurred and shone and then disappeared as he again sat upright. 'I didn't mention it through the week when you were crook,' he said.

Latty asked him when he would get the blazer, when would he be able to wear it?

'This weekend,' Len said. 'He'll bring it out this weekend. He wanted a presentation when the teams were there but I put the kybosh on that one. Bad enough strutting round in the thing without all that.' He laughed softly and Latty thought yet again how his friend had kept so naturally, so easily, his simplicity and his delight in things, in gossip and warmth and the easiness of sitting talking like this, as if it were a young bird he had carried for all those years in the breast of his coat.

'You know what it looks like?' Len asked. 'The colour and that?'

'I've seen the girl on the bus wearing one. The girl who works at the office,' Latty said.

'That sort of lovely blue colour? You don't know really whether it's light or dark.'

'That's the one she wears,' Latty said.

Len raised his right hand and rested it against his chest. 'And the monogram?' he asked. 'Have you seen the monogram?'

'Not up close,' Latty told him.

'It's all worked in white on the pocket. A Maori club affair sloping one way and a spade the other, and they're sort of roped together with little fine flowers, like a chain or something.'

'I have not seen all that,' Latty said.

'You need to look pretty close mind otherwise you miss it.'

The men were silent then while Len smoked a cigarette and the light altered about them. The day was gusty still but so full of brightness, Latty thought, it's as if the light itself was being buffeted and blown about. And then there were long minutes when there was no wind at all, when the branches and the new leaves were motionless and the scraps and stretches of light at their feet grew focused and clear.

'It's an emblem for the district,' Len said. 'The flowers growing over the war things and the farming and that, it's supposed to mean peace.'

'That is a good idea,' Latty said. His broad head nodded at his friend.

Suddenly the sun was directly above the lake and its reflection flashed up as from a mirror. Latty squinted against the glare and Len laughed again as he saw his friend's heavy face fold up so that his eyes quite disappeared. You'd swear he had no eyes at all sometimes, Len was thinking. You'd think he was a Chink or something. They stood up and said perhaps they should be moving back? 'You don't want to wear yourself out and that,' he told him. 'Not your first day up out of bed.'

7

There had been only once in seven years when the weather wasn't fine for the Lions' Fair. 'Old Hughie knows who his boys are all right,' Mr Dryford joked.

As the day approached most of the women in the office were pressed into some kind of service for the Fair. Anyone who volunteered for baking or sewing or novelty goods was allowed off a couple of afternoons. The two men who sat at neighbouring desks in Latty's office had offered themselves, one for the wheel and the other for the stall where you aimed pingpong balls at the plaster heads of clowns with great gaping mouths.

'Just as long as you make it clear what people are aiming for,' the boss explained to the office. 'If you didn't tell them they mightn't know, like,' and he had winked very broadly and moved his head slowly from side to side, his mouth gaping. The young chap who had volunteered for that job wasn't the brightest, so they all saw the point of that one. Then on the Friday before the Fair Mr Dryford stood with one hand pressed against the doorway to his own office and his other hand caught by its thumb in his belt.

'Right,' he said. He nodded his head as he glanced from one employee to another. 'That takes care of you all, I reckon.' And as a final joke he added, 'Anyone with too much stuff for their car need a company bus laid on?' A couple of women sniggered and he said, 'There's no back seat in this one, love, so you can rule *that* out.' There was a roar from the men and Mrs Cleary, who did not go in for the risqué, shook her head and smiled very slightly at the same time.

'Right,' Mr Dryford repeated after the amusement died down, 'that takes care of most of you. Ones who know what a community's supposed to be about, anyway.' His barb was directed at Latty, who had not looked up from his papers while the entertainment was taking place. The large foreigner with his florist's hands, Mrs Cleary thought, you can hardly blame him for not knowing what a Lions' Day's about. She glanced across at him, prepared to offer a sympathetic raising of her brows, but he was engaged at the long roll of figures which was unravelling between his hands. His right hand held a thick white pencil. Between those pale, slightly puffed fingers it was rather like the stem you saw in St Joseph's hand in certain statues. Only that was a strange and irreverent thought, surely, she considered. Again she coloured slightly and wondered what put such things into your head. She was glad, anyway, that she had done her share for tomorrow. She had telephoned Mrs Dryford who was in charge of the sweets and home bakery stall and asked her what it was she most needed, Mrs Cleary was willing to take on anything. She had hoped for sponges, but over the phone she heard that quiet voice say anything but, there were so many of them promised. So she had ended up with half a dozen things, toffee apples even, and butterscotch, and caramel fudge. She had packed them neatly into shoe-boxes and tied them with coloured tape. Mr Dryford had called her a treasure. 'Of course my wife will take all the credit for these, you know,' he said. She had thought he was hinting perhaps that she should take a stint on the stall, and she explained, 'You appreciate my circumstances don't you, my caring for an aging parent . . . ?' She had left Mr Dryford his opening to say something consoling, but what he had said hurt her rather more than perhaps he intended. He had spread his arms and it might have been no more than an expansive movement, but she couldn't help taking it personally, not with her weight problem, could she? He had opened his arms up like that and said, 'Not for a minute, Mrs Cleary. You've done enough making them, surely. We don't need you there eating them as well.'

Mrs Cleary eased herself between the desks and moved the papers spread out on her blotter. She hated people to see how sensitive she was. She searched her top drawer for the tin of paper clips and thought how you couldn't pretend for a moment that any of them in the office was *delicate*, you could never use that word about them. If it came to that, she supposed, it was why these days she took a much softer line with Latty here than the rest of them. You couldn't be sure how much of it got through to him, mind you. How many of the jokes about his beret and Mr Dryford's jibes and the way some of the younger ones doubled over and pretended they couldn't abide the smell of garlic if he opened anything in the lunchroom? And now when he looked up from the strip of figures moving slowly between his fingers and settling in loops on his lap, she made sure she caught his eye. He was a gentleman anyway and she had a soft spot for that, who wouldn't have in this place? He met her glance for a moment, his eyes closing as it seemed, his own smile slighter than her own. He looked up from the strip of paper and acknowledged her and returned to the column of figures without losing his place.

There was nothing he could do, Latty thought, *that was always the story.* He accepted Mrs Cleary's kindness and wished that he could do more than this simple folding of his slab-like cheeks, this bunching of his eyes. He understood how this woman beside him, in her late fifties and wearing her tasteful fawns and greys and today a scarf which he believed was called cerise, wished to stretch out her hand to him, to say how she longed to share his own quietness there in his corner desk. He recognised that as he knew too that Shirley was his friend, and yet he had spoken how seldom to either of them? He had known Mrs Cleary's embarrassment when she returned from giving Dryford the boxes of her baking, when she searched about for the paper-clips but also for the tissues she kept in her top drawer. He had wanted to speak to her, to say—but what was it he could say? What words in this foreign tongue which he knew better than any of them suspected, or in French which he loved to read or in German which he disliked and yet found still came to him at times when he lay awake in the mornings, or in his own language so far now behind those others, his own speech like a secret well—what word from all those to ease that gross aging woman, to comfort her? Or to speak to Shirley, with her exquisite fall of pale hair and the grace she carried in her movements? And at times he was ashamed that he had thought of that girl as he awoke from sleep, her breasts and the colour of her limbs. He had observed how Dryford looked at her, his joking to make her mouth open with laughter, to see her tongue held softly between her teeth. *I am an old man*, Latty thought, *there is nothing in these, in this quietly hopeless woman who sits day after day beside me, in this child whose body I cherish and envy, nothing for Christ's sake is there which I understand?* He kept his attention to the papers in front of him, the accumulated trivia for which he was paid and tolerated by a man who detested him, for whom he represented, in a way which again he did not comprehend, both threat and malice. *Yet to him*, Latty thought, *I am a mirror, I give him back what he demands to see.*

For almost a month Latty had heard talk of the Lions' Day. He hoped with the others that it would be fine, that the record of favour or luck would not be broken. 'It means so much to them at the office,' he said to Len, and his friend answered, 'Not only to them, Latty. It's the first day the kids are marching again so it's pretty important all round.'

'It had better be good weather then,' Latty agreed.

'You can put a ring round that,' Len said.

There was nothing to disappoint any of them. Saturday began with an early sky that lay as though painted, so still were the broad flat layers of cloud behind the town. Latty looked, as he did every morning, through the window opposite his bed to the rise of the hills. In three hours' time that cloud would disperse and the sun break over them. By nine the men would be up at the park, by ten the booths and tents and stalls erected and in place. It was a strange thing, Latty thought, this day when money was raised for charity, when people whose houses were filled with convenience and clutter would rifle through old clothes and stacks of books, tap dilapidated furniture, test rejected radios and third-hand sewing machines. His landlady would be picked up by one of her friends at eleven o'clock. At two she would return with her two string kits stretched with jam and fruit she did not require, a painted gourd which would gather dust in the wash-house, a purple tea-cosy which a few weeks later would be included in a Christmas present to the friend who drove her home. She would carry sword-fern wrapped in damp newspaper, an elegantly potted begonia won in a raffle. And Len would be down at the park even earlier in the piece. The first team was marching just after noon, between the pipe band and the lolly scramble when the Liontamer, in his frayed and weakly leonine fancy-dress, rode through the park in a jeep, hurling into the air the papered toffees donated by a firm in Frankton. Len would need to check that the club-rooms were A-1, he would be there at ten and sweep the already dustless floor, switch on the newly installed zip heater, open the windows so the rooms were fresh when the girls arrived. He would be wearing his blazer for the first time.

A week ago Latty had inspected the new garment, which was pale and soft, with almost a plush feeling when it folded and one's hand sank against it, as his own had been invited to do. 'You like it then, do you?' Len had asked. He spread it out on the table in the bach. The monogram was pure white against the blue, the threads neat and careful and taut. 'I like that,' Latty said. 'I like the colour and the feel and this bit especially,' and his fingers lay against the embroidered crest.

Len grinned across the table as he slipped his arms into the sleeves. He checked that the collar was lying flat, then placed his hands in the pockets. 'Good fit?' he asked. Latty nodded and Len said, 'Feels pretty right anyway.' He had left the blazer on while they drank their bottle of sherry. They had joked about it and even when they were not speaking of it, it remained the centre of the room, the living colour against the drab walls. Latty surprised himself by thinking *he is like the open doors of a church or something*. He supposed he had not been in a church, not in a way which was real, since he had gone with his sister at home, and then it was a habit like his brother-in-law's standing at the kitchen window, a thing so often done it did not make sense to stop it. *He had stood near the font at the baptism, the boy was turned over and his sister had undone the little bow at the back of his gown, and the priest's oiled thumb had moved in the creases of the infant's neck. And why that?* Latty put to himself, *why remember that now?* A child's dedication to divine providence and his people's church, a child dead for over thirty years, a church which no longer stands, *which I perhaps am the last person in the world to remember, as I look across the table, to the blue arm of my friend lying along the plastic cloth?*

'I'm wearing it Saturday if it's fine,' Len had said. The bottle was empty between them and he stood doing up the buttons which were a matching blue. 'I wore it into town today but I had my plastic coat on as well. You don't want them thinking you're swanking about in it.'

'You'd see the colour through the plastic coat though,' Latty remarked.

'Ah, well,' Len smiled. 'That's still not really wearing it, like.'

Latty switched on the radio and lay back, his fingers laced behind his head. He supposed this was the best part of the week, on Saturdays and Sundays, awake and ready to get up yet still lying there, listening to music and the news. It was good that he was no longer feeling ill. 'Not since I have been in this country have I been sick,' he had told the doctor. That was a good thing a man could say after so many years. The doctor was looking at the card he held between his hands, where he had written all the answers Latty had made to him. He smiled across the desk where the stethoscope lay and the bit of wood he had placed on Latty's tongue and the little silver wheel with the black tyre which he had tapped against his knees. He had wanted Latty to stay away from work for a little longer. 'Make it a month,' he had said. 'No,' Latty answered him. 'That will be quite enough, two weeks is quite enough.' And for that time he had lain each morning like this, his hands behind his head, watching the sky through the window which was really four small windows together, happy that he could lie and think of nothing.

On Saturdays he made his breakfast at eight o'clock and read slowly the paper which Len's sister left folded for him on the step. For two hours he read the stories from different parts of the world, and then the pages which told him about the country where he lived, what crimes were committed and what clubs had met, the things which took place in farming and teaching and sport. Latty enjoyed such details, surprised that so much happened where what he saw himself was no more than the habits of peace and work, the occasional surfacings of love and hate. It was more interesting to read a paper than any book. He had explained to Len, 'It is like it is in a story, you know? And then you say to yourself but this is not a story, all this is for a fact, and it is where you live. It is your own story that you read, and yet you don't know it until you read it. That is always strange.'

Len said, 'But it's only the *Herald* after all.' And what pleasure there was on a day like this, to leave his carefully tidied room and stand in the doorway of the bach, such colour and freshness to the morning, to the new fruit trees in early leaf. At the end of the section there was a row of citrus trees. A few weeks ago the lemons had been plump and large, they glowed like yellow globes among their shiny dark leaves. Later in the afternoon he would look across a heaped tray of similar fruit, six or seven hours later when the declining sun was tangled in the oaks at the park, and he stood before an almost depleted stall. There were a few pots of jam on the trestle table, their grease-proof paper tops stretched like small tight drums. The sun shot through the trees and picked out flags of brightness on the grass, and tipped the row of jars.

'I couldn't tempt you?' a voice asked him. Latty smiled and shook his head. His hands were deep in his overcoat pockets and he turned to move from the stall, to where a man stood on the back of a truck, shouting to the crowd milling about that this was definitely the last of the hams, there wouldn't be another chance after this one. The man's hand was on the wheel with its narrow strips of colour, the numbers painted near the rim. There was a crush of buyers round the ticket-sellers in front of the truck. Latty handed across a fifty-cent coin and was given a piece of board with the number 2 written on it. The man barked on from the back of the truck and then the wheel was spinning with a soft whirr above the uplifted expectant faces. The wheel stopped and a teenager who already stood with one leg of ham balanced upright between his feet called out, 'Right, I'll have that one too, thanks.' Latty felt his own card taken from his hand and again the man on the truck was shouting his encouragement, this time holding a box of groceries level with his chest. 'Take it or leave it,' he was telling them. 'Don't want this lot for twenty cents then just keep walking.' Latty moved on, brushing against the rope that enclosed the used furniture mart. He saw Len leaning on one of the long iron pegs the rope was threaded round. His friend was talking to a woman who crouched to examine the scratches on a small dressing table.

Len called across to him. He waved his hand at the jumble of dismantled beds and misshapen sofas, tables and dulled mirrors and nests of chairs. 'Offered my services for the afternoon and got lumbered with this lot,' he said. 'Either this or leading a donkey round with kids on its back for a couple of hours. So ask yourself.' The woman spoke to him and Len leaned forward again, one hand crossed over the other on the top of the iron stake. Then he took a school notebook from the pocket of his blazer and wrote down the name she spelled out to him. As the woman left he said, 'Missed my calling, Latty. That's the second dressing table I've got rid of, and that tallboy over there like a coffin, that one with the old-fashioned handles.' He patted his side pocket where he returned the notebook. Then, 'See the girls?' he asked.

'When I first come over,' Latty said. 'They march like an army, eh?'

'Don't know if that's what they had in mind,' Len said. He supposed that if you had been through the War and that then you wouldn't be likely to watch any marching in the right spirit. He said, 'Everyone seemed pretty pleased for their first showing this season.'

'They practise up and down a lot,' Latty said. 'March, march.' He moved his arms slightly and smiled at the notion of it, those girls from offices and factories and schools rushing their tea two nights a week, then up to the park, to wheel and stamp and obey like sheepdogs the whistling and the shouts of their instructors. There was something Latty simply did not understand in their pounding one spot of grass, swinging from the shoulder, raising their knees high at the sudden turn, swishing their skirts against their thighs. It was so unlike the elation of sport, there was not the pleasure of making music as with a band. The delight he guessed must come from group response, the precision of the obedient unit.

'Of course the uniforms give them a hell of a kick,' Len had told him once. 'And there's the admiration bit, too. There's always a line-up of young bucks when the teams are out.' Latty walked again around the park. The Lions' Day was coming to an end. The last raffle tickets had been sold and the gambling wheel on the truck was now lying flat. One of the boys from the office was dismantling the white faces and scarlet peaked hats of the plaster clowns who sometimes swallowed the lobbed celluloid balls. The young fellow waved across to him and Latty gave back his greeting. There were ladders against some of the large trees and the steel-meshed speakers were unhooked and carefully handed down. The crowd had thinned out, litter lay strewn across the grass. It was like wreckage after the receding of a tide. A few gangs of young boys kicked through the cartons and the screwed papers and discarded cones in their hunt for bottles. The only activities which kept on were the large platform with dodgem cars, and the donkeys at the corner opposite the bowling green. The children waiting for the animals were smaller than those who queued for the cars. Latty strolled towards them and leaned against the trunk of one of the trees. As he watched the children mount and clutch at the man who led them, he broke into fragments a piece of loose bark he lifted from the trunk. The scent was faint and pleasing, the bark springy against his fingers. He watched a boy who had been waiting quietly by himself now take his turn at the head of the queue. The boy stepped into the man's cupped hand and swung himself onto the donkey's back, and took the thin reins into his hands. As the donkey carried him the length of the short track the boy was oblivious of those who still waited or the man who walked beside him, holding the bridle. The child looked frail as he sat absorbed and stiffly upright on the animal's back, his hands closed tightly around the reins. 'Give him a belt,' one of the older boys called out. Another said, 'Go easy, he's nearly crapping himself as it is.' The boy seemed not to hear. The animal turned close to the edge of the park, where Latty stood against his tree. The aging man saw the thick vein in the boy's pale neck, the excitement pulsing as he disregarded all but the beast beneath him, the fact of himself straddling it. As the man led him back the boy laid one hand along the donkey's neck, leaning far forward, his hand small and white against the broad muscular arch. At the end of the ride the boy threw his leg across the animal's back and jumped to the ground before the man could help him. He moved through and past the other children without speaking and without disturbance, as self-contained as when he had sat with the reins in his hands. His dark hair fell straight forward over a high forehead. He began to walk across the park, through the litter and the dismantled stalls. Latty felt for his loneliness, for that and for the small precious private world he carried with him across the grass, to where his mother waited for him at one of the park benches. Latty recognised her from where he stood, that woman who came to the office on the past two Christmas Eves, each time as Latty, after his one glass of beer, was about to leave before the party really got under way. Mrs Cleary said last year, 'Stay a bit longer surely, won't you?', but he had said, No, it was better that he went now. He had stepped back from the doorway to let the boy's mother pass into the paper-streamered lunchroom and the chatter which hushed as she stood there. Then, 'Ah, the little lady,' Dryford had called out. 'Better roll in another couple of dozen, lads,' and the laughing had started up again, the boss had broken the ice.

Latty watched the boy go up to his mother, her laying her hand briefly on his shoulder as he turned to her and spoke. The woman smiled and she tapped the boy lightly on the side of the face. She then pointed to a large paper bag which the boy took up and raised his knee to balance, before carrying it across to a car. He saw the boy sit in the car beside his mother, speak to her again, and buckle the safety belt he drew down across his shoulder. The boy's forehead and his hand raised to brush against his hair made Latty think of the other boy, *his face pale in the light from the lantern, the pool of light they stood in and his sister holding the tired child, his brother-in-law speaking quietly across the horse's broad and shining back, the capital had fallen he was saying, they cannot be far from here.*

'Just give us a lift here will you, Latty?' Len called out to him. He went quickly to where his friend and a younger man were dragging a wardrobe up a short ramp on to a large covered truck. Most of the furniture from the second-hand mart was already loaded on. A few of the better pieces were muffled under scrim. Latty stepped onto the ramp next to Len and hoisted at the wardrobe. The driver who would not have been half their age lifted the lower end. 'Right there, grandad?' he asked.

'I'll last you out, you young bugger,' Len told him. Then the driver said, 'You might as well come for the ride if you like,' and flicked his thumb towards the cab. He said he'd take the truck down to the plant where it came from and leave it there for the night. The Lions' blokes were going to help him with delivering the stuff in the morning. 'I'll be bringing my own car back so I'll drop you here if you want.' 'Might as well,' Len said. 'Ages since I've ridden in one of these.' Then he said, 'How about you, Latty?'

'Not since the timber days,' Latty said. 'Then I drive one, oh, for years all together.'

'They've come on since then, though,' Len said. 'Just get a dekko at that.' He tapped his fingers against a large radio attached to the dashboard. 'Everything except sheilas eh?' he said as the driver swung himself in behind the wheel.

'What do you think's under there?' the young man joked. He nodded his head back to the space behind the seat, to a long folded tarpaulin. He eased the truck onto the road. They drove three or four miles out of town, to large corrugated iron sheds where fertiliser and coal were held in bulk.

'Be worth a bit,' Len remarked. 'All they keep in there.'
'Take a lot of men to flog it anyway,' the driver said. He backed under a roofed section of the yard.
'Old Harvey's come on all right,' Len said. He pointed to the name on the sides of the other trucks in the yard. 'I went to school with him and you mightn't believe it but he was as thick as they come in those days. Talk about slow.' The driver laughed good naturedly and said, 'Still is, Len. Thick as pig-shit.' Latty was glad that the driver enjoyed talking with his friend, that beneath his crude bluffness there was a warmth towards the older man. 'Anyway we'll have a drink on him before we head back.' He winked at Latty as he spoke and led them to a shed in the corner of the yard. He opened the lock with a key he singled out on a keyring that was shaped like a hula girl. He pulled out a couple of chairs from a bench that was strewn with papers. 'Don't spill your piss on them,' he advised them. 'They're the dockets from last week.' He crouched down and lugged a carton from beneath the bench. 'Treat ourselves on an old schoolmate, eh Len?' the driver said. He placed a bottle of scotch in a space he had cleared among the papers. He brought out three glasses which he rubbed quickly with a soiled towel that hung behind the door. The bottle was a little less than half full, and the young man almost emptied it as he poured into the glasses. Len looked up from beneath his untidy hair, an ancient schoolboy delighted at the adventure of it. 'Makes a nice change,' he grinned.

Latty said, 'Thank you,' as he took the carefully handed glass. The driver himself sat on the floor, his head leaned against the support in the middle of the bench. He raised his glass to eye level and said, 'Here's mud in it, then.' Len chuckled as he sipped at his glass, his eyes closed for the unexpected pleasure. Latty's broad face turned from the younger man towards his friend who had now opened his eyes. 'Here's good luck,' he said.

When the driver dropped them back at the park it was almost dark. You could make out the shapes of the trees against the sky, Latty noticed, but only just. The strong drink was singing slightly in his ears and he closed his fists in his overcoat pocket. There was a kind of joy in the evening. He looked directly above him, to the few stars he could see stirring between the delicate leaves. It was like they were chips of shining glass on a soft rich cloth. He braced his feet firmly as he leaned back and looked up, he felt the freshness of the air and the simple goodness of standing here, slightly drunk, beneath the clean falling of the night.

'I'll wait here shall I?' he asked Len.

'What on earth for?' his friend said. 'You walk over with me.'

Their feet scuffed against discarded papers as they crossed the damp grass towards the clubrooms. 'Sorry to drag you over Latty but there's that other bag of stuff my sister left for me to take back. She'd go butchers if I left it here.' And then he said, 'The walk'll do us good anyway, after that young bloke's hospitality.' The wooden pavilion took shape in front of them. Len had given the verandah its second coat earlier in the week, and the odour of paint came to them above the smell of the grass. There was another scent too, mingling with the others.

'There's laburnum or something near here,' Len said. 'Must be from that boarding house across the road there, it's all down one side of it.' Latty did not know if it was the same flower but he thought of hanging purple clusters, dying almost before they had fully blossomed. They had been in one place, hadn't they? He tried to remember where it was. He saw himself hidden in a barn, that sweetness carrying through a gap between the boards as he sat in near darkness, in the dry catching odour of piled sacks. The memory came into his mind with a strange clarity, the sacks, the gloom, the sweet heavy flowering somewhere outside. He remembered that a bottle had been given to him when his food was brought, and each time he had raised it to his mouth he lowered it carefully on to the pile of sacks. There must have been some danger he no longer recalled. *Not remember if he waited to kill or be killed. Only the raising and the replacing of the bottle, the intermingled smells of life around his darkness and his fear. And yet not where it was, not why or for whom he waited.* That is strange, Latty thought, to remember and to forget at the same time, *the sacks and the perfume which were nothing then and now are all that is left.*

The sound of the traffic carried over from the main road. This side of the park seemed withdrawn and quiet. There were lights from some of the houses across the street, but no noise. A blue television flicker showed behind drawn blinds. Latty looked across and stood on the edge of the verandah while Len took a key from his trouser pocket, fitted it to the lock, then felt for the switch inside the opened door.

A widening carpet of light fell brightly and suddenly across the verandah and out onto the grass. Latty saw the sheen on the newly painted boards, the cartons stacked at the end of the verandah, the pair of white boots one of the girls had left tucked beneath the seat that ran the length of the wall. He saw these things and heard the cry and the shout from inside the room. He took the few steps to stand behind his friend. Len was as though struck into the position he held, his hand resting still on the light switch. Across Len's shoulder, past the large freckled ear and the reddish hair tufted above the blue collar of his blazer, Latty saw the girl's breasts swing as she turned, the smear at her thighs blurring as she moved from the light, the opened door, the two aging men. Her blonde hair arced out behind her, settled across her shoulders as she crouched and grabbed at the clothes untidily spread across a chair and partly fallen on the floor. Latty removed his eyes from her lithe animal panic to the man who stood facing them above a coat spread out on the boards of the floor, exposed as he fumbled into his trousers, his shirt and net singlet rucked at his waist. He was shouting at them, threatening them incoherently. His face strained so that from the neck of his opened shirt he was like a throttled man. One hand now held the top of his trousers as he rushed towards them, and as he raged a thread of spit leaped from his mouth and fell across his chin. His free hand was raised and his fingers grabbed at the pocket of Len's blazer, there was the quick rip of stitching and Latty's own hand came up towards the straining throat. His spread hand waited there without in fact touching flesh, the two men separated by no more than inches in the absurd silence, the girl faced to them now, her clothes partly on and the rest held in front of her while she shivered, as though she had come from bathing in icy water. Dryford's eyes were on Latty. 'I'll get you,' he was telling him, his voice lowered now and unsteady. 'I'll get you, you wop cunt.' But he let his hand fall from the pocket he had ripped. He knew as he stepped back that he had cowered before the older man. Latty touched his friend's sleeve and said, 'We must go now, Len.' For the first time since the opened door and the flooded light, Dryford spoke to the girl. 'I'll drive you back,' he said, and the girl told him, 'No, I can walk back from here.' The three men stood and waited as she pulled a sweater over her head and turned again towards them. She looked at Latty and he said to her, 'You need not be worried. No one will know we came here.' She looked at him still as though his words were not clear to her while she sat to pull on her boots. Then she brushed between the men, she began to run as she stepped from the verandah on to the grass, her white boots flickering when nothing else was visible, and the gasping of her breath came back to them until the flicker too was gone. Latty turned once more to his friend, he said again, 'We must go now.' Len took a leather bag from the corner of the room and passed in front of Dryford. Then he and Latty followed across where Shirley had run, over the dozen or so yards of the broadening fading wedge of light thrown from the opened door, and then across the darkened grass to the other side of the park. The headlights of the traffic were picking out the trunks and branches of the trees.

Len said no, he could manage all right, when Latty offered to help him with the laden bag. They walked without speaking past the quiet shops and the cinema and the bank with the large pillars on the corner. Each place they passed had drawn a story from Len at one time or another, the crockery shop whose owner had lost a fortune on horses, the hotel with the haemophiliac barman, the gardening and hardware store where incest was not only verified in court, but incest that was knowingly and encouragingly observed by the town councillor next door. The two men walked on, across the pedestrian crossing to the front of the post office whose tower had been removed after an earthquake scare more than fifty years before, its graceful structure reduced to a squat hulk. Len stopped to change the bag from one hand to the other. 'Well that sort of took the shine off things Latty,' he said.

There was nothing Latty could think of to say, no word he could dredge up which might alter the truth of what his friend had said. And not only the shine but an innocence too which had dropped from things, a disillusionment which Len would never redeem. They walked from the spread of street lights into the cavern, as it seemed, beneath the large trees further down the road. They emerged again beneath the naked skies as they came to the incline towards the bridge. And as they stepped from the pavement to the bridge Latty raised his right hand from his pocket and slid it between the broad lapels of his coat. There was a sudden uncomfortable heat inside his chest, a glowing which was also pain. 'Wait,' he said to Len. 'Can we wait a bit?' He stopped and breathed the cold black air from the depth beneath them, the quiet slipping of the river between its banks. He leaned forward against the rail. 'Over here,' Len was saying, 'over here Latty.' He was leading his friend to the other end of the bridge, holding his arm as he sat him against a concrete pole. 'Take it easy for a minute eh?'

The feeling in Latty's chest expanded. He felt the altering of his pulse. *Ah* he was thinking *we are near the river*, and he must have spoken aloud without awareness, for Len sat beside him now and had his hand across his back. 'Of course we are,' he was saying, 'we've just crossed it, Latty.'

Near the river he was saying and then he said it in words his friend no longer understood. He was listening for the voice behind him, for the boy's voice to break the monotonous soft progress of the cart, the tapping of the stick against the side. Soon they would notice that light from the surface of the river which was not reflection, an emanation scarcely less dark than the night itself but which spoke the broad presence of the curving water. And then the gushing against the wooden supports of the bridge. 'Not far,' Len was telling him, 'Not far once you've got your wind back.' Latty kept his hand between his lapels, his fingers now on the smooth fabric of his shirt and the button he was attempting to undo. Len leaned above him, cradling him. 'All right?' Latty asked in that other language now, the boy had not answered and he supposed he was nodded off against the sacks of grain. There were the lights already across to the left, the river beneath them now, its washing against the piers. The boy with his sailor's cap pulled down, imagining the fullness of the sea curling against the bows, the line across the pale forehead when Latty raised and lifted and handed him to his sister, and the cap fell back.

Palms and Minarets

'You're the one who will have to decide. You're the one who knows whether you're run down or not.'

My wife sat under the lampshade made from a sheet of old monk's music we had brought back from Spain.

'I'll decide,' I told her. 'I'll decide before next weekend.' Her needles clicked while she knitted. The shiny pages of a pattern book lay open on the sofa beside her, and even as she spoke her eyes moved from the needles to the instructions in the book, then back to her work. I looked past her to the red lines drawn on the curved stiffness of the parchment, at the heavy black squares to tell a monk's voice where exactly to go, where in the huge cool greyness of a church his voice was to rise or fall, the light from a high window over the shaved heads of the monks. Because I saw that once in Spain. My wife was looking for a shop that sold filigree work, the kind she had seen in Toledo and decided not to buy, and had then thought about and spoken about for the next three days. We were in a town whose name I forget, where we had not meant to be. She lay down in the afternoon and I walked through streets which were high white walls and stiff shadows. Then late in the afternoon she had decided to go after her filigree and I walked into a church, into the rise and fall of the voices behind the heavy leather curtain at the door, the black squares on the red lines behind my wife's head.

'If you don't decide to take a rest now who knows where we'll finish up?'

There had been a smell in the greyness like concrete, like water spilled on concrete. There was a young monk with a beard who looked like a movie star.

'I told you I'd go next week.'

'You know very well with a specialist you need to make an appointment well ahead.'

'I'm sure I'll last that long,' I said. My wife's needles clashed, they were steel and clashed softly but she may also have been cross that I kept putting things off. Her hair which once I had thought so lovely was drawn close against her head. It was red in the light from the monks' singing, from the music which had no tune to follow, no notes I could read although I had learned the piano for several years. My mother had said, *He'll never be a concert pianist mind you but he sticks to a thing.* She had said it to my aunt while she stood at the kitchen sink. She wore pink rubber gloves which almost made me feel ill if they touched my skin. *You can play that piece you did for the examinations* she told me, *the piece you played last night for your father.* But it was for *him,* I thought, I am not playing it for anyone else.

I'll play it when she comes round next week I told her. I watched her pink gloves shine each time she raised them from the water and their pale dry insides when she peeled them off. *Next week, auntie. I'll be better at it by then.*

Only a few times, once or twice in the Army and another time in a church group, have I been with men who talked about their fathers. I do not mean the way one reminisces with friends, because it is likely they would have known him or heard about him anyway. I mean the times when men try to tell others what their fathers were like. That doesn't happen very often, and I think that when it does, most men will tell lies.

My own father was short, his features as sharply fine as if clipped from paper. In these past months I have thought of him a great deal. I believe I remember the first time he walked down the street with me. He held my hand as I stepped across the dappled footpath through circles and patches of brightness and moving shadow, when I was still too young to know that the pavement wasn't shifting but the flickering was from the trees that grew right along the street. We would come to a puddle of light and when I paused he would take both my hands in his and say, 'Over we go, digger.'

I am the only person I know whose father was a dandy, a man who failed at almost everything except keeping his shoes polished to perfection, and at a kind of kidding all the time that he was more melancholy than anyone understood. He loved standing on the back porch with his jacket off but his white sleeves rolled down, the cuffs held with slender jade cuff-links, his waistcoat buttoned and his watch-chain shining across his lean stomach. He would stand with a book open and resting on one palm and in the sunlight (it is never winter when I remember him), from the distance, he was lithe and solitary, a kind of figure from a western who held a book instead of a gun. But he would take books up and lay them down as though there were something in them which roughness would spill.

My father's single hobby was pool. Several nights a week he went out after we had eaten our dinner. My mother would say it was all very well having an interest but it would be nice if it was something that put food on the table. One of the delights of my childhood was to be taken to the saloon which was across the road from the library. Children were not meant to enter the bluish darkness with the great pyramids of light from the lamps above the tables, but my father nodded his head to the man at the doorway and said, 'He's keeping an eye on me.' He looked down at me and said, 'Don't you break the place up, do you hear me?' The tables were so brilliant and green that my hope for weeks was simply to touch one. It was my fourth or fifth visit before I asked if I might, and my father surprised me, he gave a quiet laugh and pressed my shoulder and said, 'You just go ahead and touch it if that's all you want.' He spoke as though it was nothing at all that I had keyed myself up to ask, and I ran my hand along the side of the table on the smooth varnished wood, then on the table itself, backwards and forwards on the pliant crushed firmness of the felt.

My partner is the one who really makes the money. He brings ideas to me for new lines and especially for new promotion methods and at the board meetings he always begins 'We've decided' or 'We came to the conclusion' and the board believes that when he says 'we' he naturally means the two of us. He is loyal because ten years ago I brought him in against opposition. He had no official qualifications and he is as ugly a man, I suppose, as you are going to get. At the staff barbecues (it is there, I mean, one most notices it) he wears a short sleeved shirt and his guts sag over his belt. His arms are fat and pale and hairless, his hair has receded from a forehead which shines always in a slight glaze of sweat. One looks at him because one must. There is no way of working with a man, of sharing with him the responsibilities of a company, and avoiding his physical insistence. Nor would one ever call his wife attractive, but at least she is not gross, she does not make you want to reach out your hand to remove plate or glass, to spirit away both food and drink because one knows how it will sag and weigh against the strained belt, puff those disagreeable arms. She is a smallish woman and when he stands beside her she seems less than half his size. The lines of her clothes hang parallel from her shoulders to below her knees. It is of no consequence of course what she looks like, whether she is all rotundities or a breathing pencil, but I notice because she is so incongruous beside her husband. They are each a kind of distorting mirror to the other. She lays her thin fingers on the cushion of his forearm, he sometimes rests his arm across her shoulders, his hand hanging loosely in front of her slight breast as though to protect it. Perhaps because her skin is so sallow, so much the colour of a kind of tawny soap, I am reminded of an Eastern woman, perhaps an Indian I may have seen in *National Geographic,* with a plump snake relaxed about her neck. Yet I admit one has so little right to be fastidious with the lives or the choices of others.

Sometimes I see his eyes slightly puckered as against a drift of smoke, and he is taking in my wife and myself. I wonder why he is so meticulous to present me favourably to the board, to share with me what he has a right to keep for himself. Or why when he speaks to the staff in his joking way does he pretend it is my way as well? There is nothing more he can get from the company, he is my full partner although I took him in when the board said quite openly did I know what I was doing? Even then he was fat and smiled. When he covered his eyes with one pale hand at the very first meeting, had opened his fingers and looked at them like a child to see if he was going to be attacked before he explained his figures, they had laughed and they had loved him. Several times over the years they have said they have me to thank for him. And over and over when he begins in those meetings 'We decided' or 'We think it best', he is saying over and over too that he has me to thank for them.

I sat on the bench in the hospital corridor, leaning my head on the wall behind me. I wore one of those shapeless blue-towelling hospital gowns and sat cross-legged, while nurses pushed at the noisy swinging doors of the x-ray rooms. An old man sat a few yards from me in a wheelchair. His eyes were receded and his hands constantly smoothed the blanket across his knees. I feel uncomfortable among the sickly, but I continued to watch him. I was wasting the better part of an afternoon to satisfy a doctor I had visited because of occasional digestive pains in my chest. ('We don't know however that it's nothing until we see these,' he told me a few weeks later. He slipped a large negative from its brown envelope and held it against the window so we both could inspect the overlapping of shadow and outline, an aerial photograph it might as well be of a city I did not know, taken through cloud and gathering darkness.) I looked down at the incongruous shoes and socks which the attendant had told me I could keep on, and across to a young man opposite me who sat with bare feet, in a gown identical to my own. Again I glanced at my watch, I suppose with some impatience. A woman beside me said, 'Would you like this to look at? It might pass the time.' She held towards me an *Australian Post* which had become dog-eared with handling by the bored and the ill. 'No, thank you,' I told her. I saw her own hands joined together on her lap, the band of a wedding ring on one of her fingers. Beneath the sleeves of her gown the bones of her wrists stood up like little domes. I went back to looking at the old man, at the gleaming lino along the long corridor, hearing the squeak of rubber soles as the nurses came and went. The woman beside me was Eva, and for as long as I was to know her that was her way of sitting, knees together and the fingers of her hands interlacing as they rested across her skirt or her paisley housecoat at home, or her naked legs during the summer.

We would joke that we met in a hospital corridor, in our ill-fitting gowns among the clattering of metal trays and the constant swinging of the doors. Later when she went for other x-rays or for tests, I would wait in the larger room at the end of the corridor. It became so much easier to take time away from my office than ever I had thought. I would leave at ten or at twelve or at three, whenever I wished, and I felt the freedom of a boy deciding simply to walk away from school. We would drive to Cornwall Park to the grey constantly stirring olives which Eva loved or to the kiosk in the Domain and once, on a flawless day in early September, we crossed the harbour bridge and walked on sloping paths between the dark green of native trees, above the glitter of the sea. Or more often, and what I preferred, was to sit at Eva's home, a small state unit on the other side of the city to where I lived. In our one winter we would sit on a settee in front of an open fire, burning thick lengths of pine which her brother had sent down to her from his farm. The ends of the logs hissed at the oozing sap and gave out a clean delicate scent. In the part of our one summer we sat in deckchairs at the back of the house, on the small square of grass, protected from neighbours and from wind by a screen of corrugated plastic sheets I had erected for her.

When I think of us it is seldom of one particular time, hardly at all of what we spoke about. I think of that simplest of things, the closeness neither of us needed to work at. It is as though when we were together we moved always under a canopy of content, like some ikon in a procession (which again I saw in Spain). And always Eva's physical stillness is in my mind, her voice which was almost harsh, which knew and carried more of life than any other I have heard. Yet she had not even been to the South Island, where her husband had settled with another family.

For the past eight years, since she came to the city from a small town in the north, she had worked at a warehouse I drove past every day. From the window behind her desk she could see our factory, with my name along the side.

I have said to my wife that I do not want to go out in the next few weeks, not to dinners nor parties nor to the Old Boys' Ball she has mentioned several times. 'You go by all means,' I tell her. 'We have gone with the same group for ten years, you will know everyone there.'

'I wouldn't dream of it,' she says. She smiles to let me know that her disappointment will never show. My partner has said to me several times, 'She's a brick, that woman,' so I do not fuss when she is heroic. I say simply, 'You may change your mind. You may want to go when the time comes.' She smiles again and shakes her head and there is the faintest of metallic sounds from the movement of her earrings.

My wife is the kind of woman everyone says has charm. The last time we were out together, the week before last at another company's social, the woman I was dancing with said, 'Your wife's got him eating out of her hand.' She meant one of the directors who wore a hairpiece and who slid his spread hand over my wife's buttock when they turned into the shadow at the further end of the hall. She took the hand and raised it back to her waist. I danced with this younger female because I was obliged to. She was the wife of one of our up-and-coming men, a boyish petulant man who sat drinking in one of the booths at the side of the floor, his leg out stiffly in front of him in the swathed bandages of an ankle sprained while skiing. When his wife spoke she smiled at me and shook back her hair and I presume I was meant to be a little taken with her charm too. 'Oh,' I said to her, 'has she?' And the young woman I held and turned with and was bored to death by said, 'There, every man with a lovely wife likes to play it down.' She gave her gay young executive wife's laugh, and it was like a stick being run across a child's xylophone. I thought as I glanced at the young throat and the breasts raised up by her dress and the folded lace handkerchief affair tucked like some small animal between them that Eva, without looks or charm, was all that mattered in my life after even fourteen months.

As on that night, dancing with the young wives of my staff, or at any other time I think of, alone with my family or going through the hoops with my equally well-trained guests, it is all much the same. I look at the faces in front of me as though at cardboard and plastic; I think of a woman who is nothing and nowhere, and she is more real to me than my own hand. Always as I think of her I am tapping my thick square nails (which Eva liked to play with, to snick her own nails against or press the bands of cuticle towards their base) on whatever happens to be near me. The vile marble thing on my desk at work or on an ashtray at home, until my wife says, 'I don't like to nag but would you mind stopping that? It gets on my nerves.'

'So would breathing if you could hear it,' I answer her. Or once when she asked me if I did it simply to pass the time I said No, it was more than that, it was hearing time pass as well, and she and her daughter looked across at each other 'significantly', as I suppose they would think it. Their look is to say observe how husband and father is over-strained, is in advanced depression, when in fact I am bored, bored. Recently I dreamed of myself fishing a lake. I was sort of trawling with several lines from the back of the boat as we moved along. There was no water in the lake and the hooks dragged at the bottom like the teeth of a plough. As far back as I could see were the neat parallel lines of the dragging hooks. But while I tap my nails against ashtray or table or the wooden arm of a chair, my wife turns her head and raises her hands when she speaks, and her rings and earrings sparkle and her voice 'tinkles', as she likes to be told. She sheers like late-afternoon water, I see her standing in life and splashing as a child in the shallows of a river. That is where she speaks from, and I answer from the dry floor of my lake.

My father stopped with me one afternoon at a house much finer than our own. I had been with him at the library for the whole morning. At two o'clock he slipped his jacket over his long white sleeves with the jade links, and the dark waistcoat he did not take off when he worked. I liked to be with him in the room where he did his tasks, and breathe in the odours of glue and aging paper and the shiny leather chair. His job was to sort out all the papers which came to the library, and put them in the wooden frames that held them together in bunches. There were brass hooks in the frames and the frames hung in rows, and between the rows was like being in a tunnel of papers.

He took his hat from a high shelf and turned it as he always did against his sleeve, while he held the edge of his sleeve in his hand.

Sometimes on Saturdays we would go to the snooker saloon where I watched him play, or sometimes to the afternoon pictures. What I remember are stories about the desert and sheiks in long flowing robes and headpieces which flapped behind them as they galloped their horses in a smear of flying sand. There were often clumps of palms where they spoke to women inside silken tents, or cities with wonderfully white walls and high thin towers. After the pictures I would hold his hand when we came onto the street, and everything was so grey and ordinary and dull after what we had seen. But this day he said, 'Nice afternoon to stretch the old legs, wouldn't you say?' Often I did not quite know what he meant. Yes, I would say to everything. He took up a parcel of books from the table where a stack of folded newspapers were still in their brown paper wrappings. We walked up the long street to the bridge and then across the tops of the trees. I looked down on the gully through the flicker of the gaps in the concrete fence. Towards the end of the bridge he lifted me right up and I held the small squares of wire and pressed my face close against them. I could look down to the rounded crowns of the trees, and in the bright summer light some of the leaves were shining like glass.

We walked until we came to a house with a verandah around three sides. A lady opened the door and when we stepped inside it was like going into a deep cool cave. My father placed the books on a small table in the hallway where there was a leaning white tower she said was carved out of one tusk of ivory. My father and the lady sat in a large room with heavy curtains folded like in a picture theatre. They sat in there and drank tea from cups which had little flecks in them that you could see through when they were held against the light. The lady took out to the verandah a little tray with a glass of lemonade, and cake I did not like with seeds in every mouthful. I walked round and round the verandah and put my hands through the spaces between the railings, and pulled over a stool from where wire baskets of trailing ferns and creepers were hanging from the roof. I knelt on the stool and leaned against the railing as though I were on a ship. I could look over the gully we had walked across, see the whole span under the bridge like part of a huge hoop. And far down was the harbour, so brightly blue I am sure I remember it as more brilliant than it was.

After our visit to the lady we walked back across the bridge and it was back to what was ordinary. We would just say we had been for a walk when we got home, my father said, this would be our secret. We waited on the safety zone for the tram to take us home. Usually my father let me sit on the thick curved end of the platform while I held on to his arm, but I remember that day we only stood. When we were walking down the small hill towards our own house my father said, as we came near the gate which always snagged for a second because part of the catch had come away, 'Mecca, eh, old man?'

'Yes,' I said to him. I knew that was a kind of secret too, long before I knew whatever else it was.

There is a marble inkstand on my desk, a present my wife brought me back from Mexico two or three years ago. I find that I tap my nails against it most of the time I am sitting at my desk. The lump of marble is off-white and yellowish on different sides, the veins merely darker unattractive streaks. It is like snow when it begins to thaw, that seeping and trickling and discolouration you see in diminishing banks stacked against the side of a road, when it is eaten at the edges and irregular and stained. This is what Zelma's present has reminded me of since the moment she placed it on my lap at home and said, 'This is yours, señor,' while the children pranced about in their broad-brimmed and sequined hats. She had loved Acapulco even more than she had thought she would, miles more than Spain on our trip before we had the children, when we had pretended to ourselves that we would return there to live.

'More than Honolulu?' my son asked.

'You don't have to compare things, silly.' She tipped the boy's hat forward so that the brim rested against his shirt front. The shirt was a present too, blue linen with eagles embroidered on the shoulders.

'I almost bought you a shirt, you know,' she said to me.

'Almost?'

'Would you have worn it?'

I looked at the bright embroidered wings and lied, I said, 'You just never know.'

'Of course he wouldn't,' my daughter said. 'He'd die if he wore anything with colour in it.'

'You can see him with this hat on too, can't you?' The children held their arms stiffly and strutted as we used to for marching as wooden soldiers, but they were being their father. The boy put his head a little to one side as I suppose I do and gave the curtest of nods several times, his father acknowledging the neighbours. He and the girl and their mother became quite hysterical, 'The idea of him in that gear!' My wife had to sit back and flap herself with both hands until she said, 'Now that will do, you've all had your joke.' I put my folded hands beneath my chin and watched them, the eagles moving when the boy's arms moved and the hats flashing as they turned.

'Did you see a bullfight?' I asked her.

'Do you think I'm sick or something?' she said. 'He says did your mother go and watch those barbarians torture a bull to death?' she exclaimed to the children. She closed her eyes at the thought of it and the girl said, 'I'd certainly hate to see one, I know that.'

'What about you?' I said to the boy. 'Reckon you could face a bullfight?'

The boy was turning the hat in his hands now, his thumbs edging the brim round and round. He shrugged his shoulders when I asked him what he thought about it. 'Not interested enough to even know?' I said, and my wife and my daughter looked at each other and each raised her eyebrows at the same time. 'We'll leave it there shall we?' my wife said. 'Before we're fighting again.'

I have noticed time and again that they are so close they do not have to speak. I have seen them at parties, they circle and move about like two animals you think are unaware of each other, and yet once they get home each knows exactly what the other has done, to whom the other spoke and when. As they sit together and talk of something again they are feline, precise. They sit above whatever they speak of and nose it, as it were, prod it about with swift careful taps.

One night very recently they were discussing bridal patterns when I came into the lounge before dinner. They were speaking rapidly together, unaware that their husband and father had come into the room until they heard me at the bottles, and I asked them why there was no ice. 'There's ice all right,' my wife said. She moved to stub her half-smoked cigarette.

'Don't you go,' my daughter said to her. 'I'll get it for him.' While she banged at the refrigerator, inserting her arm behind the frozen vegetables and the television dinners to where the one small tray of ice was stuck fast against the back wall, my wife placed her hands palm downwards on the arms of the leather chair, and closed her eyes. She was like an Egyptian statue, something at the door of a monument.

'You'll have to get it for yourself,' my daughter called out. 'It's stuck too hard for me to move.'

'It must have been back there a long enough time,' I said.

'Hard to see how that could happen, the way you go through ice.'

'Well?' I asked her. 'Is that leading up to something?'

'The carving knife's there if you need it,' she said. I chipped between the wall and the metal tray while the girl went back to her mother. As I tugged at the tray to edge it free my hand slipped and my fingers caught against one of the sharp fittings inside the icebox. Suddenly on the white encrusted ice I saw the small blooms of my own blood, splashes that opened like minute flowers. I looked at the drops for a moment, at the close sequence of stains across the ice, and felt my stomach lift with a kind of disgust. I must have stood for quite some time, fascinated at those vivid splashes that were myself. The others picked up the silence after my chipping with the knife and my daughter called out, 'Managed, have you?'

'I've cut my hand,' I said.

'On the knife?'

'On the fridge.' I waited because I thought one of them might move. I pressed my finger in my handkerchief but there was no depth to the cut. Yet I still expected one of them to come across to say is it all right, even to take the tray out for me and put the cubes into my glass. When I turned towards them I saw that both of them were looking at me.

'There's plaster in that drawer,' my wife told me. 'That one right beside you.' I opened the drawer and moved my other hand through the jumble of papers and stamps and rubber bands and tins.

'Manage?' she called again.

'It'll be all right,' I told her. I had found the spool but when I took it from the drawer it was not plaster but masking tape. I left my finger wrapped in my handkerchief and attended again to my drink. I ran the hot tap on the frozen tray, the ice cracking under the stream of steaming water. Neither of the women—for she is that, too, I suppose, my daughter—asked me how it was when I went back into the lounge, my hand concealed in my pocket. I sipped at my gin, the ice cubes nudging and clicking against one of the thin Danish glasses which my partner had given us last year for a Christmas present. 'Not that I believe in Christmas,' he had said as he gave the box with its gay seasonal wrapping to my wife, 'but I believe in presents.' That was the first night—last Christmas Eve—when I knew how clearly I was watching something on a screen. I have thought of that comparison many times; each time I feel more strongly that what I watch does not really have much to do with me. I now watched the two women and turned my glass slowly to hear the ice. They spoke of whether my daughter's hair would need to be cut if that style were to suit. I watch them as if there is an audience between us, like a man who wonders when he sits in a cinema what those actors must be like once the cameras stop filming, is there any small movement, any inflection in their voices, which tells him what they are really like? There is no one I know who is not behind make-up, not across a deep pit. I try to think of people who are not on a screen, and I think only of two, of my father and of Eva.

I have said that my partner's strength is that he can get on with people, whether he knows them or not. He tells me that is what selling is about. It is a way of putting your arm around someone's shoulder, talking to him so that he knows you're his friend. I have heard him explain this several times, to the staff or to the board. His hands open and close while he speaks. His face eases into its broad smile or he looks at whoever he is talking to quite solemnly, sincerely. When he opens his hands and shows his palms he has let out the dove of confidence and intimacy. It hovers over the heads of his audience and they feel its presence too, they look back quite as solemnly. Then when his palms meet and close and his thick fingers interlock or rub over each other in a kind of love-making with themselves, the bird has returned, it has disappeared into the magical hands, and those who have listened smile back, or laugh at his own laughing. It is like a man performing in front of a mirror, and his mirror is people.

Once my partner said to me, 'I know you think my methods are brash but they are also twenty-six per cent better than those anyone else in this outfit would think of using. That's not a bad return on brashness.' He sat opposite me while I tapped my nails against the marble inkstand. His hands were folded across the rise of his guts, as they usually were when we spoke together. He is far from being a fool and I believe he knew very early on that I did not believe in the dove. He had just delivered his latest advertising thoughts onto the broad unstained blotter of my desk. What he had placed there was a coloured photograph of a foetus, the tiniest veins in the creature's disproportionate head quite visible through its surrounding transparent sac. There were words typed beneath it. *Nobody packages more carefully than we do.*

'I can't claim it's my own idea altogether,' he admitted. 'I've seen it in an American magazine, but no one here's to know that.'

I looked again at the glossy photograph and the words on a narrow strip of paper gummed beneath it. The hands in the picture were like small fins.

'It's a logical extension, though,' he went on. 'Remember that one we used last year of a girl sealed in cellophane for the new Airtex Lunchwrap? Remember that?'

Yes, I told him. There was still a lifesize enlargement of it on the wall of the staff cafeteria.

'We're all a lot more ecologically aware now than we were even twelve months ago,' he said. 'That free advertising we did for the beech forest buffs on our food cartons for example. People associate our name with caring about such things.'

'The public?' I asked him.

'People,' he repeated. 'That's why we can't go wrong with this one.' He leaned forward on his thick thighs and a length of pale pink cuff was exposed as his hand spread above the foetus. 'You don't use a photograph like this lightly,' he told me. 'It's something pretty important, after all, pretty delicate. People would know we were serious because we're serious about what we market. Serious the way nature is when it wraps this up, if you like.' The features on the oval face were obscured by the square jut of his index finger. 'We want them to know we take packaging as seriously as that.' I continued to look down at the photograph when he removed his hand and settled back in his chair. His legs were crossed and one foot jerked slightly as he waited for me to speak. I was amazed at the clarity of what I looked at, the fine detail of the utterly vulnerable and trusting curve of the uncompleted body. I had read once how an embryo goes through the whole of evolution, through various stages of fish and other life before it reaches the fully human. I remembered how appalled I had been twenty years ago when the doctor had called me into my wife's room and shown me my newly delivered daughter. The nurse was washing her with a wad of dampened cotton wool, and there were streaks of blood and foam over the tiny chest and legs. The doctor had said *Well aren't you pleased with her?* and I watched the wad move under the mottled arm, the look of discomfort or even pain on the tight screaming face.

'We'll go ahead then?' my partner asked.

'You'll go ahead anyway,' I told him. 'Everyone else will think it's splendid whether you kidnapped it from an American magazine or conceived it yourself.'

He laughed broadly and said, 'But you think it's shit?'

'You know what I think of it,' I said.

'Like a bet sales are up fifteen per cent at a minimum on this line within three months?'

'I'd rather bet we'll be into glass coffins before the year's out,' I told him. 'Your concern for the living and the unborn can be carried further than this.'

He stood with one hand on the handle of my door and his other rubbed the back of his neck while he clucked and shook his head. 'Don't know what we're going to do with you, pardner,' he said in a drawling voice.

Before he shut the door I called to him, 'Don't you need the photo?'

'I've had half a dozen run off for Friday's meeting,' he said. 'You're welcome to it.'

I slanted the photograph towards the light to examine it more closely. There were even little fingernails on the hands, branched veins in the sac which enveloped the body. I wondered at the minute and intricate being which in time would become one of my partner's people, one of our tenfold profit increase for total additional production costs of maybe five per cent. And then a curious feeling stirred in my stomach as I realised that of course the thing was dead. There could not be a photograph like that unless the child had been removed from its mother. The idea disturbed me, and yet I was amused at my partner's self-congratulation that our care for the people was a huddle of human meat perhaps an hour or two from the first workings of decomposition.

As I said, I watch them. And now they are watching back, even addressing me, which people on a screen or stage should never do. And I remember once I said to Eva when we were in Wellington together, standing at the window of a hotel from which we could look across the clutter of streets beneath us, would she like to go to a play? I had seen one advertised in the *Dominion* we read together in the taxi from the airport. The paper was spread out over our knees like a sheet, and her hand rested on mine while she leaned close to the page to read it, because she would not wear glasses. I had kept the play for a surprise. Through the afternoon, between two meetings, I found my way to the theatre and bought the tickets. We could never go out together like that in Auckland and so now I said, as though I might have asked it any night, did she fancy the theatre? *Love,* she said, *let's not waste our time together.* I said nothing about the tickets and instead we simply walked about the city. She held my arm and we strolled along the finely curved road beneath the hotel. Every few minutes she would press my arm, bring us to a halt as she pointed or remarked on something which held her eye. When it was dark the lights twinkled up and down the hills. Right above where we stood, as though supporting itself, was the large cross illuminated on the wall of a monastery. I began to say something about religion. Eva said nothing and we were walking on, her hair lifting and blowing across her face and touching my own cheek. She raised her hand to draw back and smooth her hair, and her skin seemed so pale against the darkness. A little further on she said, *Do you mind if we rest a while?* She sat on the wall which ran along the seafront, and now we were drenched in the orange glare from the lights along the Parade.

'Tired?' I asked her. And she said to me, *Never, I just want to soak it up.* The harbour was streaked with the broad flowing band of a moon which had risen above the hill across from the city. It seemed almost exaggerated, like an enormous backdrop. I sat beside Eva on the wall and I said we would never be more contented than this, which of course was true, but at the time Eva said, teasing me, it was because like so many rich people I am sentimental.

'Not that rich,' I said to her. The sea slapped against the wall a few feet beneath us and Eva sat with her head rested against my shoulder. A little later I said that it was turning cool, and although she said she did not notice it, when we stood she asked, *Could we take a taxi back, love? is that all right?* At the hotel she lay on the bed and told me to switch on the television, it was the night of a programme she knew I usually watched. She lay there with her hair spread across the pillows. *You'll wake me if I nod off?* she demanded. *I don't want to miss a minute of this.*

Eva's brother was a tall man about my own age, his face lined and weathered, with the same grey eyes as his sister. He waited on the top step leading up to the foyer and reception desk, and he moved down the steps as I came towards him. It was eight o'clock in the morning, March the twenty-third. There was a cool wind coming in from the mudflats which lifted the soft corners of the man's checked collar. The girl at the reception desk was standing and looked down on us. She must have pointed me out to him as I left my car in the carpark on the other side of the road.

'I'm Eva's brother,' he said. 'I don't want to spend any more time with you than I need.' He looked at me with the hard stare that some men who work the land seem to take on, a hardness that dismisses all divergence as weakness, other ways of life as directly hostile to its own. I have seen his face a hundred times at football matches and on the streets of country towns. Eva had told me, when she first spoke of going to stay with him for a few weeks, that he belonged to some small religious sect. His wife was his only help on the farm, they worked difficult land with the singleness of prophets. She had felt the rest and the country air would help her pick up some of the weight she had lost in the last few months. I said I would drive her north but she had demurred at that, she said her brother wouldn't approve of us, it was better if he didn't know. 'I've come to see you because I could not avoid it, because Eva is dead.' I saw the blue-checked collar rise with the wind and lean back against his jaw. I saw the girl still looking down at us from behind the shine of the plate glass, and Eva's brother cleared his throat. 'The service and the rest of it is over,' he said. 'She wanted to make sure I saw you.'

'She knew?' I said. The words were like dry flakes in my mouth, they were colourless sounds.

'She knew she was pretty sick,' her brother said. 'I'd have thought you'd have known that much. I thought there was more between you than sin.'

'She didn't say that?' I asked. His tongue moved quickly along his lips, he turned from me to look over towards the sea. 'She said nothing very much,' he told me.

There was nothing now I wanted to say to her brother, nothing more for him to say to me. I walked up the steps and through the doors with their gentle hushed closing and into my office. I sat among the routine noises of the morning, looking out between the various factories and across the open patches of land to the slight caps of foam on the shallow inlet, the mud-brown shoreline. I watched the odd movements of wind from inside the stillness of a closed room, watched the rocking of an empty drum in the yard behind the factory. There was the stretched emptiness of the sky above the buildings and the low slope of the hills. 'Eva,' I said. *He would scoop the coloured balls into their wooden triangle and then lean at the end of the table for only the slightest moment, because he seemed always to know what to do, while the other men waited and took practice shots and stooped until their chins were tucked back and quite disappeared, and their eyes were level with the table. His cue was back resting upright in his hand before I had seen it move, the packed balls were scattered and brilliant and flowing across the cloth. Then he would pick them off one by one, tock and tock, then the soft catching noise as the first fell into the pockets, and the different kind of click as one after another bulged out the nets in the corners or in the centre of the table.* As I said Eva's name I had stood for a second in the intensity of what never comes back, in the curling bluish drifts of smoke and under the bright pyramid of light which I had not thought of for years. And yet now I seem to think always of two things at once, or of one person who immediately brings to mind the other. They are not ghosts, they are what everything else is seen by, is paled against, until what I look at in front of me is not even a film. It is a negative hung at a window, I see by the light from the other side.

They have come to look at me and so to sympathise, to take my elbow on one side with the wifely hands of concern and duty, my elbow on the other with the feeling and the intimacy of having spoken with me daily for a dozen years. I am part of their rights, I am what they have worked at and are entitled to. I am their guarantee that *they* are sane. I let them take me across the yellow earth to where my daughter's fiancé holds open the door of the car.

My daughter with tears in her eyes and my wife who does not wear make-up because her paleness is the marking of her grief, now sit one on either side of me in the back seat. My fat partner accelerates and the white line in the middle of the road disappears beneath the long shining bonnet of his car, an endless ribbon he devours. I sit quite calmly and consider how I am branded because I have stood for longer than usual in one place among the machines and graders of the extended motorway, looked down into a hole where a beautiful house once stood. There was a verandah on the house, and leaning on its rail, my knees supported by a stool, was like leaning over the rail of a ship. I stand on the wet clay and remember my father, and a woman I loved, who are also gone into smaller but identical holes. To think of that seems to me the very best of reasons to stand so still, to wonder what there can be to make moving a matter of any consequence. I have looked things in the face because they are not there.

Yet my wife and my daughter, my partner and my daughter's boyfriend, for all their love of things, their touching and their endless talk and their hating to be alone, do not believe in what they see. All *that*—the bodies, the cars, the Mexican ink stands—is for them no more than a sketch of what is real, of what might be. They believe that reality is something they shall make from all these things, not these things themselves. They now look at me from either side, in discreet glances in the rear-vision mirror. I am smiling slightly which confirms all that they suspect. I am smiling because I am with four people who think that our travelling at forty miles an hour along Great North Road, in the silence of tact and apprehension, will make some difference to anything at all. They are like those mad saints of centuries ago, men who would not believe that the world is what it is, but a distortion from its true shape that love and charity and worship could somehow wrench it back to.

We are now travelling past the used-car marts with their bright strings of flapping plastic flags, with words spelled out in little metal discs which shimmer endlessly against the light and wind. We are coming towards the turn where a church sits high on one's left, a tall grey finger of stone against the sky. I consider for a moment with some amusement that we are a procession from that old time I was thinking of. My partner who is like St Francis opens his thick hands and the doves of fifteen per cent hover at his shoulder, move with their strutting walk along his extended arms. My own wife with her eyes cast down, my daughter like a novice, my devoted son-in-law of two months' time, beside and behind that Franciscan flesh as he leads me to where I shall be questioned, dressed in a special robe, touched and tampered with by men who will work towards that miracle, to turn my world to theirs. They shall give me the cool pastures of a private room, the quiet waters of their choice. And on the green slats of their garden seats I shall be silent as a boy who walks from a picture theatre holding his father's hand, who looks at the bald streets with eyes fresh from palms and minarets.

The Corner

The woman sat at the kitchen window in her corner fifth-floor apartment. Through the foliage in the small park on the other side of the street she could glimpse the streams of traffic across on Broadway, hear the endless playing of horns and the sustained acceleration of engines. It was August, and the night so hot she felt even the heaviness of the cotton robe she wore over her underthings. Her husband sat in the next room, his bare feet on the table with the row of empty beer cans beside the TV guide. Damn them, he had just called out, not a decent can worth drinking in this whole city because those goons over in Milwaukee or wherever got themselves running at what their union boss tells them, whatever little Commie comes along and tells them how about us just messing up this country, boys? He tilted a can to his mouth and when he returned it to rest on the rise of his stomach he said, 'Should be a law, you know that? Stop people selling stuff like this?' 'I got the only ones I could,' the woman said. 'And it's not them out there it's the transport here in the city. The ones over Milwaukee got nothing to do with it.'

She leaned forward to the sill. What was going on down there, she wondered, down on the corner across the way? Round into the avenue a small crowd was suddenly forming and shoving on the sidewalk. It was after twelve now and the walkers from downtown should be thinning out, yet in a few seconds there must have been a hundred people down there. Usually this was when things became quiet for a while. An hour or so later the transvestites would begin their stand over at the same corner, their shouting and their dirty talk and dancing to the blared music from their transistors until three or four in the morning, hot nights like this. Right out there on the street, *cha cha cha* and their elbows close against their bodies as they turned and snapped their fingers. Sometimes the woman was entertained by the get-up, the piled wigs and the artificial breasts, the rather lovely calves tilted above

81

their high heels. Her husband would get into a rage when she talked about them. He had yelled down from their bedroom window one night when three of them were screeching and smacking at each other with their handbags, he called, 'You don't get off this street I'll come down there and kick your rocks off.' They stopped their brawling and screeched right back up at him, the black one who seemed to jig endlessly while he stood there, his inflated breasts wobbling under his shiny satin blouse and his large earrings tapping on his cheeks, he yelled back up to her husband that he just better try, he just better come on down and that ass of his going to eat a lot more than boot, feel like coming down? When her husband came back to bed the woman had gone through into the kitchen and poured him a large glass of the rye he kept in the cupboard above the sink. She could see the strain on his face without turning on the lamp, see it in the glare from the streetlights outside. The transvestites kept on calling up at the tall apartment block with its rows of darkened windows. In every bedroom there must have been someone lying and hearing the noise but no one else looked out or shouted down. Maybe two hundred people lying there and being kept awake and saying to themselves what's it got to do with me? Her husband shook as he took the glass. And they don't want jails for them! he said. They want to bring more of them up here and give them our taxes so they can powder their butts right down there in front of us, Holy Christ!

She watched the crowd pressing close to the middle of the sidewalk. A tall man who might have been one of the insane boarded out by the overcrowded hospitals in local run-down hotels, stood at the centre and his hands moved rapidly while he spoke. When he thought the crowd ignored him he spoke louder, moving his hands more wildly. The woman made out only the rising pitch of his voice, and the drunks and the drifters around the small patch of green with the statue of Verdi in the middle picked up the agitation going on across the way. Some of them dodged or swayed between the traffic and stood at the edge of the crowd.

'Something going on down there all right,' the woman said, and her husband asked her, 'Some guy drop his tits?' There was the whine of brakes as one of the drunks stepped into the stream of traffic. A taxi swerved to avoid him and horns blared back along the line of cars.

In a sudden movement of the crowd the woman saw something lying at their feet. She said, 'Someone's dead or something.' She held her hand flat to the top of the robe where one of the buttons had come off, and leaned forward on the windowsill. She heard the springs of the settee in the next room as her husband stood and crossed to the window in there. He belched loudly as he stooped between the hanging pots with their trailing ferns. 'Knife each other at last, huh?' he said.

The woman said, 'It might be an old person with a heart attack,' but her husband said, 'What's an old person doing down there this time of night? Unless it's one of them loonies,' he said, 'could be one of them loonies.'

The crowd was constantly reshaping. People would stop and edge towards the centre until they could see. The tall man was at the outside now, still talking, still waving his hands. There was a younger man she saw then, he might have been black or Puerto Rican, it was difficult to tell from here. He seemed the centre of whatever it was, he stood without moving while the crowd flowed and changed. The group always wheeled slowly to the left, with the direction of most of the walkers. The drunk who had almost stepped into the taxi was now back on the other side, near the park. A friend who had not moved from the bench handed him a bottle in a brown paper bag. The man removed the bottle and threw it across the back of the bench, at the marble opera characters who stood beneath the composer. From where she sat the woman could not hear the smash, not above the noise of the traffic, but she saw the falling arc of the bottle and then its springing back again in fragments, in brief glittering shards against the sides of a statue.

'The cops are here now,' her husband said, 'they'll sort it out.' A blue and white car had pulled into the kerb. The officers walked quietly into the crowd, one with his hands on his hips and the other waiting at the kerb, his hand flapping at his side. The dark young man spoke to the officer and the woman leaned further from the window. She could see it now, a still huddle like a coat that had been thrown down.

'My God,' the woman said, 'that's a dog. That's a dead dog down there.'

Her husband grunted from the other room. His bare feet slapped on the kitchen floor as he went to the icebox and took out another beer. 'Did you see that?' the woman asked him. 'That's a dead dog.' The strangeness of it excited her. She had expected to see a person lying there, an old man or a woman with a crumpled skirt like the epileptic who had thrown a fit in the deli once, in front of the imported cheese counter where she worked. There, she could see more clearly now. The officers were moving folk on. She could see the dog was a large alsatian with a pale head. The legs stuck out from the thick dark coat, thin and very straight. It hadn't been hit by traffic, she thought, she couldn't see any blood. It just lay there bang in the middle of the sidewalk where it must have dropped down dead. Somehow it seemed worse than a person lying there even. You would *expect* to see a person, there were always old ones taking sick or something, or drunks bowled by cars, but she had never heard of a dog just dying, dropping down so it lay as if sleeping, only a crowd watching it, and police.

The dark young man who owned it was kneeling now, he was taking the collar from its neck and the long chain he led it by. He stood up with the collar in his hand and slowly, while he talked to the officer, he wound the chain round and round his fist, until his hand looked swollen and gleaming when he moved it. The other policeman now squatted on his heels and took the dog's feet. He staggered with its weight when he stood up. He hunched and half ran with it to the corner, to the side of the drugstore where he laid the dog against the wall. But it no longer looked as if it was asleep. One front leg was hooked right back under it and the tail instead of lying out behind it had been folded back and was held under the body's weight. The woman couldn't take her eyes from it. She couldn't think how a dog could be trotting along a street and die so suddenly, just falling and lying there while its owner must still have been holding the end of the lead, thinking perhaps the dog was in step behind him before he felt the tug at his arm, and in the mystery of the animal's body the heart had already stopped. She spoke again to her husband and raised her voice when he failed to answer, but he had gone through to the bathroom. She heard the cistern flush and he called through to her from the bedroom door that there was enough to keep him awake most nights without dead dogs, he was going to bed.

She switched off the light and knelt down on the floor, her arms flat along the sill. There was a little movement of sweat in the hollow of her throat that she rubbed at with the collar of her gown. She looked down and wondered what was there for the young man to do now? When the officers returned to their car one of them spoke into a microphone and then they turned across the top of the narrow park, into the traffic going down Broadway. For a few moments the man stood there above the dog, before he knelt beside it, raising it slightly to straighten out the tail, to set the front legs side by side. Then he stood again and leaned against the wall. He folded his arms and looked now at the animal at his feet, now along the quiet street to his right. The main roads continued to carry traffic but here between the apartment blocks and the brownstones there was nothing but a few late strollers, the black plastic bags of garbage stacked in piles or placed singly beside steps. He waited until a grey sanitation truck moved along the street and pulled in beside him. Huge wire brushes pushed out from the front of the truck like carnival moustaches. Sometimes they swept the street at five or six in the morning and the noise was enough to wake you up, the way the brushes whirled and scraped. When that happened the woman would lie very still, hoping her husband slept too heavily to wake.

The driver jumped down from the truck's cab and walked over to the young man. He was in overalls, and perhaps twice the young man's weight. The owner said something and crouched beside the dog while the older man stepped back. He slid his hands and then his arms beneath the dog as though he were going to lift a sleeping child, while the driver went to the back of the truck and pulled down the metal lip. The woman could see how heavy the dog must be. The young man's face was fixed with the lips pulled back and his teeth showing, the dog was rolled in against his chest and the legs flopped at each step he took. As he stepped from the sidewalk the driver grabbed the back legs, and together the two men swung. The dog rose and was balanced on the metal lip above where the garbage was tipped, where the huge blunt blades of the cruncher thing dragged in and crushed whatever was thrown in. The young man saw or only then remembered the blades. He held firmly to the front legs as the driver heaved the rest of the body across the lip. For a moment it looked as though the dog was reaching over a wall, its head rested on the ledge and the young man clutching at its front paws to help it across. And then an elderly woman shouted from the other side of the street, from directly beneath the woman at the window. She had stopped her slow movement along the street as she saw the men heave up the dog. She shouted as she might have done at someone stepping in front of traffic, a rising strain of panic in her voice. 'Get it out of there!' she ordered them, 'Get it straight out!'

The driver already had jumped on a supporting bar and was straining to heave the dead hulk back up, so the whole of the dog's weight tumbled back onto the young man. He grabbed at it but the paws tore from his hands and the woman at the window heard the thud as the dog smacked onto the ground. The driver was shaking his head like he couldn't do anything more, it was all too crazy for him to cope with. The elderly woman was now stopped halfway between the opposite sidewalk and the truck. She waited there in the middle of the street and seemed lost in her agitation. She kept calling, 'Don't you go touching him you hear?' The driver was now at the side of the truck, sliding back a doorway that opened onto a dark space several feet across. He returned and grasped one of the hind legs. He dragged at it until the animal bumped over the kerb and lay beneath the opened door. Then quickly he had hoisted it and thrown it into the dark.

The young man was no longer watching the driver but the elderly woman who continued to call to him. Then he was shouting back himself. 'You get out,' he yelled at her, 'You the one get out!' He spoke like a foreigner, like he was Spanish or something. 'That my focking dog,' he shouted. His hand was pointed to where the driver now had closed the door in the side of his truck and already was climbing back behind the wheel. 'That my focking dog I do as I like!' He stepped back and knocked against a fire-hydrant as the truck moved off. He took up the chain and collar from where he had placed them beside the wall and stood there, drawing out a length of chain then pressing it together between his hands. The elderly woman had gone back to her own side of the street and up a shallow flight of stairs. She was turning a key in one of the doors. Then the young man bent forward as though he had been struck in the stomach, he bawled along the street at her before she disappeared, 'My focking dog, you hear that?' Then once more he wound up the chain on his fingers, like winding up a ribbon or a ball of wool, and laid it with the collar on the papers and junk that rose from a trash can at the corner. He pressed them down carefully and watched that the rubbish did not rise up and throw them on the ground. He then turned and walked in the other direction, until the woman at the window lost sight of him.

There was a pause in the sound of the traffic. There were no cars beneath her nor even there behind the trees, over on Broadway. The drunks on the benches were sleeping and there was only the tick in the fluorescent tubes of the sign at the side of the drugstore, a tiny tick she could hear for once from up here where she knelt. There was nobody in the street for a minute, five minutes, while the woman looked down on the well of light and stillness. Then she heard the tap of heels beside the trees across the way, she saw the shimmer of the red jacket the transvestite was wearing. The figure came over and stood against the wall, above where the dog had been put down and then picked up. He took a tiny transistor from a sequined bag, and held it up against his ear.

That's the Apple for You

Joe ran an off-the-hook fashion store up from the rail station in Bridgeport, and lived with his partner above the shop. Every Tuesday he went down to New York to see what seconds were going among his Jewish friends on 38th Street. 'You don't look for yourself,' he said, 'you don't get the pick of the bargains.' His partner said, 'That's what the telephone was invented for, Joey, so people don't have to visit the Apple.' And Joe would say, 'Look, only kids call it that. Tourists. Smart-ass guys who buy their shirts with fancy French labels. Far as I know I'm none of those. So do me a favour, will you?' One Tuesday after he'd seen a woman knocked down right by the taxi stand at Grand Central he crossed further along the street and went into a small bar. He would say when he got home, 'OK, people get run down every day, I know that. But I don't see it every day, do I? So I go into a bar.' But then each week Joe went back. He took the train half after eight, instead of the one he used to get a little before six. His partner would say, 'You're too late for that show you like about the cops, Joey,' before he had hung his old-fashioned hat on the peg inside the door. 'I been busy down there,' he told her. 'You want to try that crazy town sometime.'

There were never many people in the bar, that was one thing he liked about it. The bartender minded his own business, rubbed glasses with a white cloth, held them up against the light like it really mattered to him, you know? Like it was really something to have them that polished. But if you did speak to him he was friendly. He'd rest the cushions of his palms against the edge of the bar and the greenish light from the fake Tiffany lamp shone over his balding head, like he had just gone under water. That's it, Joe thought, it was precisely like that, as if he had just gone down and was coming up again and that's why those strands of hair were slicked down so smooth on his broad head. And he thought isn't it weird the way you think like that? And everybody must do it. Everybody in every bar from down at the Battery right up to those spic bars in Harlem you wouldn't be seen dead in, everyone sitting with these ideas going on, no one else ever really knowing what's happening in someone else's head. And there was this old broad sat along the bar a bit Joe used to look at. Suppose someone comes up to you and says, She a hooker? you wouldn't think twice, you'd say, Sure, what did you think she was, Queen of the May or something? She sat on a stool down the far end near an advertisement with Mount Rushmore and those big carved heads right over her shoulder. Her skirt was up above her knees, she was selling something all right. But the only time Joe saw some guy approach her she burned him off. So he had his doubts when he saw that, he thought, You can't even tell about people's outsides, let alone their minds. But if she ain't a pro, he thought, she's the best reserve he'd ever seen.

About the third week he came in he said to the bartender who had told him to call him Buck, 'Hey, you got a match there?' Next thing a folder slid down from where this broad sat. He lit one of his stubby cigars and turned to give them back. 'Keep them, mister,' she told him. 'Make like it's your birthday.' And she went back to looking straight ahead where she must have caught herself in the mirror behind the spirit bottles, and turning her glass in front of her like she always did, round and round, very slowly. Sometimes there was this other guy who came in and sat between them. Boy, was he weird. He wore this GI's outfit, green and dirty like fatigues he'd kept wearing since he was shipped home. Because he must have been a Vietnam veteran all right, he had a metal disc round his neck and a name tag sewn on his jacket, although it wasn't any real name he wore but 'Ask me again, Uncle' sewn there above his heart. But that was nothing. He had a crew-cut and blue eyes that made Joe think of Montgomery Clift in that movie about a soldier loving a girl in Hawaii, and sometimes this kid talked crazy, did he ever. It didn't matter a damn if Joe turned to listen or the broad just looked ahead or if Buck kept wiping those glasses and holding them up, looking for the pure light through the pure glass. Didn't matter one bit. This guy would tap the edge of the bar, tap, tap, like he was going into some routine with a drum. He'd close his eyes and click his tongue and when Joe looked at Buck the bartender held out his opened hands, like he was saying, No good asking me, buddy.

Joe got so he used to look for him. And when he came in on Tuesday night if the broad wasn't there he would think, Wonder what's keeping her? Or when only the other black bartender was there Joe asked, 'Buck

OK is he?' The black would say, 'Sure, he's OK.' He went on with what he was doing, which usually was leaning back against the bar with his arms folded, looking up at TV. His bow tie was on a piece of elastic, he kept drawing it out a little and easing it back, all the time he was watching a football game. Buck said to him once, 'Reckon you never have to eat, huh? Or even breathe. That box up there does it all for you.' The black guy just laughed at that, showing his front teeth where one overlapped the other and said, 'You jivin' me, man?' but he said it somehow like a comic, not the real black which he was. 'I'm not jiving you,' Buck said, 'I'm just telling you one of these days they're going to switch you on and off, not that thing up there. That's all I'm telling you.' But this black guy wasn't listening because he was watching the game again, he was shaking his head low over his folded arms and saying, 'Where those teams out there ever get the idea they could play this game?' He looked along the bar briefly. 'Anyone tell me that?'

But if the young guy wasn't there Joe missed him more than the others. Wow, as Joe said once while Buck was talking with him, that boy was something else again. Still wearing his gear like that you took him for one of those veteran heavies, lost because he had no shooting left to do. But in fact he was so polite he could have been a six-year-old talking with his teacher. 'Sir?' he'd say, if you nodded and spoke to him. Sometimes he would talk out loud to himself, or as if he was having a conversation but it wasn't with anyone in particular, it was like a sermon, like a piece of a play. One night he said while he was looking between Joe and Buck but never straight at either of them, 'I been exercising this Descartian gamble for so long it don't matter, see? Though I look through to the interstellar spaces and think like our literary fisherman from Arrowhead that while I watch the Milky Way, I am stabbed in the back with annihilation. I neither believe nor disbelieve. Reckon that's some place to get at.'

'Come again?' Joe said. And the young guy looked sideways and said as though someone had broken in on his thoughts, 'Sir?' He looked so goddamn forlorn sitting there, that young boy look yet the face kind of wizened too, but not with age, just pure misery if you can talk about it coming that pure. Joe felt it so sharply he said to Buck, 'Give him a double bourbon.' And the young man turned again when the glass was placed in front of him and he said, 'I appreciate that, sir.' Other nights he would sit in his usual polite silence and then perhaps break out into talk about music, about jazz of which Joe knew not one thing apart from the fact that it was black music, not white. And the kid—because that is what they all called him now, Buck did, and the old broad, she'd say, 'OK kid?' when she caught his eye—he would use technical terms that Joe could not follow, he referred to groups, to combos, to the best bass player who ever lived, he said, who was now dying, dying of you know what? He tapped the bar softly and started this snapping with his fingers and began to half chant over and over, *amytrophic lateral sclerosis,* until the tears began to move down his cheeks and the broad said, 'Buck, give him a shot of something, will you?' The kid smiled when she said that. He looked at them with his soft grin and said excuse me, and a few other words too, but in some foreign lingo, probably in French, Joe thought.

The next Tuesday Joe gave the bar a miss. His brother was visiting across from Springfield, the brother who still made firearms believe it or not, in the town that won the Civil War because of the quality of its guns. (That anyway was what Joe had always believed, what his father had always told him.) So he sat with his brother and his brother's wife and he thought at eight o'clock I know where I'd rather be now, damn it. So next week he was early. He walked up from 38th Street in a bright and pure evening, the silver leaf on the top of the Chrysler Building like it was minted that afternoon. There were kids climbing on the stone lions outside the Public Library, there was spring in the air, imagine that, spring on 42nd Street in the middle of all that garbage, all that filth. The bank building with the curved glass front slid with the evening light. All that dirt, Joe thought, looking along to the cinemas lit up and garish with their porno advertising. He stepped into a small store to buy himself cigars. Then he lit up in the doorway before stepping back onto the sidewalk. That smell too, on this kind of night, Joe thought. Funny how smells peeled the years away, like lifting a veil, that same smell when he was a boy and holding Pop's hand and he looked up for the first time at the Empire State . . . Well no point thinking back, Joe thought. No one gets nowhere doing that.

He turned into the bar. The coloured squares of glass in the lamps were bright against the gloom. He removed his hat and placed it down on the bar, beside the packet of cigars he was carrying still in his hand. The others weren't there yet, only Buck who had his back towards him, checking off some list.

Joe said, 'Nice weather out there.' Buck turned and looked at him and raised a glass to a spirit bottle without waiting to be told. 'Have this on me,' he said.

'All righty,' Joe answered. 'I'll just do that.' He lifted his eyes to the

TV screen. The president was walking along some guard of honour but the sound was turned too low for him to catch what was said, there was only a distant drone from a military band. Then Buck put a square flat parcel on the bar beside his glass. 'That kid,' he began. 'That kid comes in here Tuesdays sometimes while you're here, remember? Sits over there?'

'Sure I remember,' Joe said.

'Well he comes in last Tuesday, see. He asks me, Where's that old guy drops in here regular? So I tell him I serve people liquor, I'm not a private agent, am I? And he says, OK, just give him this, will you? Make sure you give him this.'

'For me?' Joe said. He lifted the piece of tape at the top of the folded plastic bag and took out a record.

'So I told him, Yeah, I'll give it to him,' Buck went on. 'Then we thought the kid had gone. Mary who sits over there, she thought he was gone. I did. The other bartender did.'

And Joe said, 'Huh huh', and read the writing on the record. It wasn't the original cover but one the kid must have made himself, pieces of cardboard clipped at the corners and written across it in large letters was MINGUS, and in smaller letters below that, 'Goodbye Pork Pie Hat'.

'That a joke or something?' Joe asked.

Buck kept telling him. 'We thought he was gone, see, then this customer comes hollering up from the men's room, he says, Christ, there's someone dead down there.' Joe looked at the man across the bar, the shiny green light on his moist head, the thread of frayed cotton at the side of his collar. 'Who's dead?' he asked him.

'The kid's dead,' Buck said. 'He's got this bit of thin cord tied to a pipe and he's just leaning away from it. Not even hanging, got that? Just *leaning* so he kills himself.' Joe put the record back in the bag. He emptied his glass and said, 'Better have another one, eh?' and both men tipped glasses before they drank. After a pause Joe said, 'Mary not in then?' 'Hasn't showed all week,' Buck said. 'Her health—you know?' He put his palm level in front of him and tilted it a little from side to side. 'Everyone's got problems, huh?'

On the train home Joe looked out at the lights in the high tenements and the refracted shimmer when they crossed the river. He watched through his own reflection in the window so the glaring freeways and the occasional glitter of water and even the roseate sky above the distant towns seemed inside his head, behind his face, as well as out there. He laid the record across his knees, opening his fingers and smoothing them across the plastic bag. Then again he looked out of the window, watching the oval of his aging face, the dark and the scattered lights of the moving night.

When he stepped from the train he dropped the record in a trash can. Take that home, Joe thought, how was anyone going to understand that? He could see himself trying to explain it and he knew it wouldn't work. Just his partner looking up as she heard of it and then saying like her goddamn dumb phrase explained everything, 'That's the Apple for you, Joey.'

The Witness Man

While Clem ate his sardines and toast he also fed the cat, handing down crusts dipped in the oil at the bottom of the tin. 'You old thing,' he said, 'you'd scoff on until you burst, wouldn't you, eh?' He scraped at the corner of the tin with his fork and tipped the flakes of fish, as well as what oil remained, onto his own plate. Nan would have had something to say about that now, wouldn't she, using the same plate for himself and puss? The cat hummed like a small engine as it rubbed against his trousers, then raised itself to tap at the plate with its paw before the food reached the matting under the table. The elderly man ran his fingers in the thick fur at the animal's neck. There used to be a collar there but it had worn thin with the years and the randy old blighter had probably lost it in a fight. He might be twelve years old but he still came in some mornings with scratches on his face, or a chunk torn out of his ear. 'Real old soldier, aren't you?' Clem told him. The cat licked the oil from the plate and moved away from the man's hand. He's a cool one, Clem thought. Wouldn't miss me for a second as long as someone was giving him his tucker.

It amused him to think of how he sometimes waited for the cat to come in and the darned old thing didn't give a damn one way or the other about him. Nan used to tell him he was a softie about it, about cats, about everything. They almost rowed just after the war when her brother had put up with them for what at first was meant to be a fortnight but lengthened out into four months. 'You can't turf him out like that,' Clem said. 'We don't know what he's had to put up with, do we?' Dear old Nan, she couldn't see softness had nothing to do with it, it was what you owed a bloke. Yet if it was sentimental you were talking about, well Nan was the one there, all right. She'd cry up at the pictures at the Britannia on a Saturday night even when the story had a happy ending. Her favourites were the ones with soldiers saying goodbye to girls on bridges, or the women waiting and looking up while squadrons flew away above them, and you knew by the music that was that. And he'd say to Nan, 'It's only a picture, remember.' She would tuck her hand in the pocket of the heavy coat he used to wear then and he'd squeeze it tight in his own as they crossed at the Three Lamps then took their time walking down St Mary's Road. The light always seemed softer, the night more fresh or something, when you had just come out from the pictures. And walking round was safe as a church in those days. You'd see a group of young fellows walking towards you and you'd never think of crossing over, not even if they were smart alecking about or drinking from bottles. And now here we were, Clem thought, no wars or anything to set people off, and you thought twice about going up the road the moment it was dark. The other day he heard two women talking about it on the steps of Leys Institute. One of them was saying, 'His head was caved in like a pumpkin or something.'

'They must have been after his money, were they?'

'Like hell they were. It was just for the fun of it.'

Clem picked up the plate and ran it under the hot tap. He put out his hand to stroke the cat again but the old beggar raised itself from the chair it was lying on, and hopped down to avoid him. 'All right,' Clem told it, 'I'm not going to maul you.' He opened the door and stood there above the cat for a moment, looking across the small sloping lawn with its one tree, and on down the sharp fall of the street towards the motorway, the sea, the arc of the harbour bridge. Must be getting on for twenty years since that was built, mustn't it? Since he and Nan used to sit out here in the late afternoons. They had watched the whole thing, from when the bulldozers first came in and started ripping up the beach beneath the park until the two steel arms narrowed the space between them, and at last they met like that, in that arch he liked to look at, the lovely easy line that took the traffic up and flowed it down the other side. And across the grey web of the bridge he could still make out the Chelsea sugar works, his eyes weren't doing too bad were they? Before the bridge was even talked about Nan needed her glasses to make things out on the other side. He looked across now to the clutter of buildings against the blue bush on the hill around them. He wouldn't mind a tanner for every time he'd crossed that stretch of water.

The first day on the job over there one of the lads called him colonel because of his neat clipped moustache. The name had stuck with him, right until he retired. He never let on that it covered a scar from when he was a boy, from the day the old man pushed him out of the way in the shop and he'd caught his face on an opened biscuit tin.

'Here's the colonel,' one of them called out when he came into the lunchroom. 'Left the bloody horse outside, have we?' The clerks weren't the most popular blokes at the best of times, but Clem made out all right. The thing was you didn't try to have them on in return, that was the answer. Come at that boy and you were a goner. They'd never let up if they got a rise out of you. There was one bloke there, for instance, he used to read the Bible at lunch-time and he would answer them with quotes, this mild almost silly smile on his face even when they asked him which way the missus liked it, talked to him like that. Or another one, an Italian, they never gave him a break. So when Clem had first turned up they naturally worked on him for a bit and then they let up, there wasn't enough sport in it. 'Once they know they can't get at you the penny drops soon enough.' He had explained that to Nan soon after he started there, when someone had filled with sugar the leather bag that he carried his lunch and the odd book in. She was in tears about the mess it made and he had tried to tell her, 'Look, they're always doing someone over. Don't create about it and they'll lay off.'

'They sound like animals,' Nan said.

'They're no worse than anywhere else,' Clem defended them.

Funny how those days came back to him more strongly since the trouble began. It had stirred the past up, Clem thought, like shoving a stick into a swarm of bees. When he looked across now to the distant works he could smell again the hot sweetness he took months to get used to; and the odour of the sea, when he had leaned over the side of the ferry and picked out their house, and Nan was a speck on the verandah with a tea towel waving in her hand. Even the smell of their bedroom—that came back too some of these nights, Nan's own smell and her way of clutching at his shoulder when they were man and wife together. As if I'm not a bit past that, Clem thought, as if with his dicey ticker and all he shouldn't be taking life pretty quietly, instead of waking with the old memories disturbing him. Then thinking of that led him on to other things and sometimes it was hours before he slept again, the old sadnesses about Nan's illness and even years before that, when they still thought they might have a family.

The cat had returned from scratching beneath the tree. 'We can't do much about it now, eh boy?' Clem said. 'Just two old cobbers getting along quite nicely.' This time the cat allowed Clem to finger the deep soft fur of his chest. Right under the doubled front leg he could feel the cat's heart going nineteen to the dozen, although the blighter just lay there, rolling on its side.

Clem hadn't spoken to a policeman since before the war. The last time was at the safety zone in front of Court's in Queen Street, the night the Labour Party won its second election. Earlier that night he and Nan were sitting over their tea, listening to the wireless and talking about how it had been only ten years ago say, what a different world it was now. The way Nan had to call people Sir or Madam when she opened the door of the house in Mountain Road. The retired dentist she worked for gave her a fiver at Christmas and a glass of sherry and then got her against the fireplace, his hand trying to go up under her dress and even while he was doing that Nan was saying Sir to him. 'Don't be silly, sir,' she kept telling him. She knew if she lost that job there wouldn't be another and Clem had been laid off only a few weeks before. She hadn't mentioned it to him for another two years, until he was working again and she was off sick herself, sick for the first time. She was sitting up in bed reading the paper and she saw the name of the people she used to work for.

'See he's dead,' Nan said.

'Someone we know?'

'That poor old sod who tried to handle me that Christmas.' She told Clem the story like it was a joke. At first he thought, By Christ, I wish he was still alive and I'd fix him all right. But then he was angry with Nan. She said, 'Oh, don't go on about it. I hated it more than anything in my life.'

'But you felt sorry for him didn't you?' Clem insisted.

Nan had shrugged at him as if it didn't matter. 'Well I suppose I did.' And that was in Clem's mind as they sat there the night of the election. It had been raining earlier and the earth outside the opened window smelt alive and wet. The leaves of the lemon tree near the clothesline glittered when he moved the curtain back and looked out at the yard. He was thinking of Nan pushed up against the carved mantelpiece she had told him about, that the old bitch at the house used to make her clean with a special tiny brush. Well the bugger was dead now and he supposed it didn't matter. But he thought of how he had got away with it because of his money and how Nan used to get up early and walk to Epsom sometimes before the first tram, to be there when they had special visitors staying and they wanted their breakfast early. He had looked out at the November sky above the house next door. 'By God they'll never come at that again,' Clem said.

Why didn't they walk down town? Nan asked him. They might as well get the excitement of it when Savage got back in. Everybody said 'Savage' in Ponsonby, rather than 'Labour', because you were talking about the same thing, about the ordinary people who wouldn't be kicked round any more, about better things than money to judge life by. Clem had never been that shook on crowds yet he didn't want to miss this one, he was glad Nan had suggested it. So they walked from their cottage on the corner to the end of the convent grounds, then down the little lane to Jacob's Ladder. Who on earth had called it that? Nan used to say. And Clem would tell her, 'Those nuns, don't you reckon?' They owned half the land between here and the Lamps, they gave the streets those saints' names and the Bishop's Palace still rose up among the workers' houses like something in a history book, turret and all. Anyway, it seemed a good name for that long flight of steps. There were a hundred of them, he supposed, dropping steeply down, close to the face of the yellowish clay cliff. At the bottom you could pick your way round the rocks or you could walk the other way, to the broad park with the tall oaks all round it. And fifteen minutes after that you were in the middle of the city. 'It's mad this, you know,' he said to Nan. They had turned to the left at the bottom as they always did, because Nan couldn't pass the water without dabbling in it.

'What is?' she said.

'Living like we do in the centre of Auckland nearly, the tram along the road and that, and here we go picking our way round rocks like there wasn't any other way.' Nan laughed and looked out over the harbour, across the stretch of mud where the tide had fallen back. 'I love that smell, don't you Clem?' She stood awkwardly on a slab of soft crumbly rock. He thought how she loved the beach yet she never looked quite at home away from streets and kitchens and things, she looked as though she would lose her balance any minute and tumble forward. But God she looked lovely standing there all the same. She wore her coat with the fringe of imitation fur at the cuffs and a hat that came right down over her ears. It was nearly dark by now and he looked at her raised above the little beach, the lights over the other side twinkling away behind her, across the water that was now lighter for some reason than the sky. 'Come on,' he said. They had gone across the park with the leaves freshly out on those great trees and the racket from the birds, a city of birds just settling down. And funnily enough Clem had forgotten the rest, wasn't that just the oddest thing? Not a thing about the crowd in front of the newspaper office or the cheering when the results went up like the results on a totalisator or the noise when they saw how they had put Savage back with the biggest lead in the country. He had forgotten those things although he had talked about them enough and not so long ago there was a display of pictures of that night up at the Institute. The pictures were in a glass case and there were political books with their pages held back like birds' wings and Clem had thought, Well it's just about like that now, it's all pretty near museum stuff for what it matters any more. He had watched while a couple of young women came up and glanced at the photos then turned away, their faces as blank as though they had looked at a wall. And the once or twice he had talked about those days to clever young people he had felt it was lost nearly as much as it was with those two women. 'You must remember something about that night, you must have sensed its significance?' one of them had pressed. He had sat there in his grubby enough clothes for a clever young bloke. He had a notebook on his knee and it was like Clem had to answer charges. 'Well I don't,' Clem had said, 'I don't remember a thing, I wish I could help you some more.' He was blowed if he was going to say about Nan there standing on the rock when the sky was almost dark but the sea was silvery like an old mirror, or about the poor devil they'd seen after all the excitement was over outside the *Star* office, and they came on this other crowd gathering round the safety zone at Court's. He and Nan were suddenly among the closest to the low concrete platform. A tram had stopped halfway across the intersecting streets and they saw the conductor jump down, his bag jolting in front of him and the loose change jangling as he jumped. The conductor ran back towards them and picked up something from beside the shining grooves of the rails. At the same moment, he and Nan had noticed the well-dressed man who was sitting on the safety zone, one leg across the other, his knee supporting the ankle that he held in both hands. When the conductor stooped down he picked up a boot with a foot inside it. He carried the boot in both his own hands and knelt down beside the man, as though he were a salesman showing it to a customer. The man looked at him without speaking. Clem remembered how there was no expression of pain on the youngish, surprised face. Then someone broke from the crowd of watchers and started shouting, 'Get the ambulance, will you.' A woman screamed and Nan had pressed against him, her hand holding onto his. And before two policemen came running and thrusting through the crowd Clem watched the black stain spreading on the knee of the man's grey flannel trousers. With a kind of careful modesty the man's efforts now seemed to be to protect his wound from those who watched him. Both his hands were cupped over his ankle, he hardly moved his head when the conductor put the foot beside him on the platform. Clem heard the conductor say, 'I don't know what the hell I'm supposed to do.' But he kept kneeling beside the man and put his arm across his shoulders. Even as he watched Clem was thinking, Why do I notice such unimportant things when a man is bleeding to death? For he saw how the street lights shivered down the leather strap across the conductor's back and the way the boot was standing by itself, a flat lid of shadow across the top, and so highly polished there was a pip of light winking on its toe-cap.

That was when Clem had last spoken to a policeman. Because he and Nan were at the front of the crowd it was assumed that they had seen it all. 'But we didn't even notice the tram until it stopped,' he said. 'Until we saw the conductor getting off.'

'We'll still need your names,' the policeman said. That was a few minutes or so later, after the chap had been taken off in an ambulance and the driver had lifted up the foot and placed it inside, beside the stretcher, with a towel draped over it. That long ago and Clem had never really spoken to a cop since, not like that, not about questions and times and where exactly he stood. Now this young rooster who looked as if he still didn't know what a razor was had flicked his book open while they sat at the kitchen table. When this boy policeman said, 'Where would you like to begin then, eh?' he suddenly saw that other book opening, all those years ago, the hand slowly writing their address down while the crowd still milled round.

'I'd better begin when the girl first went past me,' Clem said. 'Is that the bit you want to know about?'

The policeman said, 'I want to hear about all of it. Sooner or later it'll have to come out in court, won't it?'

They asked him the same questions over and over. How could he be certain about the time? Surely his sight must be extraordinary for an elderly gentleman? And his observation, too. Wasn't that out of the ordinary?

'I can't say what ordinary is,' Clem said. 'I can only talk about what I saw for myself. I've always had good eyesight so I just sort of take things in.'

'You see what a perceptive witness we're dealing with, my lord,' the police lawyer said when the business had got that far, when Clem stood with both his hands resting on the polished wooden ledge in front of him. He felt that the man didn't like him, it was not just a matter of doing his job. He wanted to trap him somehow, he was trying to say one way and then another that because Clem was old they could hardly expect him to get things correct. He asked him questions about what work he had done before he retired, then he made it all seem so unimportant, being a tally clerk for most of his life, working in the Corso store for the last few years. Clem was annoyed with himself when he said, 'My wife was very ill for a long time then. I had to get a job where I could come and go more easily.' The lawyer just looked at him when he said that and he was left standing there, as though he had said something foolish. Clem had raised his hand and passed it across his neatly clipped moustache and a voice from beneath him told him he could step down. As he turned and left the box he knew he was right about it, knew in the way you sometimes do by intuition, that the lawyer had disliked him because of his moustache, because of his careful answers. He wasn't dumb and senile the way the lawyer wanted him to be, that was what the pleased-with-himself bastard had been hinting at, wasn't it, with his shrugs and hitching at the folds of his gown?

Why on earth would he be inaccurate about it? Clem thought. It wasn't properly dark anyway, there were lights halfway up the steps as well as directly above where he had been standing. There was nothing so extraordinary about noticing two figures who stood at one of the landings halfway down, a man and a woman arguing together. He had seen the man's high fuzzed hair and he had thought why do girls go round with them in the first place? If it came to that he had never seen what men saw in dark women either, all that nonsense you used to hear after the war from blokes who had been up in the islands or over in Egypt or wherever, and they'd say you couldn't beat them, there wasn't a woman back home who could touch them when it came to the dinkum thing. Nan laughed when they spoke about it, there was nothing he couldn't talk to her about then. 'I bet the Japs'd be saying the same things about us, if they'd ever got here,' she said. 'You don't have to know much about men to know that one, Clem.' The dark man had put out his hand and rested it on the girl's arm. Her head tilted back as though she was trying to look straight up at the stars, because Clem saw the whiteness of her throat before she tried to break free from the man who held her by the wrist, who tried to move towards and over her. She strained away from him and was drawn back again. Clem saw the girl's own hand come up slowly as if she intended stroking the man's face. Then he heard the man call out, he shouted at her obscenely as she lunged away from him, falling against the steps as he freed her wrist. She scrambled up and then began scaling the steps to where Clem stood back against the railing at the top to let her pass. Her face was raised towards him. When she saw him she stopped running and walked past him at a normal pace. ('How do you know what a *normal pace* is for a young lady?' the lawyer smiled.) She was breathing heavily and her eyes turned again to look at him, but she said nothing as she went by. When she was further along the alley towards the street she began to run again, a clopping awkward run, her wooden-heeled shoes loud against the surface of the path.

You're quite sure she didn't speak to you? both the lawyers in due course would ask him, as the policeman had the next morning when Clem answered the knock on the glass panel in the front door. *What did you see?* I saw a dark man about thirty talking to a young woman who was twenty say, or twenty-five. *How long did you watch them?* It wasn't so much watching as that they just stayed halfway down the steps while I was standing at the top. It is where I stand most evenings if the weather's fine. I like the view from there over the yacht harbour and I used to stand there with my wife. *Would you say you saw anything unusual occur?* I saw a man and a girl talking and then arguing, I saw them struggle with each other for a little and move as if to make up and then the woman must have scarred the man's face, although at the time I thought she was touching his face and not scratching it. I just saw what men and women have been doing for ever, I suppose. The lawyer turned and smiled at the jury when he said that too. And the questioning went on and on, over and over. *You didn't realise something more serious was taking place?* I thought both the man and the girl were serious. *We mean did you realise it was something criminal?* No, Clem said to the policeman, No sir, to both the lawyers who asked him that as well. And when they asked him what did he notice about the girl he said he noticed she ran up the steps, he guessed she simply wanted to get away from the man. The man called her bitch several times as she ran away from him. He continued to shout words of that kind and probably in another language also, even after she had crossed the road and was gone. She wore something, a medallion or a cross or a locket, around her throat. It glinted in the light and it jumped up and down in front of her as she ran. Clem went over most of what he had said as he sat after his tea, and thought about the court. It was all so clear in his mind but he hadn't been able to get the feel of it through, had he? Not so they saw it as he did. She had simply run away from the man and there was no terror in it, as the smart lawyer wanted him to agree, no fear nor panic as she ran up the steps, her breasts moving inside the tight jersey thing she was wearing, and the chain rose and fell at every step she took. *She looked at the witness?* Not directly, no. But her eyes sort of slid across, they were shining but there were no tears either, that was another thing the lawyer had wanted him to say. She was no more than a few feet from him, how could he be wrong? The down on her neck beneath the close-cropped hair was touched with light, he could see that even, that's how close he was. She couldn't have been crying without his noticing it. Because later it was so obvious the man was.

But you didn't wait for the accused to walk up the steps? I was back near the wall where the convent playing courts are, when I heard the man behind me. He was wearing sandshoes so I didn't know until he was nearly right beside me. Then when I turned I looked straight into his face. No, he did not speak to me, no, I don't think he even saw me. And the lawyer said to him then, You thought? Shall we confine ourselves to what you *know?* So Clem had said nothing. He felt his hands slip against the wooden edge of the witness box and the flush, the warmth, rise at the back of his neck. He is wanting me to lose the thread of what I have to say, he is making me seem an old man who cannot remember what he has seen.

There was no way of telling the court so they might see it as clearly as he had himself, the broad dark face with tears streaming across it, glazing in the light from the lamp-post on the other side of the street. Not that, nor the smear of sweat and tears and snot that spread on his upper lip and at the corners of his nose, the three seeping lines dragged across one cheek by the girl's scarlet nails. For they were scarlet when he looked at her hands in court, when he heard her say that she marked the man in self-defence. 'It's when I scratched him like that he let me go. Up till then he was saying he would do it again. He would drag me back to the side of the steps where he had done it before.' The court was shown a grey plastic raincoat the accused had been carrying when he passed Clem, although the older man did not remember seeing it. *This,* the lawyer said. He held up the coat for them to see. It was creased and smeared with mud, and the prosecutor asked might he draw their attention to certain other stains?

Clem's confusion grew as the day moved on, as he heard others stand in the box and the judge warn them to take their words and weigh them, and for a moment he saw that too in his mind, the ancient image of scales in perfect balance, then one pan tipping slightly, those could be his words that made it tip. He looked carefully at the girl when her own turn came to be questioned. She answered very clearly in a voice he nevertheless leaned forward to hear. And then the man. He spoke so quietly Clem missed some of what was said. Twice the judge halted him to say that he must speak up. The second time he instructed him to look up as well, there was no point mumbling down at his chest, the court was over here. There was another Islander who stood not far from him, who sometimes translated phrases for him when he was not sure of what was asked. And the translator spoke to the court when the man once answered at length in his own language. That was the one time he seemed confident. He raised his head and gestured with one hand, he turned to where the girl sat and turned again towards the judge, coming back to English as he said, 'You listen to him again.' He pointed to where Clem sat. 'You ask him, you ask the witness man.' The lawyer smiled and said, 'But we already have. Surely you must have heard him?' The man's face became passive again, he looked down at his hands, one laid across the other on the railing in front of him. *The jigsaw,* the lawyer said. He stood in front of the jury. *You must piece it together.*

So the court put together its picture. Its figures were the man and the girl who worked together in Fanshawe Street. They cleaned offices after most of the staff went home. They had worked together for three months, and sometimes, because they both lived in Ponsonby, they walked home together. The girl said, Well it was natural wasn't it, she felt safer when he walked with her. If she was by herself she would never think of taking that short cut up the steps, she would go home by bus. Her mother said, Yes, that was true. Her employer said she was a good worker, the lawyer read a letter that told how last year she gave a month of her time collecting for Telethon. And the girl herself then told them how once or twice after work the man had wanted to kiss her. The girl had laughed and told him don't be silly, he was married wasn't he? And then he had begun to get heavy.

Heavy? the judge queried. And she answered, 'Just pushing his luck a bit.'

That night, then? she was prompted. That night when they were on the asphalt pathway between the motorway and the steps, the man had dragged her from the path, between the clumps of toi-toi. The traffic sped past them twenty yards away and no one else had walked along the path. He had grabbed at her and struggled at her clothes. The girl told them in that same clear voice how he had put one foot behind her leg and forced her back onto the coat he threw down beneath them. And how could she call out when she knew no one was round? That he carried a knife? Then the court was shown that as well, a dull horn-handled pocket knife. *He carried this,* the lawyer said. He passed the knife to the foreman of the jury. Some of them touched its edge with their thumbs and turned it over in their palms before passing it on. But he had not taken it out, the other lawyer said, he had not even mentioned it. Ah, the smart one smiled. He hitched again at the shoulders of his gown and said, 'Ah, I doubt if one needs to remind a young woman about a knife when she is undergoing assault.' The girl spoke out at that, she said, 'He told me at work once he never went anywhere without his knife. He never knew when he could need it.' The man's own lawyer tried to answer. That could mean anything, he said.

'It could mean he liked peeling fruit?' the prosecutor said. In that stagey way of his he simply held the knife up again and for once he said nothing. And somewhere through it all—because he could not remember the day exactly, that was half the trouble, Clem thought—a doctor said there was no doubt what had taken place. There was bruising on the girl's wrist, and contusion on the leg Clem had seen knock against the steps. The doctor confirmed that the marks on the man's face were clearly from the girl's nails. Yes, he agreed, they were the kind of wound a woman might well inflict who was defending herself.

Clem was dog-tired after the day in court. He had not looked forward to it and then it was worse than any expectation. He now kept coming back to the one thought, that somehow he had let down the man who had passed him, who had never noticed him. And yet for God's sake he couldn't do much more, Clem told himself, there were all those others as well, they believed them and not me. Yet it was two people fighting in distress or regret or in anger after sex, it wasn't what the court believed. He remembered the sly movement of the girl's eyes as she saw and at once dismissed him at the top of the steps. Yet in court she was like a child almost, as she looked down when the doctor asked her questions, when she went back to sit beside her mother. While the man had looked like a liar or at least a fool when he took so long with his answers and refused to face directly at the court. His hands washed over each other while he was questioned, his shirt had been tucked up with the collar of his suit coat so that he looked untidy as well as dumb. He was like a man who wanted to say he was guilty, Clem thought, while the girl stood there well-dressed and confident, she was one of our own. Her mother held her hand much of the time. And further back in the court among the Islanders there were two women in bright long dresses. One of them was elderly, her tight springy hair changing colour, neither black nor reddish nor grey, so that it made Clem think it seemed singed. Beside her sat a much younger woman, perhaps her daughter. He watched that woman at the recesses during the day. When she stood with the group of dark men by the patch of lawn outside the courthouse there was such quietness about her. Then it came to him that she had the look of people who are balancing something, alert yet self-absorbed, while the older woman leaned against one of the men and cried. Her hair was smooth and drawn back with a clip at the side of her neck, then flowed out again across her shoulders. When she moved the light glanced off her hair and Clem wondered if she was the man's wife. He wanted to go and say to her, I've told the truth even if it's not enough, even if he made love to her it was only that, it wasn't more than that. The woman raised her eyes and looked at him and then looked past him.

That night before he slept Clem lay with the cat on his chest, his fingers moving in the soft fur. The animal's body vibrated with contentment. Clem was too tired to watch a programme he usually liked, too shot for anything. But next morning he awoke too early, and felt unwell. The unhappy time with Nan had kept returning to him in broken yet realistic dreams. There were those days again at her bedside when she would no longer speak to him, and the night not long before the end when she had turned, suddenly conscious and alert, watching him with her bright sunken eyes. She had said to him as he covered her thin speckled hand with his own, 'It doesn't matter in the long run you know.'

'Matter?' he had said.

'Whether we had those years or not.' And there was a pause then, he had leaned forward so that his head was close against her own.

'Not mattered.' She spoke lucidly and quietly, and he had sat there at her bedside appalled at what she said. A nurse who was in the room said to him, a few minutes later, when Nan's eyes were closed, 'It's all confused with drugs. You mustn't think she knows.' The nurse even touched his shoulder, she was trying to cover up for the dreadful clarity of death. He sat on with his fingers meeting around Nan's wrist. He knew that what the nurse had said to comfort him was wrong. He knew Nan had never spoken so surely to him in all their lives together. And what held him then was *that* was her final truth, the fact he must sit and watch with until the machinery stopped. For that is what we are, he was thinking, we are machines for pain, for these last days of dissolution and denial, as though the sun had never shone on us, as though everything we ever took from music or family or God or whatever it might be, must now be paid for with words like that, the indignity of denying what we always loved.

He had sat on with her until she stirred and asked for water, which he gave her from a teaspoon. She then lay back and watched the corner of the room, and then her lids again were lowered. He had sat until an hour later when the nurse again had touched his arm and led him from the room, because in his thinking of Nan he had not noticed when she left. Then like anything else, as he liked to say, Clem adapted to the silent house, a new routine. There was then a life of shopping and library books, watching TV and taking walks. Once a week he had a meal at his sister's, he visited a friend at the hospice off Shelly Beach Road, he fed and talked with his cat. Those things too were mixed in his dreams, the night after the court. Then he watched the sky lighten, and from the greyness of the first light he saw the day pick out the gilt frame of Nan's old-fashioned mirror, the bright towel at the end of his bed. He closed his eyes again and this time he slept comfortably. When he woke for a second time his mind was calm. He thought without distress about the people he must face again in a few hours' time, the girl who he knew was lying and the Islander who was like a wild thing caught in a light too strong for it. It was so clear now that he thought of it. He would ask the Islander's lawyer to question him once more. If the lawyer drew him out, that was the thing, the way you saw them doing it all the time on TV. Then that dark young woman in the long coloured dress, he would watch her face when it began to dawn on all of them in the courtroom that the man had told the truth, and that it was Clem who made them believe it. If he could only watch that.

How odd it all is, Clem kept thinking as he moved about the kitchen, tidying up after his cup of tea and his piece of toast and his glass of Ribena. Odd how our moods can change even at my age, how much in these past couple of weeks I have passed through, feared, remembered, been ashamed of . . . He shaved and looked at himself in the bathroom mirror. He snipped at two loose hairs at the side of his neat moustache. The scissors were Nan's, something she had kept from her girlhood, from the years before they had met. There was a paua shell inlay along the flattened grips for your fingers. Clem tilted the scissors for a moment and watched how the iridescent greens and blues ran against each other, merged into a kind of soft remote fire below the smooth surface of the shell. He snipped again at hair growing from his ears. You had to watch yourself all right, you could see it with some of those elderly ones he spoke to up at the library or swapped a few words with in the shops. Suddenly you noticed how they had let themselves go, there were stains on their cardigans or they weren't properly buttoned, and there were others even worse, the ones people moved away from. As long as you watched yourself, Clem thought, you were probably all right.

He was dressed and ready well ahead of time. He could stroll up to the bus-stop and even walk round Queen Street for a bit, before he took a second bus to the courthouse. That hill was past him now, although he liked it as much as anything in Auckland. The big palms in the park, the clumps of flax-like leaves with the orange flaring blooms like flying birds, and further up those trees with the huge grey roots lying along the ground—he would come back that way this afternoon. Along past the university and the floral clock that used to have begonias set out to make the numerals, he wondered if it still had those? God, it wasn't so long ago either to before the clock was even thought of, and he walked along there with Grandma. When he remembered that he could almost smell the warm fusty odour when the sun fell on her black skirt and he walked along beside her, his hand stretched up, clutching at her own. 'Don't snip your nails on my rings, love,' she used to tell him. And at the corner where once there was only rough grass he had stood looking up to a woman she spoke to, then at the great fat iron lady over there on her stand. She was as much the Queen of New Zealand as the Queen of England, didn't he know that? And the woman had given him a white lolly like a tiny satin cushion and asked him, 'There, won't you talk to me if I give you that?' And Grandma had puzzled him because he didn't have any money of his own and yet she said while she jiggled his arm, 'You'll get no change out of this one.' Clem enjoyed the walk up to the bus. After yesterday's fleeting patches of sun, it was now clear and fine. From his gateway he looked down towards the water. The bridge and the yachts in the boat-harbour were softened by a skein of mist. But up here one was above it. Mornings like this he used to lean on the rail of the ferry and watch the cliffs and the houses slide past. Days like this the colours seemed more vivid, even the brick sugar works lifted up its yellow walls like—well, something more than you expected, somehow, and the sheet of water between the ferry and the approaching wharf was that deep green that slid off into blues, tilting and shimmering like those handles on the scissors.

Groups of girls from the convent passed him. They walked properly like young ladies and there was no swinging their bags about and hollering to one another the way you'd see with some of those other kids up on the main road. He liked it that the older ones wore gloves when they walked past his house on Sundays. If he was on the verandah some of them would look up and say Good morning to him. Some of them made him think of horses, or of foals, rather, that long-legged grace a few of them had. He began to walk up the road and was caught up briefly in their current of youth and litheness, the sudden breaking of laughter from a group on the other side of the road. And then he knew there was a grey car slowly following him, drawing in towards the kerb. It stopped when the policeman caught his eye. It was the same young chap who had come that morning several weeks ago and questioned him for the first time. Only then he had worn his cap down over his eyes, and now he sat with his blond hair combed high, a kind of puff above his forehead. He beckoned Clem over as he opened the door and stepped out. Clem thought they must be giving him a ride to court for some reason. The policeman nodded up past the library to the main road. 'Got you just in time, eh? Saved you a trip.' He spoke while the old man watched his mouth so closely that he saw the way one of his bottom front teeth slightly tilted back, out of kilter with the rest, and there was the grey filling he could see in another tooth further back. The policeman said again, 'Saved you the trip.' He touched the sides of his tie, carefully. 'Our rapist did himself in.'

When Clem said nothing the young man explained it again. 'Cut his wrists,' he said. He moved the side of one hand against his other wrist. 'Had this razorblade tucked somewhere and that was that.'

'Last night?' Clem heard himself ask.

'Last night, early this morning. There wasn't a chance when they found him anyway.' Then the policeman gave this kind of laugh, his breath caught in as though he were going to cough. 'Shows he must have done it all right. It's one way out of facing it.' And now Clem was looking at the shining metal number on the uniformed shoulder and the slight golden growth of beard along the man's jaw-line. The man must be finishing work, Clem thought, he can't just be starting or he'd have shaved. Then the policeman rested his hand for a moment on Clem's shoulder. 'Don't you think about it any more, Pop. Nothing we could have done.' He stooped back into the car and placed his cap on his head. He glanced up for a second into the rear vision mirror and made sure the cap sat straight. 'Right,' he said to the driver. As the car edged from the side of the footpath he spoke again, leaning from the lowered window. 'Not to worry now, OK Pop?'

'No,' Clem was saying. 'I won't.' He had no idea why he said it, or why he repeated it when the car had gone. A woman going towards the shops saw him speaking to himself and looked away from him. He continued to walk up the road, up the little distance to the post office and the green slatted seats near the taxi rank. The first time he knew Nan was crook was when she had said, 'I'll have to sit here for a minute, Clem.' It was pension day and they had just left the post office. And now Clem sat there again and looked past the brown iron railings at the top of the men's public lavatory and across to the corner opposite, to the Islanders near that travel shop that advertised Pacific flights. One of the men wore a deep collar of flowers round his neck. There was a woman with them too, he could see her mouth open from here while she laughed and for a second rested her arm against the shoulder of one of the men. *Cut his wrists*, the policeman had said. He had moved his pale hand like that, like a saw, against his own wrist. The blood and snot and tears on the man's face running up the steps and passing him under the light at the end of the street, and now this, that movement at his wrists—it's as if there was no time between that pain and then this, Clem thought, that man breathless and crying because of the girl, waiting in his cell, taking the blade from where it was hidden. And he must have been thinking of her when he did that too, and of the woman with the face that looked like it was carved, the one stepping onto the grass outside the court, turning from the men, the bright patterned skirt pulling tight against her body. *His wrists* and that would mean waiting too, Clem had read once how many minutes. And in the dark he supposed he would only feel his bleeding, it would have no colour. Does a man keep his eyes say on a light outside a window, on a corner of a room, until these things ebb, until they waver maybe, waver as though they are dipped in water? Or lie with his eyes closed so that the last thing is not the ordinary things, the table, the chairs, but the last thing you decide on to fill your mind, the last gift to oneself? Can one bring that off, Clem thought. And he said aloud as though he was at home and not where people moved close to him, up and down the steps of the post office, 'I want to know that. I've got to know it.'

The Professional

I decided pretty early on that if the only way you can survive this tangle we call 'life' is by telling lies, then you can't be too careful about the lies you're going to tell. Before I was ten it occurred to me that the kids who were great liars, who were caught and thrashed and stood in corners were the lesser brotherhood, they were bad liars. They were fabulists, fantasists, they in fact wanted a different world to the one they existed in. They wanted a lie to be like a cowboy film that they suddenly lived in, as if their doctoring truth would set them on the dappled horse, make the pearl-handled guns blaze in their hands. They are the ones who never knew what the true point of lying was—that its gift is balance. It is carrying across a room a glass with the water not only to the brim, but a little above the brim, while everyone expects it to spill. A lie is that meniscus. It's the arc where you control the appearance of things.

Let me start with a story.

Zeta Adams was a girl in my class at primary school. She was at least a foot taller than any other girl, and her face was nearly flat. I mean her chin was level, exactly, with her forehead, and her broad nose rose only slightly from the plane of her face. Freckles crowded on its bridge then spread out more sparsely across her cheeks. She had a younger brother called Leo in another classroom. He used to foul himself occasionally, and his sister would be sent for. It was a kind of sport for the rest of us, when the crisis arose, to line up along the windows of the standard four classroom, above the school hall, and look down on the pair of them. Tall Zeta, her legs shapeless and dead white beneath the gymfrock which she wore without the plaited gold girdle that the girls were supposed to wear; and beside her, holding her hand, her young brother walking awkwardly, comically, towards the school lavatories, where one supposed the crisis somehow would be attended to. When she came back to class she would grin at the calls that went up. If she was provoked too far, she would pick up a book, an inkwell, a pencil case, and heave it towards whatever angered her.

Of course, Zeta was several other things besides her brother's keeper, and as tall as a grown-up. She was also dumb, and fairly dirty, and the skin on her neck tended to flake. Anyone who sat next to her moved over towards the wall and called out, 'Snow storm. Watch it!' She was always worth provoking because her temper could run to teachers quite as much as to her fellow-pupils. Once she threatened to jump out of the window, to leap twenty feet to the asphalt playground beneath, if the bitch of a teacher, as she called out, took another step towards her. And so she was sat finally by me.

I was the smallest, and the cleverest, and perhaps the best-behaved in the class. I think the teacher thought I was the last chance of shaming her into some kind of couthness. Zeta took her books, and a ruler with the figures almost totally hidden beneath layers of red ink, and shifted in next to me. I made a point of helping her, which no one else would do, and I believe that marginally her pages of grubby confused schoolwork improved. I told her what the simple words were that she baulked at, and once when the message came through from the other block of classrooms that Leo needed his sister, I offered to go with her. The teacher insisted it wasn't necessary, there was no reason at all, she said, why other people should be roped into a family concern. So Zeta once again walked from the classroom, her broad face silly and flushed with the attention. A few minutes later we looked down on the pair of them, Leo bow-legged, clutching his sister's hand. But she had heard my offer to go with her, and from then she was as attentive to me as a pet dog. She would have torn anyone apart had I sooled her onto them. And knowing she was at heel like that pleased me, I suppose, more than actually using her. The less she could do for me, the more she wanted to do. A few times she picked up imaginary slights, and jumped to defend me. She would stand between me and the supposed enemy, a wall of defensive and stupid flesh. 'Leave them, Zeta,' I would order her. And as the minister who used to talk to us about religion recently had gone over Easter week with us, and explained that strange part of the story where Peter cut off the soldier's ear, and Christ joined it on again, even though that soldier may have been the very one who scourged him a few hours later, I felt a sense of virtue when I restrained her.

There's nothing more interesting to say about Zeta Adams once those few facts are told. The point of her story is that about six weeks after she became devoted to me, I stole a green propelling pencil from Irene Duffy. It was a present from her aunt who had travelled round the world, the kind of souvenir that could be bought for a dollar, but was a thing of exotic beauty to the whole class. There were tiny holes near the top, and when you held these close to your eye, and turned towards the light, you saw St Mark's Square in one, and the Houses of Parliament in another, and in the third an avenue in Paris, stretching on and on, trees in leaf along its sides, a great stone arch in the distance. I had never coveted a thing so much. I thought of it when I was at home, and walking to school, and years later when I first saw those places for myself, there was an excitement that went back to Irene Duffy's pencil, held up against the light. After a week, when its glamour was wearing thin for everyone else, I saw it lying on her desk while the class was at the windows, watching a truck dumping earth for the new playground. In the same second I saw it, and knew no one else was looking, I took it in my hand and slipped it under my desk. I then joined the press of children at the window, watching the earth on the raised back of the truck begin to slip, slowly, then gather force, then rush in a brown rapid arc from the tray. The teacher said, 'Go back to your desks now,' and a second later the cry went up that Irene's pencil had disappeared. We all had to change rows and search each other's desks, and the pencil was found between Zeta's books and mine. There was confusion for the next few minutes, the class turning and pointing and accusing, the teacher calling for silence, demanding that Irene stop bawling, for goodness sake, the thing had been found, hadn't it? We were told to go back to our places, whoever was responsible would be properly punished. This long after, I don't remember what that was. What survives is the feeling I had while I stood and faced the teacher and said nothing for Zeta, nor against her. It was a feeling of great clarity, as I saw what power there was in saying nothing: a feeling that control and indifference are perhaps the same thing, as the plane of Zeta's face turned towards me, and I saw the afternoon light fall across her paleness, her eyes a little distended like an animal's in panic, her new and sudden confusion because she did not know whether I lied or not, whether I should be defended or not.

I could tell you three, four stories like that. One would be about my husband, a tall, gentle man who forty years ago had to hold onto the rail of a verandah to cover the trembling of his hands when I said to him, 'No, Desmond, I am sure about it. I know it was from that weekend.' I was twenty-six, he was a year younger, we were on his uncle's farm and I didn't look up when I told him but wound a thread of clematis stalk, I remember, around my finger. 'Who else?' I asked him. 'Who else could it be?'

That would be one story, say.

Another could be about Desmond's friend, the partner in his firm, and the man he sailed with half the summer. He was a widower, and my lover. And Desmond asked me once if it was true, and I said, 'Ah, poor Tom. Why did he have to spread stories like that about us? Because our life is something he doesn't have?' There are one or two others. If I want an image for them it would be something like a boat running before a breeze on a splendid day. You move the tiller to make your course a little finer, you don't do it to overturn. You do it for the excitement of control.

The children come to visit me, my dark son, my fair daughter, my grandchildren who prop *their* children on the foot of my bed, and I pass the young ones the grapes they have really come to see me for. There is a girl like Desmond in early photos of him, who looks down and doesn't know what to say when I ask her does she like me best, or me and my big bowl of fruit together? And a boy, a little younger, who is my favourite, who tells me, 'Oh, you don't have to say you like one thing more just because you like something else as well, do you Gran?' The staff here tend to fuss me because I'm a 'good' patient. That means I'm not senile nor dirty nor complaining. I know there's not a thing, in the long run, that can alter things by a jot, so why perform about them? I've never been one to ask for that dappled horse, for that blazing pistol, so to speak. But there's a young man who used to call once a week, who now pops in every day because, as he says, he just happens to be passing. He puts his bible on his knee and smiles at me, he works on the principle that a bald man couldn't sit with a wig salesman every single day and not *hint* at the little bag of samples, could he?

So I tell him, 'Yes, do come again,' and, 'It's very good of you to drop in.' And when he says a short prayer just before he goes, I close my eyes until it is over. One of these days we may catch each other in the right light, the way one had to turn Irene Duffy's pencil. If I'm that impressed again, if the trees look as leafy and green and the lagoon shines still just as brightly as it used to, then I may well want this little window to peer through too. I may want the young man to talk on about what he's waiting, of course, to tell me. Hold my hand, I may ask him, help me to cross the room without spilling a drop.

Dandy Edison
for Lunch

You could tell the Edisons were somebody not simply because their name made you think of the old geezer in the encyclopaedia (and of course they said they were relatives) but because Dick who was the father wore a little RAF moustache. It was because of that everyone called him Dandy. There wasn't another man within ten streets who wasn't as clean shaven as a bread board. And by the telephone table in the Edisons' hallway—we called that bit at home the front passage-way—there was a set of Winston Churchill's war histories, with gold writing on their fat blue spines.

The mother was taller, paler, than anyone else's. She kept to herself, and every evening she walked up the road, and round the top of the park, leaning on her husband's arm. Dandy smiled if you spoke to him, but anything he disagreed with made his mouth purse up as though he'd tasted a bit of lemon. The neighbours liked to say he reeked of sarcasm. This was a phrase I waited to hear when they spoke about him. Two or three women would sit round the kitchen table and the Edisons would come up. Then I'd sit with my hands beneath my thighs, pressing them flat against the chair, and look from one face to another, waiting for it to surface. 'Sarcastic though,' one of them would say at last. Another of the women would turn her cup about on her saucer or give a little snort. 'Reeks of it,' she'd say.

There were two children. There was a boy called Davie who was my age, and a girl five years younger. Another thing the neighbours said was that Janice was the apple of her father's eye, he couldn't see past her. The family had shifted next door while we were all at primary school, and I remember Davie because of two things. One was when he came round to our back porch and waited for me to open the high lattice gate to let him in. I was playing with a cousin so I told him he could get back home, he could scram. Then he began to bawl. I had my arm raised up to the metal catch on my side of the gate and kept snipping it as though any moment I might let him in. So he waited there and when he bellowed through the squares of the lattice I saw his opened mouth, and a pink lolly resting on his tongue. I watched him take from his pocket a white paper bag with the top screwed tight. I knew then he had come over to share the bag with us and on the way across he must have put one in his mouth. He handed the bag through one of the gaps in the gate. But he said nothing and he kept up his crying and I watched the pink lolly with the spit welling round it. I kept saying, 'You'd better get out of here, hadn't you? You better get back home.'

The second time was down the end of their yard. There used to be a creek running there before the state houses were built, so the grass was lush and tall. Davie's father also had this vegetable garden that made my own father say, 'Can't that man think of bloody anything else?' But there was this strip between the garden and the wire-netting fence where he let the grass grow.

'What's he do that for?' I asked Davie.

'He likes the look of it. He likes the colour and the way the wind moves it. Something like that.' So we used to sit in the grass and talk, and one day I told him he would probably go to hell. The next day his mother came over to see mine because Davie had been too afraid to go to sleep the night before. He was scared of burning forever the way I described it to him, how the flames are never burned out and when it seemed like a million years had passed it was only beginning, it was as if it hadn't yet begun. The nuns shieded off that kind of stuff by my time. I think I must have heard my father talking about what he had heard himself when he was a boy back home. But Mrs Edison stood there at the back door while my mother kept drying her hands on a tea towel.

'It's not what we believe,' Mrs Edison said. 'We'd rather not have your son instructing ours.'

Things were tense for a little, but then blew over. Dandy gave us a bag of nectarines and my father arranged to have firewood dropped off on the Edisons' front lawn. When the wood was piled there, the end-cuts and the scraps my father had spent ten minutes tossing from the back of his truck, Dandy walked down the road wearing his little cloth cap that would make anyone know he was an immigrant. He looked at the wood then said to Dad, 'All we need's Joan of Arc now, eh Jim?' That night none of us spoke while we had tea because the old man was so mad. Last time he'd do that sod a good turn, he kept saying.

'He mightn't have meant it,' my mother said. 'He needn't have been getting at Catholics.'

'Meant it!' Dad shouted. Then he began to cough and his breath caught and while my mother was holding a glass of water for him she said, 'I don't know why these things always have to come up.'

I remembered those things at my father's funeral as we came out of the church and I saw Dandy Edison standing at the back. I hadn't seen him for over twenty years. He was leaner, his hair was a touch greyer, that was about the only difference. And he had shaved his moustache. With my arm round my brother's shoulder and the coffin resting between us, I glanced up and he looked across at me, and then nodded as though we were passing on a street. I remembered in a kind of flash as they say, the pink lolly in the dribbling mouth, and the way Davie looked at me while I told him about hell, he couldn't go away from me although he had wanted to, he squatted in the long grass beside me while I gave him terror for the first time in his life. And what he had given to me was the fact that words hold power, that saying 'No' to someone, 'You can't come in,' saying, 'Yes, there's hell all right,' is to put him in a cage, to be outside it oneself and run a stick along the bars.

We shook hands outside the church. The undertaker moved behind us, taking the wreaths from the church porch and arranging them on top of the coffin. We talked about Dad and the old days in Westmere and I said why not come round for lunch one Saturday? There was more to talk about than we could get through then.

He said, 'Yes, that would be nice, sometime.' I told him, 'Let's make it definite then. Let's say Saturday week?'

Karen demanded, 'Why in hell did you ask him?'

I said, 'He's a decent old bloke. He's probably a bit lonely.'

'Oh Jesus. Aren't you just the little chap for sentiment the moment you start sniffing the old incense.'

'He's not a Catholic.'

'Who said he was?'

'He's an old man. He turned up at my father's funeral. What's the crime in asking him to lunch?'

'Why not feed the multitudes as well?' she asked. 'Cure a few lepers for afters?'

When we get this far I can tell precisely where my wife's next thrust is going to be. As predictably as sunrise she said, 'Why not throw in your bit about the stars turning with love? You know, your little swotted up quote from that old dago? He was one of your boys.' She raised her hand and moved her fingers and rolled her eyes while she recited how divine love sets in motion such beautiful things. She had done languages at university and told me those lines before we were married. I had asked her to write them down for me. Then a year ago she found a letter of mine that said something almost the same, but to someone else. It was about love enduring anyway, about how it moves the spheres, etcetera. She had said, 'Nothing oils the odd screw like a bit of cultcha, eh?'

This is the last flourish that is supposed to take my breath away, the magician producing rabbits from his hat, a hippo from his arse, or whatever. I'm so used to it now I sit back and applaud when she brings it up. '*Very* good,' I congratulate her. 'Clever little read of a private letter and now all this as well.' As likely as not she'll go on then about secretaries without a brain in their heads and turning it on for the boss and I simply wait until she winds down, which she always does. She hasn't the stamina to be a total bitch. And it amuses me while she rages that I've never, but never been so bored with anyone in my life as I was with that little scrubber she is fuming about. *Raylene*, if you'd believe a human being could be called that. She was separated from her husband, she had blue eyes and curled blond hair like a child's doll, and she believed, as she put it, that true love was for keeps. She actually said so! (She went further down the line after I'd burned her off, down to one of the junior copy writers and she said exactly the same thing to him, after their first bash on the very same office couch. 'Love isn't just something you do for fun, is it?' she said. Ker-rist! I lushed up her beau with a touch of company scotch and it was like hearing the same record played over again. I said to him, 'She's a cross section of our market. Look at it that way and you might as well charge the company for overtime.' He was more pissed than I was and he thought he had to pay me a compliment in return. He said, 'If you'd written the press release for the first Easter there'd have been no doubting Thomas.' Then he said, 'Good tits though, eh?'

So Karen raised Raylene's ghost until she tired of it, then went back to Dandy. 'Why just him?' she demanded. 'We could always advertise. Old neighbours. Old school friends. The milkman when you were three. Your first Plunket nurse. Sister Mary Sanctuary Lamp from primer one. Get them all together for Kevin's M.S.P.'

She was sitting at her desk, working on the next morning's script. As she spoke she jabbed out the initials in the strong block lettering she uses these days. (Five years ago it was intertwining italics in purple ink.) I knew the game too well to ask her what she meant. 'What the hell's M.S.P.?' I was supposed to ask. It was an old trick on her broadcasts and her interviews. She would drop in some privately invented initials like that and throw someone completely. R.F. for Royal Family, that kind of brilliance. 'Top marks for S.E.,' she had complimented an aging visiting actor after his third marriage.

'S.E.?' he stumbled.

And Karen said 'Sexual Endeavour' and brought down the studio audience. She was ticked off by the Chairman himself over that one. She said he had sat there in his dark suit with his silver boyish hair glinting in the subdued lighting and his hands joined in front of him, as though he intended inviting her to prayer, or was simply waiting for the dove to descend.

The trick became a hallmark that viewers would wait for. You would hear her latest *mot* repeated at parties or in the pub. Once one of our brown brothers with a beard and the compulsory whalebone pendant, who didn't know me from the Maori Queen, orated as we waited at a bus stop, 'Call this a bus service? F.A. of that round here, as Karen would say.' Baby, I thought, that's fame! But when she came at it domestically I didn't rise to cue. 'There, there,' I told her. 'Back to letters, is it? Whole words too big for little Karen's tongue, is that it?'

We're good at being vile at each other. Often our sniping works up into something quite demanding—a kicked door, a poster ripped from the wall. Once I threw a rug on the fire and once Karen took my John Lennon spectacles, when they were the in thing, and folded them round themselves so they looked like some kind of perverted insect. I describe her outbreaks to her as a kind of emotional menstruation. Once a month, every six weeks at the latest, we simply have to brawl. Then we make it up and ask people to dinner who may have thought we were unhappy simply because they watched us slang each other at their place a week or so before.

Naturally, then, there was no asking her, 'Now tell me what that means, Karen.' Instead, I walked across the room and shut a window. I explained over my shoulder, 'The neighbours' children, you know?' Then I went to the bar beneath her McCahon. (*Lord, what shall we do in this darkness?* and other sundry slogans in a white, black, rat-grey mix. If the government could only commission posters like that, I say to visitors, we'd go back to candles overnight. We wouldn't waste power, we'd pay not to use it.) I opened a bottle of Russian vodka a client had given me and added the requisites. 'Real drink for you?' I asked her. 'Or your usual sherry?'

But Karen wasn't losing a good line because of my distractions.

'Where were we?' she said. 'Yes. Kevin's M.S. bloody P. Menopausal Senility Party.'

'Confusing me with your hack politicians aren't you?' I said. 'Your geriatric stick men?' I stepped aside when I saw her shadow raise its arm. The pad she heaved at me skidded across the top of the bar, then fell at the other side.

'N.F.M., that one,' I announced. 'Near Fuckin' Miss.'

'Oh, piss off,' she said. She ran her splayed fingers back through her long hair, raising it like a heavy mane.

All this, then, because I had told her Dandy Edison was coming to lunch. When Karen asked me the night before he came if we had to wear our Salvation Army hats, or was it permissible to have our old men's dinner in mufti, I smiled at her and said, 'Quite fancy a bit in Sally gear, actually. Don't you?'

On the credit side of our marriage is that we look so good together. I have very pale skin and dark straight hair that flops forward a little over my forehead—the same side as Hitler's did, Karen likes to point out. In a dark suit, and when I move my pale hands as I speak, I'm sometimes rather taken myself when I catch a glimpse in a mirror, in a reflecting window. When I'm with Karen, who even in winter looks as though she has just come in from the sun, we're the kind of couple people like to fuss over. 'Let them,' I always tell her. They recognise her voice first, because a lot of them hear it every morning of the week. Then after the voice there's her teeth, her figure, her sense of fun—they can't resist her. She is good with men in much the same way as we say some children are good with pets. She doesn't know how *not* to be. She has also had surprisingly few lovers, although she likes giving the impression that she knows the score, has been around, roots like a rattlesnake—whatever your patois is.

Last year she was tied up (literally, one wonders?) with a senior politician whose motto, as I told her, was if it moves, screw it; if it doesn't, tax it. And when she tired of trampling him, or whatever their number was, she repented and confessed to me with a few genuine little tears. She told me as she knelt in front of me in a long frock, after a champagne supper we'd been to. We had come home early and lit a fire. She told me while the pine logs flared and her head rested against my knee, and we both sipped scotch. It was pure *New Yorker*. (It actually came out later in one of my commercials. A similar fire, blonde woman, dark man, crystal glasses, on a rather crappy brand of carpet we were putting across. 'I've a confession to make,' she says. 'So have I,' he answers. Then together, 'We both love it.' A bar or two of melting Mozart, and the Voice-Over declares, 'We sell it by the roll.' A bit *risqué*, a bit cheap even, but we got away with it. I expect by now half of Otara spills its Kentucky Fried over inferior shagpile, thanks to Karen's line.)

'Why are you telling me?' I asked her. 'I'd never have found out.'

'Because it was wrong,' Karen said.

'Silly, don't you mean?'

'No, wrong.' So I patted her head and was understanding about it. We were caring and forgiving because that, quite simply, was what the role asked for. That's a feeling I have about our best times together, when we have the odd weekend away or we stroll through the Domain some quiet Sunday and I snap off a rhododendron and slip the stalk into her hair, it's as if we're watching a movie of ourselves being happy. Perhaps it's because when things go well between us it's like we've been scripted by a real pro. 'If life's not performance, then what is it?' I say some nights when we talk by ourselves, and I'm being what she calls especially H.P. (Heavy Philosophical). When we work as a team there's not much we're after that we don't get. It was teamwork for example that linked us up with California, the one LA-NZ connection that's not only viable but actually fully operative. We had already cut into the Sydney commercial market where they least expected it, you could hear the squealing from here. Then Hersch himself dropped down from LA and I told him, 'You'll only tell where the opposition is from the corpses before long, Herschy.' He's an overweight tit of the Hebrew persuasion who wears magenta sports jackets and calls the tune in half the advertising we have. My kind of confidence makes him smile right back to his gold-stopped molars. Then when Karen got him on her morning show he was chuffed as a haemophiliac with a foolproof razor. She took him to lunch and when she introduced him to people in the corridor outside the studio she began with, 'You'll have heard of Mr Hersch, of course?' Later in the year when we got the call to LA I think it was as much her efforts as mine. As I tell her, when we dance in step, kid, you've really got footwork. When we were over there Herschy palmed us around like Beautiful People. (One night we drank with Jon Voight, among others, in the revolving bar of the Bonaventure. We saw the city sparkle out as far as your eye could reach. I remembered the nuns' story about J.C. up the mountain and Satan offering him the lot, I thought if it was anything like this and he didn't buy it, then they didn't have the right copywriter.) We picked up exclusive rights to one of their biggest cosmetic outlets. Back home I did a male deodorant clip shot in the changing rooms at Eden Park, it was the first commercial from here ever to sell in California.

'It was that parcel of lovely bum-meat that did it. Don't get swelled-headed,' Karen reminds me. 'That and my boobs in Herschy's face in the lift.'

'It's your way with old men,' I told her.

So I thought now, even if Karen didn't care for Dandy, he would take a shine to her. He'd see I did all right for myself there.

I phoned Dandy and offered to drive him round, but he insisted, No, if a man was too old to travel, he was too old to arrive. He dropped these wise saws into his conversation like saccharin pills into a coffee cup. So he took a bus to the bottom of the hill, then walked up. When Karen opened the door he stood there with his cap held in his hands at fly level. He wore a wine-coloured shirt, a pearl grey tie, and a cinnamon-coloured suit that was a little tight under his arms, a shade too loose at his waist. I thought he's had that handed down from someone.

I stood behind Karen and for a moment Dandy could see only my wife. He did this incline as though he was one of our Asian neighbours, a little bow because he was meeting a lady.

'Mr Edison, I presume?' Karen said.

'Do they still say that?' he asked her. 'Perhaps I'm not as old then as I thought.'

Karen turned to lead him in and I saw her eyebrows raised. I stepped forward and shook hands with him. I offered him a drink which of course he refused. This isn't going to be easy, Kevin lad, I told myself. Karen already had whipped off to the kitchen. I heard the blender suddenly burring, the clicking of plates.

'We'll have a look outside, shall we?' I proposed. 'Before the rain beats us to it?' There wasn't an earthly chance of rain, but one had to say something. I thought it was worth looking outside anyway, unless old Dandy's eyes were shot. The glimpse of sea we had down the end of the valley, the dip of the native trees beyond the edge of our section, there was nothing wrong with that, even if my old neighbour wasn't with it enough to admire how on one side our house hung out across the bank on poles. I mentioned the architect on the off-chance he may have heard of how class was actually spelled.

We had had the patio done a few weeks before. Karen dredged up some gifted little foreign chap from Parnell who worked wonders with old bricks. We had heard about a hall at a local convent that was going to be demolished, I was down there like one of my old aunts on Indulgence Day. I fed the good sisters the right line and next thing the yellow bricks were piled at the side of the house, at half the price I'd have got them anywhere else. ('You know I'm getting a bargain, now, don't you Sister?' The nun's lips did that classic convent moue. 'I'm sure you wouldn't offer us anything that wouldn't be a fair price, Mr Grant.') Once Karen's man got to work he chipped and fitted and buffed and we now had our own yellow brick road, as I tell her. I said that at the party we had to christen it and my senior partner did the whole bit, the Judy Garland routine I mean. 'He's pissed out of his tiny mind,' someone said. Anyway my partner did this take-off and all of us except my lady wife were in fits. Leary was so pleased with himself, the pathetic old bugger, so egged on by the clapping hands and the shouts from the rest of us under the fairy lights strung out between the trees, that he did this little dance where the bricks whirled into a circle. He made like he was going to undo his belt, to treat us to a down-trou, and someone shouted out, 'The Wizard of Ass.' Precisely where I stood now with solemn Dandy.

I said, 'We had a little party to launch it, a few weeks ago.' He kept up that smile which seems more for himself perhaps than for whoever he's talking to. I explained how by the end of summer we'd have a punga fence round the whole yard. Dandy was still looking down at the bricks. 'Made a nice job,' he told me.

'Come off it. You don't think I did it, do you?'

The old man tapped at the beautifully levelled bricks with his shoe. 'Pity,' he said. 'Do your own jobs like this and you get twice as much pleasure from it.' He walked across the lawn to examine the brickwork round the barbecue. He ran his palm along the sides. 'That's all right too. That's pretty good.' Karen came and stood beside us for a moment. She said, 'I'll set the lunch out, shall I?' Then before she went in, while Dandy was still above the bricks as though he were looking like a detective for some kind of clue, she said in a whisper, 'Polonius Mark II, eh?'

'A thousand bucks in that lot there,' I said. 'Pay through the nose for anything like that these days.' He was now touching the metal shield at the back. He seemed not to believe things until he had touched them with his hands. I'd noticed that when he first arrived, when he stepped inside and one hand moved along the brocaded back of a chair.

He'd never have recognised it for what it was, of course, a new Belgian weave Karen had picked up in Sydney. And he told me now, as he left the brickwork to face me, 'It'll last you out, Kevin.'

That's rich, I thought, I wouldn't go in for too much of that talk if I were you, old cock. But I laughed to jolly him along. 'Not like that fence in Westmere, then?' I meant the one my father had put up at the end of the yard. It was a bush-carpenter's shambles, bits of wire that sprung loose, uprights that leaned off centre from the moment they were driven in. It was supposed to keep us in our own place, away from Dandy's nectarines, away from his lettuces where the ball kept falling every time we played cricket. There was a permanent sag in the wire where we balanced for a moment before leaping down to the other side. I brought the fence up now because I thought he'd like to be reminded of back there. (The line to play the oldies with is always the sentimental one.) I didn't tell him I drove down that way after Dad had died, the first time I'd gone back since we moved out. The state houses looked smaller, the streets drearier. The patch of park that used to be at the corner was gone, the big gum tree that stood at the end of the street and that I could see from my bedroom window, its grey strips of bark hanging down like unravelled bandages, that was gone too. It had grown at the end of Carpenters' section. The Carpenter girl had died of polio in the summer when we couldn't go back to school. I used to look at the tree in the night-time and it was the street's death tree, it was the closest I ever came I suppose to reverence. Of course it was bullshit, it was the dark regressive stuff our old mate Freud made light work of once and for all. But Christ, at the time I used to kneel on the bed and pull back the edge of the brown roller blind, and look at the spread arms, the tufts of foliage at the branches' ends. I could hear my parents talking in the kitchen and there was a bar of yellow light under my bedroom door. When someone moved in the kitchen the strip of light was broken. There was one night in February, a night when it was so hot that my father stood at the end of my bed in only his pyjama pants. I had woken up with pains in my legs and I had called out. My mother was crying and pretending not to, I knew they thought this was how it began with Doris Carpenter. Of course it was something else I had, I don't now remember what. But I told my father to make sure the sides of the blind were flat against the window. They thought my telling them that was some kind of fever, but it was the reality of the tree out there, dark against the sky. My father went in next door to Edisons and telephoned for a doctor. I heard his steps on the concrete path pass outside my window, and then his steps coming back. And now old Dandy was stepping across the patio and in the drift of my thinking, for the slightest fragment of time, his steps and my father's were the same.

He didn't answer me about the fence, so I presumed he hadn't heard. I stood closer to him, looking at the tuft of hairs that sprang from his ear, catching the light like a spray of fuse wire. I reminded him again because I thought at his age what else can there be except nostalgia? But he didn't rise to it. He turned quietly to look at the white-painted garden furniture, the hard lacy patterns in the cast iron.

'I think of those days quite a bit,' I told him. 'Isn't that curious? And the other families down the street, the Stoddarts, the Jeffreys, all that crowd.' I told him I'd seen one of the Jeffrey girls lately.

'Oh. Which one?'

'Valerie,' I said. I had seen her a month before in Queen Street. I was walking with one of the artistic design people from the office and I had turned almost full on towards him when I saw her coming. I didn't want her speaking to me, I didn't want her looking at me and perhaps not speaking either.

'She was the prettiest,' Dandy said. She had been tall as a girl, with lovely English skin. The sisters had long hair and a drunken old man who was mostly out of work. And their silence, that was it, their way of looking without answering back when most of our mothers thought of excuses why they couldn't play with us, had made them seem wild, defiant. They were the exotic ones amongst us. Davie Edison had crouched under the house with me one day, in the mixed odour of dry earth and firewood and a rotting canvas tent, and told me Valerie Jeffrey did.

'Did what?' I asked him.

'You know.' And in our newly learned jargon he told me she Father Uncle Cousin Kinged with the oldest of the Stoddarts, one of the other boys had told him down at the reef. The reef was the narrow strip of lava rock pushing out from the mangroves, across the shallows and the sometimes bitterly reeking mud where for some reason one always wanted to talk bad things, the territory of disorder and excitement behind the slope of houses, the tilt of streets, where the suburb leaned down towards the sea.

'His brother told me,' Davie repeated. 'Down the reef.' I thought of the two boys crouched and confiding while I waited for Dandy to speak, to step back towards me and to Karen who was at the opened doors. She watched him with arched amused eyebrows, tapping the front of her blouse just between her breasts, signalling me to note his jazzy tiepin with the red inset stone. I thought if you could only hit on some image to set people off as I had been, some slogan to dredge up instantly the old emotions, what you couldn't sell with that!

I now examined his old man's skin, that bloody awful pink tenderness around his eyes, the skin at his temples so thin you could see the soft blue branching of veins underneath. You're as good as dead when you're like that, I thought, your hands speckled and dry and already cold too, cold because I'd felt it when we had shaken hands, it's as though life is already drawing back. Then from my own little nostalgia gig I went into something darker, an unexpected anger with that careful old man who was now watching me. The feeling swept me so strongly that for several seconds I wasn't able to speak nor even hear him although I saw his prim mouth begin to move. At last I asked him, 'What? What are you saying?'

'I don't,' he said. He faced me with his bland level gaze as though I were under inspection. 'I don't think very much about them, those Westmere days.'

'I suppose a lot slips your mind,' I said. I knew that might sound offensive.

'No, you remember all right,' he corrected me. 'I mean you don't go out of your way to dwell on it.' Then he laughed, his new teeth grotesque in that dry, papery face. He put his fingers around my arm. We walked inside like that, pretty much as he led me round the side of the old house when Davie and I cut up his daughter's doll, and the sawdust guts spilled out on the apron of concrete near the underhouse door. He now surprised me by saying, 'Live in the past, Kevin, you're good as dead already.'

As we came inside he did an odd thing. I hadn't noticed that he had picked anything in the garden, but he now opened his hand, holding it out towards Karen. There was a twig that branched into two or three pinkish tips. I didn't even know we had something like that growing. But Karen took it from his hand and raised it to her face. 'Yes,' she said, smiling at him. 'Daphne.' Then she was talking to him about that, about how it must be one of the loveliest scents there was.

'And verbena,' Dandy said. 'Daphne and verbena.' Karen told him how she had loved it when she first found out what that kind of bush was called. 'I was reading this book of Greek stories, you know, myths and things? It was a book I thought I should hide from my mother anyway because it had photos of statues that showed ladies' bosies, you know that kind?' Dandy was laughing with her, enjoying her casting back to when she was a girl. 'Anyway it had this story in it about Daphne. It was written in that stilted old style, *Apollo loved her, and as she would have none of him, pursued her.* I had only an inkling of what it was about, but once I knew she turned into a tree instead I thought well *anything* would have been better than that.'

'*Almost* anything,' Dandy wisecracked back at her.

'Exactly.' She was flirting with him now, she tapped her hand on his when she said that. I thought, Shit, you can't resist it, can you? See a corpse with a smile on it and you'd come on strong.

From then it might as well have been Karen who had lived next door to him when she was a kid. A couple of times I tried to bring the lunch back my way, he was eating my food after all, he was on a chair I'd paid for. When Karen went to bring the soufflé from the kitchen I said, 'Davie doing all right is he?'

'Still with Air New Zealand,' Dandy said. 'But I've told you that, you asked me earlier on.' He began to build a little tent from his table napkin and set it upright between his hands. He tapped at the side of it, balancing it, then took his hands away.

'Advertising doesn't have quite the same—well, the same thrills,' I tried to joke. 'I mean it has its moments but there's not the same glamour, is there, as flying those jets around?' I wanted him to say at least that we looked as if we were doing nicely too, to give some flicker that he saw you didn't buy furniture like ours in some bargain store in K Road, that the big picture with the writing on it probably cost more than he'd ever earned in a year at the Electricity Department. ('An inspector,' I'd explained to Karen when she asked what he used to do. 'Got trouble with your connections and old Dandy'd sort them out for you.') I knew even as I thought this that it was a bit vulgar, a bit downmarket. I don't mean that I wanted him to feel our gold, as my partner likes to say. Not quite. But I wanted him to know we had taste, and that taste wasn't cheap; that our imported glass-topped tables and Swedish lamps and Karen's collection of paintings were a far cry from Taihau Crescent. I wondered what sort of stuff Davie had. I expected that for all his wings and his flying hours he had wooden salad tongs from Fiji and carved Singapore tables. I suppose I didn't give a stuff whether I was crude about it or not, I wanted Dandy Edison with his Churchill histories and his prissy voice to know that I wasn't playing in the back yard of a state house any longer, scoffing a bar of chocolate before my sister came home. Because he'd seen me do that, fuck him. He'd come round with a phone message in those days before we had a phone of our own, and seen me ferret off into the wash-house with my mouth crammed. He had pushed open the door and looked down at me with his high quizzical stare.

'Mrs Mississippi wants your mother to phone sometime.' I looked up from where I stood edged in against the curved concrete surround of the copper. I felt my cheeks bulged out and the heat of embarrassment prickling up from the neck of my shirt. 'It's important she knows the name,' he said. 'What is it?' I remember how I repeated it, breaking up the word into its slippery syllables. He had told me, 'I need to know that you get it right.' So I had to say it to get rid of him.

'Mississippi,' I attempted. A dribble of chocolate saliva leaped in a dirty arc, I could feel the oozing at one corner of my mouth. Then Dandy laughed as he took a piece of paper from behind his back. 'Here, the number's on this.' The paper had some name on it as well, a name like our own, or like his, something as simple as that. I slammed the wash-house door and the tears danced in my eyes. I said whatever I could lay my tongue to.

I had that in mind now, watching the fastidious movement of his lips as he smiled at whatever Karen said, as he dabbed at his chin with the corner of the napkin he had unfolded from its temporary tent and laid again across his knees. They were onto cooking now, on how he managed by himself, the kind of dishes he found it most convenient to make. 'Time's never a factor you see,' he confided. 'I can take the whole afternoon preparing it, for all it matters.'

'More soufflé?' Karen was holding the dish in front of him, the server ready as though she were about to feed a child.

'No, I think I've had sufficient.'

'Go on,' she teased him. 'It'll build you up.'

'That's never worked before.' He raised both his arms from the table and his sleeves fell back. He showed her his skinny wrists, and the inch or two of thin forearm below his cuffs.

'But I love a challenge!' Karen opened her eyes wide so her eyelashes stood out like spokes, then they were goofing off together again, old mates, Jesus! I thought why push this little number any further, I've done my bit? I went and poured myself a decent-sized gin and clanked in ice from the fridge. Karen glanced across at me while she continued to dangle her geriatric fish (as I'd tell her later). Just to see if her lines still worked, was that it?

'Janice,' I interrupted when I returned to the table. They were onto talking about desserts by now, how to eat crap and save five dollars a year, that kind of recipe swapping.

'Guavas,' Dandy was telling her. 'So few people eat them and yet they're a joy. They're exactly that. A joy.'

'And the colour. That lovely deep pink.'

So I threw in, 'Janice.'

For once my spouse was startled at what I said. I had told her there was some kind of tragedy there somewhere, I wasn't sure of how the details went. But apparently no one ever spoke of it, it was something Dandy himself would never mention. So we wouldn't either, I had warned. Ask about Davie as much as you like, but leave Janice out of it. 'Oh,' Karen had said before Dandy arrived, 'but that's the only bit I want to know.'

'You haven't mentioned Janice.' I stirred the ice about in the glass and smiled across at Karen, then at Dandy. 'Or have I missed it?' I waited for what she calls the N.U. on occasions like this, the Nasty Upshot.

'We're onto recipes, love,' Karen pointed out. There's nothing like a touch of affection to show when she's close to panic.

I continued to smile at them. I lifted the glass and tapped it against my teeth. 'Funny,' I said, 'I seem to have kept up with Davie's movements over the years, but not Janice's. I met one of the Jeffrey girls lately, I think I told you, and she seems to have got through her net too.'

Karen was driven back to asking gaily, 'Janice?'

'Kevin must have mentioned her,' Dandy said. He pushed his plate away from him slightly and laid his dry speckled hands side by side on the cloth. I noticed one of his nails was dark blue, as if it had been jammed. When he looked up he held Karen's eyes, not mine. 'She was my daughter, you probably know that much.' Then he said, 'She used to be a stripper.' Without moving his hands, and in a voice that might still have been talking of guavas, he told us that she took her clothes off first in Wellington, then in Christchurch, because it was the easiest way she could make money. From time to time he smiled slightly while he was talking, when he said, 'She was lazy, you see, but she was also intelligent. I mean she could see the moral objections someone like myself might raise, but she could also talk herself out of them.' Then again, after telling us she had crossed to Sydney, he explained, 'They seem to pay more there for the same thing.' He went on with her career, almost laboriously. Although she was lazy, he repeated, that didn't mean she wouldn't rather do something else than have men look at her. So she bought a massage parlour she called 'Tropic Palms', and then another that was already named when she bought it. Finally there was one that we would probably call V.I.P. It catered only for the rich and was named very simply 'Lolly'. 'And so she led a life of what we call vice. She told me her one weakness in the business she had chosen was sentimentality.'

'What did that mean?' Karen asked.

'I don't know the details.' But he told us other things about her. That she wrote to him often, for example, and that he always knew, more or less, what she was doing. They agreed not to let her mother in on it. 'She always thought Janice had some office job over there. She knew she was doing well.' 'Davie,' I said at last. 'What did Davie think?' 'Oh, he wouldn't speak to her. Not even about her. Did you think he would?' And again there was the slight smile, and the odd feeling he gave that for all his frankness what we were witnessing was only on the surface, some stirring of what went on far off. I felt I had been outmanoeuvred by the old man owning up that his daughter was some kind of seedy call girl. I could tell Karen was moved and that somehow Dandy was untouched, that saying all that filth about his own family seemed almost incidental to him, that because it was Janice it was somehow not so bad, was that it? I was unsure of everything about him. And then he was tapping the red stone in his tiepin and saying, 'She sent this over to me once. It's not imitation either.' He moved the pin slightly for our benefit, so the light streaming in from the window opposite him glanced across the stone. 'Ruby,' he said. Then the old bastard threw his trump card, the one he can never be forgiven for because he must have known all the time he was setting it up, that Karen would go down in front of it like some whore in front of a customer with a hundred bucks, oh mustn't he just. Because Karen already had an expression on her face that I had never seen, not simply shock nor surprise nor wonder. It was like the look on some of those old women who used to go up to St Joseph's when I was a kid, who knelt during the long hours of Exposition when the host was stuck up on the altar in a glass disc and from the edges of the disc gold spikes rayed out, it was like they were gazing into the centre of a dulled sun. And these old hags would stare on and on and the look on their faces was this crazy mix, as if they saw and yet were blind at the same time, that what they looked at was a kind of veil and what they sought was on the other side. It bewildered me that I'd ever think of Karen like that, that I'd put her in that same clutch of mutter and superstition. I sat now without speaking, without any of us in fact moving until Karen tapped his hand and said, 'Is she dead?' And Dandy said, 'Yes, of course.'

We gave him coffee and got rid of him just after three. I'd put away a few more gins and thank Christ we'd got off the morbid line, we'd left the late-lamented Janice stroking the koozers of eternity and the last half hour was Karen's usual fund of chat, travel and work and a touch of politics about which she knows B.A., by which I don't mean Big Amount. But the moment he was gone and I stood beside her and my hand moved across her arse she said simply, 'Don't,' and she went out into the yard. She opened the door to the garden shed and took out the shears. Then she attacked a hedge at one corner of the section, a shaggy mound of a thing that I'd been meaning to ring someone to come and trim for weeks. She was so inept she was comic. I thought, She'll be inside in ten minutes, she'll want me to put band-aid across her angry little blisters. I was wrong about that one too. I don't know how long she worked because when she came in I had nodded off, I was sitting in the Ezyboy chair with the headphones on, listening to The Who.

'Time to dress up,' she told me. 'Not that I feel much like party times.' But of course she managed. Her gay station manager announced half way through the night, 'Our Karen's nothing if not an old trouper.' He leaned within inches of my face to tell me, his breath rotten with halitosis. I know now why studio producers sit behind a pane of glass. And at midnight when we said we would have to go there were calls of 'Piker' and 'Off for a bit, eh?' and a general sigh of regret that I was depriving them of Life and Soul, as the fat hostess chided me.

'You'll survive without it,' I told her.

Karen put her head on my shoulder during the ride home. We covered the four or five miles without saying a word. Later when she leaned over me her hair fell across me in one broad brushing swathe, a kind of golden tent. It must have been all that old Westmere stuff being churned up earlier in the day, because I raised my hands to run them through her hair, I spread it to either side of us and said, 'Tabernaculum Dei.'

'Some of your old mick talk?' Karen teased. I lowered my hands from her hair and moved them to her tits.

'More a trade name than anything else.' Then I told her, 'Blame your visitor this afternoon.'

I felt her weight move across me, her nails run lightly across my neck. She said, 'Good old Dandy then.' Her hand stretched out and groped for the switch on the bedside lamp. Then it was dark as when we first pushed open the door to Edisons' under-house in the summer evenings, when we'd hide from Janice, and Davie would tell me 'Shhh!' We'd crouch until we heard her walk past, then begin to talk about our secrets, about the Jeffrey girls and the Stoddart brothers and the things we heard down the reef, and sometimes Davie opened his hand and gave me a badge, or some stamps, or once, a foreign coin he had taken from his father's desk upstairs.

The Club

He is sixty-seven, which makes him perhaps the youngest person in the room. The trouble is he looks no more than in his late fifties. He feels that he is out of place. For when he enters the Club it seems to him that the large central room is full of old people. He is also very nervous. For a moment he remembers entering classrooms as a child, changing sheds on Saturday mornings when he played rugby as a boy. There was the same shyness as he feels now. It is as if all conversation stops, and all those eyes turn to take him in. He is the new boy. The new old man.

A woman whose teeth look to him as though they have been soaked in tea smiles and comes up to him. She says to him, So you're the gentleman who phoned? He tells her, Yes I am. She continues to smile at him and he feels obliged to add something else. He says, I mentioned I was recently bereaved. Then there is another woman beside the first. This one is taller, and smiles with her lips. She also holds out her hand, which he takes. She must be English, he thinks. This one holds his hand firmly. There are sessions she tells him on bereavement some Thursday afternoons. There is a minister and a psychologist who are quite informal, it's remarkable the way reservations fall away and people are willing to speak quite openly about their grief and just everyone benefits from it. That's the point of the whole thing. The woman said all this in so quiet a voice he had to lean forward to catch her words. He is close enough to tell that she smells of peppermint.

The first woman then says how she had occasion to benefit from those sessions over the last eighteen months. She shows her dark teeth. Say what you like, she says, a shoulder to cry on is half the battle. Only then did she say she was Mrs Weston, and the other woman was Mrs Boyer. But for the moment he must of course meet some of the others. If the Club wasn't social then it might as well be nothing, she says. She takes his arm and turns him towards three men who sit and watch him.

He thinks of the picture that had been pinned to the kitchen wall for years. A picture by a Frenchman who made his paintings look like stained glass windows. There were thick black lines of lead between his figures. That picture had been called 'The Judges', hadn't it? Lou in any case was the one who put it up, on the wall between the fridge and the door into the hall.

The three old men look up at him. Then one of them holds out his hand and tells him, They'll be bringing the tea round any time now, it's as well to be in early if you want your pick of the cakes. He tells them his name is John. The others are Stan and Dick and Leo. Mrs Boyer is the wife of Leo. Then John sits on an old armchair with the mock leather flaking away from the canvas beneath. The chair smells sour. He thinks of waiting-rooms in a hospital, the dog-eared magazines. All those articles he had read on Queensland. Lots of girls in skimpy clothes.

The old men have gone back to the game they were talking about. Is that Stan or Dick talking now? It's so easy to get things wrong when you are first introduced. Then he has to say No, he didn't watch that game. Nor the other one they mention. He doesn't know Essendon or Collingwood or Carlton or anything else. He never watches football. He does not say so, but he finds the whole subject boring. Brought up here though were you? one of the men asks him. He has to answer Yes, he was. Christ, one of them says. In pure amazement.

The cakes come on a trolley, and the tea in a big pot that one of the volunteers, a woman with firm brown arms and a word for everyone, pours into cup after cup. One of the men snips a little container and drops tablets into his tea. But there is a lady beside him now talking to him. She laughs and he smiles at her. He is feeling almost panic. He looks about the room, at the old people and the three volunteers. The woman explains to him that once every month they are taken for drives. To the Botanical Gardens or sometimes out to the coast. Sometimes there are theatre parties although not as many as there used to be. All this gloom she says and dirty talk even on the television. I haven't got television, John says. Well I don't want to miss out on this, the woman tells him. She means the plate of strawberry cake that was being handed round.

He is standing then by himself. He notices that the room smells of clothes. Clothes and soap and when the women move past him, there is the odour of scent and powder that he turns away from. He watches the eating and the soft pink mouths, the crumbs that some are so careful with, dabbing at their chins, brushing briskly across their chests and stomachs, but that others are not aware of. He is uncomfortable at how easily he finds it all distasteful.

Then another woman speaks to him. For a moment John believes that she is speaking to someone else. Until she touches his arm. With one plumpish hand, one finger pinched in by its broad gold ring. I'm sorry? he says to her. She says simply but in the tone of saying something for the second time, are you all right? Excuse me but I thought you mightn't be all right? Her face has broad cheekbones and her eyes are blue. She wears a black coat with an astrakhan collar. It makes her look old-fashioned, even here. But she watches the tall man she has spoken to, and he knows it is not mere politeness, her asking that. She gives him the feeling that there is no hurry at all, about anything. She is slow and certain as she waits. I'm simply new here today, he says, that's why I'm quiet.

He was there because he found the house too painful sometimes to be in by himself. He would try to read or to spend an hour in the garden or to prepare his evening meal in that leisurely, careful way that had been Lou's custom for years. But he would find he had read a dozen pages and barely a paragraph had sunk in. Or he would stop with the secateurs poised in his hand, the reddish-green stems of the rosebushes, the exquisite fine curve of the thorns so vivid. The garden seemed to pulse at him. Even the heap of cuttings at the end of the yard seethed with its rich rankness, those small things moving through it if he leaned forward to inspect the mulch closely. And he felt his own blood churn more clearly. Like seeing the cat one morning with a tattered but living finch tapped from paw to paw, the fine teeth so careful not to pierce it as she saw John step towards her. The bird's eye a pip of reflected light, the cat so elegant as she slipped past to the side of the shed, the billowy fur like trousers on some exotic dancer. She had once left the remains of a rabbit lying in the hall, the ears and the tiny legs. The dark pink veiny ears that felt cold and slightly waxy when he picked them up, like tulip petals. He had said, You're better at this kind of thing than I am, and Lou had taken the pieces from his hand. He had never bothered all that much with what you call 'nature'. Lou was the one for that too. For pointing things out. Arranging flowers. Watching from a window and calling him to look at the beads of rain on the olives in the yard, at their silvery dry flashing when a big wind tossed them. So now it puzzled him at how much he saw. The breaking of trunks from the earth for example, that urgency he had never noticed. Or the gape of some of those flowers he didn't know the name for—a sort of hibiscus, were they? Their mouths turned towards the sky, funnels that could never be sated, that drank and drank at light so desperately, so briefly. He found that he was so often standing, merely looking at such things. It was all like standing too near a flame. Yet Lou must have stood there always. That upset him more. That only now, this late, he saw as Lou had seen all the time. He thought of the white small fangs holding the bird, the coursing white flakes that eat a blood stream, a human body. John felt an anger that oddly pleased him as he looked at the rage out there in the yard. Which had always been there, as he now knew, while he had seen only the flat planes, the two dimensions. He thought of how he had gone off to work at the library and come home pleasantly tired and they had eaten their meals together, and listened to the radio or read, and gone to bed some nights to love but mostly to lie and drowse together, their hands at ease across each other's bodies. He had lived he thought with someone who was so ordinary. He remembered that design of a bird nested in flame on the back of a red set of books in the literature shelves. Ordinary as a phoenix, Lou was, in its ordinary fire.

The woman who calls herself Joyce watches the new visitor carefully. It is the second or third time that he has come, and she knows how nervous he still is. Because he does not fit in at all, does he? He finds it difficult to talk with the other men, for instance. He sits this afternoon in front of the television. He is the only man in fact who does not speak while he watches the game, although he smiles when a fat man beside him raises his arm and shakes it at one of the players and calls out, A pansy or what are you? Another man shouts across not to be hard on him Fred, can't he see the poor bugger's never handled a bat before? The banter goes on along the rows of chairs around the screen. Joyce thinks how they are like a caricature of a classroom.

She gives half her attention to a funny little thing who has perched beside her. A marquisite brooch bobs up and down as the smaller woman flings herself about as though words alone can't manage, there had to be this 'body language' as well—isn't that the phrase she has heard her daughter use? If there's anything in it then it goes for him too, of course. John, that new man there, in his tartan tie and his suit, stiff there among the open-necked and blazered old blokes shiyacking each other. He'd rather be miles away from here, that's what *he's* saying. Yet

Joyce decides he must prefer even this to something, this raucous and aging equivalent to the yobbos out there on Brunswick Street some nights yelling and revving their motors and making their girls squeal out.

He's bereaved, of course, the other woman says. In her special voice, so the word slips a wreath around his neck. It is like the oval at a country show, Joyce thinks, the red and green and blue sashes handed out for prizes. There are different words with their different colours, but bereavement is the best. That kind of exultation—yes, it is even that, she thinks—each time at the club when a new death ripples among them. *Only last week in that chair beside me. Only Sunday and we were playing bowls. A great bloke, all right. A proper lady.*

The wind shaking the shrubs outside the window quivers the light inside the room. The winking brooch beside her says no one in the district knows him really, that's a bit odd isn't it? He must come from somewhere further out. You'd think there'd be places closer to home he could go to, wouldn't you? Her own husband mind you says he's too stand-offish ever to get on anywhere. Makes the other lads uncomfortable, just sitting there like a moke. There are people like that, the woman keeps on. There are wet blankets by nature and nothing's going to change them.

Joyce sees past the little face beside her to the spiteful girl in grade four, the young wife jealous of a neighbour's car, an old bitch whose only surviving weapon is a husband who is supposed to say the words she gives him. Joyce tells her I don't know anything about him. I'm not interested in guessing. She goes to the counter where the large pot of tea squats between the cups and saucers. I can manage, she tells one of the volunteers. She wonders, without being disturbed by it, why women like that have always grated on her so much. Why their common femininity irks far more than it gives—as her daughter says it should—a sense of sisterhood. Dear Delia who carries the world on her shoulders, so solemn beneath her banners and would sell her soul to make the world a better place. She tells her mother there can be no future unless we give ourselves to caring and concern. There is also a male force and a female force, but the female must always triumph, apparently, the woman is replete when the male lies exhausted. Joyce remembers her own mother with her novenas and spiritual bouquets, the Lourdes water sprinkled for whooping cough and Our Lady on the front lawn the night before her wedding. Sure enough the sun shone out and the wedding photos were perfect. They are closer together,

Joyce thinks, mum and Delia, so much closer than I am to either of them. Sisters holding hands across my head while I stand too sceptical to take up what they offered. There is no self-congratulation in her thinking this. She lifts the heavy enamel pot and pours the steaming tea.

She says to the new man, You look as lost as I feel myself sometimes, and hands him one of the cups. He says with a wry frankness that pleases her, I didn't know what hard work social life could be. They sit together on a form against a wall. He tells her that he came to the club in the first place because it became intolerable at home. So it didn't matter really whether he enjoyed it here or not. The important thing was that when he looked at the kitchen clock and closed the door to go out, it was one o'clock. When he opened the door and saw the clock again it was six. At least an afternoon had gone.

How recent was it? she asks him. He tells her, Four months. It is worse now than it was in those first few weeks. Joyce says, There is nothing to say, really, is there? Nothing much helps. And John, blowing softly on the scalding tea, says No. There is only the hollowness. And the distaste for time. Then he looks at her and smiles, You know what it's like too?

Joyce's Andy had been a clerk in a bank. When he was a young man he wore his dark hair sleeked back so smoothly that she thought of a currawong's brilliant sheen. He was tall and lithe and as he grew older his angular features made her think again of a bird. His leaning above her chair, his swooping on bits and pieces the children left about, snapping them up, demanding tidiness as evidence of parental rule. He lived with the regularity of those figures who come out on the dot on ornamental clocks. The season altered on the morning he took out his blazer, or reached for his twills at the back of the wardrobe. He smoked his pipe each evening at seven o'clock. On Tuesday nights they went to the movies. They made love twice a week.

Andy collected recordings of Eddie Cantor and Fats Waller and especially of Al Jolson. He liked to sing the words softly as he did jobs around the house.

And when it's raining, have no regrets,
Because it isn't raining rain you know, it's raining violets . . .
Joyce liked to hear him singing. He didn't attempt to imitate the intonations from the records, but sang in a light tenor voice that made him sound young.

He was kind and bought her lovely presents for her birthdays and for their anniversaries. He liked to be quiet and warm in the way Bing Crosby was in some of the films he enjoyed so much. She knew although Andy never said such a thing, that he would have loved to be an American. The last time they went out before he became ill, was to *Easter Parade* at a festival of old-time movies. Judy Garland looked like a doll someone had dressed up. And Joyce had thought how that world with its comfortable houses and blatant accents had nothing to do with their modest home, their flat diffident voices. It all might as well have been in a foreign language. Yet in a sense it was the last time that her husband had been to what spiritually you might as well call home; to where a man who did not believe in God, and who found it difficult to put his tongue to words that carried emotion, might go and return refreshed, where his life opened into brighter lights and warmer sounds than the brick house in Gallipoli Avenue could ever have offered him. She thought how sad it was, even sadder than the slow encroachment of his death, that the vitality and flaming colours there all the time in the world around him, came to him only through tinselly movies, in songs that grew from lives that were nothing like his own. And when the disease did come they were the deepest things.

Her sister tried to tell her how his humming those tunes, those snatches of song coming to him sometimes when he had said nothing else for days, meant that he was happy in himself. And the specialist explained to her as well how the mind's connections jumble and cut out, how what does emerge may seem random and fragmentary, yet there is no reason to believe that people with that deterioration either suffer, or are aware of their own condition. She said, How can we know anything like that for certain?

The boys dutifully sat with their father in front of television and Delia made him scones even when he refused to eat them. Stephen brought cans of beer for when they watched the football, until Andy's hands would jerk and the beer slosh away from his mouth. Then above the mopping of the sofa, the whispers of how their father was going downhill. The light is drawing back from him, Joyce would say, everything he loved is being lifted from around him. Oh mum, Delia said, do you have to go on?

Thank God he had slept for so much of the time. And when sometimes she led him by the hand into the small garden at the back of the house, along the path between the scratched earth where for years he had coaxed up lettuces and radish and skinny sticks of corn, down beneath the big peach tree where she placed the cane chair for him, his face would glimmer with fragments of comprehension. He would try to rise from the chair to embrace her, to call her over to him if she knelt at the weeds that had moved into his garden. It's called Alzheimer's, she explained to the man at the club. What Andy had.

They sat near a dried fountain in a stiffly formal park, where Joyce thought of people in old-fashioned clothes. John was beside her on the concrete ledge. Over the past weeks they had become friends. Then they met by chance in a delicatessen. Joyce said she would wait outside the shop for him. With their shopping bags they had walked along to the park. It was so much easier talking there than at the club. That picture of the Queen and the Duke to begin with, John said. Joyce liked him for that too. She kept telling him the story she had begun at the club, while his fingers ran against the smooth cracked concrete where the water had once played. She said Andy took two years to die. He would go for a month without knowing any of us, then stand in front of me and mumble words from a song. What kind of song? John asked her. In a clear voice she picked out the notes for him.

Rock-a-bye your baby with a Dixie melody,
When you croon, croon a tune from the heart of Dixie . . .

He watched the woman beside him. Her eyes were so like a young woman's and now her voice as well, while her old hands fidgeted in her lap. A man reading on a bench looked up from the paper he held in front of him with wide spread arms. He lowered the paper and raised it again at once as soon as he took in the old codger with his natty tie, the crazy woman next to him singing clearly enough for it to float across the clipped lawns, the raked pathway, past the bed of recently turned earth where one good rain would release the frail plants into colour. John saw how her skin was soft and creased as crumpled calfskin gloves. She said quietly, looking straight ahead of her, her heels like a girl's tapping at the concrete wall, I hated my husband before he died. Andy who was the kindest man the only one I'd ever given twopence for, I hated him. His songs and his silences and his slobbered food. When he died I was in the room with him alone and I sat at the window and looked out at the pure sky for oh I don't know how long, say twenty minutes before I phoned the doctor. There was a clock ticking on the dressing-table, one of those little square travelling clocks. And each tick was like a fragment more of a huge weight being taken away from me. Then I had this oddest picture in my mind. It was of rows and rows of trees, like a forest you see in photos of England or somewhere. The trees had been quite bare only now the leaves were falling back up, do you see what I mean? It was like autumn in reverse. The leaves beginning to rise from where they lay on the ground and then simply pouring back up. I knew it was all inside my head but I saw it so clearly while I looked out at this cloudless sky. Until the whole forest was full and swaying and I could even hear it then, like every leaf was moving in the wind and the leaves were the ticking of the clock as well. Do you see all that?

John was watching the traffic on the main road while Joyce talked on to him. He felt such tenderness for her even as he thought yes, she is a bit crazy, a bit off centre. He had never heard anyone go on like that. And yet what she said also made its lovely sense. He could imagine himself and Lou looking out there at the same trees she told him about. Then he surprised himself by saying Lou's arms were branches towards the end. I'd see them lying along the outside of the quilt and I always thought that. They were so thin and brown and were like old thin branches.

It was time for them to make a move, Joyce said. We've been sitting here a couple of hours, know that? The man with the newspaper had gone off some time ago. An old Greek lady was on that bench now. Her eyes were closed and her hair was held down tightly with a black scarf. Joyce said as she looked at her, If you're one of them you might even have loathed your husband from the word go, and you've still got to wear black like that forever. John felt how the woman beside him covered her own guilt as she said that, denigrating the love of forty years which after all meant so much more than her feelings at the end, her natural animal distaste at seeing another die so badly. But there was no way he could put that into words. So he joked, he pointed out to her, You're wearing black yourself. He touched her astrakhan cuff. Ah yes, she said. But this is the oldest coat in the world. I had it dyed years ago because it was frog-green once and hardly ever worn, it was faded so much you wouldn't believe it. I got it for our honeymoon, that's how old it is. It can't be, John said. She said, Oh yes it is. To go to Tasmania where I'd heard it was so cold you even needed a coat in March. They both laughed when he asked her, Was it then? As cold as that? And she told him, I can't remember wearing clothes for the whole two weeks.

It is the Thursday in the month when the chaplain and the social worker join the group that gathers in the special lounge. The small room is called special because the furniture there is better than in the larger clubrooms, and there are flowers arranged in a vase shaped like a swan, the stems tucked in between the wings. There are seldom more than a dozen people at these meetings, only those who reasonably come under the heading of Recently Bereaved. The social worker is skilled at weeding out the voyeurs, and the chaplain speaks discreetly if someone becomes upset. There is also a special trolley, and sandwiches brought by the volunteers, for those who sit down to hear the chaplain read briefly from the New Testament. The social worker then holds up a book with many photographs, an American book called *Living Through*. It is a book about terminal illness and how, unbelievable as it may seem, there can even be joy at the end. Well there's nothing wrong with hoping for it, Joyce supposes. She thinks of the dead man in the bed behind her and the leaves, the teeming seconds, the purity of an immense sky outside the room. It is still beyond her to make the two events connect—that afternoon only six months ago and that other day far back, her veil snagging she remembered on the outside safe as she walked round the side of the house, Andy turning slightly as she walked towards him in the church, his face pale and smooth as soap. Yet she knows there is a line between all things, a connection she must work towards. She smiles now as John comes into the room. She can tell that he is tense, that normally he would hate such a place as this. She knows that privacy is a jewel to him, and yet here he is this afternoon, about to make himself public. His eyes move about the room, his hand touches gently, rapidly, at his tie. They look at each other, the youngish old man and the dowdy woman in her black coat.

John raises the tweed sleeve of his jacket and sees it is a few minutes from two o'clock. They will hate him of course, he knows that. They always do when they know. But he has no more choice now than if Lou were there beside him, telling him he must speak for them both, as he had done that other time at a meeting for civil rights. His legs that day had shaken against the back of the chair in front of him. There were nudges and turned heads round the hall. There always had been. In shops and from neighbours and at work in the library, as if the world waited to bestow its one certainty, its sense of anger at them both. But the social worker is leaning forward now, his hands clasped round his knee, talking to them so calmly. He is explaining as he does each month that they are friends together. There is only sympathy in this room, he says, we have all felt the same things, we are friends who will understand. And John finds that he is speaking. He knows his voice is steady and that they look at him with interest. He says I want to talk about my own loss because the words to say it out publicly are the words that help it heal. He sees that the minister and the social worker are both surprised at how he speaks. He knows that some of the others in the room will think that his voice is snooty, that he is educated and so at once to be held in doubt. He says, We were together for over thirty-five years. From soon after the War. We met on the steps of St Paul's during the Victory celebrations. Half the people in London that day seemed to be Australians. And the room stirs because they like that, it means that all of them could cast back to the massive crowds outside Flinders Street Station and the hooters and sirens in the smallest towns even throughout the country, the flags decked across the streets and the bars chocker and the singing late into the night. So they begin to warm to him while he went on, while he said, We have to say the truth because that is the last thing really we can do for the dead, the last and most enduring thing we can give them. As he speaks he is looking at Joyce's placid face. It is as much for her in fact as it is for Lou, this truth that no one wants and that none of them will thank him for offering. He feels the prickling discomfort beneath his collar and the heat at the back of his neck. How Lou used to have him on about his blushing when they were first together. But it was only Lou who had given him confidence in so much—to go to library school, to finish his degree, to sit at last beside that bloody hospital bed for days and then into weeks and to be able to say finally how that was a privilege too, to see how death wins of course but that is not the point. That mere brute massing of the dark. The victory is in defying it, in saying to the last breath you may take this body but never me. He knew how his words would seem wild now. He sees how the minister is softly tapping a ballpoint pen against his thumb. And for Joyce's sake now he will tell them. It is his gift to her for what she has given him, that awful honesty about the husband she had loved and then hated, and now that he was dead, could love him again. I lived with a man, he is telling them. He feels the sweat gathering beneath his eyes. I slept with a man for nearly forty years and it was as true as anything any of you could know, although you will not believe it. He is only able to say it now because his eyes are on Joyce, on the slight smile that remains there while already there is a stirring in the room, the minister glancing at the social worker beside him. Already a couple of the men are on their feet. The cleric says to them benignly, opening his hands in that practised gesture of acceptance and blessing, Shall we break here for tea? He quickly carries a cup to John, and asks the woman at the trolley to pass over the sponge-cake. He is deliberately jolly as he places the tea in front of the recently bereaved. Something to perk you up, he says, thinking this one's going to take some smoothing over, the poor old sod. He is glad to see how the social worker is covering the other front, speaking expansively to the group around the trolley, anxious to hold them there, to delay if only for minutes the word that shall spread out to the other room, among the rest of the club. That the new geezer in there with his tartan tie if you please and his tweed jacket and his la-di-dah voice he's a poof would you believe it, one of them flaming arse-bandits as Fred Weston will say when the women are out of earshot, shaking his close-cropped head, honest to Christ would you credit that? With the Queen and the Duke on the wall and half of them ex-servicemen and now that kind insinuating himself into a club where there'd never been a pervert of any kind. Out on his jaxie that's where that bugger belonged. For a whole afternoon attention would waver from the TV set in the lounge, and the air shimmer with the odours of the hunt. But that will come later. As the chaplain now keeps up his carefully off-hand remarks and the woman who carries over the sponge wonders if she has actually seen one of them before, one of those queers close up as this, Joyce crosses to her friend. She puts her hand on his arm. Come on, she says to him. He sets down his cup and follows her to the door and across the TV lounge and through the tiled entrance to the shallow fall of steps, out to the main road and again towards the park where already they have sat, the open spaces that are always there as Joyce is telling him, talking to him quietly but without pause, the pure sky is there that you can fill with looking, where time is a great tree shaking through never mind what season, it is now and it's part of ever, it has to be. He is not sure what the woman means but he says to her yes, as they pause to cross the street, yes again when she says, You must know how good it is, don't you, being brave enough to say it? Her black coat bobbing beside her companion's tweed. And when she is not talking to him she is humming one of those songs, one of those tinselly things that Andy liked to think were the last word.

The Last of Freddie

When he went at sixty-four his friends could hardly believe it. Indestructible old Freddie! They all knew his paintings had not been up to so much these last few years, but as for dying—if Freddie came at that, then who couldn't? Although that was said discreetly. Critics liked to say—now he wasn't there—what a gap he was going to leave. On *Kaleidoscope* Bonnard would be mentioned as his master and a constant influence, as a quick comparison of selected canvases confirmed. Bonnard of course through the eyes of the Moderns. But that same preference for intimate domestic scenes, the shortened perspectives, the delicate sense of colour. If the phrases came rather too easily, as Maddy suspected they did, this was not the time to point it out. Oh yes, she thought—he painted, he screwed around, he drank himself to death. Caesar's neat little triplet hardly matched that as an epitaph. But it was a limb lopped off, wasn't it, hearing his death announced that morning over the nine o'clock news? She had poured herself a stiffish drink and switched the radio off. And she thought at once, oh won't they be swarming now, the academic maggots. Not even waiting until the meat had time to go off.

When June phoned her a little after ten she said that to her friend, although she knew June's son was at work on a *catalogue raisonné.* A few weeks before she had said, 'You can't *raisonné* before someone's dead, for God's sake.' She had been amused. But now she was angry, and a little drunk. She thought of Freddie wearing a green paper hat and not a stitch else as he lumbered down on her after a party at the old place in Kelburn. Angus already was out to it in the lounge, a gold cardboard crown slipped over his forehead as he lay squashed into the piled cushions of the sofa. It was after Freddie's finest show. They wore silly hats because it was Angus's birthday as well. Earlier in the night they had blown whistles that unfurled long paper tongues. They had danced to a Glenn Miller record and Maddy livened up her husband's drink with something somebody had brought in a black stone bottle. All it did was tumble him like a tree trunk. Then the artist had raised his long pale arm and groped for the glass-bead cord, like a row of raindrops, beneath the yellow shade. 'Painting be stuffed,' he told her. He said it vehemently. Then he had collapsed on the bed beside her.

'So you've heard?' June asked her.

'I heard it on the news.'

'When you think how well he was looking.' Then after the slightest pause, 'Had you seen him lately?'

'Not for a while,' Maddy told her. (*Madeleine*, Freddie used to enunciate back in those days. Why the hell can't people call you that, why that ridiculous abbreviation?)

'Last time he was that frisky. You'd have thought any of us might have gone before he did.' June reminded her how Freddie of course visited every second Friday. Surely she couldn't have forgotten that? 'We always had such *rapport*.'

Maddy could see her friend, red-eyed and big-busted, sucking at grief like a child at an orange. She thought, you ridiculous old cow, Freddie was into anything. But she said the required things until June had to tell her, 'I can't talk about it now. Not this close. I'll have to go.'

'Take three or four disprin.'

'As if that'll help.'

'They worked when John went missing, didn't they?' Maddy thought, I'm a bitch saying that, aren't I? June had told her time and again how she hadn't shed a tear when the police came to her after the accident. It had taken weeks before it sank in. She had taken all those disprin and simply gone to sleep. But this morning she had drawn the curtains and cried until she knew her face would be puffed for days.

'You never know how death will strike you,' Maddy said. After they had talked, she sat by the window that looked out across the valley to the irregular line of hills, her comforting glass beside her. She stroked at the glossy cover of a book she had for review, as though it were a cat. Each of them had forgotten to say so on the phone, but the women took it for granted Lydia would drive down for the funeral. How could she not? The three of them together again, to put their man away.

They met in the porch of the crematorium chapel. A northerly blasted along the valley and across the gravestones, driving people into the porch. 'How he'd love those hills,' June was saying. She nodded to the darkened slopes, the cloud shredding along their tops. 'If he could see them he might,' Maddy said. Why, she thought, do people have to talk such damned rubbish? Then at the same instant she and June called out, 'Lydia!' There was a brief trio of embracing among the mourners.

'We'll talk afterwards,' Maddy said. 'We're late as it is.' She took the smaller woman's arm and directed her to where they should sit. June walked on her other side. 'Oh,' she was saying, even as they stepped into the pew. 'Our meeting up like this!' Lydia smiled without looking at either of them. Then they sat, two tallish women with a shorter between them, listening to what was being said about Freddie, who lay on a slightly raised platform, a few inches of stained pine coffin showing beneath the flag that draped him. Maddy thought of him lying in bed, watching her dress, with his feet extended outside the bedclothes. Once her clothes were back on he would say, 'A gin'd go quite nicely for afters. Know where everything is?' She heard the minister talk of his war service and his art. Then more importantly in the eyes of God, his generosity, his lack of malice. 'Balls,' she thought. In over thirty years, how often had she heard him say a good word about a painter younger than himself? Although he could be very open-minded with the dead. 'Weekes was brilliant,' he used to say. 'He was so very close to being good.'

Lydia heard June sobbing beside her into a handkerchief tugged from the top of her frock. It was one of the handkerchiefs Freddie had made in that period when he used to say, in his best proletarian voice, 'What are us buggers painting pictures for anyway? Why don't we make things people *use*?' This had meant at different times curtain fabrics, wooden toys, neck-pendants with local polished stone. And that spate of handkerchiefs—coarse linen made by a friend in Levin, then treated by Freddie with his own vegetable dyes. Lydia wished for a moment that she had brought hers, a sombre green that Freddie insisted was as natural a dye as it was possible to get. No one could mistake them for anyone else's work. Their size, their big hems that the artist himself had stitched on an old Singer treadle machine. Then she saw a woman at the end of the row in front of them—a woman in a fur coat and with heart trouble it must be, the way she panted, breathing through her mouth. Or asthma. She was dabbing at her throat with the same kind of coloured square, only dun brown. Freddie had given Lydia a tablecloth he must have dyed at the same time. It had been on the table the last time he visited her. He had taken it between his fingers and said it wasn't lasting so badly, the colour had kept quite nicely too.

Must be twenty years, he said, since he made those things. Nineteen, she remembered. The year she went to Sydney.

'Get on with it,' she heard Maddy say beside her. Lydia felt confined between her friends. She looked straight ahead, at the pillar of sun that fell from the windows high in the wall. It picked out the line of powder on the sweating woman's throat, and made the ears of the man next to her quite transparent. The tiny veins and splotches seemed unpleasantly naked. What was that story about June and Freddie on the riverbank or something? A light shone on them by surprise? She had an image of their white limbs, of June's rotundities and Freddie's lankiness, caught in the flicker of a policeman's torch. The torchlight falling then and the sunlight now. June's wedding ring blinked where she crushed her handkerchief in her lap. Then Lydia noticed too that Maddy's fingers drummed on her crossed knees, a sign of irritation.

After the prayers and the eulogy a curtain was drawn across so theatrically that a bow would not have been out of the question. Then there was a hymn chosen by Freddie's wife. Everyone sang the words from a printed sheet, and the chapel swelled.

> *There is a blessed home beyond this land of woe*
> *Where trials never come, nor tears of sorrow flow.*
> *Where faith is lost in sight, and patient hope is crowned,*
> *And everlasting light its glory throws around.*

'He'd be bored shitless!' Maddy said at the end of the verse. June looked over sharply, her eyes interestingly pink, as Freddie might have thought, against the dark linen held at her cheek. Lydia continued to gaze ahead, at the stirring in the front pews as the family prepared to leave. That odd little smile of hers, June thought. I wonder if she quite knows what is going on? God knows none of them were any younger. It was senility with some, that was simply the way things were, just as it might be a weight problem unfortunately with others. Though the last time Freddie grabbed at her he had said for the umpteenth time, 'Can't stand these bloody women with no upholstery to them.' He had nuzzled into her as eagerly as at the University Extension weekend all those years ago. It had been a life-study class. Rather a pert little woman sat partly draped on a desk in front of them, her breasts as small and sharp as the last inch or two of ice-cream cones. That was exactly what she had thought of then, and it came back to her now. It was so silly, June smiled. And the way life goes on, she thought. She watched

Freddie's wife walk down the aisle, her arm linked with her son's. What a gift, a wife as innocent as that had been! You'd have thought, though, wouldn't you, that a relative or someone would have told her the little cap thing she'd been wearing for years wasn't quite the thing for a funeral? It made her look like a jockey. And years ago when her own husband took her to the races, June had noticed the little men used to carry their saddles in the birdcage rather as Jos now carried that big old leather handbag across her arm. She wished she had thought of that while Freddie was still alive. He had liked her flair for putting things.

'Outski,' Maddy broke in on her. She jerked her head in that rather masculine way of hers, as though it was simply the movies they were leaving, or the end of a concert. Then for the first time since coming into the chapel together, Lydia looked from one friend to the other. She smiled shyly at both of them. She was thinking how they had all lain and sighed with and been loved by Freddie, hadn't they? There were times when June at least had become unfriendly about it, having to share him around like that. Although Maddy always laughed when they met and his name came up. 'He's fun the old wretch, isn't he? If you want more than that of course you go to someone else.'

They moved slowly from the chapel, the man with the thin pale ears shuffling in front of them. Perhaps a stroke, each of them supposed. There was something wrong with everyone, if only you knew about it. In a few moments they would be in the porch, then out again into the pelt of the northerly, the dappled scudding of the afternoon. There would be a quick embrace with Jos and others in Freddie's family, and words with people Lydia had not seen for so long perhaps she would have forgotten their names, and she would feel awkward because of it. Then the laughter that always began soon after a funeral. She and Maddy and June would separate, come back together, observe at more leisure the encroaching signs of age that marked them. And a man in a vaguely imagined room at the back of the crematorium would turn a jet—she supposed it was something like that—and flames would leap up, a bright engulfing calix with Freddie at their centre. While they were talking, glancing out of windows. It struck her as very strange.

Lydia was a widow as her friends were, but the widow to nothing spectacular. June's husband had quite a name as a surgeon, then drowned a few years ago when he fell from a yacht off Banks Peninsula. Maddy's became a big wheel in theatre design. He had dramatically up and disappeared because of some homosexual flurry just after the War, and died before he was fifty. In other company Lydia perhaps would mention Cliff's Cambridge degree and the edition he had been working on for years when he died. Compared with the others, she supposed, Cliff didn't cut much ice. He now seemed so far away in any case.

'All of us widows!' June said rather gaily, just as Lydia was thinking that.

Young Richard came up to them and said, 'I'm glad you could make it. It's nice so many of his friends could be here.'

'As if we wouldn't have!' Maddy said. As if we'd miss out on seeing how the others were taking it.

Richard was the only son. He was tall like his father, with the same hank of hair falling across his brow. It had always made the self-portraits look lop-sided, that sheet of thick ochre slapped across the thinnish face. The young man smiled at the three elderly women, saying enough for each of them to think yes, what a charming boy he was. They could quite see Freddie coming through in him.

'That same profile,' June said. 'Can't both of you just see it?'

'At the same age!' Lydia said. She had been the first to know his father. 'You'd swear you were twins.'

'You knew him that long ago?'

'When we were students, would you believe that?' There was a vivid memory of swinging along with a group of friends, their arms about each other's waists, across a Gothic quadrangle forty years before. It was late in the evening, after a party. Between the cloisters and the ginkgo tree in the middle of the quad, Freddie had put his hand under her skirt.

'You saw him recently, did you?' Richard's question was to all of them. 'Saw Freddie?' June hesitated then said, 'Oh, not so long ago.'

'I hadn't seen him to talk to for a year or so,' Lydia had to admit. Then she asked herself aloud, 'Would it have been that long?' Richard had taken their wine glasses to refill, holding them between the fingers of one hand like a clump of transparent tulips. Maddy said, 'After our last *contretemps* it was probably better for everyone if we kept our distance. After that portrait.'

A couple of years ago Freddie had exhibited a nude, the female figure aging but attractive in a butch, chunky way. And anyone with half an eye could recognise Maddy. The figure was sitting cross-legged on a chair, in a splash of greenish light, starkers except for a pair of long suede boots. Silly old bugger, she had said when she saw it. He hasn't seen me like that for ten years! It still made her hot to think about it.

'Well, as if you didn't have reason to,' June said. She was thinking thank God the one he did of me was *The Pink Hat,* the one the National Gallery had snapped up. It was impossible to guess who that one was. The tilted plane of the hat was all that interested Freddie that day. He had come in the morning, painted, had lunch, painted, then even after John came in he turned down a gin to get it through in 'one bash', those were his very words for it. Until, 'That'll do,' he said. Then he sat down in front of the telly and went to sleep. It was romantic though, June considered. It was how artists should work. She could have paraded about that day in boots and suspenders and it wouldn't have mattered twopence to him. She had reminded him of it only a year or so ago. They were sitting in the garden, it was in the early weeks of spring. They had been there for an hour and he had not even suggested that they go inside. 'Fancy a bit of the old one two?' was what he usually said. It always amused him that June would have liked him to put it more delicately. 'Christ,' he used to shout at her sometimes. 'Your whole life's like those bloody pink doo-dah things you've got over the spare dunny roll in the jakes. All frills and puff and cover-up.' But this day he simply sat in the white cane chair under the lime tree and tapped first the sharpened end of a pencil on the table, then the flat end, over and over until June had said, 'I was just working it out, Freddie. It's exactly fifteen years since you did that picture of me in the hat. That was October too. There's that same light falling across you now.' Freddie had looked at her, surprised. 'You've got a good eye,' he complimented her. Then he told her something else. 'Fifteen bloody years since I've done a decent picture in that case.' But as though saying that was a door he had partly opened and at once regretted, slamming it before June had time to enter, he leaned forward and pressed the swell of her thigh beneath her new wrap-round skirt. 'Still there, is it?' he asked her. He threw his head back and bellowed when she slapped at his hand and looked across, quickly, to where a neighbour's window might have given someone a view of her entertaining.

With the same slight smile she had kept throughout the service, Lydia said now, 'I don't know how I'd feel if it was me. I mean a picture like that, Maddy.' Then she added, 'I suppose as long as people are only thinking of it as art.'

Maddy looked at her friend, at the neatly parted grey hair and the grey suit and the benign fey expression like an aging doll's. What the hell Freddie ever saw in *that* one. But here came Richard with their glasses again, there was no need to answer her.

'You *are* a darling,' June told him.

'There we are, ladies,' Richard said. Carefully he handed each of them a brimming glass. 'I know they're not supposed to be that full. But it cuts down on travel.' There was such a press of people around them that Lydia wondered how he had carried the glasses so well.

'You'll be all right?' he asked them.

'We won't go dry,' Maddy promised. She gave him one of her broad rare smiles, showing the perfect teeth that had made his father sometimes call her the Piranha. June watched her friend and the young man who now laughed with her about something that was lost in the hubbub of the wake. No wonder Freddie had that nickname for her. Here she was devouring Richard, drawing him off so that she and Lydia were simply left standing there. That'll make her day, June thought. Although not quite a victory like the old days, not like that writer's funeral in Auckland when a much younger Maddy had waltzed off with the dead man's brother onto the side of One Tree Hill. She had come back inside without even brushing the twigs or whatever from the back of her dress.

'Oops!' Lydia broke in on them. Someone had jolted against her arm, so that half her wine leaped from its glass. Richard was with her at once, mopping at her skirt, telling her he didn't think it would stain, in fact he was quite sure it wouldn't. Red might but not white. Then the man from behind the bar was there as well, handing her a dampened cloth. June raised her eyebrows as she caught Maddy's glance. But Lydia was turning from one friend to the other, asking 'Why me?', her face crinkled comically, her little-girl voice that hadn't done so badly for her over the years either, Maddy thought.

They had not met so often over these last five or six years, but Freddie always used to tell her, 'By God you're the one who matters, Lydia.'

'Oh yes,' she would smile.

'You are,' he insisted to her.

'And the others?'

'The others?' He would raise his arm from where it lay above the bedclothes and snap his fingers. He always did that about 'the others'. It made her think of a bank teller, contemptuous of the notes he was counting out.

'You believe me?'

'Yes and no,' she used to say. She said it about liking pictures or people that they knew or in this case what she meant to Freddie. And he so easily became angry when she answered him like that. 'There's not a mind inside there,' he would tell her, pointing at her head. 'There's a bloody see-saw.' He told her she was like the whore he had heard about during the War, who had 'Mild' tattooed on one breast and 'Bitter' on the other. 'You try to please everybody, that's your trouble.' He was so jealous. Then she would put on a face like the one when the wine spilled and Richard sweetly made such a thing about attending to her. 'I please you, don't I?' she used to ask. She would draw herself across him and Freddie always spread his hand across the back of her neck, gripping her as one might hold down the head of a kitten so it couldn't move. 'I love that,' she would tell him.

June broke in on her with the coffee she placed on the table next to her.

'I was just admiring this,' Lydia said. She tapped the marble table beneath her cup.

'Florence,' June said. 'John should have been an auctioneer, the stuff he picked up.'

Maddy took her coffee and said, 'I hope this isn't the strongest drink you're giving us June?'

'Scotch then? Glenfiddich?'

'That'd do nicely,' Lydia said. Then they sat without switching on the lights, the three women facing the broad window that commanded half the harbour.

'Even on a dull day like this,' June told them, 'it's worth watching.' The northerly still pushed the clouds in ragged packs along the hills behind Eastbourne. The harbour itself might have been made of pewter.

'It depresses me,' Maddy said.

'What does?' June asked. She was kneeling at the gas heater, adjusting the bright whispering flues.

'This view. This weather.'

'Freddie used to say that if we could remember things exactly, things like colour tones and the movement of shadows and the rest of it, there wouldn't be more than half-a-dozen days in a life-time probably that were exactly the same.'

So the talk came back to the man who had died. They spoke of him warmly, without envy of each other, as the evening darkened outside. Maddy at least was thinking, he is never going to exist so fully as this again. Next time we meet we may talk of him, but not with this ease, this intensity. Our talking is letting him go slowly, slowly. The last time a man is spoken of is when he finally dies. Then she clucked her tongue sharply. It annoyed her that the vague pool of dimming silver in the mirror behind June's head, and that luminous lift that comes to the harbour when the sky itself is all but completely dark, were making her sentimental. How much she disliked June's own love for 'atmosphere' she thought. Her friend's finicky arrangement of camellias and looped Italian candlesticks and such. Those frothy blouses and pastel shades that June wore because they were the 'kindest' to her years. The moment you give way to sentiment, Maddy had always instructed herself, you blur the present as much as the past. You lose the lot. For a moment she held the hot swill of malt in her mouth. Then she asked, 'Can't we have the light on?'

'Is this making you jumpy?' June said. She liked the way the panel in the gas heater glowed there in the darkened room, while outside the night came down. 'There we are,' she said. She had touched a switch beside her. Two carefully angled lights were thrown across the paintings on the large expanse of wall. Only one of them was Freddie's, a gutsy still life of simple brilliant forms. What treasure that is, Maddy thought, after sitting in the gloom. Coming back from Hades. She thought of those favourite lines of hers, the great hero unrecognised in the swirl of fog, the twittering voices as remote as birds.

'The way he gets that orange,' Lydia said. 'Doesn't he?'

'The whole thing's *alive*. That's what matters about it.'

'Drinks again all round?' June offered them. She went to the kitchen for ice. Lydia knew she should refuse if she was sensible. She looked up at the painting and saw the fruit was already slipping when she tried to focus. The orange kept losing its roundness, smearing towards the bottom of the frame. She took a handful of nuts from the dish Maddy held towards her.

Lydia thought what a pity the light went on when it did. She had liked the sense that they were suspended somehow, as though in a transparent bell with the outside world pressing against its curves, a place where their voices came to each other clearly yet mysteriously, where surfaces ran with shadows and the last silvery core of light. There was no way she was able to put it, really. And she had almost made the mistake of confiding in them. It was good that hadn't happened. To have almost said, 'When I woke on Friday morning before it was light I knew he was there with me.' *Who?* she could hear them say. Who are you talking about, Lydia? *Freddie*, she would have had to say. They would not say much back, how could they? 'I opened my eyes, I often wake just before light, but the moment I woke I felt his weight.' Because it couldn't be anyone else. And they might ask her then, 'You'd already heard he was dead?' And she would answer them, 'How could I have heard? He wasn't even dead then. He was dying.'

'You're a quiet lot in here,' June said. She carried through a tray with sandwiches as well as the bowl of ice with claw-shaped tongs lying across it. She placed the tray on a table at the end of the room. Then before she attended to their glasses or handed each a plate, she briskly drew the curtains. She snapped on other lights, the room lifted into a glare of colour, of vases, bookshelves, more pictures on other walls, a brilliant clump of proteas.

'My God!' Maddy said, when she saw the flowers. She stretched out her hand to touch the stiff waxy blooms. With the press of dark leaves that backed them, they made her think of a burst of skyrockets, frozen and held against the night.

'They are lovely aren't they?' June said.

Yes, Lydia was thinking, what a lucky stroke that she hadn't tried to tell them that.

Then June went on, 'He never painted flowers. That's odd, isn't it?'

'It's because he couldn't draw them,' Maddy said.

'Couldn't draw them?' June looked down at her friend. 'But he drew beautifully.'

'He said he couldn't ever do flowers the way he wanted to. They don't have dimension the way fruit does.'

They certainly wouldn't have believed her. June would have become puzzled and flustered, her hand running along the chain of her gold Victorian locket. *There was this weight, how could she explain that?* And Maddy might have said, but isn't it only a coincidence anyway? That she had this feeling and thought of Freddie which was natural enough for *her*, she had hardly played the field? Then later that morning she had heard. It was curious, but not so much more than that.

June was adjusting the wall-lamp, directing it more clearly across the painting of the fruit. 'Haven't I seen that jug?' Maddy asked. 'I'm sure I remember it.'

'That one?' June looked more closely at the canvas, at the few brush strokes that gave the shape of the jug, a dab of whitish-blue along its rim that made you think all the light in the picture was gathered just there.

'It's the one he kept his brushes in,' Lydia said. 'Isn't that the one?'

'As if it matters now.' Maddy spoke quietly, her impatience tailed off. But Lydia was looking at her own hands, thinking again that it was not a thing to tell to others. How her bedroom had been completely dark when she had closed her eyes. Then after—how long, five minutes, ten?—the weight was withdrawn and when she looked again the morning already had come with that feeling of such stillness, and yet such energy too. The furniture and the mirror and her clothes across the chairback near the window, the frames on the photographs even and that oddly sad painting he had done when they spent an entire week in Akaroa, her red dog in grass as stiff as spears—how they had all been steeped in life, immersed in it. Full of that exuberance she had lain there and thought of him. *Dear Freddie.*

'Come on!' June was ordering her. Her friend stood in front of her, holding the fresh glass and with her other hand offering a plate of sandwiches. Maddy was standing too, one knee supported on the arm of a leather chair. She rooted about in her handbag, saying she was after a photograph she had brought to show them, the three of them in summer clothes outside the Takahe, three young women Christ knows how long ago.

'Dreaming, eh?' June had always teased her about that. Lydia smiled up, the 'drifting' smile as Freddie used to tell her, that bloody batty look as he had joked about it to Maddy and to June, there was a screw loose somewhere, there had to be.

She took the glass and an anchovy sandwich. 'Yes and no,' she said.

Good Heads

I hold as I've done for years the mirror this way and that behind him and then to each side, revealing his neck and profile and three-quarter face in a tilted silvery flow. I lean close towards him as I flick the talc brush above his collar. I say, That's a month now then, Sir? Since the *contretemps?* Sir says, Seems more like a century I can tell you that, George. I see Greta raise her scissors behind her own head and snip snip the air with them like snapping castanets. Because she of course knows the other side only too well, Madame telling her a different story and at more frequent intervals. I ask quietly, You don't see any end in sight for it, then? The disharmony? In what Peter calls my seduce-them-slowly voice so that I've said to him more than once, At least Peter I do *have* a manner. Which is more than many I can think of in what used to be a profession. He puts both hands behind his head and flicks his loins and I refuse to bat an eyelid. But that's another story again.

Sir and Madame have been among our clientele for oh, so long. I always do Sir of course and Greta occasionally Madame, and such are life's ironies neither actually knows that the other comes in to *Mister George's*. Has she got herself another lover? Greta asks. Has Sir another friend? Ah ah! As if speaking of the dead I remind her. Style and discretion is all we have to offer. It's not even having your hair fashioned any more like is it? Peter says when he hears us discussing them at morning tea. More like going to confession. Then wouldn't you expect, the boy intrudes, that true professionals would simply keep confidences to themselves but? So that Greta takes up his words and says to him, Listen lolly darling I don't mind a mick and I don't mind a poofter either but a mick poofter is more than I can actually stomach. Makes me want to throw up. To heave my ring, in a word. I'd take the chance while I have it then darling, Peter comes back at her, the closest you'll ever get to the real thing. He flaps the medal he wears on a gold chain against his brown winter skin. Solarium lamps in the Wakefield sauna is it? Greta has said to him before. Isn't that male luck all over? A nice grope in the rec room and you get a tan on the side. His buttocks tight little bundles as he flounces off after *that*. Knead them like scones couldn't you? I said to Greta and she said back loud enough for him to hear, Couldn't you just, Mister George?

But Sir. Sir is all of sixty and Madame is, shall we say, forty-eight? Greta my assistant is almost thirty. Peter the so-called trainee who carries a hand-towel over his shoulder because it makes him as he thinks dear boy not unlike Florentine David only clothed is all of twenty-two. Such details of age you might say, what is that? *Everything*, I will tell you. My own small horror for example when I see by accident—catch in mid-flight you might say—striations on my flesh as I step from the bath, the slightest withering of my haunches, that shiny fragment of scalp I comb over expertly. You're as vain as a peacock Giorgio, Madame has told me. And in the banter she loves I tell her no dear lady, vanity is merely excitement at one's own presence. Mine is something else again. A metaphysical leap from the fangs of time. Which delights but pisses her off no end. She is not sure a hairdresser has a right to the larger emotions. And I bend close to her ear, dab at a twist of frankly exhausted hair, Madame lying back with the sprig-patterned cloth tucked over her slightly flaccid breasts, a little of that terror reflected in her own grey gorgeous eyes. I lean above her and say to her (meaning her eyes), My shield of Perseus, my deflected fear. (To have had a schoolteacher for a father is as good as being educated oneself.) But Madame poor ignorant slut is not noticeably impressed. As I so often think, for all the family jewels and the rest of it she is untamperably thick. As indeed is Sir, spiritually. For his years of course he is in perfect physical nick. All that squash that jogging those manly slaps against decrepitude. I've seen him myself when he enters the steam-room, his arms raised to run his fingers through his hair, knowing how his chest rises as he does so, that lithe line of his body down to his compact thighs. Oh Sir, indeed. And so he had told me again as I dabbed his high cheekbone and deftly razored the hairline level with the juncture of his ear, That's a month George since she has actually spoken to me, do you find that hard to believe? One's wife? Well yes Sir I do, I find it very hard indeed. The eau-de-cologne pooled in the palm of one hand, with two fingers from the other I applied it to the tender flesh that perhaps only a hairdresser knows so well, the pure touching nakedness where the razor has just skimmed. I thought I had spoken quietly but I saw Greta in the mirror as I turned, hanging on every word. The metal blades again opening and snapping shinily above her head, above her plainish face.

Retroussé, I once described Greta to herself. She said back to me, Like I've had my nose jammed against someone's jaxie for the past ten years? And Peter called across from behind the screen where he is supposed to be making up one of the mutes for the Deaf Institute play, a charity on our part every twelve months, Wouldn't be so lucky would you darling? Snipping his own scissors. But quite a different timbre to Greta's doing that. A quick metallic excitement, a congratulatory laugh transferred to the tools of his trade.

But Peter. Peter another day in front of Madame mind you. Prancing in with one wrist at waist level as though looking for something in my cubicle, and then his attention caught by the folded morning paper, my biro beside the scarcely marked crossword. My he said not so clever this morning, are we? So I said to him, Just check one down three across for me will you there's a good boy. My voice steady as a spirit-level. And he read out, 'As well as common flower sometimes one of those.' Reading it slowly—what else?—and oh the most natural blankness over his tanned face. Even Madame getting it. She shrieked. I said to her softly, Not now Madame please they'll think you're in the throes. But loud enough for Greta to pick up and so her own little cry of amusement. And Peter with the paper in his hand suddenly getting the word! Positively scarlet behind the ears.

Why do you do it? he taxes me later. His boyish pretence at being hurt. The *salon* is quite empty, my fingers massaging his smooth firm pectorals, easing the tension in his shoulders. Do you do it just to hurt me?

Peter! I have to say. Then, Just turn like that again, I ask him. The gold stud in his ear catches the light and winks brilliantly. The planes of his jaw and cheekbone, the facial muscles playing into and out of shadow as he chews his gum—that delicate brevity which indeed all flesh is, and the hard bright pip of metal—oh yes yes! Greta, I call, come and look at something lovely! That makes them both so cross. A week later I enrage them even more by calling our new cat Dorothy. After both of you my dears, I tell them. Oh the sexual innuendo! In her cubicle Greta has Dustin Hoffman life-size and full-length in his sequined spectacles and slinky dress. I have told her, Don't let Peter see that dear heart he'll eat your poster for lunch instead of his custard squares. And so much better for his acne. After that of course they will join forces against me for a day. *Mes pauvres enfants* as I tell them, all I know I pass on to you!

Two days—their alliance lasts two days. But then I book in our snatches as we call the lovelier clients with Greta, and Peter silly boy positively stamps against her. A greying actor AC/DC if ever the theatre threw one up and a creature from the Post Office with the most exquisite string shirt, Polynesian *macho* with the faintest smidgin of eyeshadow. It's *play* I remind them, is not all life play? But for an afternoon Greta and Peter speak neither to each other nor to me.

The first and longest snatches of course are Sir and Madame. They are in a sense my professional touchstones. To maintain clientele of that class! To be *confidant* to both. And each for years it must be now not knowing how the other confides! No wonder young Peter there thinks of that word *confessional*. I have had them in the same chair within twenty minutes, the same talc falling gently onto both, the same soap in delicious lather. Fail to see the *frisson* of that and frankly what is there anywhere to see? There is a French book I have heard about in which a man plays mental symphonies by combining different perfumes, running together different colours. At times with Sir or Madame in the chair, the rich tang of tamarind shampoo (they choose it independently!), their reflections in the smoked glass screens—I say to myself, George, is there more that one can reasonably expect? I feel brother to that Frenchman.

But the screens, now that we come to it, to the pivot shall we say of the story? How often have I said to my assistants, there are salons and salons, my dears, just as there are lovers and lovers. I mean you can begin at one end of Cuba Street and by the time you get to us—well a person would know what *decor* wasn't, even if he/she had no idea what it was. Quite frankly you'd have seen the lot. Those zebra skins on the walls at *Zirca's* for example, need I say more? An establishment for tarts if ever I saw one. Tip them all in, I say as I see the heads that come out of there. Up end them all in the one tub of dye. As much individuality in that place as there is in drenching sheep. Walk down the street and look what you come to there. Bamboo screens and Eastern music and Shiseido I wouldn't be surprised footing the bill for the whole parcel of tat!

What about *Manila*? Greta has the gall to ask. *Manila*! I scold her. Brothels I presume look much the same the world over? And when Peter the young Turk puts in his *Ramon's*, now *Ramon's* is class, I really do get quite cross. Oh, Swedish furniture then is it? Sterility at twice the price I'd ask to *give* away work like theirs. Of course Peter if your thing happens to be operating theatres then it must seem like paradise. Personally I'd get more pleasure from visiting my dentist. And I try to tell them how there is *no one* who does not show to advantage against smoked glass, be it male or female of any age. And to provoke them both I say if all those eager little fags hadn't so overworked 'ravishing' after their *Brideshead* splash I'd be tempted to use it now, for the way anyone looked with the decor at *Mister George's*. (The name etched darkly against the bluish-tan glass.) Of course, I say, if it's a failed monk with the hots for a teddy bear you're after . . . And Greta looks at me wearily and says, Do you think one of these days you might keep up to date? Or even try to?

And then it comes, like a bomb thrown through that plate glass. I see Greta glance at Peter and he nods at her and I know without a doubt, oh not a shadow of it, they're in cahoots about something. If this is the nips for a raise we'll see about that. And Peter the pup for the first time ever drops the Mister and says to me outright, *George*. So we're high and mighty with our suntan are we, I think? With our little gold chains and the rest of it? And I see Greta's head is lowered over her nails so her eye won't catch mine, crafty little slut. Well? I challenge them. Permission to leave the classroom is it? Yes Peter says, we're starting out on our own.

Well! The shelf of shampoo bottles is suddenly so vivid as I look at it. There is silence among the dark chairs and the chromium plating and a distant siren from the other end of the city. Until I laugh at them and say, Don't fart anybody the youngsters are in church. Peter raises his eyebrow at Greta, his what-are-we-to-do-with-him look. While *she* comes in then if you please, We're sick to death of this place George, she says. And then, *Sorry*. Of course once the ice is broken Peter is away. I must admit mustn't I—that's how he puts it to me—admit surely if I gave it a moment's thought etcetera. That the place was indeed, you had only to look around you, there was nothing personal in the observation and, I really mustn't mind, but surely a touch *passé?* Even *déjà vu?* (*My* words, notice that?) Fucking clapped out do you mean? I demanded of both of them. In a word but, Peter sighed. Greta snipping her scissors nervously so that I said, At least you'd be good enough dear girl not to wear out my property before you actually leave? And she puts them down so quietly on the marble ledge near the washbasin. The merest chink.

I look at them both and give them the benefit of my years. I tell them, You don't set up places like this for nothing you know. You don't get *quality* at the drop of a hat. Indeed not, Greta agrees. She snickers across at him. Then oh I begin to see it. I begin to pick up the stench of grubby little intrigue. But I keep my voice calm. I say, There is also more to business partners than hopping into bed. At which Greta snorts at what I am implying and tells me, Now come off it, Mister George. I say back to her, Not left the rebellion already have we? Not scuttling back this soon? But Peter says, Money's not the problem George. Money is no worry at all. He must catch my look of surprise. Inherited the family estates have we? I ask. I think of the humble little houses of Newtown, Berhampore, wherever it is he tucks away. So when Greta says to me, Don't be such a bitch eh, I ask rhetorically, Where then? I ease back the brown slats and look from the window. Raining shekels for God's people is it? Or have we benefactors? Have we secret admirers?

If you must know, Peter begins. While Greta signals Hush! from where she leans now, arms folded, backside against my ochre marble. And as if they have practised it Peter tells me, If you do have to know then, and the slag says at the same breath, the identical instant, *Sir*, as Peter tells me, *Madame*.

Greta goes and sits in my clientele chair. Of course they are both crestfallen now their little climax is over. Rather sentimentally I touch Greta's shoulder. Sir? I enquire of her. She answers, Oh, Madame as well. *Both* of them. Well there's two of us remember, Peter puts in. He turns and goes behind his screen, a delicate youthful shape against the smoky glass. And then blasé as you like, It's purely business. If *that's* what you're thinking.

My scissors are in my hand. They have been there all the time. I begin to snip at the ends of Greta's fine brown hair, at first more or less absently, then with skill and precision. Never forget, I tell her. Forget what George? she asks me. The little minx is close to tears! That whoever the customer is, I say, the head's the thing. We're like executioners in that. She tries to smile at my joke. And I begin to hum a tune, as I often do while I work, bend my legs a little to take a side viewing of my line, and pat her hair, oh so gently. There, I say, there. Which always works with Madame. And I tell her, *Whatever* happens, Greta. Yes George? So I say, We mightn't be quite the oldest profession we cosmeticians, we *friseurs*. I'm not claiming that. But the second oldest, I'll put any money you like on that. I tell her, You never know when you'll need this one to fall back on, dear heart.

Survivals

It was November. In the afternoons the paddocks shimmered under the early summer heat and it always seemed at one-thirty, so he thought, at two o'clock, as if his watch must be at least an hour slow. He used to think, 'I can quite imagine dying on an afternoon like this. It's the time when it seems that death could slip in with less flurry about it than at any other time.' The roofing and the walls of the house snapped in their expansions beneath the sun, small clear explosions inside a well of stillness. The poplars across the paddock were bars drawn stiffly against the sky. In front of them lay a narrow stretch of water, a swamp which in certain lights could look as beautiful as a lake. Beyond the trees there were further paddocks stretching flatly out, a few far houses, an occasional car distant and small as a toy, raising a smudge of dust on the unsealed crossroad. The poultry gathered in the shade beside the barn, the rooster with its fall of bronze feathers occasionally scraping out its mechanical cry.

In mid-afternoon, as the woman's motor-scooter passed Dutchman's Orchard half-a-mile down the road, he would pick up its sound and then lose it again where the highway passed beneath a stretch of pines. When the bike emerged from the other end of the windbreak its engine beat more strongly. Another quarter of a mile and it would turn into his drive. Then she would burst from under the boughs of the apple trees at the corner, her foot already stretched out to take her weight when she cut the motor. Everything about her was as decisive as that. On a fine day she rebuckled her safety helmet when she had taken it off, shoved her gloves into its dark crown, then slipped it across the higher of the handlebars. When the weather was bad she carried it to just inside the door and put it on the varnished boards near the Turkish rug. It rocked there for a moment like the half of some huge egg.

Sometimes when Richard picked up the even throb of the approaching bike he pushed the papers in front of him to the centre of the table and piled his books together. When he walked back up the stairs with Monica she would ask him, 'How's it going?' Each time he would give her the same answer, 'It's coming on.' She knew after several weeks this wasn't true, but that in any case it hardly mattered. It was only someone else's story, it had nothing to do with them. They would stand in front of the wall-length windows and look right across, past the pines and the Dutchman's neatly ordered acres and the distant line of English trees. Beyond all that, to the greyish smear of the town. And again Richard had the feeling of looking across at miniatures, a profusion of models set out on a board. That feeling was even stronger from the bedroom that was reached by a ladder at the side of his desk. Only in the bedroom there was no large span of glass but a circular window surrounded with black painted metal. Monica said looking from that, at the top here of this crazy house, always made her think of looking from the window of a space-ship. She said, 'The swamp could be a great sea from up here.' From the bed there was nothing of course but the sky to look out at.

Monica had been in the last intake for the Children of Mary before a new post-conciliar priest, replacing the Irishmen who had run the parish for years, came and put an end as he said to all that old hat stuff. 'Or should I say old biretta?' He talked of trimming the Church back to its Christ-lean essentials, phrases that embarrassed most of his parishioners who didn't care a rap what tremors were coming through from the European theologians. But they missed the comforting details that to them were inseparable from the one apostolic church. So Monica had worn the silver medal on its broad blue ribbon no more than half-a-dozen times, standing in front of the Fatima statue and reading in unison the vows of the sodality. In the next few years, habits her parents' generation had been used to since their childhood were bundled away in the spiritual spring-cleaning. First there were no purple cloths across the statues during Holy Week. Then The Holy Name Society relinquished the gold-rimmed shields on their long poles that used to be set at the end of each row of dark-suited men, the insignia stacked under the convent hall with the backdrops of the nativity plays. The screen was removed in the confessional so that instead of getting the pepperminty breath of the old priest through the mesh that reminded Monica of the outside safe at the bach, there was the face in full daylight of the new priest chatting away to you. Her father said why didn't the fellow give up the whole shooting-box and call himself an agnostic, at least you could admire him then for being honest. 'You have to keep up with the times,' her mother said. Her father told her irritably, 'He'd rather talk about milk-biscuits in Africa than the Holy Ghost.' 'Spirit,' her mother said. 'These days you call him the Holy Spirit.'

Monica was not what the family would call religious, and so the swing of the tide did not matter to her a great deal. But on the Sunday after the Epiphany, in midsummer in fact when the pohutukawas were in full bloom along the low clay cliffs above Shelly Beach, she turned at the sign of peace to see a tall man leaning towards her from the seat behind. She noticed a trace of gold along the edge of his front tooth. He held her hand for the brief time it took to say, 'Peace be with you.' She repeated the phrase back to him.

The man's name was Tom Winton. He came from what everyone called 'a good background', which in his case meant his family's holding a block of land somewhere in Hawke's Bay in a line of descent that led back to the original purchase from the Maoris. A deal made, so his mother used to say, on a July day between a wall-eyed chief and the however many grandfathers back it was who had some vague but profitable relation with the first Minister of Maori Lands. But the memory of the local chief with the bad eye had stayed with the family for a hundred years.

After Mass, when Monica was introduced by her friend Margaret Stein, she thought two things. It struck her first that the tall man she spoke to was both attractive and oddly reserved. And she knew from the minute he looked down at her that he liked her in a way that had more to it than just wanting to reach his hand under her dress, although it certainly would include that as well.

A year later they were married by the new priest who had gone a bit over the odds, both families felt, by telling them in his homily to make the most of physical love. At the reception Monica's family had felt they were under scrutiny. But Tom's people to their credit could not have made it clearer that although they may have issued in a broad prosperous stream from the day the chief held the deed of sale against his good eye and then carefully placed his name in broad missionary script, there was no landed gentry nonsense about *them*. One of Tom's uncles, a bachelor with a striped regimental tie, said, 'You won't find any of that Canterbury shit in our outfit.'

Her father said afterwards that their all being Catholics together was obviously the thing that saved embarrassment about one side having so much, and the other so little. 'Which wasn't quite accurate,' Monica explained. 'Our side had nothing at all.'

They had been married for only a month when her mother was in a car accident and Monica returned to Auckland for the next six weeks. When she came back Tom went with the first New Zealand farming team invited to China, which took another month and a half. Then it was straight back into lambing, and the farm next door came on the market and his family decided it should be bought. And at the start of the summer holidays, her mother had a 'relapse', as her father called it on the phone. In fact it was a heart attack that may or may not have had something to do with her car ploughing along the culvert outside Tuakau several months before. She died the week before Christmas. Monica stayed on with her younger sisters until it was time for school to begin again. Much later she thought what a good well-trained girl she had been, believing you didn't let go of your family—or them of you—just because you married a man to begin a new life three hundred miles away. When she looked back to that year she felt contempt for what she had been, for the sloppiness of her feelings as she drove back and forth across the Taupo Road and through the bland Waikato farmland. She had tried so hard to fit everyone's conception of what she ought to do. But had she told Tom how since adolescence she was bored and irritated by everything her mother thought and said, he would have been as hurt as though she were getting at him. She had told Richard though, who said very little, and stirred his coffee, and touched her hand as she spoke.

They sat in a coffee shop above an area selling unpainted pine furniture and cane chairs from Singapore. There were piles of bright cushions and a rack of Indian scarves that a couple of teenage girls turned round and round. One of the girls drew the scarves out across her pale forearm or slipped them through the ring she made from her forefinger and thumb. They laughed and fooled about and when they walked out onto the footpath Monica said, 'She nicked one of those scarves, did you notice that?'

'Yes, I saw that,' Richard said. 'Was she one of yours? The thief?'

'Come off it! They'd have spotted me and scarpered, my lot.' She grimaced at the thought of the school where she taught, the enclave of privileged mums and dads tucked into the hills behind the town. Then she laughed, resting her hand against her friend's. 'Nothing like seeing a thief to test your social responsibility though, is there? Both of us watching it and not doing a thing.'

Richard said, 'I've been involved in two political acts in my lifetime. One was being patted on the head by Peter Fraser at the Empire Games when I was a kid. The other was in Athens.' He told her about a café near the hospital in Kolonaki. He used to sit there and drink cup after cup of sweet grainy coffee and watch the fashionable women raise their dark glasses onto their hair when they stopped to look at the displays of confectionery in the window. From the same table, by turning his head but not needing so much as to alter the angle of his chair, he could look to the side entrance of the enormous yellow hospital, and occasionally see the poor lugging their unvarnished coffins to the back of waiting trucks. But the point anyway, he said, was that he sat there one day and saw the jokey little proprietor give a smart young bastard the change for a hundred drachmas when it should have been a thousand. 'The young man slapped the keys of his Lamborghini on the counter and shouted abuse. Then he turned to me because my table was only a few feet away, I could be his witness. No, I said. I used one of the few phrases that I knew. *Then zero tipote.* I know nothing. I have no idea. I'd turned into a sly little peasant in a matter of seconds.'

'Were you playing at Robin Hood?' Monica asked.

'A lie for the workers against the bourgeoisie. Then the man I told it for was the first bloke in the city to stick up a photo of the Colonels after the revolution.'

'The right thing for the wrong reasons. We all do that.'

'It tells you about my nose for social realities.' And he thought then of one of the last times he had been in the café. He had just walked up past the tanks outside the Royal Palace, past the flower stalls which had been boarded up for the first few days in deference to military power, then returned to normal, to the banks of geraniums and potted oleanders and the huge wreaths an armspan across. He passed the closed doors of the Byzantine museum before he took a turn into a narrow modern street shaded like a canyon, with fingers of trailing vines from the iron balconies. He had let himself into their basement flat. The steps down to the door were made from marble that the landlady told him came from the same quarries as the Parthenon. 'That's no big deal,' Jane had said, 'the whole country's one great fucking quarry.' He opened the door and saw that the Samos rug had gone from the back of the settee and the transistor from the table. Both of them were hers so he knew before he walked into the dark bedroom that Jane had gone, that the muslin dresses would not be hanging there and the poster of some saint who was dressed in heavy vestments but had the head of a dog would be removed from the wall. 'Don't tell me that isn't Anubis in some new gear,' she had said the day she pinned it up. 'Just don't tell me that.'

Monica asked him now, 'Watching the time are you?'

'He's never on time. He's always apologetic and red in the face when he gets to surgery. Rushing in from golf.'

'More then?' She rapped the pot with her knuckle.

'Not for me.'

She stirred in half a spoon of sugar and said, 'I've a chart at home that says I need to walk ten minutes to burn off that many calories.' Richard's hands lay on the table in front of him, the fingers laced together.

'Now you look like you're praying,' Monica said.

'I was brought up to believe that if you had the right disposition and were in a state of grace, everything you did was a prayer. *Laborare est orare.* That was my school motto.' He played with the strap of his watch that rode loosely round his wrist. 'I'll have to make another hole in this thing.' Then he said, 'I've read girls are having bangles welded on that are too small ever to slide over their fists. You have to wear them for the rest of your life.'

Monica said, 'Archaeologists of the future will think it a significant religious shift.'

'A change from bracelets of bright hair,' Richard said.

'Oh,' Monica laughed. 'That. I used to think that was the loveliest poem I'd ever come across.'

'If only you knew what pits of gloom you dig for your young ladies every time you teach them that.'

'Nothing the latest heavy metal recording won't atone for. Or a quick grope at the weekend.'

'You're not getting cynical?'

'Donne doesn't mean a thing if you're actually screwing your boyfriend.'

'Culture is anticipation, you mean?' Richard said.

Monica took her cigarettes from her handbag. Richard moved his chair to allow a couple from the next table to ease past. He pushed the ashtray from the corner of the table to the centre, and looked down into the well of the shop. There was now an elderly lady touching the scarves where the girls had thieved, and a tall man stretched out his hand and let it run along the scrollwork of a cane chair. Monica lit her cigarette then snapped the dead match into smaller and smaller pieces. The last section she split with her thumbnail.

Richard asked her, 'Is it a free period this afternoon?'

'My mob are doing a UE paper for practice. The HOD'll keep an eye on them.'

Richard laughed, which pleased her. 'You sound very military when you say that. Like HQ and DMZ.'

'What's that last one?'

'Just journo talk.' He was playing again with his watch strap. The looseness seemed to bother him. He said, 'Of course I could get one of those expanding ones, you know? Like a garter so it still fits even as you get skinnier.'

'You're not losing weight though,' she said. 'You're holding your own.'

'Just,' he answered. He went to move back his chair as Monica smothered the cigarette that was not yet half smoked. She asked him, 'Wait a minute, do you mind? It's no great hassle if he does see us but I'd rather he didn't.'

'Who?'

'That man looking at the chair. He's my husband.' They waited until the man had left.

'It's an odd time for a farmer to go shopping,' Richard said.

'Sale day if you remember.' She saw the Stock and Station Agents calendar held at the side of the fridge with magnetic clips, the red and blue and green circles ringing various days of the month. There was another circle Tom had drawn in yellow crayon. It marked her birthday, between the last sale day of the month and the date for car registration.

She was speaking about him to Richard for the first time. She said lightly, 'There's the enemy for you surely, if you're still hitting the bourgeoisie.'

'That's a basic contradiction. People on the land can't be middle class.'

'That's only Europe you're talking about.'

'What are we here, then? If it's something different we haven't worked out what it is.'

'If only you knew his ideals,' Monica said. She spoke kindly, and with exasperation.

'Tom's ideals?'

'Would you believe that? Bred with all the care of a Charolais you might say and then this desperate desire to get in among the Jerseys. I mean, a socialist from that crowd!'

'You know what Chou En Lai's background was?'

'I'm not mocking him,' Monica said. 'He's actually a very good man.'

Without cynicism, Richard thought how women almost always say that, about the man they are being unfaithful to.

They lay together in the room with the circular window. A scraggy sky streamed past the glass. Richard's head rested in the cradle of his hands. It was the second time she had asked him what he would do when it became too difficult to climb the ladder? 'Put the bed downstairs,' he told her. 'That may be the last and the most difficult decision I have to make.' She thought, how long do you have to know someone to tell how sardonic he's being? But she was wrong. He was being quite level with her. He stretched out his hand and ran his fingers across the smooth cap-like fall of her fringe, and admitted how he sometimes didn't feel like the climb even now. But there was no problem in the long run.

'Problem?' she said.

'There's no pride involved, I mean.' He liked this room and he would stay here as long as he could. And when he couldn't, he would shift. He looked at the sky as he told her.

'You know you never take your eyes from that porthole thing when we're here in bed,' Monica said.

'You wouldn't be in bed with me if that was true.' She slapped her hand lightly against his arm. 'Don't talk bawdy.' And he laughed properly then, as he rarely did. He told her, 'You don't know what bawdy is, do you?'

'Is that a disappointment?'

'It goes for me too, I suppose.' He thought, if Jane's word was anything to rely on. It would have been on *that,* anyway.

Monica said, 'It's always seemed a bit out of my grasp. Gymnastics or whatever.' There had been only one lover before Tom. She supposed it must show one way or another. And she thought of the night of their first anniversary, she and Tom at a restaurant in town, the curve of mock-Spanish arches in the dim lighting. She had touched his hand on the red cloth and said, 'You know the way this first year has gone, love.' She pointed out to him how in twelve months they must actually have slept together about a third of that time. She didn't think much of that—did he? Tom drew back his hand and slipped it along the sides of his glass. 'Oh,' he asked her, 'did that matter so much?' He didn't look at her as he spoke, he didn't return his hand to hers as she had wanted him to do. She had been as shocked by what he said as by anything in her life. She went over it so many times. Her own hand had stayed resting on the cloth, while her spirit drew back. That was the only way she could think of it. But something altered between them in the restaurant, among the tourist posters and the hard, insistent music getting on Monica's nerves.

'You're not upset are you?'

'Upset?'

Richard jogged her head in the hollow of his shoulder. She brushed her mouth against the side of his body. The raised outline of his ribs behind the flesh reminded her oddly of the supports in a tent, their bending and pressing against the strained canvas when they were at the beach as children, her father always dickering with the tent-pegs he found so difficult to get right. 'My mind's all over the place,' she said. 'Did I look vacant?'

'Withdrawn.'

She shook her head shortly. 'I always look like I'm at a funeral when I'm thinking.'

'Not of me then, I hope.'

'Oh, don't joke like that!' She closed her eyes against the warmth of his side. She could hear the pump of his heart, the silky even push so close to her ear. Yet her mind went back to it, to the shame she had felt and tried to cover when Tom said that about their love-making. They drank champagne and drove back to the farm with his hand occasionally touching her knee. They had made love, and when she woke at two in the morning she heard her husband in the next room. She went to the door and asked was everything all right? He looked at her from the desk where he sat in his dressing-gown, papers spread in front of him. He had smiled at her and she thought how touchy she had been earlier in the night, she was so wrong to take his words as she had. 'Come back soon,' she said. She lay expecting him any moment. But when she woke again at six the bed was empty beside her. At breakfast he told her, 'You were so sound asleep I didn't want to wake you.' There were worse things, she said, than being woken by your own husband. And she asked him, 'What was all that paper anyway? It's not time yet for tax, is it?' And he explained no, they were family papers as a matter of fact.

'*Family?*' She tried to say it lightly, as Tom spoke himself when he mentioned his mother's harking back towards some pure source. But she could not stop herself saying, 'I didn't know you took all that so seriously. To get up in the small hours with it, I mean.' Then for the second time that night—or that night, and the morning after—her husband surprised her. He said how of course on one level it didn't matter, not in the absurd way it did for his aunts who lived in the fiction of their breeding, the 'Merinoes' as he called them sometimes, fat-throated, dull-eyed, happy at their grazing. 'But on another?' Monica had prompted him. Yes, it mattered there all right. Because it was fact, didn't that count for something? There are lies all about one, he went on, we live in the thick of them. 'You must know that from school as much as I do from politics. That's why I enjoy looking over these. I might even turn them into some kind of book.' His hand brushed at the array of papers and documents and dark-bound diaries his father had collected and annotated for his last half dozen years, the family stuff that his son now stood beside at the desk. Monica did not ask, although she felt the urge to do so, why aren't there lies in there too? He watched her and smiled as he had last night when she came from the bedroom to see what he was doing. She thought of him in photos as a boy, as a first year student in a football jersey (still on his mother's wall), or as he stood on the steps at St Joseph's with herself leaning on his arm, her veil billowing across both of them. Something is happening, she thought from the breakfast table. I am beginning to see him for the first time.

Richard now moved again, and she took her weight from his shoulder. 'Do you want to tell him yet?' he asked her. 'You know. Tell Tom?'

'I will soon,' she said. 'Not for a while yet.'

The affair had begun six months ago.

Monica sometimes rode out to Dutchman's Orchard on the way back from school. There were other places closer to town where she might have bought fruit quite as cheaply, but what she bought and what she paid were not the point. For one thing there was the long row of pines with the afternoon sun cutting down not in bars so much as in constant streaming flickers that gave her a deeply sensual pleasure. She had read once that people with epilepsy could be brought to the brink of seizure if they passed through strips of light and darkness, if they sat in a car say as it drove through late afternoon woods. Such people were taken as far as she was, she supposed, with what must seem a similar elation, then hurled so much further than she could go. She thought always of that as she entered across the first dapple and mix of light. And then there was the old foreign man with the heavy cheeks, weighing out the asparagus in September, the peaches at Christmas, the apples sometimes as late as March. His hair was clipped to a grey stubble across his high narrow head. He wore lengths of string around his neck which he drew off to tie the sugar sacks for those who ordered in bulk. When he stood in the doorway to his shed the shadows lapped across his face and he reminded her of the book in the school library which fascinated her so disturbingly that she set it on the top of a shelf where none of the girls would find it. It was a book of photographs, detailed and morbidly beautiful studies of bodies taken from Danish bogs, the bronze-age corpses lifted from the long preserving night of their interments. Some of the bodies still wore in such awful detail the folds of their capes, the caverns of their hoods, one of them the rope that had killed him. Monica thought how they held their fascination forever, they were so like ourselves, the hooded man and the girl chosen to die, confronted with those final rites that must have been only moments ago for them. They were there still for us to gaze at as closely as at the faces of our friends. She watched the old Dutchman's face and thought of the photos in the book, the long glass cases in the museums that must be in darkness while she watched this man here in the light. Then she would go back to her motor-scooter and turn south as she left his drive. The road home took her past the pa at the corner of the main road, its sharpened stick fences and the carved figures at the gate.

She would begin preparing dinner as soon as she arrived home. She and Tom would tell each other about their day's work. They seldom argued, or even disagreed. They spoke kindly from conviction that people should be courteous with each other, as they should be honest and fair-minded. Tom was putting far more time into the Labour Party, a fact which puzzled people when they first heard of it. What's he in *that* for? What about his family? The land that's coming to him? Those are the knives are they, Tom would ask, that are meant to trim back everything, common-sense, responsibility? He put such questions quietly, disconcerting the party people he worked with almost as much as he did family friends. His uncles pointed out that his father had been into dynamos run from windmills, into anything except straightforward farming. It was that same craziness taking a different turn.

Tom asked her one night, 'If I had anything to do with another woman would that put paid to it? As far as you were concerned?'

'Paid to what?'

'To us.'

'No,' Monica said. She supposed he asked for the only reason that occurred to her.

'One has to tell the truth.'

'Yes,' she agreed.

'Otherwise.'

'I know.' They meant otherwise trying to live like this, civilised, considerate—all that would go in a scribble across whatever careful order one tried to make of life. And while her husband spoke she felt she was watching him again on that night when she woke to an empty bed and had gone to find him in the bright circle from the desk lamp, his pencil running along the lines of the special calendar that gave him the day and the month for a hundred years. What he was saying seemed that remote. Neither of them spoke of love, or whatever the word should be. Then quite angrily Monica thought, as though on the other woman's behalf, that it shouldn't be like that. It should be passion or being carried away or swept off his feet. It should be so he didn't give a stuff what his wife thought of it, instead of adultery neatly stacked like his old diaries, his political papers, life as ever under control.

'So it's all pretty clear then?' Tom asked. He meant, so you won't leave because of it? We won't dislocate our lives absurdly?

'It's better that you've told me, certainly.'

The next Sunday for the first time Tom stayed away from Mass. For a long time Monica had attended only occasionally, at Christmas and at Easter and the Sundays when her father was down staying with them. 'Of course you mustn't go if you don't feel you should,' Tom used to tell her. 'It means nothing if it's compelled.' She sometimes sat on the verandah, a mug of coffee warming her hands, on those Sunday mornings when he drove along the valley to church. She often put to herself whether she had stopped believing, 'given the show away' as her father would say. There was no answering even that one simply. She thought of the sentence she had underlined at university in her favourite book—'I neither believe nor disbelieve.' Yet any intelligent woman should know at least that much about herself. She considered her brother in Australia. He had turned so strongly against it all, against as he said those years out at college at Glen Innes, a memory that was nothing but the dreariness of rugby changing sheds and teachers inflicting scraps of learning as though you could expect nothing without paying for it, not in this vale of tears. But then there was her cousin too, her favourite. He was now a solicitor in Auckland, he served on the committee for Corso and carried a small scar from one of the marches a couple of years ago that showed like a strip of white cotton if you moved his hair aside. He called it his liberal's stigmata. He still believed he said because it was logical and it satisfied him emotionally. And probably, he joked, because he didn't fancy a bit on the side. He meant he wasn't like Jack in Melbourne, who had left his wife for a girl with an Italian name, and then left her for another. But now she envied Tom that between one Sunday and the next he could pull down the whole edifice of his religion and level the section and have it planted in ornamental shrubbery, as it were, exactly seven days later.

'And now?' Richard said to her. They had been talking of God, and then of Tom. They sat on the thick flokati rug in the centre of the room.

'He goes to church again, of course.'

'Of course?'

'Since Margaret dropped him.'

Rain was pelting down outside. Monica hoisted the blanket she wore closer about her shoulders. She stretched her feet towards the bar heater and the undersides of her calves gleamed as she raised them. The blanket fell back from her thighs.

'Come off it,' Richard said. 'Not trying to excite me *again?*' He took her feet and rested them in his lap, across the red Chinese-patterned gown. His hands ran along her warm flesh. 'So you got to meet her anyway?' he said. 'The woman he'd taken up with?'

'Remember I mentioned Margaret Stein? Old family friend? Bridesmaid? The one Tom asked what's a girl with a nice Jewish name doing in a church like ours? Well her. They met up again at some Labour Party jamboree.'

'And then she dropped him?'

'She pleaded conscience. Husband of her school friend and what have you. In fact I think she became bored more quickly than she bargained for.'

'With sleeping with him?'

'Even more with his politics. Margaret had jumped in the Marxist end of the pool by then and thought she could entice Tom into joining her. Radicalise him, as she said.'

'Why in bed?'

'Where better to start? One of her catch-cries was that only one in fifty women thought differently to the men they slept with. I suppose she liked the irony.'

Richard placed her legs again on the orange rug. He said, 'Let's have a drop of something to warm us up.'

'I'm not all that cold,' Monica said. She watched her lover raise a fringed cloth from in front of a set of shelves. There were postcards of various places—Vienna, Nepal, the Tholos at Delphi—pinned on their plain wooden side. It made her think of undergraduate flats, although everything else was sparse and tasteful.

He turned to her with each hand carrying a glass with an inch of brandy. He rubbed his knuckles against her cheek before she reached up to take her glass. 'Come on,' he said. 'No being sad now.' They had promised each other that after their first time together.

They met in the first place because her motor-scooter had spluttered out a mile after she left the orchard. She pushed it as far as the next drive, leaned it against a post, and walked towards the odd-ball house she had glanced at often from the road. A modest enough cottage had been added to haphazardly. It made her think of those interlocking bricks that children built with, adding crannies and half-storeys and unbalanced extensions to whatever might have been an original plan. Her old Dutchman had told her something—what was it?—some old joker years ago had tinkered on and off with the place. The side of the building that faced her as she turned from the drive was primed with pink daubs. She supposed he was some old gaffer amusing himself, 'filling in time' as one always euphemistically put it. But then she saw a man not so much older than herself walk from the shed at the side of the house. He carried a can of petrol as though he knew for certain what she was after.

'I only wanted your phone,' she said. 'If I could ring my husband?'

'You can do that too if you like. I'll just put the petrol in first.' He walked with her back down the drive. She saw that the man had not shaved that day, and that his arms, as he raised them and balanced the can against the lip of the tank, were thin beneath his shirtsleeves. She remembered then what someone else had told her about a man who lived along this stretch of road.

When they were back at the doorway to the house, the man said to her, 'The phone's up there.' Monica followed him to a room with wall-length windows and a ladder rising from the far side. She saw the

typewriter and the manila folders and photographs held together with coloured plastic clips. She tried phoning home to say she would be late.
'No luck?'
'Farmers,' she said, shrugging.
'You mean you wouldn't expect an answer?'
'I mean you're not surprised if there isn't.'
Monica noticed a small crucifix on a white expanse of wall. The man picked up her glance. 'Vestigial,' he explained. He smiled at her for the first time.
'Am I being nosey?'
'Why not?' Richard took a book from the shelf behind him and held it so that she saw the gold lettering on its spine. 'I read this too.'
'For old time's sake?'
'It's the story I've known longest. Those are the ones we're supposed to like best, aren't they?'
She saw that his grey eyes were flecked with darker dots. She tapped the folders on the desk and asked him, 'Are you writing a book?'
'A local history thing.'
'Why?' she said.
Instead of answering her he said, 'An enthralling story about bigots and carpetbaggers and rip-off merchants and the lower orders scrabbling to put the boot into someone further down. It's the story of our country in miniature.'
She heard the edge cutting across her own words when she said, 'Why waste your time on people so much beneath you?'
'Because some of their descendants are paying me to do it. The local council in fact. They think if your grandfather is in a book then he couldn't have a been a shit.'
'And you'll enlighten them?'
'No.' Richard sat on the arm of a leather chair drawn close to the expanses of glass. He smiled at her again. He said that he used to be a journalist, and this was simply work he could do at home.
'Try the phone again if you like.'
She said, 'You must be the one who's supposed to be dying.'
'I know you too,' he said. 'Your husband's a Tory radical posing for the time being as a centre-left Labourite.'
'Goodness!' Monica laughed. 'Have you got spies?'
'It's called research.' He was glad that she had taken it as a joke. 'I also hear he's got journals and things I'd like to borrow.'
'I don't think he'd let you have them.'

'Never mind,' he said. He moved his hand towards a chair, inviting her to sit down. 'We've both heard things that are half true.'

Her husband had said some months after his 'openness' with her, after the honesty that had cleared his behaviour in much the same way as his no longer going to Mass had done, 'It's all over, Monica. That whole business with Margaret.'

She had thought, 'This is like the second act of some play about adultery. The audience has been out for coffee after all the pain and now it's back to see how the stitches are put in.' She and Tom were sitting as they had that other evening too, the same papers probably on his desk, she with the stack of exercise books on her knee. She cuffed them with her palms so they sat square.

'It was a mistake.'

'Everything is when it's over.'

Tom uncrossed his legs. He said, 'You know that's pretty trite.'

'So's fucking for a few months. If it's only that.' She knew putting it so crudely disturbed her husband. She felt she was like the bitches she had seen on television or read of in books, now that she had the whip hand. She said, 'It didn't take long for her to get bored with it.'

'It wasn't boredom.'

Monica set the exercise books on the floor beside her chair. 'Sorry,' she said. 'I thought ordinary old grabbing a bit would follow the ordinary old pattern of it wearing thin after a while unless there were spiritual depths I wouldn't know anything about.' Then she caught herself at what she was doing. Never mind about Tom, she was demeaning herself. She cleared her throat and told him, 'I shouldn't go on like that. It's not what I mean to be saying.'

'Well?' Her husband waited for her revision. He had picked up the ivory paper knife he used for a marker in the farm diary. It had been a Christmas gift between his grandparents before they married.

'I only mean we need to make an effort. You know, that we don't sink ourselves in brawling. I'm just reminding myself of that.' Tom put down the paper knife and walked across to her. He began to unbutton her blouse. It was not like him to step aside from habit even in a thing like sexual advance. He fumbled the catch on her bra and undid the buckle on her leather belt. He continued until she was naked in front of him, but her own hands had not moved. He looked at her and told her to sit down again and then he knelt between her knees. She thought Margaret must have taught him something, after all. She felt his head against the inside of her thighs. His hands, folded into loose fists, rested on either leg above her knees. Then he remained still like that, her own hands now on his shoulders which she rubbed at gently. She thought how behind the sex there was something even stronger. He was a man who liked being humbled more than anything else.

They remained like that until Tom believed he was pleasing her. There was the occasional distant sound of an animal from across the farm. The curtain moved at the open window, swaying out slowly across the desk, its hem whisking softly against his papers. Her hand moved across the back of her husband's neck then began to unbutton the shirt she had given him at his last birthday. She supposed afterwards that she was the one finally who had behaved like the man. She might have done anything to him, as they say about submission.

'Fourteen years!' Monica said. 'Fourteen years away from everything here and you wanted to come back!'

'You know the old saying about going back to the mat.'

'I know it but I don't see the point of it. Not with you.' Richard told her he came out of the doctor's rooms in Clapham, after the first tests had come back, and his mind was already made up. 'Twenty-four hours later I'd booked my flight home.'

They were walking on the far side of the swamp. Its level was high from recent rain, and lay still as a mirror. Richard swung at the grass with a stick. He had thought of here, he said, the minute he heard.

Monica was still puzzled. 'But throwing in all that because you hear you're not well. I mean if you get better and then you've left your life over there?'

'All that?' Richard took her up. 'A number of people I worked with, went to the pub with, walked round parks or galleries with on Sunday afternoons? That's all we're talking about.'

She shook her head. 'I'm out of my depth. If you knew what I'd give even to get there.'

'There were about a dozen of us, close friends. Some were married, some weren't. From time to time one of us drifted away from the group and someone else floated into it. We all liked much the same things and it was civilised, if you like, in a way I'd never have known here at home. I lived with one of the women for a couple of years, then she took a job in a museum in Cambridge.'

'That's not far. Is it?'

'Distance is how many people there are between two points quite as much as it is a matter of miles. In English terms it was a long way.'

'But there's no one here at all,' Monica said. 'Not ones that matter to you.'

'You can't compare either, if things are too far apart.'

'Oh!' Monica flicked a rusted can from her path with a rapid turn of her foot. 'I can't run a measuring tape over everything as easily as that.'

They said nothing then for several minutes. A horse in the neighbour's paddock ambled towards them. Monica plucked handfuls of lush grass from beside a log that must have lain there for half a century. The horse's mouth quivered along her sleeve before it nuzzled into the feed. The lips felt rubbery against her palm. Then she and Richard walked further beside the placid rim of water. The horse kept up at their shoulders, waiting, breathing heavily, until they both stooped to gather more grass for it.

'You know I see a place on TV or get a letter from somewhere and I think for a moment that I've got a whiff of what it's like, but it's not even that much really.' Monica's hand lifted as she spoke. She meant the place here, the district, the town over there and the private school in the hills and a little beyond that, her husband and the farm, the quick drop to the coast, the stretching out and out of the sea—all that for the moment was balanced on her hand. 'That's about my world,' she said. 'I don't even know enough about the rest to miss it.'

'I still write now and then,' Richard said. 'Maybe for the first pint on Sunday mornings someone says, "Heard from Richard", and someone else says, "Christ that reminds me, make me drop him a line sometime will you?" That's about all it means once you've left.'

More sharply than she meant, Monica asked him, 'Why should any of us expect more than that?'

The man beside her raised the willow stick he carried and tapped it against her arm. 'I'm not whimpering,' he said. 'I'm not asking for special favours, miss.'

They were at the far end of the swamp. Trees grew at odd angles from the low bank above the water. It was difficult to say of some of them whether they were alive or dead. The trunks and the leafless branches reflected blackly in the water beneath them. A fantail cut in rapid bursts a few yards from where Richard stopped and Monica came up behind him, circling him with her arms and resting her head on the back of his suede jacket. They stood in the heightened silvery light, the bird piping thinly as it darted about them, and Monica thought how if they stopped like this for only a few minutes, the fantail would perch on them. But they turned to the impacting clatter at the far end of the swamp, the mirror sheered off into fragments where first one duck, and seconds behind it another three, slapped down onto the water.

It was several evenings later, back at the house, that Monica said, 'What does it give you here, then? I mean what are you after?'

Richard said, 'You're always saying "I mean", do you know that?' He stood up from where he sprawled in the leather chair. Monica sat on the floor, her head leaned back against its arm. She watched him draw his gown around him and she thought how gaunt he looked as he did that. The token of his illness. 'Token,' she thought again. For it did seem only that, a sign and not an essence; not the defining and corrupting force which of course it was.

'Don't prevaricate,' she said.

'The "gift" then, if you want to call it that. What I'm after is stillness.'

'Stillness?' She heard the slight rise in her voice that completed the statement for her—*is that all*?

'Since I was a kid, you know? The thing I've always admired because it really is so simple yet it's hardly ever been around me. Not in my family to begin with, not my marriage with Jane nor with anyone else I ever had to do with.'

It was important to her that she understand at least this about him. 'You came all the way back for *that*?'

'The only reason,' he said. He leaned back against the ghost room in the reflecting expanse of glass behind him. 'The day I heard—the *minute* I heard—what was probably wrong with me and how long it would take for this or that to happen. It was like an instinct. This place came into my mind although I suppose I hardly thought of it at ordinary times, I mean.'

'There. You're saying it now.'

But he passed over her banter. 'I didn't need to think of it much I realised later because it was always there, underneath the rest. Behind whatever else I was doing.'

Monica watched the man she loved as he hunched against the glass, one naked foot set across the other, his fists weighing like stones in the pockets of his dressing-gown. She was thinking how absurdly lives converge, strands draw together. She could see no more sense in it than that. And she remembered his telling her on one of their first days together, at the distant beginning of their friendship, how he was here at all in this odd-ball house on these few acres of rough paddocks with the swamp she looked down on now, a greyish smear out there in the night. Here as he said because a half-inebriated grandfather had met another man in a bar in Onehunga, beside the wharves, in the same November week as the First War came to an end. The man was known always in the family as the stranger. He is with an Aussie mistress who looks exactly what she is and talks of racehorses he has owned or is going to own. He has also (all this in Richard's words, his mother's words, presumably at some stage his grandfather's too) a contempt for almost everyone he knows, he sees already that the ending of the War is as much a farce as its beginning. Some years later according to the story he disappears off a ship between Melbourne and Perth in weather so calm you'd think it was part of a painting. But in the Onehunga bar, in the reek and bonhomie of scotch, the celebrating racket of distant victory, the stranger says he's got this bit of land it's going for a song, you wouldn't find a better piece, dirt cheap. *To cut it short* Richard had said several times while he told her. So his grandfather comes here after parting with his last hundred quid. He clears the scrub and carts in gravel and digs pits in one place to throw up mounds in another, anything rather than admit the stranger might have sold him a pup. He builds the cottage and drags stumps from the swamp except for that far end where the trees still sloped above the water because he believes one day that will be an ornamental garden, it is only a matter of time which he thinks is the one commodity he's not likely to run out of. Only one day thirty years later his heart stalls and the Maori woman he has taken up with the minute he gets out from under Richard's grandmother's eye, turns him from the sacks he's slumped against and he's already dead. But that is how the cottage was built and the swamp first cleared. Then a son who has never married, who the rest of the family accept as more than a few bob short, who walks always with a limp although no physical reason was ever found for it, takes over from the old man and turns his energy and inventiveness against the house itself. He runs up bits and pieces from the walls and above the roof and out at defiant angles, until he in turn dies on the afternoon of a Ranfurly Shield game because his body is found in the kitchen several days later and he's wearing the black and white woollen cap that he always wore, the closest he came to ritual, whenever he listened to a match. 'From then on,' Richard said, 'there was a string of tenants who knocked the hell out of the place and a while when it was empty, until I started coming here as a student. Because nobody in the family ever thought it worth selling any more than it was worth doing up. That was when I put the glass in place of one wall and made the bedroom upstairs you can see nothing from except the sky. At the time it was the most romantic thing I could think of.' And this talk coming back to Monica now as she watches him against the dark glass, as though the glass itself is water and the reflected objects of the room, the armchair and the bookcases and she herself sitting on the orange rug, are receding into it. We are what brings the story this far, she thinks, we shall press back as it goes on and becomes someone else's. Her eyes were tired from crying earlier on. She had decided months ago she would never do anything as crass as that, Richard must never be yoked into some awful sentimental thing because of her. But today they had sat here in the room for hours while the late sun drained off from the hills and the night had risen as it seemed from the ground, until now they floated on it. The water outside moved with quick running lights when cars turned at the corner near the Dutchman's bend. They had decided—Richard made her decide—they would not tell Tom after all. Not tell her husband she loved another man, as she wanted to do. He had brushed his hand across her hair, spanned her wrist with his fingers, talked so calmly to her until she saw how right he was to leave things exactly as they were. 'Talking her down,' wasn't that the phrase? A suicide on a ledge, a test pilot—where did the phrase come from in the first place? But down, certainly: from hope, from her fears of grief, from expectations of oneself or of others. His hand moving smoothly across her flesh, adroit as oil.

Billy Joel
Her Bird

Billy Joel her bird. Betty's bird. He move along his stick in the cage, the cage swing out, Billy Joel make it swing. His whistling then all morning, afternoon. His cage on a hook over the cut-out bench and Betty talk him every little while. Sometime the other girls make Betty mad, they run the scissors along Billy Joel's wire and he stop singing. He shaking in one corner of the cage and the girls laugh. Fat Frances say or Rachel, look, where his whistle Betty? Then they hide down behind the bench because Betty throw her markers at them, hold up her scissors like she going to stab them hard, you dirty cows! Come on, Fat Frances tell her, where's a joke? So she hand over this bit of lettuce from her lunch box and Betty fold it over careful between the bars. Here my Billy, she say to him, here my darl. Betty she so pretty everyone in the factory like to walk past her. Her hair fall down shiny right pass her shoulders, over the pink line beside her ear she hate people to look at. And she got this radio nobody to touch that except Betty say to, and the tapes inside her drawer. See, everyone like giving Betty presents that how she get all these tapes. But only her favourites she ever bother to put on. There, she telling her bird, this one ours. She makes her mouth go with the song.
   But I'm taking a Greyhound
   On the Hudson River Line
   I'm in a New York state of mind.
Fat Frances tell her, you pretend you know that Betty? Not even saying them properly. That no worry Fat, she call out. No worry either Gunga and Frig come pass when they pick up the big bin of scraps and they touch her on the arse, Betty just flap her hand, push them off like it nothing much. It's Rachel shout out youse leave her, youse touch her tit you cop this. Rachel hold up the long weight like a ruler she keep her patterns straight with. Touch yours too had any, Frig tell her back, all drop off or something? And Rachel tell him then wouldn't know

where to put it would you Frig. Frances say, not even for practice, those just two wanker. Betty not caring one way or other. She turn her tape over. Listen darl.
Sing us a song you're the piano man,
Sing us a song . . .
Betty only twenty-two. She so pretty, Betty, I think I tell that. She wear jeans every day Rachel say her mother want to hide her legs from the men. Stop men reaching up their hands. And best tits. Everyone reckon that. Should be in movies, Rachel tell her. Rachel always try to make it nice when Betty cry and her friends say don't Betty, everyone your friend, even the mongoes standing up you get on the bus, want to carry your bag. Then Betty smile again like she forgot already why she start to cry. Put her tape on, Fat Frances shout across to me, stop gawping at her. She let me touch her radio Betty but no one else. Everyone else scare to. But I find a tape I say this one, Bet? Listen Rachel laugh out he calling her Bet now. But she tell me that the one, that the one she want on. And she shove her hair back and smile. When I push the button I say that alright then? Fat Frances watch me, she say to Rachel Hey, Mister Ronnie Corbett chasing Betty's pants, you watching Rachel? Mister Ronnie Corbett my joke name with everybody. I see him Thursday night in his big chair and nice pullover and glasses a bit like mine. And I smile big like him. My hands between my knees in the lunchroom that like him too. I watch him careful, how he walk next to his fat mate, I walk like that next to Fat Frances sometime everyone piss himself. Betty some days she come right up there behind me, her hands squeeze my shoulder, she say when everyone else looking, see my best mate here, everyone? I lean my head back on her. Not on her tits, not talk like that, on her *chest*, that the polite way to say it. I smile so my teeth look good, I sing in a voice come a surprise to everyone,
Friday night I crashed your party
Saturday I said I'm sorry
I was only having fun
wasn't hurting anyone.
Anyway Billy Joel this morning I think of, he lie there, both his feet these little hooks, his eyes still open but sort of rubbed. I mean the shine not there, only this dull old dead eye. Betty look at him at first, just not believing Billy Joel dead as all that. She think he having a game or something. Then she turn the cage and swing it round so sudden Rachel turn her head only quick enough in time, and *thwack* the cage belt on the edge of the bench and all the wire bits make me think of

straight stiff rain when the cage hanging there on the nail those wires spring out all over the place, and Billy Joel just this fucked dead yellow fluff there on the floor. Then all week, every day, Betty not even playing her tapes, her face swollen up like someone bash her. Fat Frances and Ruth make their joke after a while but not so funny now. Every day at the canteen I bring Betty back the cake she like, you peel the paper off the side and see the little ribs. She eat them all right but not as good as before. So I think what to do to make her happy then? The whole workroom different too when Betty like this. The forelady scream and carry on that the work not done right and Rachel hold her scissors until she past and shove them up and down in the air behind her, says cut her arse to pieces one of these day. So all this time I thinking what to do for Betty just across the bench and her lovely hair over her face like she inside this shining tent. Then I think well we get her another bird. I tell Fat Frances and she say she ask Rocky fix that shagged cage. Rocky her boyfriend in the metal shop, Fat say he do anything for her if every now and then she go in the storeroom with him. She got these other boyfriends too, she laugh and shout out when sometime they punch and kick out in the yard because she nice to them all. Enough to go round everyone, that her joke. Rachel tease at her, room for Mister Ronnie Corbett in there too? I hope Betty not listening when they talk dirty things. Anyway Betty only smiling, she touch my shoulder, she say out loud jealous of you, that their trouble. Anyway I make up my mind. I go into the pet shop near to Coles where the man let me watch the puppies and hold the kittens and sometime when he too busy I sweep the shop for him. One day I even mind the shop all lunchtime on a Saturday when he go down the road. So when he out the back where he keep his straw and the big lot of food for his shop I open a cage and take out a bird got blue wings on it and like someone draw on him with a pen, these little black marks. I think it all out very careful before I go there, I take this rubber band that hold his wings down at his side so there no flying off. On the bus I feel him warm and jumpy in my pocket and he shit white and runny over my hand. Then I run up the workshops before the others get there. Fat Frances there though because we plan it and she hold open the cage for me and I take the rubber band away. At first though the bird not jumping and flying like we hope, he sort of drag over to a corner and just bunch up. Fat say I reckon you half kill him Ronnie. And now he go all ruffly like he been rained on and not quite dry out. Then Betty arrive and funny enough she think it my bird, see, because no one say it a present for her, because it too sick to say that. So she hold my hand and she saying never mind, never mind, and when it stop moving about morning tea time she take it out carefully and wrap it in a piece of material they cutting from this week and when she come back from outside she say I put him somewhere quiet for you, Ronnie. And she smiling at me whenever after that. Ruth and Fat Frances look at me and behind Betty's back move their fingers rude as they can. Hey bitch! Ruth shouting at her friend, the peppermint on her tongue showing like it sit on a dirty cushion. And Betty say suddenly like it just struck her, someone fix up this cage? Then she lean over and say to me, for the first time since Billy Joel dead, because no one else ever allowed to touch it, she ask me, push that tape on for me, Ronnie Corbett. She even put her own finger on the button next to mine. And the music start again, after what seem ages. Her old favourite then, Betty's mouth talking with the words, *I was only having fun, wasn't hurting anyone.* Nice one, Fat Frances call out. We all tapping our hands on the bench in front of us like Billy Joel never die, like it was before and good as now, just about.

Putting Bob Down

It is usually assumed that if a man has two mistresses or two wives, then they must be physically quite contrary types. Perhaps literature has corrupted that part of our thinking irretrievably. There is always the 'dark she, fair she', as the gloomiest of English poets once wrote. Or what we drew from those books we were reared on. Walter Scott. Nathaniel Hawthorne. There is a blonde girl who embodies the domestic virtues, who wears a plaid shawl, looks after an aged father, and gazes at the hero with eyes so blue that ice floating in the coldest fjords is not to be compared. Truly. And there is a raven-haired woman who speaks directly from the blood. She is Mediterranean, and behind her we see the temples of forgotten faiths, a rage for existence which that blonde girl knows nothing of. She carries phials in her pocket, while the Anglo-Saxon angel has merely an address book in her reticule. Which is introductory to this simple fact: when Bob Roberts died, there were two women at his graveside. They were almost identical.

Helene, whose name had always enchanted him, said as they walked away from the dark gaping hole, 'We all get finally I suppose what we most deserve.'

The other woman was called Frith. She hated her name intensely because of that mucky story about the bird. She said, 'If only we did.'

Metaphor is something that Helene hates more than anything on earth. A plate is a plate. A fish is a fish. A plate can never be a fish, even if it is shaped with fins and painted with scales, and signed Picasso in the corner. Because there is always the irrefutable test. Give a hungry man a plate painted like a fish.

Frith does not think like that at all. To carry metaphor in one's emotional arsenal is to carry a thin stick that snaps open to a gorgeous fan. There is a semicircle of wonder as close as the palm of one's hand.

Japan, as she once explained it to Bob, sits waiting in Dabtoe. There is holocaust in every match that is struck correctly.

At the graveside both women stepped forward simultaneously, to take a handful of clammy yellow earth. One had removed her glove while the other had kept hers on. The better dressed of the women reached out her right hand to the trowel which the undertaker offered them. The other woman took her handful from the left. Frith thinking of a cake offered on a cakeslice, Helene looking only at the clogged crumbs of earth.

When Helene threw that clutch of dirt into the grave, onto the polished wood and the freshly engraved metal plate, she knew quite absolutely she tossed dust to dust. So did Frith. But she was thinking how she knew beyond any disbelief in resurrection or anything else, that she was throwing eternity onto dear dead Bob. That all of us, walking or sleeping, wear bodies which are indeed the merest tip of the past, the arrowhead that shall then lie round for a million years. She thought, I am throwing the dust of today onto the ash of stars.

Bob had said to them separately, 'You cannot expect me to choose between you. You just can't.'

Each of them had said in her own way, which in fact was very similar, 'We're not cannibals, love. We don't believe for a minute that one has to devour the loved one.' Helene had spelled it out. 'Isn't that what we've been fighting against for millenia. That old *mine, mine* nonsense?' Frith put it like this. She said, 'If we could only think of sex as an aesthetic experience too, as well as a mere tingling of nerves.' (In her mind she saw the telephone exchange her mother worked at while she herself was a child. And on some days too many bells ringing in that small town for one operator to cope with. Until mummy's hands finally across her ears with the room ringing about her and the lights flashing on the switchboard and simply not enough hands for too many wires. With mummy crying *oh shit oh dear*.) What Frith in fact was saying: 'If you own a painting I mean. You don't turn it to the wall if someone else enjoys it too.'

At the graveside she wore a plain grey suit and Helene a black frock with a cut-away matching jacket. From not very far away they might have been sisters, one of them clearly richer than the other. They had both taken a taxi to the cemetery. Neither thought it important which of them had known the corpse the longer time.

Even now, if it came to the push, Bob would not have known what woman he preferred. Thank God though there had never been anything sneaky about the liaisons. He had told Helene quite openly. He had said, 'I don't consider myself a particularly randy sort of man but there's something I'd better tell you.' It was almost as if she had expected him to say it. She had stroked his hair as she leaned across him. He had thought, I'm buggered if I'd have taken the same thing from her. But another time when he had forgotten an appointment with her, Helene threw things at him when he next came into the house.

Frith was so much milder. Yet she wore exotic underthings and said the strongest words when her breath caught and her hands fluttered across his rump.

A point to be made here is that it's not at all the same thing as looking through a doorway, although it's easy enough for writers to imagine that it is, when the figures pull back from the sunlit and lovely oblong which is the top of a grave. To imagine it is like friends going from a room. As a matter of fact the legs are absurdly out of proportion to begin with. They are positive pillars. The heads too such disproportionate bumps above the big swinging handbags, the hands the women held together in their dark gloves rather like the mitts of boxers touching as they prance in their corners. Then when they drop those handfuls of dirt. Honestly, the way the clods come pouring in you'd think they had it in for you.

'I'm only a journo,' Bob used to tell them. 'Only run of the mill in the least elevated of callings.'

'It must be so marvellous to use words at all,' Frith said. 'With that freedom, I mean. That control. All I ever do, day after day, is hear children recite their grammar. Hear them conjugate, decline, fumble with sentences they will never know how to use. Languages!' she sighed. 'Those complicated and dreary ladders. Where do they expect them to reach?'

She liked it when he nuzzled close against her, ran his hand down her stomach and left it lying there. 'A man is like the *Zeitwort,* do you understand that? The verb. Women are so many nouns.'

When both of them stood back from the long bright space hanging there above him, he thought how lovely a patch of pure blue could seem.

The women turned away and walked for perhaps a minute in silence. Then Helene was saying to Frith, 'In the six funerals I've been to in this cemetery this is the first one it hasn't rained.'

They were cutting across the rows of the buried towards the road. A champion billiard-player's monument with its slate table, its marble cue, struck them as too absurd. 'God knows what Bradman will have. A whole oval made from brass.' They touched each other's arms in amusement. 'Imagine what Bob would think, us talking like this!' They remembered how he believed that women knew nothing about sport.

As it happened, he thought a great deal. He thought of Helene's knee on the side of his bed, her preparing to throw herself across him like the great Jim Pike across Phar Lap himself, and his telling her, 'You are lovelier than anything I know.' And her playfully putting her hand across his mouth so that he bit at that fleshy part just down from her little finger. Her saying to him, 'Never say *than*. Never say *like* or *as*. Do you hear?' Pressing with her strong knees against his sides. And his saying quite seriously, so that she roared with laughter, 'There's not a love poem I bet you in the whole of literature for that part of a woman's body. That little soft bit there on the side of your hand.' Helene would even laugh sometimes in the middle of their loving. With Frith there was either no talk at all, or those words she would never think of using anywhere else.

The first time he had ever seen them together. At an art opening he had to write up for his paper because the critic was down with the mumps. He was terrified at the thought of speaking to both of them at the same time. He leaned close to Frith as he came in and saw her by the table with the catalogues. 'There's an awful lot of people I have to nod to tonight. Or the paper does rather. Know what I mean?' He brought her a glass of wine and looked at some pictures with her. She knew the names of all of them without referring to her catalogue.

Helene said out very loudly, 'This is the most boring exhibition I have ever seen.' He had been shocked. He looked at the famous black figures against their ochrous background, the flashes of gums and flowers like gunshot in the violence of the light. She said, 'Introduce me to her anyway. She can't be worse than this.'

They had reminded him of a Moore exhibition as they peered down at him a few minutes ago. Their heads so small and distant, mere tufts on pyramids of flesh.

Helene, he had sometimes thought, liked to be with him so that she could *hone*. On anything. On politics or race or people they knew. 'Private money makes it so easy,' he would say to her. 'I could sneer at half the price.' She sat with her legs tucked under her, her glass of wine reflecting like a great coin. Folded on her knee was the paper with his column. 'What would you do if you actually had to look at something? Come into the open without your clichés? Your little images? Run like a nigger flushed from the cane-brakes, I wouldn't be surprised.' Her teeth when she teased him like that! So white and even and gleaming. She enraged him. And then so deliberately looking at her watch, declaring that her husband already had left his office, was stroking this very moment life into his Bentley. But the excitement never really wore off, because there was one lesson he learned very early. To root above one's station is the first step to the stars.

It is surprising how little it shocks one to hear that a friend is dead. It would surprise one more at times to hear that he had won a fortune or written a book or even that he had remarried. Death, when the chips are down, is a very ordinary thing to come to terms with. No sooner has one heard it than there are those meetings with other friends, the ceremonies that nudge it so easily, so gently, away from the warm place where we stand ourselves. To buy a hat, for example. How much of grief can be absorbed in that. To buy, as indeed Frith did, new black underwear for the funeral. Appreciating her own dark joke as she tried it on at home, for a moment there Bob was alive again, watching her from the bed, assuring her she was a bit of all right, bloody oath she was! That other time twenty years ago when she had surprised him with what she wore beneath her dress. The day she had opened the book that he gave her at the end of their first summer. In the tiled vestibule of the Seacliff Hotel! The dark pines on that space of lawn across the street, a solitary girl walking there in a white frock. *Munch!* Bob had said when he looked at her. One of his dreadful artistic puns. Just before he gave her the brown-paper wrapped present and told her to open it in the car. 'I'll open it now!' she had said, and they were tussling, fooling about, people giving them the oddest looks as they passed at the foot of the big staircase. She tore the brown paper and saw that marvellous gilded face. The thick black lines on the eyelids. The cheekbones of pure gold. All because she had said once, *wouldn't you love to go to Egypt?*

After the women withdrew, there were minutes in that oblong of brilliant light when almost nothing happened. A palm frond waved across bottom left. A flight of longnecked birds that could have flown from a Russian movie flicked over very high. Then a man sat there briefly with his feet dangling down as though he sat on a wharf, and smoked a cigarette. When he stood up again he hitched his belt and shouted across to another bloke to move his arse. And the earth started to rain in. Bob tried to remember something. Yes! That quick flowing across of girths and bellybands as ground-level cameras caught the jumpers at Beecher's Brook. The clods flying out from the impacting hooves. The clods now pouring down and the blades of the shovels flashing above there like aircraft in low flight.

And by Christ to hear them now you'd think they had been cobbers from way back.

Helene said, 'You must have known him as long as I did?'

'I suppose I must have,' Frith said. 'At least as.'

Helene said, 'Did he mention me much?'

'You know what men are,' Frith said.

Helene asked again. 'Did he ever mention me?'

'Only to denigrate,' Frith said. 'To say he was chained to a cunt the way men used to be tied to benches in galleys.'

Helene said, 'Whenever he mentioned you it was like he spoke of a disease.'

Bob enjoyed their saying that. He thought how even here you could write your own column. But the women refused his script. They did not squabble as he had hoped. What Frith said in fact was this: 'He lied to both of us, of course.'

'He was a liar all right,' Helene said. 'And he wasn't even that bright, either.'

But there are ways the dead unsettle the living. There are casual remarks made long ago in the warm rooms of the flesh which become weapons in neatly-cuffed and buried hands. Bob thought, it is the least I can do for them now.

'Metaphor is shit,' Helene had said to him once, putting down his paper. His livelihood and his skill dismissed just like that. He had told her you have to be well off to say that. Only the rich were content to be exactly where they were. All very well for her with her fat books of philosophy she could read all day, her picture of Bertrand Russell on her desk like a boiled chook.

'If it wasn't for imagery life would be one long walk along a gutter.' That was Frith. Her blue pencil in her hand, saying that to be able to put 9 out of 10 on a schoolgirl's work was indeed *délice*; *10* out of *10* was *jouissance*. They had a silly game in which she came to bed only after a pupil had scored the top mark. While Bob lay thinking then as now, that for a heavy smoker life indeed could be worse than keeping a gutter eye out for what his old man had called derbs. 'For every ten drowned butts there is one that lies there dry enough to light.' Not every father has that much wisdom to give a son.

He thought very hard about cigarettes, and the room where the women were talking.

In the large quiet room above the park Helene saw the walls flare sharply at her, then return to their tasteful white. It frightened her because she knew there had been no alteration in the light. She said to Frith, 'What were you thinking just now?'

Her dead lover's anterior and it seems always concurrent mistress said, 'I was thinking how life is like a rainbow when we come to think of it.' Strangely, for a moment there Frith had felt as though she bent back on space, her head and heels drawn towards each other, the ether as the poets call it so sparkling about her. *Arc-en-ciel—c'est moi.* Her eyelashes had seemed like the spokes of an iridescent wheel. She wondered if Bob was trying to get through to her. While Helene, because she was the cleverer of the two, thought: if that dead bastard is coming at this one . . . Talk of things like telepathy made her want to throw up. I am a single and finite mind, she told herself. I am not a bloody button in some cosmic jukebox.

From her chair on the other side of the comfortable lounge, Frith watched how her friend's hands met and laced and moved in the silvery light, the point of her cigarette so alive across there, so brilliant. *Alive,* she thought. As the dusk rinsed and dipped in the long low mirror that ran the length of the far wall.

He had quite expected the first night to pass slowly. The light coming up across the surrounding rows made him think of arriving at Kennedy airport in New York, one morning when it was very early, on a dawn flight from the West. Manhattan's blocks, its tall secular angels above their strips of narrow street, had made him think it was like a cemetery.

He thought, given time I suppose I shall remember everything. I shall get bored I suppose with this outlook as I have with every other until I remember this one is for keeps. And oddly, that quite comforted him. There would be the chance at last to find one experience that was inexhaustible. He would want to remember precisely what this sensation was like, the first light breaking of the first day. To recall it would be to continue it, to extend it and to know how this day differed from the second. And through memory living those two days as the third was added, and so on. The hundredth. The ten thousandth. To discriminate each moment, as he had liked to quote when he was a student, 'on that day of frost and sun' or whatever it was. Six crosses ranged to the right, then. A stone child dropping a stone rose. Those bloody Italian inscriptions he could never read! Then the college tower far over there beyond the fence, across petrol stench and the trees. There were some positions as he knew that had a damned sight less than this to pass the time. And in the distance there a corner of a building with the dawn smearing its upper windows behind which, had one turned directly about and walked through the lounge with its morbid mirror and its Aubusson birds, one would come to a passageway as they called it when he was a child in which a fumed oak stand protruded antlers for one's hat and a painted Victorian can waited for the winter months to receive one's umbrella, past which one proceeded clothed as a rule or dishevelled at times or on some few occasions starkers towards a bedroom where a woman now lay looking at the light which broke not only there for her but across a city, and given time, a country; a dawn into which she might walk from her own front steps with their small ornamental lions and along an empty street to the locked iron gates which suppose were opened, she might then pass through and walk on between and beneath the elaborately cut stones and the marble figures, the religious confectionery which made her think if not of the bread of life at least the cake of eternity, and so come to the mound where the flowers already wilted although some of them this time yesterday had not been cut, their binding ribbons straggling damp, their handwritten consolations already dribbled ink. From a point equidistant, say, that mound of the grave, the shape of the bed in this greyish light, were not so fancifully unalike. Only Helene tugging her covers close, hoping for further sleep before she had to rise and take her bath and dress. At which moment, Frith: that quite as loved but much less wealthy woman lay with the fingers of one hand spanning the wrist of the other and thinking of how at Père Lachaise she had stood at the graves of so many famous of Oscar of Baudelaire of Alphonsine Plessais Chopin Daudet it could have been of Colette too so she heard later but had missed her at the time. *The grave's a sad and lonely place,* who said? It is a bed it is a bed, she thought. I am running out of what-it's-likes!

When the women met at the Jewish cake-shop at St Kilda Helene said the moment her gloves were removed and lay like something skilfully skinned beside her, 'That old sod's been on my mind practically non-stop all week.' Stabbing the golden arse of a *pêche* concoction. 'Don't tell me he hasn't been on yours?'

'My mind becomes blank whenever I try to think of him.'

'I wake,' Helene said, 'in the early hours and my mind's as full of nonsense as that glass counter there of European gut-rot.'

'You go over the past?' Frith said. She peeled the paper from the *torte* she had chosen.

'Sometimes I remember the past like it's the present.' Both women noticed the unexpected word that established itself in Helene's sentence.

Frith's cheek bulged horribly as in children's caricatures of toothache. She swallowed the wad of sweetness away. 'I used to dream for a bit but now it's pure bareness. *Le néant.*'

Helene said, 'Every morning when I do get round to waking all I smell is earth.' She laughed. 'I'm starting to think like you!'

Bob remembered a cake shaped like a ship with white frosted lines of rigging at a Sea Scout Christmas Party in 1938. He thought of four meringues that sounded like a gravel path when he crunched them and he had wolfed them down one after the other at the wedding of a cousin who wore a military uniform. He recalled in no particular order seedcake with aunts on Sunday afternoons kisscakes with his mother measling down icing-sugar from a flour-mill lamingtons soggy as a rained out oval *Kuchentorten* and *Schlagsahnetorten* during his time abroad. Those aerated squares of pure dryness Frith dipped in her tea while she went on about Proust. He could think of every cake he had ever eaten. No two had been alike. No mouthful was identical with a following or preceding mouthful.

'I'm so sick of this already.' Helene slapped her tiny fork down on her plate. One cheek of her *pêche* remained untouched.

Frith dabbed at her lips with a paper napkin.

Back with their brandies they began to talk of God.

Helene said that when she was a child there had been a crucifix on her grandmother's wall. Two narrow strips of black wood and a grey contorted figure like a deep-freeze lizard.

Frith said she could still sing hymns quite seriously. At weddings or funerals for example. She never gave it a thought between times, mind.

Helene said she would have shot priests if she had been a Spaniard in the old days. 'I see those bastards in black I want to reach for my branding irons.' Which was not really so strong an image and certainly not a metaphor, when used by a woman who was a grazier's wife.

Bob used to joke that in any case a Christian was only a lapsed atheist. He had known so many anti-clerical jokes that he couldn't keep up with invitations to speak at Catholic men's dinners.

But Frith had perched on him once, *in flagrante*, and quoted some lines of John Donne about tuning his instrument here at the door. He had turned on her and told her not to be so bloody disrespectful.

The two women now sat in the lounge and looked over the massed trees to the black iron fence and its acres of remembrance.

'You do wonder though what becomes of one. Gauguin's great painting, *Who are we?* etcetera. Cliché that it is.'

Helene reached irritably for her cigarettes. 'Anything worth saying is a cliché.'

'Aquinas, wasn't it, thought that you couldn't use any predicate at all of God? That any statement at all was pure tautology?'

'He fucking would,' Helene said. She had hated the Angelic Doctor since her childhood, when she heard that story about a semicircle being cut in the refectory table for his bulk to sit down to meals.

The women sat in silence for several minutes. Then Frith said, 'If He is there, it makes every moment so infinitely of value.' She was sightly embarrassed that she had said it.

'If he isn't of course,' Helene said, 'every moment must be more valuable still.'

'What?' Frith sounded surprised.

'Because there is only a straight line and not a circle. There is no redeeming time, I mean. Each act stands as itself forever.'

Bob thought, 'What if you're both wrong, you smart bitches?'

A picnic in the You-Yangs. The only time he had been with them both together, apart from that art show. A busload of them during a weekend seminar on 'Responsibilities of the Press'. Frith there because she believed such questions mattered, Helene—although she would not even know the word—because she was by nature a groupie. For opera. For *The Tree of Man* during its first year out. For existentialism in its time and then for Vietnam. Only a rich woman could have afforded to care for so much. So at least Bob thought while he sat behind them in the bus, listening to an academic who had been on the same panel with him that morning. He watched the heads of his mistresses sway and bounce.

That outcrop of ancient rocks gave him the creeps. He detested people who used words like numinous, or a few years later spoke of 'the vibes'. He looked at the group about him. Thirty minutes standing in prehistory, as they liked to think, then haring back to the free piss at the cocktail party. The thought of those great grey boulders, the sudden abutments and leaps of rock, depressed him enough to make him consider staying on the bus. Which of course a good journo would never do, because he would not seem one of the team. So he walked with the sociologist who he suspected could not have written a convincing cheque, while the two women he slept with followed some distance behind. Frith said, looking up at the pure blue that hazed off towards the city, 'It's like being inside a jewel on a day like this.' Helene told her she had read how you saw further at this time of year than at any other. 'You can see a candle burning at night three miles away.' That in fact was no more true than the bit about the jewel.

Someone in the group had snapped photographs as they walked along. Eighteen years later Helene handed a print across the coffee table to her recent good friend. She said, 'Remember that afternoon do you?' Bob was some little way ahead. He was turned in profile, laughing. He looked young and happy. The collar of his sports jacket, so typically, was turned up at the back. In the distance far beyond him was the thin strip of the Geelong road. A woman's head was blurred beside him, but her hair was dark and long. Frith took her glasses from her purse. 'Which one of us is that—next to Bob there?'

Helene gave that laugh which sounded so butch Bob used to tell her it reminded him of rugby changing sheds. 'I'm damned if I remember,' she said. Her quieter friend began to laugh as well. The photograph fell as it passed back between them. 'Easy on it,' Frith said. 'One of us is being dropped.' That struck them both as very funny. Helene rubbed at her eyes as though smoke was stinging them.

The women went on to speak of something else, then something else again. While the sky either clouded over or grew dark, Bob was not sure which. It may have been a week later or a month. The two furthest crosses, and the rose-dropping child, were no longer clear in any case. The lawnmower that sometimes charged past like those bloody speedboats that used to irritate him so much the summer when he and Helene lay on that perfect beach on the Tasman Peninsula, that didn't seem to bother him too much at all. He was beginning to forget the names of horses, and football players, and the meals he had once eaten. He was not quite sure any more if *Mille feuilles à la crème* was a cake or a sprinter.

They were leaving the expensive restaurant where Helene had taken Frith to lunch. The afternoon was late as they passed the proprietor who swung back the door for them. They could see the gold tooth near the back of his head. If they wished to sit on with another coffee, he was assuring them, until five, five-thirty, what did it matter? They were not customers, but friends. Frith thought how that would sound so epigrammatic in Latin. While Helene leaned forward in front of her. She heard her friend's face scrape against the man's. She thought how the dangling palm there above the two embracing humans was like a great green hoof. *I hear an army charging,* she thought. What nonsense comes into one's mind!

Helene stood in the street with her car keys fretting in her glove, looking to right and to left.

'You left it up near Parliament,' Frith offered. 'Didn't you?'

'Of course,' Helene said, 'near that little lane where the press boys play about.' Old darling Bob! she thought.

Frith felt her eyes prickle suddenly with tears. Very aware, even now in the diminishing light and the sated aftermath of food and drink and her friend's expensive brooch not turned merely but *flashing* at her, aware of the lovely drifting of the past through the present's glint and whirl, knowing there was something on the tip of her tongue, in the back of her mind, an image just dissolved: with Helene turning as they walked up the slope to the sticks of traffic lights playing their brightness against the massive building, turning and saying with a smile, 'Do you realise we went a whole meal and never mentioned him?' People were walking between them, separating them, allowing them again to come together.

'Remember this same light that time the same at where was it, do you?'

'Dreamed it,' Helene said.

A man saying 'sorry' as he nudged against them.

'Wit then,' Frith laughing, knowing she was a trifle drunk. 'Would you believe I can't get my mouth round his name?'

'Wittgenstein?' They had talked about him at lunch.

'He sounds like a capital.'

'A brand of cigars.'

'Prestige ist eine Zigarre namens Wittgenstein.'

'Stop it!'

Oh their voices high, high and happy, happy and so thin and distant. Voices remotely clapping can one say that? Impacting anyhow softly. Like gloves say meeting hush so softly above there in the greying distance that first far day that afternoon, the praying over, the hands of the women palming like a singer's is it, her hands clasping under the notes, the most silent clapping?

On the pedestrian crossing Frith remembering, 'Was it Wittgenstein said can to dream have a present tense?'

the snow
in spain

if you could only see me the way i am now alec you'd piss yourself at the very sight. remember the way you used to love anything a bit freaky remember that. if i could work the brackets on this thing with only one hand i'd throw them up either end of this sentence and say look who's talking will you just look ha ha. i get so bored sitting here even with perth across the stretch of water there so shining and all it makes you think of oz at the end of the movie it makes you think there has to be something wrong with it, it couldn't be that lovely. the girls are off at the club and there's this other bloke standing in for me until i have the plaster off. that's in a couple of days time and in any case the show might be closed up by then, there's been letters to the papers and wowsers snooping round as it is. if only roxy had thought of it before she said i've carried this bloody portable round with me for years god knows why i don't remember when i even opened the thing. she gives her roxy laugh. thought once she says i'd do a typing course the minute i got out of the cross there but you know what those plans come to don't we all. roxy's a bit like looking across the city on mornings like this. you'd have really gone for her alec. you'd have made that little duck's arse out of your mouth and sucked your breath in and said just put my name down for a slice when that one's handed round. so i started tapping out with two fingers of my left hand because the tv is shot since mitch put his foot through it and who the hell's going to explain that to the hire people i thought i'd write alec it might be years till i get round to it another time. like it seems years ago doesn't it since those long warm evenings in the green kitchen you said just looking at it made you want to chuck, the fridge placed so you only had to lean your chair back on two legs to drag the stubbies out. we had to sit inside in summer even because if there was only one mozzie in the state he'd sniff you out the minute you opened the wire door. i'd been thinking about those times anyway before i decided to write. remember when i told you very early on about the one thing at the factory i used to look forward to. jesus the dirt used to pile up on me there. i remember i told you that and the other things the awful stink all that time from the sulphur vats. even now i can't stand the look of anything yellow not even a yellow car or a yellow tablecloth that's enough to bring back the smell, a corridor of pus at the back of my throat. and the racket of the place. by knockoff time i'd be aching with just the din of the presses and the belts slapping across above the machines. i told you all that otherwise i'd never have mentioned what i looked forward to that one afternoon a fortnight when the machines shut down at two o'clock and the sports teams from the different sections took off to the oval. at first i thought they might drag me along as a lucky charm a mascot you know how but luckily that didn't occur to anyone. no one gave a stuff much what i did. they'd yell and shove at each other in the locker room and call out to me to watch my step there samson who did i think i was leaning on. then once it was quiet i'd go out the sidedoor from one of the storerooms and there it was. yards of this deep grass and the sound of the creek. the light that was kind of dusty and red between the tall brick walls but this bloody grass alec you'd think it was painted. it was a real creek between the workshops water for some reason that hadn't been mucked up. it wouldn't have been more than a foot deep and these small ferns on the edge and moss that was plushy you know when you pushed at it. it was clear that way aquariums are in posh hotels and i'd put my hands in the water so they'd look green and different and these tiny bubbles along the hairs on my arms. and you'll say i'm boring the arse off you going on about it. you used to tell me that often enough, eh alec. if i told you what i'd read in the papers say or especially if i ever mentioned things made me think of grafton, for the love of god do you have to be so boring. probably, i'd say. and then you would laugh. you'd take the plate i gave you and not say a word until there was the sound of your knife scraping round the edges so you wouldn't lose a scrap. you'd say sometimes one thing you can do's make bloody great tucker. you'd let your belt out and raise one leg and call out duck this one, soldier, and i'd roll over making out you'd bowled me. jesus it was fun those days alec. sometimes i'd hardly be able to get up for laughing. you'd put your foot on me and pretend you were holding me down till you had another one ready to let go. you used to say yourself what fun we had. you didn't give what you called a tinker's root either for who saw us walking to the bus together, what anyone thought about anything if it came to that. you did it all so natural. and you'd have understood mitch's offer too if you'd been round, just don't give a bugger about what they think, isn't that right. well you'd love it now alec if only you'd stayed round. you'd love every minute of it.

behind everyone we call 'you' that's really special there's another you, know what i'm getting at. it makes me think of those trick ads on tv sometimes there's a man say advertising some health food let's say he's bouncing up and down, raising his arms, making you think how fit he is. then suddenly his edges blur so where there were two arms there are now four, he sort of unpacks himself one behind the other so you feel there is a line of people where at first you thought there was only one. the one in front of you at the time seems the only one, the only real mate, but there was always someone else who mattered that much too at a different time i'd love to explain it to you alec just to hear you say mother of j.c. esquire what's the wank of the day but grafton would have understood like a shot. grafton'd know alright.

some mornings i come out on the verandah and see the stretch of the river just across the street. it makes me think of some shimmery material pulled very tight and i can hardly believe i'm over here in a place like this, as if the factory and all that was just a story someone told me about someone else. when i was a kid practically grafton i heard you say you'd give anything to be able to paint or something so you could make things last and i remember i thought what on earth's he talking about, why's he want to do that. but i think that too these mornings. i think this is perth where i never expected to be and there is something i can do and i'm paid more to do it than i'd ever get from anything else. i know the names for things that i'd never heard of a month ago. roxy has shown me geraldton wax for instance and coral trees and i know my way about hay street and sometimes when i'm with her we eat pastry that's shiny as glass in a place where the waitresses dress as mountain girls and the building is like a swiss house on a calendar. you told me grafton about the spanish girl you had lived with when we were at home by ourselves until you'd get up and walk to the window and jingle the coins about in your pockets and say tempers fuckit, that's latin, old man. and when my aunt came into the room you always stood up. you were the only man she ever brought home to stay because it didn't worry you that i was there. first time you came in you saw me sitting on the sofa in that dark old sitting room and you said now if she'd told me you were here i could have brought you some toys. i remember my aunt covering her face with her hands and you realised you'd made some kind of mistake. but he's sixteen she called out. she was crying for herself though because she had had to look after me from the time i was a kid. she had said to me only a year before wouldn't i be happier if i joined some place where there were others the same. she said there were lovely clubs and social functions and i'd really love it. but this day anyway grafton you put your arms round her and patted her head against your shoulder and winked across at where i still sat staring at you both. you were letting on we understood each other, what was a bit of a mistake about mentioning toys after all. because i laughed out loud then, didn't i. i beat my shoes against the leg of the chair and my aunt thought i was going to have a fit or something. we'll get on famously, that was the next thing you said. in the posh voice i know she liked you for as much as the name she never knew could be a person's first name. after you left the next morning she was all over me. she kissed me and rubbed my hair because she was so happy. i think about that when i go into the dressing room and the girls start pawing me about. you'd be amused by that grafton as alec would. he'd have flapped that wonky arm of his and done his rooster call but you'd just lean back with your hands in your pockets and say play it again, sam. you always came out with that when you heard something you liked. all that female flesh eh grafton. those blessed sets of pliables, that's what you called them, reaching up as my aunt passed behind your chair and she would look quickly over at me and then at you, as though you shouldn't speak like that when i was there. but i'd kick this drum-roll on my chair legs and we'd all break out laughing. the jokes you could have had with this lot. and i'm thinking now as well grafton about that time it snowed. it was freezing because the oil heater had packed up and all we had were these measly pinecones to try and catch a bit of warmth from in the grate. my aunt said why are we living in a dump like this anyway, she was never out of the sight of beaches until she was in her twenties and look at her now. you had your arm around her and pulled the blanket up across her shoulders and told her there were people in spain who had never so much as seen the ocean in their lives. and my aunt was laughing and crying together and said well she had never seen a bullfight if it came to that but what did that have to do with it. when my aunt became upset like that her hair fell in wisps about her face and above where her fist held the blanket against her throat was this lovely light pink colour. but this night, you can't have forgotten that. i was the first to see it. i drew the blind back from the window and there was this quick ticking sound where the big flakes hit against the glass. look. i ran across to the sofa and put my hand to my aunt's cheek to turn her to the window. look at this. you opened the door onto the verandah and she ran to stand behind you. she said in this quiet voice as if she were almost afraid or something, but this never happens here. she put her arm around you and her thumb hooked over your belt. then you let out this whoop grafton that startled us both. you grabbed me up and swung me in this arc so that my legs were flying in the snowing before you had left the top step. and you ran down the steps and carried me with you into the yard. i looked up at the spinning ropes of snow that fell in my opened mouth. it sprinkled so quickly over our shoulders. and you held me up there above you, shaking me at the sky. esta niviendo you were shouting out, esta niviendo. then my aunt was there beside us when you put me down and i pranced my feet up and down on the pure ground. we were all shouting to each other and i was stinging with the cold. grafton she called out grafton no as you put your hands at the top of her legs and hoisted her up. her arms were round your neck and her skirt rode right up so that through the black and white flicker of the night i could see the length of her naked legs her thighs as they gripped round you and you tried to run through the spinning flakes. then the excitement had suddenly gone from it as though a light had been switched off. i went inside and waited shivering until you came in. then we all had glasses of brandy until our fingers pulsed thick with the hurting warmth and the steam rose from our shoulders. i hold the brandy in my mouth when roxy lets me drink from her glass. we make a sort of game of it. she looks towards the door making out she's terrified someone's coming in on us if monique or simone happens to almost see us she'll toss a towel or one of her underthings across the glass and say that was a close one, perfect. mind you mitch would really throw a big one if he ever caught us. he thinks if i drink it will bugger up my flight. but he doesn't like it either that roxy's even my friend. neither of you, not you alec nor grafton either, would think that mitch was worth a pinch of shit. he's supposed to be roxy's bloke but you ought to hear how he talks to her. or to the others too, the crude talk i mean in front of her. he says he pays them more than grinders have any right to expect so the door's always open, they can piss off the second it comes into their heads. he has an eagle would you believe it tattooed across one of his shoulders and a little star on his cheek, just on the side of his eye. he wears belts with big cowboy buckles and before we go on he puts a folded teatowel down the front of his leather pants so it looks bunchy as a fist. that's the real star he grins at roxy. you said as we drove down to town once grafton when your eye was playing up and you needed to have the socket looked at, most people you said are god awful shysters know that old mate. i said i didn't know.

you have to know both of you what it's like when someone suddenly walks out. the person left thinks there's been some kind of mistake for a while, as if it's not really yourself who is feeling all this but someone else who has taken your place. then it comes home that it's going to last. just leaving that note for my auntie when it seemed the three of us were set together, that wasn't on. or just telephoning from the station alec saying there was this job in the north you weren't in a position to say no. but what about your crook hand i said. it was the only thing i could think of to say. i could imagine you see at the table in the kitchen stroking the shiny skin where the accident was. with anyone else you always made sure it was out of sight. sometimes you put a glove over it when we were out. but at home you'd stroke it the way they stroke a cat or something or even someone's forehead when they're sick. jesus you'd have hated it if i said that though eh. you'd have worked up a real snorter for that one or one of those great belches when you'd pull the front of your shirt out and look down at your gut and say who fucken invited you then. but on the phone when i said that about your hand there was this gap when i knew i'd made a blue. then you gave this half grunt this half laugh, you said there's worse things than a crook arm you dopey little bugger.

so i'm bloody careful about whatever i let on to you then aren't i mitch. one thing mind apart from work you couldn't care what i think about anything. when i met those guys at the morley pub the night we went to watch their turn one of them said you were the best thrower there is. he'd seen them at the manhattan in brisbane and the venue at st kilda so he must have known. the little abo bloke said he knew people who worked with you and they all said, he's ace. holy shit one of the others said there's throwers out there smoke dope so they don't give a shit if you go into the crowd. the abo just hung on this bloke's every word. doc's done all sorts of work haven't you doc, he said, he's done the big shows, ice, the lot. but it was then you and your mates came over mitch and there was talk then about which clubs were the ones to work and how the pigs were supposed to be going to close us down for good. the abo's thrower said there's more fucken do-gooders in this state than there are fucken people. then you told them mitch how we'd never had anything except full houses, chocker, there was a demand out there the public had a right to so let the fascists rot. i could see that vein in your forehead going bump bump. then this other bloke chimes in you've got the girls as well mate you can't go wrong. that's when you squeezed my shoulder, sort of building me up in front of them all. look you told them they can see a bit of snatch at home if that's what they're after, we're the ones they come to see that right. that's right mitch, i said. but tell you what though you said looking round all of us, the girls are what bring the women in. go on, the abo said. and you told them what roxy had already told me anyway, that the women got as big a kick out of a decent strip as the blokes did. and while you were talking i thought god knows how you've hung on to roxy, even simone and monique look trashy next to her. she walks into a place even with all her clothes on and she knocks them out. you see it's grace she'd got not just what you call the goods, mitch. you'd think i was out of my tree if i told you that, you'd think i was a sniffing little bastard like that mate you had over surfers. it was different girls over there but you just got sick you said of the way he could do what he liked with them, took their bras off in the dressing room, remember you told me that, sprayed under their arms for them. you walked in once and caught him making out one of those private things of theirs was a joint, he'd even lit up and these slags were killing themselves. you said who did he think he was woody allen and kicked his arse round the room. that was before throwing ever came in, he just strutted about between strips and cracked a few jokes so you could get rid of him just like that. it made you fucken mad to see those little mitts crawling between the girls legs and they either didn't mind or even enjoyed it, the bitches. lose respect for those you work with the show can only go down hill. you were the one told me that, same morning soon after i started and you said roxy was your bird, you'd hand out more than a warning to anyone fancied he could do alright for himself there. i mentioned this to roxy later she said he's even jealous of blind people the dozy prick. that was after i'd got to know her and i'd sit reading the paper to her in the dressing room and the girls changing their gear all round me, simone sometimes pretending to smother me to death with her jugs until i'd have to shove her away to get my breath back. you came in just as roxy was leaning over me that night you mucked up the throw. i knew by the look of you something would go wrong trouble is you're thick as pigshit that's your trouble mitch. all the teatowels you can shove down the front of your jeans won't make up for that.

the girls rent this house not far from the river. what's the point of a fucken house though when we'll be moving all round the state, mitch couldn't get the point of it. look you said unless the cops make us close shop we'll work a dozen places from bunbury to geraldton, they're crying out for us. see that photo of bloody schwartznegger here in the paper last week—had to turn them away didn't we rest of the morley run. the photo showed me in mid-air my arms spread out my helmet making me look like an astronaut. underneath it said how i'd told them it was great people like myself were given a chance to make a living. i said i certainly didn't think it was demeaning, it was a skill there was a market for and it was a great way to make new friends. you'd wised me up mind about what things i'd better say. the crash helmet's light blue and matches the jump suit roxy made out of blue satin with a red triangle on the chest. the crowd love the joke as soon as i walk in, lois lane still drop her daks does she, they're shouting out things like that. that abo boy i talked to a while back said he was always having to find some new slant just to keep them off the snow white jokes, he got so fed up with a little black goes a long way sort of thing. but it's pretty good when we first go in like that isn't it mitch. i'm leading you by a chain that goes with the leather gear you're wearing and the spiked collar, your arms bare and the eagle bulging there at the top of the arm your hair sleeked down so it shines. i know you get a high out of the roar and the whistling when it looks for a moment like the freak is leading the stud. then you hold your arms up with the black leather strips round your wrists and explain how the throwing's done and although there is no chance of anyone getting hurt you say you'd appreciate utter quiet during the performance. some shows you hear of let the audience have a go but you won't wear that. it cheapens the whole thing, you say, it's just pissheads wanting to act big to haul in pussy. so when it's quiet and simone's got the drum roll going in the corner you lean down and straighten my scarf and there's that smell that tells how you're excited. it's the crowd and the noise and the smoky light when the spot's on and you're at the centre in your black gear, your face dead white. but your hands underneath my arms when you pick me up then let me sort of float there while you grip the harness must be the steadiest thing i've felt in my life. see that's the puzzle about you mitch, steady like that and mad as a snake. on the bus across when you flew on ahead i sat next to roxy all the way. that's how i know so much about you. she said she'd been with you now a couple of years. she wasn't interested in working the parlours the way monique would go back to because it screwed you in the head. or some heavy got hold of you and you tasted a bit and next thing you couldn't knock it off, they owned you once that happened. she didn't know much else she said except taking her clothes off that was the trouble, grinding her bum so the wankeroos had themselves a free fat. what's a wankeroo i asked her. every second bugger in australia, she laughed, you won't have a problem finding one if that's what you're into collecting but mostly on the trip over she'd look out at the scrub, at the red distance not changing for hours. sometimes she says to me and she's only half joking why don't we just cut loose from all this shit. when she's had a blue with mitch after one of the shows say and we sit on the verandah and look at the city reflected in the river like something massive's been killed and all this bleeding across the water. or when we're on this swinging seat thing in the mornings and one of those long green parrots with the little yellow ring round its neck slices down between the trees. just leave all that shit imagine it roxy says and settle for something like this. i think of my aunt saying one of these days it won't be like this grafton we'll be out of this dump and up the coast there where the big lights are. or you alec. it's got to come, you were always saying that, the sleeping giants, going to wake up one of these days and the bosses won't know what's knocked them. could you leave the rooster though, i say to roxy. that's all monique and simone ever call you, mitch. the fucken rooster. christ roxy says, could i what. she looks up from her knitting and she's laughing at the thought of it. come here she says, turn round. she holds the half made cardigan against my back to make sure she's measured right. and funny thing her hands against my back make me think of your hands mitch as you raise me up and i brush against the leather singlet as you begin the to and fro of the swing to build up pace. i reckon when you let me go beneath all that husky sweat and your rippling tattooed eagle you still wish you were the one with the light flaring past in this wobbly streamer and the lovely bit, never mind it's only a second or so, the bit when arms out and all i'm flying. then the racket starts up again and i thud on the foam mattresses and they're shouting out fucken beauty and terrific and did you see him go the little cunt. a few throws like that then back in the dressing room that's really just a storeroom in some places or an outside bathroom even but everything for a few minutes anyway is shiny satin like i'm wearing and roxy unbuckles my helmet and pushes her fingers through my hair. you light up mitch and you like making your eyes go narrow through the smoke and you say as the girls go out for the final number and the disco's like a hand thumping against the wall, don't give it away out there ladies there's mitch back here loves ya all. and one of the girls will ask the others as they scramble past did his mum dress him like that for spite or does he just like looking like a dork. when they go out on the floor there'll be whistling and stamping and they'll turn green and purple and yellow in the lights and the bits they take off sparkle and reflect over the walls. alright muzza are you, you nearly always say that mitch when we're suddenly left there, just the two of us. and i nearly always raise my thumb like i'm in a plane and signalling through the windscreen. i'm beaut, mitch, i'm saying. fucken beaut.

Testing, Testing . . .

Surely it is not only because of the authors they had read, nor the records they played together, that they realised, each of them quite separately, that there *was* an essence to life, however fine-beaten by everyday pressures it might be? A filament, a thread of pure value that existed and would continue to exist amid dross and distraction and infidelities, a pendulum that carried them across whatever gulfs there might happen to be?

Susan was the woman, and Max the man. They would look across crowded rooms towards the other, and know the filament was truly there. They told each other with utter frankness about the past. Max had tinkered with religion, for example, and had taken Francis as his Confirmation name. He had once had a sexual relationship with a man in a sauna in Wakefield Street. His father for years had served as a military policeman. He had never told another woman any of these things.

Susan was quite as frank. There had almost been a child, she said, when she was eighteen. The father was an accountant of almost forty, a friend of her own father's from Rotary. There was not another living soul who knew that. She had once stolen money enough from an office she worked in to fly to Sydney for a week. She had written poems when she was younger, and sent them to a paper under a Polynesian name to make sure they were published.

Those are not easy things to tell each other, they knew that. Max remembered how at school if you dipped something in liquid oxygen it became solid as stone. It might still look like a breadcrumb, say, or a slice of cucumber, but it was unbreakable. What they confided now between them became a stone of great worth.

Marriage, they were certain, would make no difference to that. They meant not to their frankness, nor to their great sense of respect, because each believed in those so completely. They wrote their own service, which included a paragraph of Frank Sargeson and a poem by John Donne. They wore bright casual clothes, and their word to each other was pledged in a friend's backyard, beneath a magnolia tree whose blooms as the evening deepened appeared both so solid and yet so hovering that without saying a word, Max and Susan knew a symbol had been dipped for them into—well, into an element that would last.

A month or two after they were married, Max said one evening to Susan, as he sat with his arm along the divan behind her, 'You know the most unexpected thing happened today.'

'Yes?' Susan said. Her head was on his shoulder.

'That new woman,' Max said, 'I mentioned in the office?'

'The one with the jugs?' They both laughed at their being able to say a thing like that.

'Well she was standing next to me just fiddling this bangle up and down her arm and out of the blue I had this incredible hard-on.'

'You never!' Susan's tone was a teacher's with a boy who was showing off.

'I did so!' Max said. 'I certainly did so!'

A month or so after that, in the middle of a meal in fact to celebrate their first quarterly commitment, Susan bit her lower lip, tilted her head, and raised her eyes wide towards her husband. 'Out with it!' Max demanded. 'I know my wife well enough to understand that look.'

'I'm afraid I've done it again,' she said.

'Tell me,' he ordered. That peremptory tone was one of the jokes between them too. It was one of the filaments.

'Well,' she began. Then waited.

'Well?'

'You know I told you once about that money? That naughty little thing I did once?'

'Susan,' Max said, 'the fact that you tell me is the most important thing.'

'I won't necessarily keep on doing it,' Susan said.

'Not if you don't want to, sweet.'

'But a thing like that is an expression of oneself, isn't it? As long as it's not a habit that takes you over.'

'Like the—you know,' Max provoked her.

'Better not be!' Susan warned. They were slapping each other's wrists when the waiter came in. 'Sorry!' they both called at once. 'It's her/his fault!'

Back in the kitchen, edging slices of avocado from a knife with his forefinger, the waiter said, 'We've got a right lot out there tonight.'

'Just keep them off the carpet,' the manager said. 'That's what upsets the other diners.'

There was soon the realisation between them that the most intimate of confidences takes a richer *frisson* from the possibility that it may really be a lie. Between themselves, their arms about each other and their tongues flicking at each other's ears and cheeks and throats, Susan and Max would play what they called Girl Guide roulette. This meant that one out of every three or four confessions definitely was not true.

For example, Susan said, 'I know Max you want to know everything about me so there was this girl whose breasts I liked touching when I was fourteen. There was this Dutch neighbour who looked at me across the back fence while I sunbathed and I'd oil myself all over as lasciviously as I could. There was once a guard on an empty train who asked me to hold it for him. There was a boy in a bathing shed whose eye I saw at a knot-hole in the wall and so I slapped myself against the wall, square in his eye.'

Max said, 'The Dutchman isn't true,' and so he won the game. Because they always owned up when the one lie had been hit on. But their roulette hadn't always to do with the erotic. He said one night after a party when they had felt close for the whole evening, 'I once asked a neighbour's little boy to put his finger on a spark plug for me when I started the motor mower. I took money from a jar in an old lady's kitchen when she was filling a form for a Lions' Christmas hamper. I loosened the wheel on an asthmatic neighbour's shopping trolley.'

'The shopping trolley,' Susan said.

'You're getting too good at this,' Max told her.

'I am, aren't I?' To expose the lie carried with it the reward of a completely free hand. That night Susan tied up her playmate with a black extension cord. It was the first time anything quite like *that* had occurred. Soon afterwards, each of them agreed they would play their game only a few times a year, or the shine would tend to wear off.

Then one evening after her parents had been staying with them for a week, and she and Max were quite honestly going spare with her father's socialist rant and her mother taking up the living-room with her quilt making, Susan said, 'The manager, darling. I'm afraid. So there'll be no trouble about that few hundred that simply jumped up, remember, into my hand?'

'The Gold Coast's on,' Max said. 'Last time I was up in head office I tapped in the info for the air tickets. No one noticed a thing.'

So Susan told him then how she had quite talked round one of the secretaries who was holding out on the other senior partner. It was amazing how a discreet phone-call could produce a cheque by return post.

No more amazing, Max pointed out, than promoting a seance where widows will do but anything for a word from beyond.

'*Evil!*' Susan shrieked. They knew then there was something with more of a buzz to it (Max smiling when he used that downmarket phrase, Susan licking her finger slowly then sliding it into his mouth) than their usual roulette. The lie and the truth now flowed into each other, so that each walked transfused.

They sometimes sat naked on opposite sides of the room, saying disturbing things. To say them with distance could be even more titillating than lying side by side. 'It's better if you tell me while doing such and such,' one of them might call across. Once Susan's hamstring was damaged at the angle Max had suggested. But then for months and months they might act very much as the proverbial couple next door.

And they never doubted the essence, for a moment. The grosser their admissions, in fact, the rarer—*à la* John Donne—was that gold between them beaten to airy fineness. Susan now had the closest rapport with the bank manager, a couple of city council night-workers, and a man she suspected was a clergyman. She gave Max the money they sometimes insisted on giving her and he enjoyed putting it on race meetings where it usually was lost. Telling each other the truth was still the most important thing they shared. And one of them might say, after months of straightest domesticity, 'Time for a picnic, isn't it, my love?' That was their code for breaking out.

One morning, remarkably, they told each other a dream at breakfast, and their dreams were almost identical. 'I was in a tree last night,' Max began, 'I was on this rope like Tarzan in those old movies and I swung across a river full of piranha and grabbed you from another tree.'

'It was actually a platform,' Susan said. 'I was imprisoned on this high platform and you flashed down in your spotted little loin-cloth and whisked me away. I woke up with this sense of such utter achievement.'

'I could have sworn it was a tree,' Max said.

'It was surrounded by trees. It would have looked like that from where you were.'

'I couldn't swear they were piranha,' he admitted. 'I think I might just have added that in.'

'They were crocodiles,' Susan said. 'Their backs were ridged like rusk biscuits and you'd hardly tell them from logs.' Then she asked Max, 'Would you actually do that for me?'

'If it was dangerous enough,' Max said, 'of course I would, Susan.'

From then on it was inevitable that the thread be tested with a final weight. As if preparing themselves for something greater, for six months they did not even play Girl Guide roulette. But on Max's birthday Susan gave her husband a black carry bag, whose contents he quite knew before touching the zip to open it. And so on her birthday too—which was only a fortnight later, Librans that they were—a small parcel arrived from the postal lingerie service they often had ordered through before, and a sheath-knife to wear with her tiny jungle-green garment, held by a simple cord around the waist.

The zoo was easier to gain access to than you might think. They had walked there for several weekends getting the lie of the land, and grew familiar with its avenues and enclosures and open space. They chatted to employees and became knowledgeable on feeding habits, routines, hours of sleep and silence. They began to sense the teeming world within its borders of high stone and knotted wire, an island of watchfulness and impulse set down among tracts of suburban ordinariness. They talked late at night about its beautiful savagery. Most people simply drove past its edges, heard the odd baying or trumpeting from inside the fence; thought they should really take the kids there more often.

As Susan moved against Max the leaves they had taken to putting under the sheets clicked and stirred against her. It seethed behind those walls, that's what Max had said, hundreds of eyes that could bide their time with a patience we'll never understand. Unlike the swaddled bipeds who gaped there behind bars and spikes and railings, the tiger and the ocelot, the gibbon and the wolf, know nothing of panic as time ticks away. Max and Susan these days often spoke like that.

Max took from his birthday bag the rope with one weighted end, and threw it across the branch they had chosen the last Sunday they were here. They shivered, naturally enough, against the cold air on their skin. Susan took her stand on the platform of the tree hut on the other side of the pit. They could hear the creek that ran between them, the low calls and shufflings and exhalations on every side. They were both pretty sure that what they planned would work. But there was, say, one chance in three that it would not.

Rather bored, a sprawled lion opened one eye and saw the blur across the sky.

Terminus

There is a woman downstairs with a mask over her face. I said that to my wife when she came in from work. I said there was this woman with a black mask across her eyes, who leaned back against the wall as I walked by her into the hallway to the stairs. I said, 'There's this woman. She must be waiting there for someone.'

My wife works on the trams. She is tall and jolly and when we are in bed she makes me think of a good-natured conductor on the trams jangling her sack of coins.

When I told her about the woman with the mask she had just boiled a saucepan of water to pour onto teabags in large red mugs. She was using the saucepan because the electric jug is being repaired. When she tilted the saucepan the boiling water ran up the side of the metal, hissing and spitting out. She had no idea of what she handled, of how the rising urgent water against the tilted metal made me want to stand back, on the other side of the room.

The woman with the opera mask has been there for several days. She doesn't say a word. Her eyes that are moist and shining in the slits of the mask don't seem to move as I pass her. I look across at her but the eyes behind the mask don't ever move. But because they are moist and glittering they seem always to watch. I mention her again to my wife, who says, 'Worry about every loony in this area there'd be time for nothing else.' She is trying to say perhaps, 'Try to look at things as they look to me.' Forget that holiday in Sydney when we bought the black and white porcelain faces on their slender white sticks in a shop that was called Venezia. Forget that masking is natural and even beautiful and set the way we want things to be against the fact of how they are. When I tell her there is the woman downstairs she pours the water like that, the hot needles leaping up from the side of the pot.

There is a woman too who masks her foot. I have seen her in the neighbourhood for years, a yellow-skinned elderly woman who walked slowly because of her foot. But I had never actually looked at her feet until the day she sat with me on the same tram. She wore an old-fashioned leather coat with panels that flared it out. One foot wore an ordinary shoe but the other was built up. It was wrapped round in this kind of leather cage, a mass of straps and buckles and overlacing threads. I looked at it for some minutes, disturbed by its shape. At first I could not understand what it was that irritated me. And then it was so clear. I realised there was no conceivable injury, no possible affliction, that could *need* a boot of that kind. There was something so pointlessly complex about the thing I looked at, I looked too at the woman's face and she was watching me, very calmly. She was watching me in that way which is not concern or interest of any kind but because I was seated opposite her and she had to look at something. But she must have seen the expression of distaste on my face, for I knew I could not possibly be concealing it. She must have known that while I would sympathise with any disability she might have, I also hated her deceit, her theatrical flourish of overlay and glitter and strapping, her indecent trussing of herself. Her foot was pornographic. It was meant to excite in a way no decent woman would want, she was like an amputee with the tawdry glitter of sequins across her private parts. All this I felt instantly, from the second I realised her fraud.

The conductress that day was a friend of my wife's. She spoke about the stifling weather and I answered politely enough. But she must have found my manner with her rather brusque. Because she soon went and stood at the far end of the next compartment with her back against the panel on whose other side the driver would have been looking along the dreary old road of closed shops and small warehouses and a few figures walking past. My wife's friend had both her hands, which were sheathed in mittens, sunk in the leather pouch she carried in front of her. The pouch was supported by a strap around her neck. She moved her hands and the coins shifted beneath her fingers, an unpleasant scrabble that made me think of claws against a tin wall.

The crippled woman kept looking at me. She leaned forward as naturally as any woman would do, say, to scratch her ankle, only this old liar, this fraudulent bitch, tugged at one of the buckles on her foot. She *picked* at it, like a scab. It lifted away from the worn stitching that held it to the leather and she turned it for a moment in her hand, letting it lie in her palm while the little finger of her other hand prodded at it, pushed it softly with a fingernail. She was fascinated as though only minutes before the thing had been part of her own living flesh. I wanted to grab her hand and press it hard around the metal until its shape cut into her. But she turned sideways, catching her reflection as she pulled at the cord to stop the tram. She then edged towards the door. Her foot dragged with her, a parcel of straps and brass studs.

My wife said to me, 'Dulcie said you were pissed the other night on the tram?'

'Dulcie?'

'The one with mittens. Her hands are that bad with rheumatism and she isn't forty yet.'

'I know who Dulcie is,' I said. 'Of course I know who Dulcie is.'

'She said she tried to talk to you and you hardly answered.'

I said, 'The bitch stood with her fingers hidden inside her bag. She sounded like a rat behind a wall.'

'God,' my wife said, 'tone it down, can't you?' My wife's nipples make me think of eyes. In the morning she raises her nightdress and stands with their naked stare towards me before she conceals them in her brassiere, hiding them away, preventing their hard gaze that I turn from rather than let on that I see. I wonder why all this had not occurred to me before, this constant play of deception that even she is good at. There is no deliberate evil in my wife, I quite know that. But I shall have to watch her more carefully. Her breasts with the dark eyes at their centres warn me in spite of her. I shall watch her if only to help herself.

The tram I take back from work passes down that long street which at one end has tall old-fashioned villas which once must have housed the rich of the city. These days they are places of obscure charities behind their iron railings, their dry cracked fountains. There are often drunks and derelicts sitting on the front lawns. Derelicts and blacks. Then further down the street has all those restaurants, Italian and Spanish, all of them foreign, even the expensive ones. People walk towards them calling out across the footpaths, carrying bottles of wine in brown paper bags. They all dress the same, in casual bright clothes, in jeans and dirty white track shoes. Then beyond this part of the street there are shops that sell old furniture and faded books, junk shops that the people who eat in the restaurants exclaim at and pull each other back to look at carved chairs, ancient dolls, hats from the different wars. Some of the shops are now boarded up. And at the terminus, right along, there is a chemist shop whose Indian owners never close. Opposite it on one corner there is a service station lit up brightly as a stage. From there the street becomes trees and small houses. After dark it is a trail of orange street lights that go on and on, for miles. There are patches of scabby grass, sections where buildings have been demolished but the rubble not cleared away. It is there you will always see cats, and groups of young people handing around their cigarettes, and people you would cross the road rather than have to speak to.

Someone once told me that the Indian brothers in the chemist shop are also undertakers, although I tend to think that can't be true. I have stood over the road from their shop so many times, my back against a doorway that a couple of years ago was the premises for a vet. There are still advertisements for different things in the window, and a small wire wheel of the kind you see mice running in, and some of those rubbery bones people give their dogs to play with. I have stood there and never seen a sign of the Indians having another trade. There are evenings when the two brothers sit on cane stools in the doorway, sit there for hours and scarcely exchange words. I have waited for the big double gates at the side of the shop to be opened and a long black car to drive out, to see its polished sides reflect the street lights in long orange smears. My wife has never heard of it either, and on the trams they pick up most things. She knows number 470 is a brothel, although no one else has ever told me that. She has heard that the old man above the shop next to where I stand at the terminus is really a priest who was kicked out of his church. So she would have heard, surely. 'It beats me,' she says, 'where you get these stories in the first place.' When the eyes of her breasts are put away we get on as well as any married couple. She does not get angry when she thinks I am exaggerating about her friend's hands in their conductor's bag or the old slut with the deceiving foot. And I hold the newspaper motionless so she does not know how much it irritates me that she has still not collected the electric jug from the electrician's right beside her depot, and that for weeks now she has tilted the boiling water from the saucepan so that it leaps and splutters from the side. It is sometimes only inches from where I sit.

Last night one of the Indians spoke to me from his cane stool outside the chemist shop. When I stand at the corner with my back against the vet's door I think that because my wife is on late shift it will not matter to her where I am, but now that the Indian has spoken to me of course I shall have to find somewhere else, although clearly the terminus is the obvious place. The number 11 pulls in here every twenty-five minutes. In general conversation with my wife, I find out which run Dulcie is on and so avoid the times when she will be on this route. But I know for certain that bucklefoot travels to here, to the very end of the line. I have heard her ask the conductor time and again, 'Right to the terminus,' she says. (Why I wonder did she get off earlier, that day of the scab?) Always she folds her ticket over and over until it is a sliver, and slips it beneath her watch-strap. It would open out again like a very small fan, a thing to hold up and lie behind, even that tiny size.

For the first time I have struck my wife. After all these years! While she lies in the dark bedroom and I can hear her sobbing through the walls, I work out on an envelope that allowing for the time we spent together before we were married, and all that time since, we have been been together for more than six thousand days. Allowing even twelve hours a day when we are not together—and that is too high a figure surely, if one considers weekends when we are always at home—it means at least seventy-two thousand hours we have been with each other, year in, year out. Perhaps half of that time in the same bed. And for less than ten seconds I have forgotten myself enough to act out of character, and to strike her twice across the face. That is less than one two-hundred-and-fifty-millionth of the time we have lived with each other. I have worked it out as exactly that. But I shall not try to explain that until the morning. I shall do a graph of it as well so it shows as an infinitesimal bead on the wire of our lives. I shall tell her it is like something the size of a fly between here and the other side of the earth. And I shall also say that she must know how the mask was getting on my nerves, she must see that? Understand the rage that was suddenly there in front of me, pulled down like a red blind in front of my eyes.

So why did I strike her? My dear wife who came in from a day's work carrying an avocado, which we both love, and a can of artichoke heart soup, and a french roll and 250 grams of unsalted butter. She was happy because from next week she had been put on to our own tram route. She had been requesting that for eighteen months. To celebrate with her I opened a bottle of Portuguese wine. I was opening it as my wife laughed and said to me, 'You know that woman you said you saw the other week?'

'Which woman's that?'

'The woman with the mask. You know, the opera one downstairs?'

My hand ceased turning the corkscrew. I could not believe what my wife was telling me. She was laughing and saying there were these schoolgirls with all kinds of get-ups. 'You know the things. Those long feathers round their necks and bright stockings and one of them with a blue mask across her eyes. It's a school thing they're rehearsing for.' She said that must have been the one who upset me.

I saw my wife's fingers easing the fat dark stone from the split avocado. I thought, for the first time in my life, why is she lying to me?

'The mask wasn't blue!' I shouted at her. 'The woman was as old as you are!' I could see from her shrug that she too was embarrassed now I had told her that. What was the point of her lying? I demanded why my own wife would defend a woman in a black mask, some rotten creature watching you enter your own home? 'Is that what working with Dulcie does for you?' I shouted. 'Cripples and whores and liars! Is that what it does for you?'

'Oh shut up!' she screamed back at me, without turning to look at me. She could suddenly have been any woman standing in our kitchen, her face turned from me and lying, having no right to be there, not honest enough to turn, to show the lie that stood there in my own wife's place. And that red blind, as it seemed, drew down closer over my eyes. I heard the bottle crash to the floor and my hand was falling twice across the woman's neck, and the double impact of her forehead against the cupboard door in front of her. 'Black!' I was shouting at her, 'the mask was fucking black!'

I am sorry I ruined our celebration and that what I hear, this minute, is my wife's grief on the other side of the wall. But there is only a little bruising, fortunately. There will be no mark on her face apart from this little bruising. And I shall have ready for her what I have copied from the back of the envelope onto a sheet of paper. She'll be able to see for herself the figures showing how infinitesimal in time my anger was. And the graph as well, the projection of a trajectory between the earth and the moon, and a speck which cannot be taken as more than the size of a fly's body. She will see how ridiculous it is to imagine that a perfectly harmonious arc through such colossal distance might be marred by a fly.

But I shall be watching, believe me. I shall be the husband I have always been but I shall watch the trams she is on and see if bucklefoot so much as tries to talk to her as the tram sways those last hundred yards towards the terminus and my wife goes as she always does to wind the canvas roll in its glass oblong that changes the destination, to say suddenly the terminus is not where they shall stop in only a few seconds time but the place they leave behind after the driver has drunk the tea from his thermos flask I'll see it if she does. If the cripple talks to her or if my wife answers. I shall see it all right.

Sometimes I wait against the door of what used to be the vet's but sometimes in between the trams arriving I walk along by the derelict houses and the sections of deserted rubble that don't look quite real, not under the orange lights. There are great blocks of shadow where the world disappears. Or I walk back the other way, past the shops that at night reflect back like a mirror as you go walking past. One of them is safe to go past because he says nothing, unlike the other one who asks things. The problem is to tell the difference before you are right up close, right there walking past them. But the point is I shall be there and I shall be ready. When the tram rackets past it looks like oil is on its sides when it rushes at night and the light slips streaky along the panels. But no matter how fast it goes past you can see if people are talking, and as it slows towards the terminus I will be able to catch up with it, or watch it approach me if I am in the vet's doorway, if I am standing there at night. I shall be ready when the time is right and the strapped and buckled and laced-up old slut limps off towards the trees and the shadows that in fact are purple under the orange lights, oh won't I just. And when my wife comes in late and tired and wants to hold her hands out towards the bar heater I shall have it switched on for her, and the tea warming under the cosy that is a black cat stitched from quilted squares, and the electric blanket on, all that will be ready too.

Hims Ancient and Modern

A thousand times if it was once she had said them to her friend, those two short, ordinary, so dominating words, said in so many ways. *Oh, him*, with so little left to it, so dull an inflection, a mere flopped pancake of a pronoun, meaning, so often, her husband Don. Or in tones of such utter dismissal, a dollop of ordure as it were scraped from a shoe, which was a lover discarded, a repellent colleague, a memory from years back, repeating on her like unpleasant food. Or occasionally, once a year or so at the most, the words of anticipation or desire, *oh, him*! Placing her hand lightly on her friend's sleeve, looking across the room, glancing over the tables in a restaurant, to see the figure of the moment, a man not so unlike all others, who stood bathed for that instant in sweet challenge and potential. Her friend never knew quite what to say.

Her friend was Alicia, and she was Ros. Friends from way back, Ros declared whenever they met a new set of acquaintances, my best friend for yonks. They had shared a room together in O'Rorke, remember that dreadful old warren of a hostel? Borrowing clothes from each other, window latches left on the loose to let the other in, when that great shambling warden imposed his curfews. That's how far back they went. Further, Alicia would say, we were friends at school as well. 'Oh, but life only begins at seventeen,' Ros said. 'We were the youngest in the hostel, remember that?'

Ros still looked very good. She was proud of Don, whatever the inflection she might put on *him*, and he was very proud of her. He had been head boy believe it or not the year she was head girl. At different schools, but good ones, both of them. They danced together at the seventh form ball. They married the summer after graduation. *The Great Gatsby* was the favourite book of both of them. And they loved each other enough to respect each other's privacy. 'Ros and I respect each other greatly,' Ron explained the one time he placed his hand on

Alicia's leg, and Alicia's fingers met round his wrist like a very firm bracelet and placed his hand back on his own thigh. 'As pure as the old proverbial,' he said, very good naturedly, very appropriately, for they were driving down from the mountain towards the lodge at Ohakune and high drifts of snow were banked on either side. Alicia's husband Frank and her friend Ros were in the long-bonneted Humber a hundred yards ahead of them, because Ros and Frank were such good mates and so enjoyed talking to each other. No one was jealous in the least. Ros said sometimes, her eyes widening with admirable frankness, that she simply couldn't understand how one could cope with possessiveness. 'It *wizens* you,' she said. 'It's so demeaning.' Don thank heavens wouldn't recognise it if it was sitting next to him on a bus.

In her even, quiet tone Alicia said, 'Frank says he could quite imagine himself killing for jealousy.' Hard-working predictable Frank, his hair already greying in that distinguished legal way, had quite amazed her when he came out with that. 'As if he'd ever need to!' Ros hooted. 'Honestly!'

'Italy!' they called, almost simultaneously. On the sundeck, on a June day of unusual warmth, the blue volcano riding across the satiny harbour as seductively, Ros said, as a Tourist Department poster. The Japs would be here in their millions if they could see it now. Then within twenty minutes a grim sky trundling in from the south, raindrops the size of ten-cent pieces splotching the wooden slats of the deck. From inside the lounge they watched the spears of rain march across the entire view, the colour drained from the blur of Rangitoto. It was cold enough to turn on the fire. The electric coals fluctuated with artificial shadows passing across the ruby patches of heat, when Frank said casually, 'That trip we've always talked about,' as if the rain and cold replacing sun and the smoothest of seas made him yearn of a sudden for quite a different world. The idea flared up between them as though it had waited for this very moment to ignite. 'Yes!' Ros said, her spread hand and its chunky silver rings slapping quickly on the broad arm of her chair, 'Oh yes, yes!' 'A break from all this anyway,' Don put in. 'How would that grab you, eh?' He grinned down at Alicia. No months and months of planning, just up and off as the spirit moved them. And because she felt so strongly the push of expectation, the sudden stretch toward new vistas, Alicia surprised herself by drumming both her own fists on her lap. 'Oh yes,' she said, 'let's just do it then, why don't we?' And without a thought between them of Hawaii or

Club Med or Lake Tahoe or the Ardennes, in one voice, really and truly, before the first had time to finish the word the others were saying it as well, 'Italy!' they called, almost simultaneously. Ros sat back laughing and Alicia smiled up at the men, who slapped each other's palms like black American sprinters on TV.

The next evening they sat with brochures and maps spread on the table between them. Ros had just phoned her niece. 'You wouldn't believe it would you? They're away that fortnight so the place is ours!' They each picked a city which they said was an absolute must. Frank said Assisi although no one but his aged aunts had called him Francis for years and Ros of course said Florence because that was where her niece was on a scholarship at the Villa Tatti and Don said ever since he was a boy he had thought about the dog frozen in ash in Pompeii. Alicia pushed about the pile of brochures in front of her, the coastlines and lakes and hills with cypresses and cities studded with domes. There was nowhere she wanted as specially as all the others did. Then a man with a dark stony face looked at her directly from a page she opened, and she caught her breath. Her hand smoothed across the page. 'Get a load of *him*!' Ros shrieked over her shoulder in mock schoolgirl shrillness. She pointed at the man in his long stiff toga although she had no idea in the world of who or where he was. They were all a little silly with excitement and Don's usual heavy hand with the drinks. 'Yes,' Alicia said, closing the brochure, opening it again, smiling in that vague way that sometimes drove Ros batty. 'I think it will have to be here all right. Is that OK?' She looked at her husband, at her friends. But there was nothing vague in the way she asked them that. It wasn't asking at all, in fact. It was telling them what they were going to do.

It was marvellous travelling together in those first few weeks—the sun, the warmth, the fun they had between them, something new at every turn of every street. Don saw his ash-embalmed dog and when no one was watching Frank crossed himself in the chapel at Assisi and Ros quite knew, at last, why the art buffs made so much of Giotto. And Alicia smiling and reading and, as Ros at least picked up, looking simply radiant.

There were days in Florence however when Ros was inclined to sulk. Her husband and Frank strolled out to the Agenzia Ippica where Don would try out his meagre Italian by placing trifectas at Palermo or Genoa, although after the one afternoon he went to the track at Florence he said you wouldn't believe they'd have the bloody gall to prop up what should be dog tucker and parade it around as horseflesh. They would stop on the way back for coffees and gallianos, a mix that seemed to amuse the waiter in their neighbourhood bar. The two men fortunately hit it off together, and at more or less the same time declared they were a bit sated with galleries, and might start giving them a miss. This, Ros noticed, coincided with their coming to terms with the local bars. Don said, sometimes several times a day, 'Should have done this years ago, know that? There's more to life than slaving to make a buck.' And Frank would tip his glass against his friend's and tell him, 'Right on, fratello.'

In her niece's minute apartment Ros closed her copy of *Look at Me, I'm Dancing*, the fifth volume of autobiography of a New Zealand author who, for all her success, had never lost her childhood values nor the bonding example of her working-class aunts. Ros wondered how her own life of travel, comfort, and tolerably civilised men could strike her at times as incomplete. She bit on the handkerchief wrapped round her knuckle and was glad when her friend came in and offered to make them both a mug of tea. Ros knew she was on the verge of melodrama, and she simply hated that. Even in herself.

The women carried their steaming mugs through to the late afternoon haze of the apartment's balcony. Across the jumble of tiled roofs and above the stacked angular blocks either side of the river, the bells of one of the churches boomed on and on. When the bells suddenly stopped there was the delicate thread of a piano, not too far off, tinkling through the haze.

'It couldn't be more perfect,' Ros said.

'No,' Alicia said. A swallow flicked up from below the eaves, circled the women, veered off behind a neighbour's wall.

'In one way,' Ros went on. Then she was silent, assuming that what she said demanded at least a query from her friend. But no, none came. She looked across at Alicia, considering as she had so often before how it was quite beyond her even now, after knowing her for half her lifetime, to guess in the least whether that pale, pretty, insipid face concealed the deepest ruminations or simply nothing at all. But Ros picked herself up, not wanting to be unkind. She is a good dear friend, she thought, only she's too solemn for God's sake, too reticent, even to know what letter fun begins with.

Alicia's eyes were closed, her head tilted back against the canvas of her chair. The sun gilded her face. It fired her lashes, her eyebrows, to a burnished copper. She was thinking of what she had read earlier that afternoon, preparing herself for their next town. She imagined those lines of perhaps forty virgins, facing across the nave the same number of young men, fresh in their white togas after fifteen hundred years. She saw the magical green hill with its allegorical flock. But the feeling she had was not connected with art, she quite knew that. She was angry too with a woman she had never heard of until recently, as much as she was moved for the man that woman failed to appreciate. She was also very calm, and very sure. She had felt rather like this, but less so, when she was pregnant with Jasmine. She thought, my face is like a mask beneath this deliciously soothing sun. Like a face in a mosaic. A mosaic in a holy place in the ancient city of Ravenna.

'He's following me,' Ros said. 'I'm quite certain of it now.'
She and Alicia had turned right from the straw market where Ros for luck had touched the brightly bronzed snout of the famous boar. Alicia had bought a leather handbag that the young vendor fetched with a pole from its peg high above his stall. They were walking back, almost at the Piazza della Grazia, when Ros made her announcement.
'Who is?' Alicia said.
'The one in brown there. Only don't let on.'
The women turned and the man twenty steps or so behind them also turned slightly towards a wall, his head tilted above the quick jump of a match flare between his cupping hands.
'If you're walking behind someone it's easy for the person in front to think you're following them,' Alicia said.
Ros clucked with irritation. 'I ought to know if I'm being followed, for God's sake!'
Alicia supposed it had to happen sooner or later in Italy. It was one of the bores of travel, didn't everyone say that? She wouldn't be sorry to leave this town of too many tourists. Marvellous and beautiful and reeking with history and all that, but a town without privacy. You couldn't look at a painting or a statue, you couldn't stand in a doorway to take in the blue and white enamel madonna with its string of green leaves and vivid lemons above a doorway across the street, without lots of other people seeing you looking. Alicia didn't care for that. She said so to Frank, and Frank laughed at her. 'Just you and Lorenzo de Medici,' he said. 'That'd be the perfect town, I suppose?' Then last night the two men had quarrelled about how best to get to the station. Everyone was getting tetchy. The glamour was wearing off, she

supposed. They were beginning to see things as they were, every day. She had said, 'Being tourists works so long as you remember it's only once in a lifetime.' Frank had turned to her then and snapped, 'Is that contributing something?' She never did say witty things, she quite knew that. Sometimes she said things too that quite missed the point. So she said apologetically, 'I was miles away, I'm sorry,' running her finger round and round the rim of her wine glass. Ros had then said sharply, 'Well we all are, actually. Tourists. This is Italy, after all.' Don raised his eyebrows at his wife and Alicia smiled at them both. She wished they would go back to the flat, where she could think quietly again about Ravenna. She thought of a huge round mausoleum whose roof was a single slab of stone that weighed 230 tons. It wasn't the sort of thing though you could very well tell people you were thinking about.

'I know I am,' Ros insisted now as they walked up towards the bridge. 'It's not as if at our age you don't know a thing like that.' At thirty-eight, she implied. You know about men by then if you're ever going to. Oh, there was a bit of a *frisson* to it, she quite knew that. An Italian following you through the streets. A tad vulgar, she admitted that, but still a *frisson*.

Next day at lunch Don said, 'What's that shady bugger in the corner there find so interesting at this table?' The man in a brown suit with the dark glasses and a folded paper tilted his head so the glasses flashed with the smear of reflected light. 'God, you're neurotic,' Ros said to him. 'How can you tell where he's looking if you can't even see his eyes?' But she looked directly at where she believed the centre of his eyes would be, and defiantly held his gaze.

That evening as they undressed Frank said 'So much for Tuscany, then. What's our next kingdom?'

In the train the others slept most of the journey across to the coast. Their last night had been a scream. They had met up with—no, we didn't dream it, Don would say later as he told it—met up with two very nice Australians. And finished up in an apartment Ros went on that she would give her eyes for, above the Piazza Santa Croce. 'Don't tell *me*,' she said, 'about la dolce vita.' Their hosts had kept insisting 'Try this one from Friuli,' implying that until you'd sampled another you wouldn't know what Pinot Grigio was. 'Italians don't drink the way we do,' the woman partner remarked. Her statement hung there, isolated, for half a minute before anyone spoke, a kind of tombstone with its line of considered grief. And the Australian, very seriously, said with understanding, 'And look where that's got them, eh?' They sang together like undergraduates. The woman, who was blonde and lovely, said they'd probably never go back. She spoke of Urbino as familiarly as Dabtoe. Alicia thought, am I really here, listening to all this? In a room four hundred years old with little painted figures and intertwining vines on the ceiling, and tomorrow—she could hardly think of *that* without pressing her knees together like a girl waiting for the curtain to go up at a pantomime.

On the balcony soon after midnight their host put his arm around Frank and nipped the lobe of his ear. 'The good thing about here,' he said, 'the great thing about here'—and he waved his other hand that roughly took in the sweep of half the city and the hills—'is that you can't only look at the loveliest stuff in the world. You can get anything you want.' There was a significant pause, as they say, above the square with Dante standing in front of the vast raw brick façade. 'Know what I mean?' the host said.

When the rest of the party came onto the balcony Frank tapped his watch and told them, 'Work tomorrow, playmates.' After they called their farewells up the echoing stairwell and came into the yellow lighting of the piazza, he broke out, 'Christ, rugby league and vino until they're coming out your ears and then he goes and touches you up. You never know where you are with Aussies.' They laughed and shuffled about on the pavements like a group of teenagers on their way back home, their voices appallingly loud as they turned into the canyon of the Via San Niccoló.

And so they slept most of the journey in the train. A man in a brown suit and wearing dark glasses passed their compartment, twice. He looked in at the three sleepers and the woman who read, glanced from the window at the rushing plains, and read again. The man put his bunched fingers to his lips, then exploded their bud to a full bloom of palm and fingers. He reminded himself of something happening in a book. A schoolteacher from Bradford, this playing at Graham Greene roles was his annual diversion from randy adolescents and sweaty gym shoes.

Alicia read slowly, and with great delight. 'A period of battle and intrigue, but also of incomparable beauty, and mysterious sighs in the passageways of civilisation.' Was it too much to imagine one might hear them still, those echoes, those sighs, hear them with attention enough to catch the very words? She looked from the pages and their visions of marble, blood, incense, brilliant stones, to the flicker of poles along the side of the railtrack, the smears of mist rising from the dark fields. St Heliers seemed ever so far away. So did the children if it came to that. So did their father, dozing across the compartment from her. She looked at him quite dispassionately. In a sense she already knew. She was very calm about it.

They stepped from the train to a cold platform and a depressing fog. The two women and Don went to the station café and ordered cappuccinos. Frank, with his list of recommended addresses, crossed the space in front of the station to the dull modern hotel. This was a town that had been here since the Romans used it as a port, where civilisation rested on its flight from Rome to Byzantium, but it made him think of Frankton. You take the sun from Italy and you turn it into a junk yard. Nothing was truer than that one.

He spoke with a surly girl across a formica desk. On the wall behind her shoulder hung an overbright replica of a mosaic dove. He asked the prices, got her to write them down, and booked two rooms that faced away from the street. He then waited for the wet gleaming side of a bus to slip by in front of him, and recrossed the square. He skirted the taxi drivers who offered their services in arrogant mocking English. He said to the last one, who came up close towards him, 'Look, piss off.' And he said to the group he had left in the bar that the hotel was no great shakes but it would do. It would bloody have to.

They sat in the cold hotel bar, the only patrons. They drank two quick brandies which did little to warm them up. Don and Frank were fractious together, disputing the difference between cathedral and basilica. 'It's architectural,' Don said. 'Like hell it is,' Frank argued. 'The difference is bureaucratic.' Then Don ordered another brandy which even he knew would make him more difficult. When the men left the bar to get a guide book from upstairs Alicia said, 'You remember that man?'

'What bloody man?' Ros asked her.

'The one in brown clothes and glasses? The one in the restaurant the other day?' She said he had been on the train.

'My God,' Ros said. She rolled back her eyes in irritation. 'Him!' It was something to be grateful for, she supposed, that Alicia bothered to tell her even now. For a few seconds she hated all of them. Then she put a Kleenex to her eyes, her nose, and looked from the side of the lace curtain at the strip of sky that was like a dirty band-aid.

Alicia said, 'I've seldom felt happier. Isn't that odd?'

'Remarkably,' Ros said. Sometimes she could not believe what a trial other people might be.

They were close to the mausoleum that historians consider unique. They walked down the steps from the road level and its hum of constant traffic to the quiet pathways and the stretch of lawn. They purchased tickets at the booth and moved towards the tomb of Theodoric, emperor, Goth, servant of God, soldier, husband. Ros said, 'Mosaics are one thing, sure, but don't tell me people come to look at *this*? A cross between an outsize dunny and a concrete silo?' She was tetchy still, with the weather which kept on foggy and cold, let alone with the hotel which she disliked, the Italian men who had done nothing more than track and ogle and elude her, and with her husband who said arse-freezing temperatures or not he had no intention of pushing on towards England ahead of the schedule they had planned. And Frank of course encouraged him to drink. Anything. Wherever they could. Their combined male memories of Italy would be a series of labels and torn-up betting slips.

On the pathway to the tomb, the massive arches set so far below the level of the present world, its chunky dome rising as it had always done above whatever age surrounded it, Alicia said, 'He was here for a comparatively short time after 526. The mortal part of him.'

'What's she on about this time?' Frank said. He too was already bored with the morning's task.

'That pattern around the top,' Don said. 'They're like dentists' tongs, eh, Ros?'

'It's better to say nothing sometimes,' Ros snapped at him. 'Just effing nothing.'

'Never knew you cared,' Don said. Sarcastic now, Ros thought. Pity there isn't a door for him to slam as well.

Frank began crooning, 'What a swell party this is,' in his Sinatra voice. Getting at her, of course.

'That's it!' Ros said. 'No, really, that's it!' She clicked across the scruffy patch of grass to a seat beneath some sodden pines. 'I'll just wait over here.' There was the pattering of small drops about her and she felt the dampness already seeping through her clothes. But she had to sit it out now. She simply had no choice. She bit her lip and was determined not to cry and thought why couldn't she be more like her friend, safe in some dull little cocoon that protected her from this kind of hurt?

Alicia kept walking, quite unfussed by the squabbling about her. She walked through the black iron fence and mounted the external stairs to the chamber directly beneath the dome, the room which architects had wondered at for a millenium and a half. She took in its austere detail, felt its magnitude and bulk. She remembered all that she had read, in a flash that plucked her from the normal currents of time. She was unaware of crossing the floor but felt the rim of the huge lidless sarcophagus against her breasts. It was like a massive bath. She raised her hands to the porphyry's solid iciness and felt a change suffusing her. She walked around the sarcophagus, right around it, her fingers stroking the broad sloping smoothness of the rim. She knew her lips were moving, she heard the incantation of her breath, but had no notion of what she said or why. Then she stood at its foot, her back to the high open door, and looked into the great hollowed block of dark red stone as though she simply looked at a bed. Had she turned she would have seen through the oblong of the doorway how the sky hung dull as canvas. But Alicia did not turn. Her hands still at the sarcophagus's rim, she felt a tremor of a kind that she hardly expected. She knew it was autumn and that there was fog between the mausoleum and what surrounded it. Yet she saw a shadow moving steadily past her, a shadow in a cube of brilliant light. She was not in the least fazed by its presence. She turned and the living mosaic was within arm's length. She was surprised only that he was no taller than herself. She then asked him quite calmly, as though she spoke to her husband when he dressed not quite adequately for the weather, 'Do you think those sandals are a good idea?' She pointed to the feet of the greatest Goth of his or any time. And then, as naturally again as she might straighten her husband's tie as he set off to the District Court, she touched the dull gold clasp with its nine surrounding white stones, the three chunky matching pendants, and ran her opened hand from his shoulder to his chest, across the prickly brown fabric he had worn now without changing for a very long time. She brushed the stubble of his cheeks, no more frightening in fact than the growth on the Whetton brothers the morning before a Test. It was though a little unexpected to see his head with only the cap of tight brown curls. She had got so used to him in his famous picture, the squashed tiered crown and the large gold disc behind his head. They were both struck enough by the novelty to laugh out loud. The funereal vault was a place of sudden fun. She asked, quite knowing how silly it sounded, 'Do you come here often, then?' She felt she must surely be the plainest woman he had ever been this close to—

no tiara, no fifteen inches at least of earrings as that empress wore. She thought, My God, am I asking for trouble mixing it with her! But he was watching her with a kindly expression and must have read her mind. 'Look,' he said, 'she was always a bitch. And you've got to remember when it was. Rotten teeth. Warts. Hygiene problems of one kind or another. You don't know when you've got it good. No,' Theo summed up, 'you can forget about that one. Slag wasn't in it.' That should have sounded coarse, even in Latin. But it made Alicia very happy because she knew he told the truth. Then the brightness was blocked by his approaching head. She felt the pressure of the sarcophagus against her shoulders. She opened her lips and his tongue was as warm as you could reasonably expect any tongue to be. She bit on it softly. It tasted of cloves and Sicilian wine. She felt his calf muscle tense against her own. 'Veni, imperator,' she said very softly. 'Will I ever!' he told her. His breath was hot against her ear and she heard him sigh, 'It's been so long.'

Marriage really is the oddest thing. It was nearly twenty years since they first slept together, in Frank's parents' beach house at the Mount while the oldies were off at a Rotarian dinner. Alicia was twenty-two and knew sooner or later it had to come to this. She had thought with some coolness well thank goodness it's not happening on the beach anyway, at least there isn't sand to contend with as well. And when Frank's parents came back they were sitting there playing Scrabble and his mother said, 'Why don't you two ever go out and have a bit of fun?' Mrs H., as Alicia thought of her even years after they were related, couldn't make out the young these days. 'You're such stick-at-homes,' she told them. Her husband belched so that his wife flinched, and announced 'That's all for now folks! I think I'll pile up the zeds.' She herself smiled wanly and went off to her own room. And the next morning the young ones said they would get married after their final exams. Mrs H. gave Alicia a family locket and said she'd help her choose her clothes from now on.

And now here she was, in Ravenna, lying beside one man, thinking of another, never quite so startled, nor yet quite so at peace, in her life. Marriage really is the oddest thing, hadn't she said that this afternoon? And Theo had laughed, exposing the molar broken in half by a glancing barbarian axe. 'Need a stronger word than that for some I can think of,' he had said. 'You must have seen her up there in all that fancy clobber? Talk about a cow!'

Alicia turned carefully, anxious not to wake Frank. Her shoulders ached from where the porphyry rim had pressed into them as Theo's ardour jogged at her. And the rash on her throat where his beard had rubbed like a pot-mitt. 'Amor,' he had said just before he moved back into the radiance and his shadow flowed across the floor again as though cast in front of a searchlight, 'amor omnia vincit.' She turned and winced from the long bruise on her right thigh where the jewel-encrusted scabbard had danced and flipped against her like a playful whip. She still felt the firm pressure of his grasp as he hoisted her against his tomb.

And it *does* conquer everything, love, that's the delicious thing about it. Back on the sundeck a few weeks later, the same harbour spread there in its marbling blues and greens, the scents pungent from the conservatory. Ros fanned the colour prints across the low table between them, and Alicia looked at them and nodded at what a scream it all had been. Don could be an Italian almost couldn't he, tucked under the archway with that silly leer? And Ros herself there, see, the very spot where those marvellous hillshots were taken in *A Room with a View*?

'Frank's talking about going back next year,' Alicia said.

'Back!' Ros declared. Her eyes were wide and expectant. Alicia told her, 'There's a man at Russell McVeagh with a time-share near Livorno.'

'Imagine,' Ros said, 'imagine all that over *again*!'

Alicia laughed and touched a print of a green and white facade. 'Remember your man in brown?' she said.

'Do I!' Ros declared. As if she'd forget *him*. 'After tracking me from city to city?'

'Wasn't it there we saw him first?'

'Where didn't we see him?' Ros said. 'Talk about *infatuated*!' Alicia smiled and looked at the images of what, after all, was only a couple of months back. She thought of how careful she had to be for days so Frank wouldn't see those marks. She thought, rather more apprehensively, of the little airmail packets that arrived every few days, the chips of coloured stone she simply didn't twig to until she had several dozen of them, moving them idly about one afternoon where she kept them hidden in the toolshed, and realised they formed—she could hardly believe it—formed a sandal, a big toe, an ankle, the hem of a toga. She laughed out loud as she had in the mausoleum, and there was the same quick echo, a fraction behind her voice. Because it came to her, that instant. That absurd dear Goth was actually posting himself to her, bit by bit! But they would notice soon, surely—there must be a wall, somewhere, a curved space in a dome, where his image was diminished by as much as appeared there, in front of her, on the bench in the garden shed. She was quite content to wait. She would manage Frank when the time came.

'His name,' Alicia said suddenly, 'his name means a special gift. Did you know that?'

'Whose, my dear?' Ros asked her. She felt so warm towards her friend since she mentioned that Latin admirer who had taken such risks to pursue her. She had thought—she was a bit ashamed of it, now—she had thought Alicia might even have been a tad envious that *she* was the one the males decided to track. 'Whose name is that?'

Alicia held up the picture Don had snapped with his Singapore zoom-lens. It showed the placid, intelligent face surrounded by the lesser figures of his rigid court. 'His,' Alicia said. 'That's what his name means.' And she said it out loud, in case Ros had forgotten it. A name that was frank and warm and took its place exactly, among colours that would hold for another thousand years.

Coasting

Brin and Fran, fortyish, academics, New Zealanders, and thus trebly anxious, drove in sudorous heavy silence while the gauge rolled over another thousand ks. It was like travelling in a clammy tin. The car smelled of food and feline presence.

The landscape intruded by its very sameness, gums flecking its edges with their archaic repetitive script. The couple looked straight ahead or to the side, but seldom at each other. Childless and bookless, although they had tried earnestly enough for both, they travelled north, always north, with their cat Palincest on a spread newspaper on the back seat. The cat they had thought a female as a kitten, an inexplicable mistake considering the close inspection Fran had given next door's litter when they were no longer a mere clot of undifferentiated fur. Yet within months it had made advances at its own mother, its gender orientation unexpectedly reinscribed. Hence pussy's playfully hypocoristic signifier. A bowel disorder, picked up in the camping ground at Noosa Head, now made it more a patient than a pal. Fran in fact detested the creature. It was Brin, anxious that all living things share his mental space, who spoke to it quietly and fed it bacon rinds at breakfast. One day, Fran thought, one day it will skulk about in the scrub and a snake will bite it to death. Good.

Fran and Brin were thoughtful enough to realise that marriages, as much as houses or one's critical discourse, from time to time demand refurbishing. This long—unbelievably long—north-eastern coast was what they hit on for refreshment. No theatres or libraries, no bright lights, but simply as close as they could come, within reason, to the solitary, the remote, to touch centre as it were and then emerge to new perspectives. Fran said, 'We're starting to talk like those bloody white male explorers used to, realise that?' Brin asked but wasn't marriage itself a site with now the flag of one empire, now that of another? *Alii alia dicunt*, wasn't that life all over? It was this alertness to linguistic slippage that now obliged them to travel anywhere except in their own country. For hadn't they been among the first, God knows, to impose self-discipline on their recognition of the word as oppressor, of vocabulary as imperialist *piège*? Adam naming the beasts, not the killing of Abel, was the first act of violence, as their students immediately understood. They refused to travel, to stay, even to cross those areas of appropriation where names had been changed, imposed, inverted, by Pakeha transgression. At least they would not go along with 'Wellington' for Te Upoko o te Ika, 'Auckland' for misplaced Tamaki-Makau-Rau. Certainly their presence would not contribute its trace towards illicit reinscription on such a massive scale. Their absence would declare, however modestly, an atoning erasure. And more than that. They had each, by way of solidarity and protest, excised a syllable from their own given names. A simple enough gesture, sure, but at least enacting within the frame of the nominal a metonymic castration that mirrored (with all the duplicities that implied!) the larger rape of the indigene as language; that carried in their own address to themselves an imperial displacement as vivid, if not as painful, as Kafka's celebrated discourse on the colonial/penal body. While behind that too, as Fran noted, one might usefully recollect and so re-enter Nietzsche's witty configuration with crime and sin, *der* Frevel and *die* Sünde, making of Eden itself a contentiously gendered site by virtue of those rabidly buoyant defining articles. Fran, to Brin's constant admiration, could articulate things like that in the twinkling of an I/eye/auie/aye.

Brin said, 'It would prevent us being here too, if we knew enough about the place.' Two hours later he spoke again, as they drove past a tiny settlement where the First People sat on a raised wooden verandah in front of a blue and yellow country store. 'Putting Blake's drawing of a native family—remember?—still putting that in front of what the people in fact are. Imposing our semantic grid. That's what we're up to, you know. Still.' 'Piss off sometimes will you,' Fran asked him, 'darling?'

In the motels in the evenings Brin read Cook's account of sailing north, Beaglehole's monumental rewriting of Cook, Hoare's probing of Beaglehole, and the articles that challenged Hoare. History, as he well knew it, was a progression—regression?—of referential drift. But so was everything else.

Fran lay on her back at nights and smoked, and sipped at gin. Every few minutes she raised her cigarette to her mouth, its pharos of incipient lungwrack intense and brief. She thought of the real estate salesman at last night's hotel. She thought of the fair complexioned teacher and his obviously non-connubial companion in the lounge after breakfast this morning, and of the photographer who raised her hand to wave from a sand-dune sixty kilometres from a phone box. She thought of her own remarks on a student's narratology assignment, reminding that language at best was a makeshift net, not a containing dish; that the mind's sharpest objective perception constantly echoed itself. She thought if this ice can't last longer than that before riding into the lake of lukewarm gin, then come back referentiality, come back boredom and hang-dog fucking realism as long as ice means ice. And she thought if that cat craps again during the night I shall not even bother to wait for the snake.

In such moments, and with some minds, stories begin. With others of course, not. But as Fran and her brighter students very well knew, not to begin a story is also a story of a different kind.

> *Sunday April 1. In the P.M. had a moderate breeze at E., which in the Night Veer'd to the N.E., and was attended with hazey, rainy weather . . . At Noon our Latitude by account was 40 12S., Long. made from Cape Farewell 1 11 West.*

At a pinewood committee-room table, imagine, there are seven people. Real people. No one person likes every other person, naturally, but good manners and complimentary wine would make an eighth person suppose amity prevailed among them all. It is a Friday evening, ten minutes before sunset. Light pours across the table as a verandah door opens on the company, a sudden flag of brilliance for several seconds until the door is again shut. A clock ticks noticeably when there is a pause between words. These people, moving left to right, do not in a sense exist until they are named. Let them be named then. Charlie and Moira, Harry, Connie, Bazza, Emma and Rex.

Across a pause, Connie Batchelor says, 'I wish someone would kill that bloody clock'.

'At least it's had its strike cut out. It's been neutered to that extent.' When Charlie Ruxton says that he grins so his tongue shows grey as a calf's between his teeth. Beside him, Moira Lucas thinks how that man turns even time itself into an animal, so he can say something smutty. She sees that Harry Buchanan on her other side is drawing small intricate wheels on a piece of paper. Across from her florid Rex Morrison, the real estate dealer, helps himself from the carafe. He then holds it up, his glance round that table asking them all, Who else? Only his young wife Emma pushes her glass towards him.

'No,' says Bazza Forbes for the rest of them. 'No thanks.' The school teacher's face, a red wedge beneath straw-coloured hair, does not turn to Rex as he speaks, but he moves a finger, his middle one, so that only Emma notices.

Connie Batchelor brings them back to the business of the meeting. She says, 'We've got exactly two months until the Event. Everything looks pretty much on schedule, wouldn't you say?' Pretty Emma Morrison answers because she fears that otherwise she may not seem alert and keen. 'We all know where to go next, then, what we're supposed to be responsible for?'

Vapid bitch, Moira Lucas thinks. She smiles, however, and says, 'I'm sure that goes for everyone, Emma.' She leans across to the desk calendar in the centre of the table and rips off the leaf which shows the end of March. 'There,' she says. 'A nice fresh month for us all to start with.'

Rex says the weeks will be on top of them before they know where they bloody are.

> *Friday 20th April. The Southernmost point of land we had in sight, which bore from us W.S., I judged to lay in the Latitude of 38 0 S. and in the Long. of 211 7 W. from the Meridian of Greenwich. I have named it Point Hicks, because Lieutenant Hicks was the first who discover'd this Land.* The great navigator was tempted to commit to his journal the observation that the baronet, brought on board at the last moment at the Admiralty's request, was for all his breeding and wealth, and his friendship with Mr Banks, a most wearisome companion at table. Yet again the gentleman had raised that his own name be held in reserve for a piece of land considerably more impressive than mere headland or estuary. The baronet's hands played constantly with his cutlery, with turning his glass and folding, unfolding his napkin. Cook noticed how Solander observed the man scientifically. He must have a word with that sober Swede. But none of this he committed to the page. Instead, he continued calmly, *In the P.M. saw other Egg Birds [Sterna fascata] and again, in numbers, the Gannet [Sula serrator].*

Mrs Connie Batchelor put her copy of Jung on the pile of books beside her bed—*The Interpretation of Signs, Time and Distance*, and a journal she subscribed to on reincarnation. She lay for a few moments with her hands behind her head, her elbows pointed high. From the ill-lit mirror facing the bed, she had the impression of heavy pale wings. Then she switched off the light. There was the faintest feeling, which she knew could well be unsettled scotch, that made her think the room gently swayed. She closed her eyes and thought of the broken pattern of the *I Ching*, an arrangement which warned her of approaching change.

At more or less the same time, Harry Buchanan was moving a series of matches into lines that were not unlike the rows that Connie thought of. In fact he had picked up the habit of moving them about like this all those years ago when he and Connie were very close. She would throw the coins and say, 'Set them up for me, Harry.' He would then lay down straight matches, or broken ones, so she could take it in, as she said, rather more vividly than you could when you simply drew the lines on paper. This way the smooth unbroken sticks contrasted with the snaggle-ended halves that Harry snapped. It was how things should always be, Connie used to remark, ideas set out in objects, even a humble clutch of matches taking their place in the eternal scheme. She said it with a laugh, of course, she hated the very thought that she might sound pretentious. And her young watchmaker friend simply listened, mostly. He liked hearing her talk and he liked her size, the arms that made his own seem emaciated and the breasts when she first let them loose from her bra and the streaks of powder he could see along their sides, making him think of flour sacks. He liked it that he was twenty-four and that she was twelve years older. All girls had stayed pretty much sisters until he met Connie. She had said to him as he handed across the counter a silver clasp that he had fixed, 'Libra, am I right?' He told her what day. She said, 'Ah, Taurus. Venus on the cusp.' He looked at the handsome big woman as she laughed and tapped his wrists. 'That's why we'll get on.'

Emma Morrison said to Bazza Forbes, 'But doesn't your wife ever suspect?' 'Nah,' Bazza said. 'Not an earthly.' Emma thought of a mechanic she had gone out with once who told her life only began when you had grease on your hands, and yet he always spoke so beautifully she said to him once that if you heard him from the next room you'd think someone was talking on the ABC. And now here was Bazza who was a teacher and an historian as well and he deliberately made it sound as though he had it in for nice English.

He put his hand further along her leg.

'I can't at the moment,' Emma said. 'Aren't I a dead loss?' She pulled a sorry-for-both-of-us face that inside the dark car he may not have been able to see. 'Jeeza,' he said, 'I'm surrounded by women this week who feed me that line.' But he said it so good naturedly Emma could hardly mind the reference to his wife.

The car rocked as though someone leaned at the side and shoved it. 'Cook got the winds this time of year too,' Bazza said. 'Blew the tripes out of him further down the coast there. Out from Sydney.'

'Sydney wasn't there then though was it?' Emma said. She knew Bazza enjoyed her playing dumb. His own ball-and-chain as he said was thick as the proverbial yet she fancied she was Mrs Einstein with her Uni external courses or whatever. 'And here's you,' he told Emma, 'You're the brightest person in this scumbag town and you make like you're the old two planks.'

'I don't mean to,' Emma said. 'I think it's just a gift.'

'That's why it's so nice.' He stuck his tongue in her ear the way he did as a kid at Towoomba High, thinking you had to do that to stir a girl up. She said, 'Settle for this then, will you?' She began to undo his belt, humming beneath her breath.

'As long as you don't sing at the same time,' he said. 'High notes make me excited.'

He watched the pin-points of light from down the coast. The moon that had ridden out there over the sea as they drove up to the look-out was tucked behind skimming cloud. He closed his eyes and thought, This'll do me! And on the way back towards town the teacher said to his old friend's wife, 'I've never actually asked you how old you are, know that?'

Emma said, 'I do a nice schoolgirl, mister, if the money's right.'

In his cabin the greatest sailor in the world put down his quill, rested his elbows in their long linen shirt sleeves on the edge of his table, and rubbed his eyes until he saw grainy spots. He thought how he must ask the surgeon to suggest some cordial for the baronet's nerves. 'It was important for the navigator to maintain a steady grip on the goodwill of his crew, as well as his own confidence in the entire enterprise, fraught with difficulties as it often was.' Two hundred and twenty-eight years after Cook pondered on the gentleman who irked him, and lay down his quill in mild irritation, a small town's historian would summarise his character in those surprisingly vacuous words, as part of the brochure for the celebration. The brochure's cover would carry a photograph of a model ship, against a painted frothing sea. A light showed at a porthole of what was taken to be the captain's cabin. A light which Cook shifted slightly before he shook the sprinkled sand from the page of his freshly written entry, and a little later blew out. He commended himself to God, praying briefly for his distant wife and their brood, and lay so that his left ear was only feet from the sea. *Stood to the N.E. until Noon, having a Gentle breeze at N.W., at which time we Tack'd and stood to the Westward. . . . . A point of land which I named Cape St. George, we having discovered it on that Saint's day.*

The town might be far from the largest on the Coast, but once Charlie Ruxton, who had sold them their cars for years, and Rex Morrison, the property wizard who promised he would have two kilometres of tasteful bungalows geared to the middling-to-well-off elderly at Touchdown Beach by the end of the decade—as soon, so the TV feature said, as soon as jaunty Chas who was the wheels of the town and Rex the man with the market initiative put their heads together on the project, then it was all on, believe you me, all systems were go. The first dozen bungalows on Endeavour Heights in fact would be opened the very week the little town paid its respects to the man who, after all, had made Touchdown merit that name in the first place. They might have got only a thirty-second slot on the southern channels but within a week there were more queries from suburban retirees down there in the damp and mist than Rex could have built for in ten years; and more offers of sponsorship than Charlie Ruxton's committee knew what to do with.

'There's a Japanese condom firm for Christ's sake just faxed in.'

'Snap it up,' Rex said. 'It'll make the ethnic factor think they're part of the celebration too.'

A lot of people knew Bazza Forbes at the High School had hit on the idea. But the word was put round Rotary that it came to Ruxie and Bucho on the fairway to the eighteenth. In fact, as the three men knew, but saw no reason to say, it was Moira Lucas who sparked them off. In her darkroom almost a year ago she was waiting on a seascape taken from the hill above the bay. In the odd jostling of molecules on their way to stability, it seemed for several seconds that one of the distant rollers was the sail of a ship, the crest behind it another sail again. In ten seconds however there the true print was, a stretch of barren sea.

Moira did not believe in the perfect photograph, although she believed perfection was what one had to aim for. Most of what one looked at was wank, she thought, every square centimetre of it. For the past months she had been after something that was, well, nothing actually like an Utamaro print, but would make her think of one all the same, the moment flared out in a delicacy that was also monumental, which said this is what you see for a fraction of a second, but what you see is absolute.

That quick fading of what she had taken to be a ship lingered in Moira's mind. She said, quite idly, as she chatted to the chemist in the main street, why had nothing ever been made of the fact that Cook, of all people, had touched down here, even for a morning? There was sponsorship money round, she said, for celebrations like that. She had gone on to imagine the canful of images you could have nabbed if you'd sailed with him! 'Think of a koala even,' she said, 'the most boringly photographed little bugger in world history. Imagine him looking down your lens for the first time! It would have been the one and only snap of the thing worth taking.'

She paid for the large packets of photographic paper and pressed them against her chest as she left the shop. She was a good six inches taller than the two men who stood back for her inside the doorway, and nodded politely as she passed. One was the schoolteacher who looked sunburned any time of the year, the other the car dealer who sported in his showroom Moira's portrait of him, going on life-size, inspiring confidence and trust with a wide engaging grin. The men had overheard her conversation. They knew that she was onto something. Onto something big.

At 8, being very squally, with lightning, we close reef'd the Topsails and brought to, being then in 120 fathoms. At 3 A.M. made sail again to the Northward, having the advantage of a Gale at S.W. Cook welcomed days when the seas were too boisterous for the baronet's weak stomach, for that gentleman, after all these months, had still not become accustomed to the elements. The captain tired quickly enough of the clever southern talk—Banks on native women ('more naked than Eve,' whatever that should mean), Monkhouse's speculations that the Polynesian and Egyptian tongues derived from some common source, the baronet, worst of all, who called himself a scientist yet spoke with tiresome warmth of the great Stone and the flasks, as of something verifiable. He spoke too of coincidences and spirit manifestations, until the captain at times cut sheer across him, addressing questions on tapeworms to the surgeon, or requesting Solander's opinion on cultivating rice on the terrain that now stood to their west. With flinty northern humour he remarked that flatulence perhaps accounted for his own meagre gifts at speculation. *Saturday, 5 May. I had sent the Yawl in the morning to fish for Stingrays, who returned in the Evening with upwards of four hundred weight; one single one weigh'd 240 lbs. Exclusive of the entrails.*

It amazed the small town that the first meeting to consider the project was so well attended. Few of them knew much of Cook's passing until Bazza Forbes stood up, produced an old-fashioned map drawn down from a roller, and explained to them. He said unfortunately precise details had not been recorded, although the name indeed was on the first maps printed after Cook's return to the Admiralty. As they knew, the iron hoops from a cask, presumably broken by accident and left at the freshwater creek, had been found over a hundred years ago. There was also the pewter dish with MONKHOUSE incised upon it, which could be seen to this day in the small museum on Sunday afternoons. Monkhouse, of course, had been on board as ship's doctor. 'And there is no conceivable doubt,' Bazza Forbes said, 'that the greatest Englishman of the eighteenth century stood somewhere not far from Rex Morrison's new development that does honour to the navigator's name.' He finished with the remark which so puzzled Emma, that any Englishman who wanted so desperately to get here indeed deserved such a memorial.

So the special commemorative committee was chosen with an eye to several factors: Charlie Ruxton as the man in town who spoke daily to more people than anyone else, who had been responsible in his time for public toilets, for gas barbies in the park, for the Premier's visit to the Assembly Church, and for Safari Enterprises, run by an old air force mate who dropped 120 Nips on the town once every two months regular, which meant motel trade you wouldn't have thought possible a couple of years back. There was Bazza Forbes of course for reasons no one doubted, for if history was your bag then Forbsie was your man. And Connie Batchelor because she ran the motels, catered like a charm, and because she told them of a seance she read of in one of her magazines where a member of Cook's crew, with an accent the medium could scarcely decipher, told a Dabtoe circle he couldn't wait to get back to the North. The manifestation had given a longitude which was uncannily close to their own. Also Connie had more imaginative flair than any of them. It was she in fact who called into Harry Buchanan's shop, carrying in a brown paper bag an old bottle she had kept at the back of a cupboard for as long as she could remember, a bottle in which her grandfather, as a lad at sea, ingeniously erected a scale model of the Endeavour. Family lore had it that the model was by way of winning a thin seventeen-year-old girl to accept a man whose delicacy of touch and steady eye could pop history so cunningly into an aperture the size of his thumb. She said to Harry Buchanan, 'Could you build me one like that? Only life size, I mean.'

Harry recognised the smell of the powder from years before. 'No probs there, Connie. So long as there's funds.'

She said, 'It only has to sail half a day. It's the next thing to building a stage set for Pinafore.'

And Harry told her again, 'No probs far as I can see.' The proposal excited him. The Sea Scouts and the Christian Youth for month after month would run up and down ladders, cart timber and patiently follow plans, as they built the sailing ship around the hull of Rex Morrison's luxury launch. Close up, Connie said, the thing looked like an abortionist's picnic, but fifty yards off it was as good as you'd see in the movies. She had in mind the Bounty dancing on little waves in front of a palm-treed shore. She thought her old beau Harry had come up trumps. Behind their many meetings and visits to the building area in the yard of the Scout Hall, there remained the faintest memory of the clamminess of summer afternoons, her hands running across the lithe young man who instinctively shook her watch and held it against his ear, after he removed it from her arm and before he placed it on the table beside her bed. That was what Harry had always been like. Meticulous, down to the very last tick.

Emma, because she could take shorthand and type, had been invited to act as secretary for the group. As the commemorative day grew closer she found she had more on her hands than she ever might have thought. Each day was a turbulence of letters received and answered, queries referred to other members of the committee, and matters for the various sub-committees (maritime, catering, publicity, coordination, transport and community comfort, finance, children's activities) those members now chaired. She handled the banking and wrote the cheques, endorsed by at least one other signatory. Usually this was the town jeweller because his shop was directly opposite the council chambers. She so easily popped over. Then one day Harry Buchanan gave her a tiny gold reef-knot, the logo all over the town for the coming

Event. He had noticed that some days she wore charms on a chain around her left wrist. She did not tell Bazza Forbes of the gift because he would have said Harry was after her pants. But she wore the little ornament to every meeting. And she found that sometimes she was inventing a cheque just for the relaxation of talking to her new friend. She found it rather exciting, even a little kinky, when she came in on him once and he raised his head and she saw his greatly magnified eye swimming there like a kind of jellyfish behind his jeweller's glass. He pushed the device to his forehead and there he was, normal as ever. She said, 'Put it on again, Harry.' She playfully leaned across the counter and went to touch his bulbous eye. 'Ugh,' she said, 'you're like a late-night movie, Harry, know that?' And when she felt his firm fingers take her wrist and lower it to the counter, his voice telling her quietly to be a good girl and not touch what wasn't hers, Emma knew she would have to face up to it. Your pulse never lies, she liked to say, does it? It keeps perfect time.

It was Emma whom Harry intended to phone, that evening when he moved the matches on the glass-topped table in Charlie Ruxton's modern lounge.

After an expanse of island-studded water which he named after James, Earl of Morton, President of the Royal Society as well as one of the Commissioners of Longitude, Cook turned from the murky channels and the mangroves towards the open sea. A gathering southerly sat behind him. For several days he had confined his diet to biscuit and claret, and a little fresh fish. Dr Solander sat with him several evenings and read aloud from Pliny, a diversion that particularly pleased him, for the loose talk of the gentlemen at dinner rather distressed the captain, especially as young Isaac Smith, midshipman, and a cousin of his own wife's, had sat with the older men. It was unusual for Cook to feel unwell. He examined his stool and found nothing untoward. *17 May. At daylight I found that we had in the night got much further to the Northward and from the shore than I expected from the Course we steer'd, for we were at least 6 or 7 Leagues off, and therefore hauled in N.W. by W., having the Advantage of a Fresh Gale.*

One day about the middle of May Emma asked Harry Buchanan, as she would never have put it to Bazza Forbes, asked straight out was Charlie Ruxton, you know? She put her tongue between her teeth for a moment.

'A what?' Harry asked.
'You know, Harry. You know very well.'
'He keeps it quiet,' Harry said. 'The town wouldn't go much on it if they knew.'
'Then how do you know, eh?' Emma's breast flattened against his chest as she leaned across him. She ran a finger down his cheek and looked at him with arched quizzing brows.
'Charlie tells me everything,' Harry said.
Emma bit the lobe of his ear. She so liked it when you became close with yet another friend. Harry would never have told her a thing like that a month ago, not even with his clothes on.

Saturday, 19th. Variable Light Airs and Calms . . . regular, even Soundings, from 13 to 7 fathoms; fine sandy bottom.

Monday, 21st. At 9, we discover'd from the Masthead land to the Westward, and soon after saw smoke upon it.

Friday, 25th. The Mainland in this Lat. is tolerable high and Mountainous; and the Islands which lay off it are the most of them pretty high and of a Small Circuit, and have more the appearance of bareness than fertility.

Moira Lucas had more work than she might reasonably handle. She had designed the brochure and other publicity material, and taken the syndicated photographs of the coastline, and simply spools of the Endeavour firming up behind the Scout Hall. The little gallery she rented from Connie Batchelor was doing a roaring trade, what with so many strangers driving through at weekends. And now you couldn't walk along the bluff on a weekday afternoon without passing half a dozen couples, the kind with orange anoraks and hiking boots, or elderly pairs sitting in the marram grass, the woman perhaps pouring tea from a thermos flask, the husband reading aloud from Cook's own account. Some of them sat with their knees tucked up, looking out to sea, to the same slanting of light, the same play of winds, that returned here over and over, since the famous captain ran his minuscule ship along a continent's rim.

Moira was out with her camera whenever she could snatch time away from town. She had been obsessed like this years ago with river gums at Overland Corner. She knew there was an image among the rest that would be that fraction finer, closer to what all the others aspired to. When she tried to explain that to her father way back in those days he had said, 'Plato, eh?' and she imagined throwing her camera so that its German fragments splintered across the caravan they camped in beside the placid bend of the Murray. But, 'Plato's arse!' she had simply shouted at the old man. Couldn't he see it was the exact reverse she was after? Not some ridiculous ideal that infiltrated particulars but a particular so real you could not imagine anything like it that wasn't already here in this. It was the last time she tried to explain anything to anyone. But as the river gums then, so this coastline now. She thought of it when she woke, and its long curdling hem of surf, its hazed penumbra of spray was in her mind as she went to sleep. She shot forty or fifty exposures at a time. She refused to crop her prints, which she knew was like cheating at cards. Every few days there was one at least decent enough to sell in the gallery.

> Cook stood at the taff-rail. The breeze boomed in the mainsheets, a halyard vibrated in his fist. From second to second, he thought, the universe seemed under control. When he held the brass sextant against his cheek, or watched the lecherous Mr Banks working so quietly at his dish of paints, giving his sapless specimens a rich second life as he transferred them onto sheets of card, it seemed a simple thing to acknowledge Providence. And then the intricate cordage would bellow with the accelerating wind. The naked feet of the crew slapped round him. He called for the alteration in tack, the ship heeling down to his command. He quite knew what the classicists meant when they spoke of the exhilaration of hubris, of facing uncharted waters through hazard and chance. He knew that he provoked destiny as his vessel took current and wind. Yet one commends oneself to God and takes no undue risk. *Winds and weather as Yesterday, and the Employment of the People the same.*

Charlie Ruxton indeed did not confide to Harry Buchanan that his sexual preferences were of a kind that Rotary would have turfed him out for, smartly. But Harry, wanting to impress Emma Morrison, had said that rather than tell the truth. For the truth was that Connie Batchelor told him on Easter Monday morning, all those years ago, when she believed in her post-coital closeness that whatever she said was safe with her young friend. She said she was distantly related to the Ruxtons, although no one in the town was wise to that one, either. And

Charlie poor dear had actually gone by another name down south and only escaped by a whisker, once it got round that he dished out fivers as they were in those days to teenage louts for opening their mouths on demand and keeping them shut later on. Young Harry had been taken aback by the language the generously naked Connie employed. 'Arse bandits,' she said, 'gob-stoppers. I don't know what they see in it.' Harry would never have thought of telling a soul if Emma, her tongue wet and provocative, had not asked him at precisely that moment. Or returned to it later, on the concealed ledge of the bluff where Bazza Forbes had taken her first and she in turn took Harry. He made her promise she would keep it to herself. Hell, he said, hadn't he known Charlie for years? Didn't they watch VFL replays together on Sunday mornings? He'd never seen so much as a flicker of that side of the man. Then because she supposed that Harry, like Bazza, would think it very sexy, and also to take his mind off betrayal, Emma moved her tongue like an urgent slug inside his ear. Evening came on. The white collar of her Canterbury was the last thing that shone out against the dark.

A long time later she said, 'Time to slip your daks on Harry. My daddy man will be wondering where I am.'

From the dark hillside Harry saw, far out to sea, a light flash very weakly. 'It must be all that peering with your periscope thing in the shop,' Emma said. 'I can't make out a thing.'

A light which as it happened Connie Batchelor saw too, from her own windows high above the beach. In daylight she looked directly down on Rex Morrison's development. She thought enviously of those medieval sieges where they poured reeking ordure on those below. It was an image that gratified her, to think of Rex with his hairy fingers mining behind his spectacles, scooping them free. For Connie had just been speaking to her cousin on the phone. He thought he might leave town in a day or so, he said, perhaps even tomorrow. 'Before the Event!' Connie said. Before the replica they had put all that money into sailed round the bluff—before the re-enactment on the beach with Charlie himself as Cook and the gala party for the whole town? 'You're not talking sense, Charlie!'

'Things tend to get round, old darling,' Charlie said to her. She was meant to pick up the sad bravado.

'Oh, not the same trouble as down south?' she put to him.

Connie sat and looked at the black expanse, to the tiny winking light.

Someone was leaning on Charlie of course, that was always the story. She threw her *I Ching*, which predicted great changes, a tempest of unresolved forces and broken lines. It's paying the little shits, she considered, that was the problem. Why did Charlie never click that people give it away?

Charlie Ruxton as it happened did not leave town until after the monster piss-up hosted by the committee the night before the re-enactment and the Floral Float Parade, and the various related functions on the oval behind the Town Hall. Connie Batchelor nursed her one glass of scotch throughout the evening. She talked to Bazza Forbes's wife when she saw Bazza nip out with Emma Morrison. She then talked with Rex Morrison when Emma returned, and left the hall again within minutes with Harry Buchanan. She decided she had seen enough of all these people to last her a lifetime. Without a tinge of regret, she told Rex she would sell him her hillside, the whole bloody lovely flank of it, that he had been chasing after for years. The figure she put to him was so reasonable that each knew without saying a word that she was saving her cousin's bacon as well. She thought with some disgust of petite and pretty Emma lying next to her unattractive husband and confiding whatever she had heard from her current lovers. She was glad to leave him, to get away from the square warm hand that continually touched her arm as he spoke to her. She moved across to Moira Lucas, who thank Christ had left her camera at home for once. Because Connie, for the first time in her life, was feeling her age. Which meant there was very little in the evening that interested her, nothing about the people she spoke to which she found charming or diverting. She closed her eyes and thought of a mandala, a white centre among frothing blues. She remembered the fractured lines of the *I Ching*, black waves that moved towards her, and Harry's hands years ago in the lamplight as he had set the matches in their squares. All patterns were like cages, weren't they? Little cubes of fate. They spoke of those deep and intricate codes that made all things possible, all things assured yet seemingly unlikely. She saw Charlie shaking hands with Rex Morrison as she tucked her sequined evening bag beneath her arm and left. Outside the hall, she took her keys and her credit cards from the bag, and left it on the low wall beside the carpark. Leaving it was her sudden gesture that a great deal no longer mattered. She had carried the thing, or others much the same, to nights like this for forty bloody years. As she turned the car towards the exit, its lights picked out for a moment the cluster of scintillations of the concrete ledge. Then the beams burrowed out into the dark.

The baronet disappeared from the ship. His recent obsessive talk of their need for 'touching down' as he called it, his monologues with Banks on the fauna he expected to discover and whose names he was prepared for, had warned the Captain of the sudden event. Cook at once ordered a boat to be put down, and several empty casks despatched overboard, in the unlikely hope that the crazed man might cling to one of them. The ship circled for many hours, before resuming its northward set. The great sailor of his age quite took the irony of his calling the adjacent shoreline after the baronet's own repeated phrase of touching down, rather than the family name which the poor man had felt a continent could scarce do honour to. He wrote that evening: *Fresh gales between the S.S.E. and E.S.E. Hazey weather, with some showers of rain, which shorten'd the Prayers I thought fit to summon Officers and Men attend.* He did not elaborate on the missing articles reported to him during the noon and evening. One was Mr Banks's own ivory-handled magnifying glass. There was also a cooper's hammer, which the insane gentleman presumably had used to weigh himself down, and a belaying pin a sailor observed him trifle with moments before he jumped. And Dr Monkhouse's dish, with his name worked upon its rim, which the suicidal baronet seized from the medical man's hand as he dashed past, stuffing it down his shirt, bidding him good day.

Moira Lucas felt the lurch to her feelings as she watched the image emerging in the developing tray. She was tired from the party the night before, and knew how hectic the next day would be. She had driven out to the bluff that afternoon, simply to calm herself after hearing that Connie Batchelor had disappeared. It was purely out of routine then that she developed the roll before she went to bed. Her mind was vague, a screen of indistinct sand hills, the deserted beach with its fringe of trees, a couple in a passing car she had waved to. And then the picture rising to her from the tray, its sense of commanding absence that she had always wanted from the sea. She realised as she looked at the grain of indistinguishable sea and sky, that normal demarcations seemed sluiced off: a sense of neither right nor left, past nor present, up nor down, an emptiness so pure nothing might encroach on it. A photograph of Zen perfection.

Wednesday 30th May. Captain James Cook writes how *I gave over all thoughts of bringing the ship a Shore, being resolved to spend as little time as possible in a place that was likely to afford us no sort of refreshment.* He glances across the starboard rail before turning in. The waves, scribbled with moonlight, are a page of indecipherable script.

'Christ,' Fran said, 'what's all this about the winterless north?' The sky was the colour of pewter. The sloping bluff, the low hills behind the beach, identical empty stretches to north and south. It was all so dull. She slipped a cardigan over her shoulders as though it were a cape, and realised Brin was droning on; imagine if Cook had landed kind of thing, imagine if he had and we didn't know, imagine if he didn't land and we thought he did, oh as if referentiality wasn't tricky enough this very minute, to know even where you were sitting, what you were looking at, what to call what you saw, let alone naïvely believe it stayed the same once you called it anything at all. Who the hell would be a historian, Brin demanded, who the hell can even write a cheque with confidence in our current foci of indeterminables? 'Pity he didn't,' Fran said. 'Cook, I mean. There might have been a tea-rooms here or anything. A pub. A library where we could read about the place instead of having to bloody be here.' She knew she was being epistemologically vulgar and simply didn't give a stuff. She moved slightly on her haunches, her sheaf of written pages ruffling beneath her thighs.

Brin sighed. He edged a wedge of chicken flesh towards the cat. Palincest nosed the gift and moved away. 'He's still off colour,' Brin said. Fran failed to answer. She was occupied in trying to flick an insect from her glass. 'Watch out!' Brin called to her. 'Oh bugger me, watch out!' The cat was close beside her, its sides convulsively heaving before a feculent gush threaded across her jeans, colon-ising the text wedged under her thigh.

'That's it!' Fran shouted. 'That's fucking it!'

'It?' Brin put to her. He carefully placed his copy of Beaglehole on his copy of Cook, Beaglehole and Cook in turn on Hoare, then Beaglehole and Cook and Hoare on the folder of essential articles. He slipped them all into a blue plastic carrybag whose lettering appeared reversed either because the bag was inside-out or because the bag was printed that way accidentally or possibly on purpose. 'What on earth, Fran love, can *it* refer to in a context like that?' He was amused at her ludic brio in assuming 'it' might mean anything at all.

Taking in
The East

She told me nothing about the fix she was in, she told me nothing that related to anything that he would want to know. That was what, at first, Kavanagh found so difficult to believe. 'So you do this regular?' he said. 'Take up ladies in distress? Buy them dinner for three days let alone breakfast?' And when he saw I was not lying about it, that I thought I was in, as he supposed, an erotic adventure, a chance meeting of the kind that doesn't happen often outside true romance, Kavanagh's eyes rolled back. He began to sing in grating American parody, 'This could have been love, this could have been Paradise.'

'Wrong musical, sport,' I said. 'Wrong ocean.'

'Haven't you heard art's universal?' he came back at me. 'It's like bullshit in that, Thomas. Like crime even.'

He was full of such asides, wisecracks, those nervous tics that he assumed were insights raising him a notch above the mere prying cop. And we each knew where we stood. He condescended to me and I detested him. He had a file this thick, he told me, on Karen. He raised his levelled palm six inches above the white cane table. But he had never actually spoken to her, know that?

'Then you don't know what you're missing,' I said. 'You'll just have to read about her.' Not that anything could throw Kavanagh. He popped one of his lozenges from its paper wrapper into his mouth and stared across at me. I knew how it fascinated him, the fact that the three of us, Karen from Surrey Crescent, me from Point Chev, himself from Westmere, the three of us from within a couple of miles of each other as kids were now playing out this cloak-and-dagger stuff in Singapore thirty years after he and I were at school together, fifteen after Karen left the same convent school I had got my wife from, first time round. 'Happy days,' he said. He raised his glass and I waited until it was back on the table before I sipped at mine. When he grinned his teeth were square and even and stained, the kind young children put in their drawings of funny men.

I was in and out of Singapore a couple of times a year. The place bored me after my first few visits. I reluctantly stayed on now in the curved white tower of the Belvedere, in a goldeny-pink bedroom that looked out from the ninth floor onto a derelict colonial mansion in a green obscured enclosure that must have been worth a wad among the highrise. I waited there for one of our travellers who had been delayed in Indonesia. 'Our', as Kavanagh already knew, is Tiki Foods, which means high-protein dairy products, milkpowder, the kind of thing the East needs and we can market and so far it's an oyster we've hardly cracked. I was simply a businessman cooling his heels in a luxury hotel and its set-piece bars when Karen crossed my path. 'My, my,' as Kavanagh said. 'Talk about Fate!' Karen, who was in her mid-twenties I thought, and was killing time too, waiting to meet up with a sister who was flying in from Heathrow. Karen who on that first day was tracked by a tedious admirer, and we spent three days together, and most of two nights.

We made love once, on the third night. She left later in the morning when I thought she was going for a stroll, as we had done before, on the grass verge beneath the dark overhanging trees that ran from the hotel down towards Scotts Road intersection. Simply a stroll before the crowds and the heat. She left her small white leather suitcase, as innocent as any other woman's with its summerweight clothes, its make up gear, its couple of novels, a case then confiscated by Kavanagh and no doubt sniffed and analysed by ubiquitous Sam and written up for that file already, as he said, six inches high. Karen who was several other women as well, and Kavanagh was interested in all of them.

'We ought to keep out of Asia, son,' Kavanagh said to me in the last few minutes before my flight. 'We ought to just fucken keep out.'

All this was September, between the 26th and the 30th of September. The *Straits Times* in Singapore, the New Zealand papers I saw later, the Australian press that month were full of Crittenden's story and his sentence in Penang. Crittenden who was apprehended at the airport with a kilo of heroin. You couldn't be in a room five minutes without his name coming up. Surely the Malaysians would back down? It couldn't come to hanging an *Australian*, could it? The expats found it unbelievable but the Singaporeans viewed it with their hard pragmatic commonsense. 'They hang so many Chinese up there a foreigner will prove racism has nothing to do with it,' our Singapore manager told me, glancing across his raised bowl of curried fish. 'It will prove what impartial justice the Malaysians have.'

Kavanagh liked to get things straight. Which was why he liked to know exactly the kind of lives his school contemporaries led, the promising stories that have ended up as bad ones, the odd bad one that turned out well. So I helped him with mine that night in the Goodwood bar. By the time he was in the sixth form I had finished my degree and worked in as conventional a law firm as a dull city possessed. At first it seemed good because I married Pauline Harkness, whom Murdoch had gone half blind over as Kavanagh reminded me, and who was stunning beyond belief. She had money of her own and we bought a spacious renovated farmhouse in Tamahere. Our neighbours were a doctor with a vigorously unfaithful wife and a German couple who bred horses. Each neighbour had a swimming pool but only the German's was set under a conservatory roof with white-carpeted steps descending to it. He and his wife were handsome enough to play a fighter pilot and his Brunhilde in a war movie. Our own house was colonial, Persian-rugged, gleaming with copper pots and Turkish vases. So our life, you see, was what Pauline, self-mocking and vaguely discontented, called *très chic*. We had no children without trying not to have them, for several years. We had barbecues with our neighbours, and dinner with them in the winter, about once in six weeks. Then Pauline had our first daughter and I became the youngest senior partner on High Street. That covers eight years. Then through the German I met two Malaysian businessmen and moved from the comfortable boredom of divorce briefs and property transactions into exporting. That, you'll remember, was the heyday of kiwifruit. We bought up early in Te Puke which became the world capital for the fruit that looks like a masochist's enema but half the earth was desperate to get its teeth into. I began to travel. First Holland twice a year, where we set up connections, then other countries. And so another five years, another daughter, another house closer to town, but with more land and a pool of our own. Pauline called the children Rachel and Emma. She and the doctor's wife opened a boutique for children's fashions that was called ETs, after Emma and Thomas, the other woman's son. But we weren't shits, Kavanagh, I want to tell him. We didn't try to make quick dirty money when the share market took off. We didn't need to *change* to Labour, like a lot of our friends. Which means, doesn't it, that Emma was four and Rachel nine just after the last election, the very morning after, when Pauline said she was going to live with the German with the white carpet at his poolside and the beautiful wife with the Marlene Dietrich cheekbones who had left, three months before, with one of the doctor's wife's former lovers.

I told that story too to Karen while we walked around the zoo that was famous for not having fences or cages, where concealed electric wires beneath pouring drifts of vine and colourful plants made you think—were meant to make you think—that you saw animals in their natural state, tigers pacing beneath thick-leaved trees, baboons jumping from branch to branch against an open sky. We had said very little up until then about what our lives were like back home. Our talk had been of more neutral things, of beaches, hotels, airlines, public figures we liked or didn't like, music we cared for or couldn't stand. She said they sang 'The Nuns' Chorus' at school and it still made her want to cry. I said Ravel should have been hanged for writing *Bolero*. 'Or made to ice skate,' she said, 'until every bone in his body was broken.'

It's amazing how much there is to talk about beside oneself. Most of it now I remember as a blur, a film as it were run on too fast, those couple of days when I waited for Hawkins to fly in from Jakarta and while Karen, as she said, was filling in time until her sister arrived. But I recall exactly when she did begin to speak of herself. Her saying, as we walked up the steps from the small stadium where the elephants balanced and swayed to the calls of their Sri Lankan trainer, that her first boyfriend spent his varsity holidays as a groundsman at the Auckland Zoo. They would meet for lunch and she could smell the animals on his hands when he touched the outside of her blouse. And then her talking on with far more ease, her hand taking my arm, my hand, as we came by bus back into the city. That same evening as we sat in the absurdly lavish lounge of the Regency Pavilion beneath its vast golden pyramidical vault, its massively kitsch twinkle of falling lights.

'*Enjoy* it,' Karen ordered me. 'Don't disapprove.' The staff in their long dark frocks moving silently between the tables, across the acres of peach carpet while a group of string musicians played Strauss, Lloyd Webber, the seductions of the west.

'I am enjoying it,' I said. 'How couldn't one?' I nodded towards the lifts beaded with lights, glittering fat insects working up and down the building's central shaft.

'You're being a prude,' Karen said. 'You don't mind the mildly rich like yourself living in comfort but you don't like the *very* rich owning whole slices of heaven.'

'You don't?' I said.

She sipped at her drink that reflected a dim circle in her palm. 'I don't have a problem with it,' she said. Then, smiling across at me, 'In fact I love it.'

I said, 'There's no end to it though. Once you start wanting things like this.'

'I'd know when I had enough.' But an edge to her voice as well now, a mocking turned on herself to prevent my thinking, as she said, that she really wanted to be Caligula's wife. Then she said, 'Here's Grapelli now,' looking towards the young Chinese man who imitated the famous sound with solemn accuracy.

After our third drink we took a taxi to hear a group Karen said had to be heard to be believed.

'That good is it?' My arm deliberately brushed the length of her thigh as we settled in the cab.

'That *bad*,' she said. 'A Filipino Elvis this late in the day?' Her deliberately pressing back against my arm. And even after Kavanagh's enlightenment she will stay as the woman I knew at moments like that. And to cover up so brilliantly is not as Kavanagh assumes a reason to loathe her as he would expect me to. Thus he will keep telling me one flaw after another, like a doctor explaining causes for alarm. And always his implication that this isn't all, by Christ, that there is more he will let me in on in time, and more that even he does not yet know. He will ask me, 'Think she cared do you how many died from ODs?' He will stand in the pseudo-Roman landing stage on the island on our last afternoon and tell me, 'If it hadn't suited her you wouldn't have lasted an hour.' He'll say to me in the cable car, 'I suppose you held hands up here at the beauty of the world?' And I will answer him with great pleasure, and total truth, 'No. She asked me though had I ever seen *The Third Man?*'

And Kavanagh will look down the sloping wire as the small sealed cabin runs smoothly as a raindrop from the last great pylon to the green mass of the vegetation and the levelled space of promenades and restaurants, as she and I had looked three days before. Karen and I.

'There's no end to that bitch, is there?' he'll say.

He walked and taxied about the city with me for several days, bringing his questions always back to her, to what she talked about, to what I thought of what she said. I put to him in the bar of the Goodwood Park where the waitresses in Gordon tartans and long white socks went through their colonial charade, I put to him that he needn't keep me company until my flight. 'You know every detail by now.'

'Put it down to liking your company.' He grinned, knowing very well how much I disliked him. Then, as he had done before, he attempted to take us back to school.

'Remember Barker?'

'No,' I said

'Strevens?'

'No.'

'Cutler, then?'

'Who?'

I knew the other two, of course, they had been my year, but I had no urge whatever to reminisce. Cutler I'd only known by sight, a slightly built boy with very pink skin, a year or two ahead of me. I said, 'If he's the one I'm thinking of he must have left before you were in sight.' Kavanagh himself I remembered as ugly and insolent, in the front row in assemblies.

'A skinny prick,' Kavanagh said. 'Wispy yellow hair. Always into some racket. Flogging stuff from Woolworths. Nicking mission money at the back of St Pat's.'

'Were you a cop even then, Kavanagh?'

'Thomas,' he said patiently, 'the whole bloody school knew if you wanted anything badly enough Cutler could get it for you.'

'I must have missed all that.'

'He was thick with Lenihan. The only cobber he had. You know Lenihan's a QC?' His expression flagged me his opinion of him as well.

I said, 'Why do people want to stay at school once they're grown up?' He patted my hand and laughed. Nothing I said could rile him. Yet he would flare up when he spoke of Karen, of 'the racket' as he called it.

'There's nothing illegal in changing your name,' I reminded him.

'Several times?'

'If she likes.'

'Several passports?'

'If she likes.'

'No, Tom,' he said, 'not if she bloody likes, I'm afraid.'

'You're mad because you've nothing on her, is that the trouble?' I knew—I thought I knew—that they would have swooped on her if there was a leg to stand on. She had slipped them simply through their not knowing enough. 'We want to know what she leads to,' Kavanagh said. 'Apart from the bank.'

'Money?' I said.

'More than you can think of, Rothschild.'

'You're raising your voice again,' I said. I put my hand on my forehead as though to shield myself from embarrassment. By then we had both fallen into routines. He simply watched me with disappointment.

When his eyes held mine they seemed ridiculously sincere. Usually they flicked about, across neighbouring tables, over faces as they passed in the street. They held me now, the eyes of an innocent, I thought, a man who wants the world to be more pure than it is. As if he had been saving it for me until now, a card he knew he could beat me with, he took pleasure then in telling me, 'Our old schoolmate, Tom, you know? Cutler? Well that old schoolmate, Tom, had been screwing the pants off her for years. His friends did too when he told her to.'

I believed him because Kavanagh knew so much he never needed to invent. And he knew of course that I didn't want to be told. He let it sink in, how 'the racket' used her at every turn. He said, 'They're bastards, Tom. Everything about them. Total scumbags.' Then, disappointed perhaps that I hadn't immediately gone along with him, he defined her even closer. 'She's big-time, Tom,' he said. 'Is that getting through? I mean, *big*.'

I surprised myself then, amused at his description, his matinée way of phrasing things. I said, 'You've never left the old Cameo in Grey Lynn, Kavanagh. Life's still the Saturday flicks.'

'Look,' he said. His eyes were darting again now, across the waitresses' shallow bosoms, the business-suited men ordering at the bar. It was his moment again to cut me down to size. 'I don't know how I can spell it out more clearly.'

I tried to set myself back from what he would tell me, to make myself attend only to the look of the man across the table from me, his physical grossness, his badly shaven chin, the sparse grey hair above his maroon sports shirt with the crocodile motif. He said, 'As long as she was with you those three days she knew she had a cover. She knew *we'd* be watching her, and then watching you, and that would keep her safe. She was in with a very nasty crowd, see. Mr Big's number was up and she knew a lot they don't want other people to know.' He leaned towards me, his arms folded on the edge of the table. He said, 'There's one thing that doesn't seem to be sinking in. She'd have shagged a leper through those three days to ensure the same thing.'

'So they wouldn't get her?' I asked him.

'So they wouldn't get her,' he confirmed. Then he yawned, showing the mouth packed with fillings, his pink gums. He fished in his shirt pocket for a lozenge.

I asked, politely even, could I in fact be alone for a bit now, even a few hours? Now she was gone he didn't need to spend more time with me, no one was ever molested in Singapore. 'It's the safest city in the world.'

'Afraid not,' he told me. 'We're being watched even now.' He said someone else of course was watching *them*. He loved the schoolboy drama bit.

'But I can't tell you anything you don't know.'

'They don't know that alas. Do they? Where you fit in exactly?' He shook his head at me. He said, 'You need to be *careful*, Tom.'

Yet Karen was even more in my mind, in my affections, if I can put it as grandly as that, since Kavanagh had begun his story. Or should I say pieces of his story, for there often seemed to be no sequence in it, no point it actually led to beyond its telling.

Kavanagh placed several notes beside his glass for the girl in the tartan skirt. 'It's not your job to know the whole story, Thomas my son. Just hold my hand and believe.'

In the beginning she was an encounter in a Somerset Maugham story. She was standing there like an apparition, as they say, when I looked up from the hotel brochure on bus trips to the Malaysian east coast. The dimmed light from the wall-brackets picked up the reddish glints in her hair. Her hands met in front of her on the wide brim of an old-fashioned straw hat. There was a band of navy blue around the hat. She wore a white frock with a billowing skirt, the kind that makes a woman look as though she is trying to be a girl. She looked quickly to her right, towards the lifts, and then her attention returned to the bar whose lighting remained unaltered for twenty-four hours a day. She saw me looking across at her. She walked directly towards me. She placed her hat on the marble-topped table and sat beside me on the leather couch. As one hand fingered the ribbon-ends of her hat, she looked directly at me. In a careful voice, as though she might have spoken to a foreigner, she said, 'In a moment I am going to kiss you on the mouth and you are not to look surprised.' Then she put one hand on my arm, and her other she rested on top of mine. Her palm was damp with perspiration. My only thought for the moment was how disagreeable it felt. Then she brought her face against mine. She turned slightly to make our kissing more visible to anyone looking from the entrance where she had stood a few moments before, where a figure now paused, a shape merely at the edge of my vision. We kissed perhaps for thirty seconds. I tasted the thin film of sweat on her upper lip and felt the heat of her cheek against mine. Her fingers pressed firmly on my hand as though to encourage me not to break the embrace. Her dress I noticed was not white so much as cream, matching the light straw of the hat. And I felt as well the warmth of her thigh along my own, before she sat back, the figure at the doorway already gone. She then looked at me and said, 'I'd better buy you a drink I suppose to say thank you for all that?'

The Malay waitress was at the table before the sentence was finished, placing coasters and a dish of cashews before us. The woman ordered without my being asked what I'd like. Two beers, she told the waitress, two long beers.

She held out her hand with surprising formality. 'I'm Karen Blainey.'

I said, 'I've a feeling we've met already.'

She said simply, 'It was quite important I avoided someone just then.' Then she said, 'Whew!' like a schoolgirl, leaning back against the dark leather behind her. She fanned her face with the broad straw hat.

Then she said, looking at me, taking me in, 'Thank you for that.'

'What would have happened if he'd seen you?'

She pouted like a child. 'He'd have made a scene.'

And that, Kavanagh will tell me, was the first dumb thing about me, believing her when she said that. As if he'd not been watching her for half the day as it was. It wasn't Houdini he was trailing, he said, it was just a dealer's little moll suddenly out of her depth. Of course she knew he'd seen her. She had wanted him to. 'But she thought I wouldn't know you, that was the point of it. She hadn't reckoned on the old school network, eh?' He laughed as though he had said something particularly witty.

As he spoke he was visually pawing the woman at the edge of the pool. 'She thought she'd waste our time finding out who you were, you see. That we'd think you were a lead we hadn't followed up.'

For the one time, I think, in the hours and days he quizzed me, a mild glance of commiseration came into his face. 'Look,' he consoled me, 'you're dealing with an expert. A pro. A top-rung slag. You don't have to make like you've lost Marie Antoinette.'

He suddenly pointed to the woman at the edge of the pool, her tanned knees pulled up beneath her chin. A girl of four or five had run up to her, a towel around her shoulders to make a flowing cape. Kavanagh observed, 'Lovely woman, wouldn't you say?' And pausing for a moment, he said, 'The house detective told me she's using a stolen American Express card.' Then after a much longer pause, 'You simply never know do you? That's all I'm saying.'

And I felt an intense pleasure that I might have done something at least to help Karen get away from Kavanagh and whatever brand of justice he fancied he served. He may have picked something of that up. He said, 'We will continue pursuing our enquiries, as we say, regarding several million dollars.'

'I don't believe you,' I said.

'Oh, not *stolen* them,' he said. 'She'd never sink to *ordinary* crime.' He made a face that took offence at the very thought. 'She's high class, our Karen. Private school. Like your wife, remember?'

On the second day we stood in a street where paraphernalia was sold by the Chinese merchants who provided for the dead, the replica treasures that could be conveyed to the lovers, the parents, the children who presumably still yearned for solid comforts in their shadowy world. I had never heard of either the belief or those who provided for it.

'There's a shop I knew in KL,' Karen said, 'that makes you fake cheque books, credit cards, gold bars. You can get anything there you'd ever want.'

'Passports?' I said.

'You can get life-size paper Filipino maids so I expect he could manage passports as well. I don't think much of his trade came from tourists.'

'Sounds like a party shop for grown-ups.'

She said, 'You've got to think of it as a lot more real than that. If you don't believe in it there's no point getting the stuff.'

I imagined piles of cheque books, stacks of currency, brightly convincing plastic cards, lasting forever while the dead beside them crumbled away.

'They *burn* them, you absurd man,' Karen explained. 'That's why it's all paper.' Then she was crying. The only time.

I looked at her but I didn't ask her why she cried. There wasn't even much sympathy in what I thought. But that grieving moment is as sexual at times as one is likely to get. I know it is not even very agreeable to say that, but men know it's a fact. There is seldom a time when you will ever want a woman more than when you see her cry for what you don't understand. (I wonder what Kavanagh would whistle to that?)

And the opposite, too. At times the distaste when a woman laughs. In that church, when she lit her candle, then mocked what she had done. For those minutes I disliked her very much, her answer scraping against something I could not define. And yet leaving the church, in the quiet space between the side of the building and the quick returning smear of jungle, in the fumes of traffic and beneath the noise of commerce against a gathering storm, I touched her breast for the first time and drew her against me.

'Right here?'

'Right now.'

She said, 'I owe you one, don't I?' And she let me kiss her, without pretence.

Kavanagh said, 'Could we go over it again then?'

I said, 'I can't very well stop you, can I?'

He lit a fresh cigarette from the one he was holding. He then let it lie there in the corner of his mouth, the smoke clouding about him, as I suppose he must have seen a hundred sleazy cops doing in the crap TV he no doubt believed was life.

'You hadn't met her, you say, until that night?' He flipped as all cops do at his pocket-sized pad with an airline logo stamped on its fake suede cover.

I said, 'Doesn't the sheer boredom of this get you down at times?'

He repeated what he had asked. 'You hadn't met her before?'

I sighed as though I too could only do what the role expected. I said, 'I'd never so much as heard of her, I've told you that. That's the third time if you check your notes.'

We sat in the garden at Raffles which Karen and I had planned to visit every day and had never got to, which may have made the story Kavanagh wanted less exciting than I could offer. There were no gin slings in the Karen story. No Writers' Bar. No shades of Noel Coward pursuing the trim arses of the East.

In the heavy filtered sunlight Kavanagh looked a good ten years older than he was, which was five years younger than myself. I had heard some time in the sixties that he was in an accident. I'd forgotten it, and then remembered when I saw the skin beneath his chin, an inch-wide flare a different colour from the rest of him, that ran down his neck to the top of his lime-green T-shirt.

I said to him after he ordered and we sat back in the white cane chairs, drinking in the last jewel of the Brits, the fan palms, the hibiscus, the colonnades and the latticed windows, 'That in the cause of duty too then, was it?' I tapped my own chin then ran my finger down my throat. I enjoyed provoking him. But he didn't rise to that either. He took up one of the frosted glasses the waiter had placed on the table between us and raised it towards me, a wordless 'cheers'. He said, 'I never heard the full story either about Pauline Harkness taking off with some kind of Kraut.' My one-time wife was head girl at St Mary's, the captain of their champion netball team, when Kavanagh was in the third form. He broke into his quick raucous guffaw. He said, 'Murdoch used to say he nearly went blind beating his meat over her, remember?'

'Murdoch was just one of those little shits like yourself Kavanagh,' I said. 'I could never distinguish one of you from the other.'

But nothing hurt Kavanagh, nothing put him off. He veered back like a man with an obsession. He said, 'Next thing you didn't know Cutler, I suppose?'

'I haven't seen Cutler since school. I haven't even heard of him.'

'I haven't seen you since school either,' Kavanagh said.

We both sat there then in silence, watching a group of tourists calling to each other that they were in the right bar. 'Tigers all round?' one of them asked from the step. While Kavanagh's head turned, keeping in view a tall dark woman in a white swimsuit who crossed the lawn. He turned back to me and said, 'It could be true like you say Tom, but the kiss bit does make it hard to believe.'

'I explained about that too,' I said. 'Until I'm sick of it.'

Then as though content to let go of that one, 'Milk biscuits, Tom,' he said. 'How long have you been in milk biscuits? Can we recap on that one?' And again, later, 'What did she talk about, can you give me that again? She must have said something in three days together.'

Karen was what my mother used to call a mine of useless information. A year later I can still think of a list of things she told me that I had never heard of and that it makes not the least difference that I now happen to know. That dogs sweat through their tongues, for example. Her telling me that on a corner in Pagoda Street, above a mud-coloured dog peering into a storm drain, its breathing bronchial and shallow. Or that corn oil did less harm to your body than other kinds people normally used. Her explaining why this was so as we lay in my room on the adjoining king-size beds, wide enough I said to play tennis on apart from anything else. We watched the television picture but had the Chinese sound turned down. A woman talked about the food while a small middle-aged man did the stirring and flipping about with a long wooden stick. Other things too she told me. That Frank Lloyd Wright's mistress and children were murdered by a mad servant in a house called Taliesen, which is Welsh for Shining Bow; that the figure with all the arms was Shiva, who destroys the world continually not out of malice or rage but to ensure new creation, a world that is fresh, over and over.

I asked her, 'Were you into quizzes when you were young?'

'What?' She had pointed to Shiva on the roof of a temple we walked towards in thick mid-afternoon heat. She told me as we crossed from the sun into the strip of shadow beneath the high wall, and then stepped into a broad bright space where the low surrounding buildings held the same reflecting shimmer as the sanded courtyard.

'You know all these bits and pieces as if you've swotted them up.'

We were slipping off our shoes at a wooden rack inside the temple's ornate entrance. The only other tourist was a tall man in a safari suit who waited until we had moved from the rack to reclaim his sandals.

She said, 'I used to be a journalist for a bit. Things stick the way things do to magnets. You can't help it.'

In the temple courtyard there were alcoves and recesses with steel mesh let down in front of them and inside, almost too dark to see when you first looked away from the glare, the brightly painted statues with bowls of dried flowers placed before them, and the ash from incense sticks fallen to the floor. But there were other figures too that weren't sealed off, that stood in well-lit rooms like chapels, life-size and crude as children's drawings. There were framed accounts of where they fitted into the Hindu faith.

I said, 'You'd need a week to work out who's actually who.' A human figure with an elephant trunk, another that could have been male or female, its face painted blue, a sword in its hand. Others with cobras spread behind them like high fancy collars.

'It's all God anyway,' she said. 'Different names for the same thing.'

'Which is?'

'Any of them. You pick the one you like best and forget about the others. It's like choosing one door into a room that's got twenty other doors as well. They all lead through to the same place.'

'There must be a boss?' I said. 'A top god?'

'They all are, once you get there.'

'I don't get the hang of that,' I said.

'There's God or there isn't,' she said. 'If there is then every part of him's just as real as any other.' The elephant head, she meant, or the blue face with the bulging eyes.

The next day in a Catholic church, a building with opened sides so there was a sense of expansive coolness about it, she lit a candle in front of a different kind of statue. And I said did she believe in God then? Still believe in all that? She turned from the bank of burning candles and said loudly enough for someone further down the church to turn and look at us, 'Piss off, will you! Do you think I'm out of my tree?'

Even a thing like that, you see, even God, she obviously had two views on. I heard her talk about it only twice, in the temple and then in the church, and I don't believe that in either she was necessarily lying.

So, 'Yes,' I said, when Kavanagh placed one by one the photographs on the desk, 'why on earth shouldn't she?' Yes for the close-cropped fair-haired woman taken when she was unaware that someone photographed her; yes for the dark fuller face who looked directly at the lens. What was his problem, I asked him, why was he trying to make her into just one thing? I said did he know what she looked like even until he saw her—saw me—in the bar that day?

Kavanagh was irritated at that. He said, 'As if I wouldn't have seen her just because she's pashing up the first man she can grab. It can't have been because I wouldn't recognise her, right? With all these photos, for one thing?'

I said, 'She's not so stupid that you've caught up with her yet.'

He swung back to me, his sunglasses smudged with fingerprints from his constantly prodding them higher on the bridge of his nose. I thought how there was not a thing about the man that didn't make me loathe him. His stained teeth. His scar. His ridiculous bulging eyes when he removed the glasses. 'Have you got a wife, Kavanagh?' I asked him. I simply could not imagine what kind of woman would abide him.

'Yes,' he said. 'But I managed to keep mine.' He beckoned across to the uniformed boy who stood with his tray in front of him as Karen had stood at first in the doorway holding her wide-brimmed hat. 'Another two,' he said. And to me, 'Where were we with Vodanovich?'

Irene Vodanovich of Surrey Crescent, Grey Lynn. He already had spelled it out to me. Although he had told me too that she called herself Lucy O'Connor, Fay MacKenzie, Rachel Levy. Not to speak of Karen. 'She might be a crook,' he said, 'but she's not a racist.' He thought his remark amusing enough to follow up. 'Irish. Jewish. Scots. A good Dally girl like her?'

I asked him if she had ever called herself Mrs Cutler.

'She's a bitch,' Kavanagh said, 'but she's not a total moron.' Snapping it at me as if this were something I needed to be reminded of.

I knew, I'd heard it before we met up, that Kavanagh must be good at what he did, at imposing his version of law on a delinquent world that would never come to heel; how it angered him that crime and deception ran riot not only against regulation but what he took for logical, decent behaviour. There had been an article about him in a Sunday paper. He'd broken up some ring. He was photographed behind a desk in a Fair Isle sweater.

I couldn't look at Kavanagh nor listen to his voice without thinking of muddied shorts and pungent farts, the wet floors of changing sheds and a coach ranting at us as though our futures, our right to live, depended on how we performed in a paddock of winter rain. It was the side of school that I hated most. The first time Kavanagh spoke about rugby, asking me had I seen the school's first fifteen came out on top for the second year in succession, I thought the man retarded, a fragment of outdated national psyche running loose round Asia. I hated too that anyone watching us on the lawn, in this dated set piece of opulence, might think us one of a kind, that I shared nationality and God knows what else with this lozenge-sucking cop. And that *he* was civilised life and Karen the outlaw, the destroyer! 'I'd eliminate her, Tom,' he would say to me on the cable car to Santosa a few hours before my flight. 'Given the chance.'

Yet only at the airport, almost at the last minute as they say, it clicked that he had been with me for the last forty-eight hours not to discover anything about Karen that he didn't know, but to prevent something happening to me. He said when we were almost at my gateway, after walking past the enticements of duty free shops, the fashion names, the stalls of batik and masks, 'Just don't come back now without letting us know about it will you, Tom? They might still want to put you away. You know. For good?'

The transparent disc of his lozenge visible there on his tongue as his mouth pulled back in a grin.

'Who might?' I said.

Kavanagh gave the melodramatic sigh of a parent explaining to a child yet again. He checked the point he was making with a forefinger against the outspread fingers of his other hand. 'One of the biggest ladies in the business spends three days with you at the very moment her loved one's in oh but *real* trouble. Now, no one gives a stuff whether you played chess together or fed her a length twenty-four hours a day. Point is *you* were the one she was with, got that? *You* were the one they'll assume she wanted to tell things to and you're the one they'd like to talk to now, boyo, believe me. Not that Dutchman in the temple who's continents away by now. He's the man with the lists, the bank codes, all the stuff they'd like to know. But only we know that don't we, Tom? *They* don't.'

'The Dutchman?'

'That tall dude in the plantation owner's get-up? Day at the temple? Size eleven sandals, can you imagine what that implies elsewhere anatomically?' He panted and gave a purring noise at the thought of it.

'In the temple?' I said.

'Got it in ten,' Kavanagh complimented drily. 'A roll of film,' he said, 'that's all it took, slipped into her empty shoe while you gawped at heathen gods. The Dutchman waited until you walked away and picked it up. They can do things very simply, that's part of the fun at this game. It's Moscow rules with this lot, Smiley.'

He watched to see if Karen's game was coming home to me. I felt as I did across the breakfast table three years ago when Pauline, pouring tea into my cup in her last moments as suburban wife, explained that the world I believed was stable was about to fragment.

'You're not even Mr Small in this story, are you?' Kavanagh commiserated. 'You're Mr Almost Bloody Invisible.'

We were at the departure gate, the light already flickering for Flight SQ288. His head jerked towards a Malay in a business suit, engaged with a folder of computer printouts.

'Sammy's spent three days watching *us*,' he said, cleaning it all up, wanting me to know it only now, at the last minute. 'Sammy's very professional. The hours that boy's put in this week. Raffles. Sentosa. One shit-house golden dome after another. Of course he looks the same doesn't he as the rest of them do? Take them anywhere, that's the advantage with Asians. I knew you'd never spot him.' He glanced across at him again. He said with mock sentimentality, 'I wouldn't feel quite safe with anyone else. That's how much Sammy means.'

'Fuck off will you, Kavanagh?' I asked him. But it was hardly anger. I was merely tired of everything to do with him, with this city I'd be away from within thirty minutes.

'If only it was that easy, old mate.' Kavanagh said. He put his hand in the middle of my back, a gesture of assurance but also I expect one of dismissal, urging me towards the gate. 'It's like I said, Tom,' he told me again. 'We ought to keep out of Asia, our lot. They're too old to play with schoolboys.'

Sentosa is the word for Peace. The brochures in the hotel lobbies will tell you Sentosa is also a treasure-trove for the tourist and the holiday maker, a repository of history, an assured delight for young and old. There are beaches (not very good ones) beside jewel-bright bushes and tropical growth, eating places to ravish the palate, a coralanium, a waxworks, aquaria and a museum of animated history where you can see the war-clips of Singapore under attack, of the island's surrender, of small men in shapeless uniforms marching tall handsome Englishmen to compounds of shame and starvation. Karen recited dates and figures as though she were reading it from a book.

How did it happen, I asked her, that she knew all this crap?

'You must have known stuff like that about tamarillos? About kiwifruit?'

I said, 'I paid people for it. I wouldn't have known where to begin.'

'I told you, didn't I, I was a journalist years back? Well I was fibbing there a bit, I'm afraid.'

'So?' I said.

'I mean it was only little articles, human interest interviews, writing up reports. It wasn't the real thing.'

'So?' I said again. I tapped her hand, making a game of what she regretted having to say.

'I was bloody awful actually. I mean I was good at being bloody awful. I wrote stuff like that very well. PR promotions was what we called it.'

'It would still be beyond me.'

'It paid. You can say that for it.' And Kavanagh of course will tell me later that it was Cutler's cover, Asian-Pacific Promotions which meant offices in Bangkok, in KL, in Brisbane. He'll enjoy telling me how our pale schoolmate with his pockets stuffed with stolen Woolworths pencil-sharpeners and Mickey Mouse rubbers went on to greater things, how among much else he picked up this not very bright floozie (Kavanagh loves words like that) who wrote tenth-rate copy for one of his fronts, and then, 'Pow, Buster, there was love as big as the Ritz.' Kavanagh popping one of his eucalyptus lozenges into his mouth, sucking on it as he wonders how I respond.

'Then I met Robbie,' Karen said. 'He saved me from a prose worse than death.' And a strange look, a quick movement of her cheek muscles, as though something bitter had caught in her mouth. But the little train we were sitting in, that ran on its fun circuit of the island, stopped at the station where you stepped out to see the waxworks, and our talk drifted off to something else, some other segment of her life. For most of what I know of her, most anyway of what and how she decided to tell me, came to me on those few acres of plastic and blaring music, cooking smells and plaster mock-ups and Singaporeans earnestly enjoying themselves, is in images rather than facts. The flood for instance when she and her lover walked one morning from their bedroom onto the balcony of an apartment in St Lucia and saw the Brisbane River level with the balcony, and a floating harpsichord turning very gently, slowly, in the brown growling sheet of water. There is always, she told me, always some detail to hold on to. She said she had once seen a man open the door on the Auckland–Wellington express and step out with no more fuss than if the train were stationary and the platform there beside him. She said that when the cord was pulled and people ran back along the track with torches the man was just sitting in a kind of bush, rubbing his ankle. Imagine she said how dreadful it would be to make a hash of simply everything. She told me the sister she was going to meet had been a stripper for six months and although men masturbated while they watched she said no one seemed to mind but if they said even a mildly suggestive word they were dragged out and thumped in the lane beside the theatre by a Tongan bouncer. 'My sister said she never really appreciated until then that it doesn't finally matter what we do so much as how we say it.' Her sister had a daughter now at a private school and a computer-software husband who didn't approve of her walking as far as the bathroom with nothing on.

Karen's stories were quick, and frequent, and sometimes I missed their point. Few of them were really about herself, apart from those few facts she came back to—the sister she would meet up with in a couple of days; her departed lover. I remember the songs she would start on, humming them, singing them quietly, when our talk tailed off and we would sit, walk, side by side. There was an ease Kavanagh could never click to. 'Can't you *see* how she took you in?' His anger that whatever he revealed to me mattered far more to him. *Smoke gets in your eyes*, she hummed as we sat in the little train, *Dinner for one, please James*, as we swung back across the narrow strip of water between the island and the city. They were the tunes of pianists among potted palms in the corners of hotel lounges, the songs middle-aged tourists expect in the glitzy bars. And *Abide with Me*, scarcely loud enough for me to hear, as we walked from the church where she lit the candle, after her quick obscene dismissal that lighting it could mean anything important. Kavanagh seemed especially to resent the church bit. 'She's the kind of woman who raises pure shit to an art form. What a lucky man you are to have seen it so close.'

'You're oversimplifying,' I tell him.

'Her greatest gift was contempt for others,' Kavanagh will come back. 'Nothing's simpler than that.'

When she turned to me on the bed, back in the hotel, and we began to kiss, her fingers at my shirt, my belt, after our two days of wandering about this city that is like a film set, when she did that, her lips not moving from mine, her hand lightly taking my wrist, directing me, I knew whatever it was on her part it was at least something like love on mine. And I told Kavanagh when he asked me, in the line of duty, had I got a leg across, had she at least turned it up for the trouble she put me to, I told him, 'What we did actually Kavanagh was *make love*. Can I spell it for you?' And in the only way he knew, he tried then to throw me with his trump card. 'Christ!' he says, 'Cutler was fucken Crittenden, you fool! *Crittenden!*' The blurred quickly turning head in the front-page photo, the only photo they had of him, I'd seen a dozen times in the last three days, and had not linked up. The pale, straw-haired leader of the group that hung about the brick dunnies beside the handball courts, the fag-suckers, the swoppers of magazines, the bait prefects fed on when it came to handing out detentions. I don't think I had ever spoken to him.

I feel the numbness, of course, the final click of the kaleidoscope that sets the last few days into the frieze that will never change. A moment of illumination, as her journalist soul would call it, with Karen there in marvellous clarity, everything brilliant and suddenly explained. No stories that might be true because truth had passed quite beyond where she now was, or ever likely to be. Karen become a mask that would not lift off, that was her own skin when she touched it, the pure animal become its camouflage. I saw her trapped and cornered and brave and cunning and extreme. I saw her as pure and intense survival, a flame where everything else was burned to ash. And Kavanagh watching me, waiting, wanting my compliance now at least in placing her, as he did, as liar and criminal and bitch. And after a moment, 'As if that matters.' That is all I managed to say.

And Kavanagh closed his eyes, as if this, my accepting it like this, was the final thing he could not take in. In fact, that is what he said. 'I do not believe it,' he said. 'I simply do not believe it.'

When I woke I didn't recall for one quick drifting moment that there was anyone with me in the hotel room. Then I heard the rasp, the soft igniting of a match.

She was sitting in the salmon coloured armchair, looking across the early city.

I lifted my arm to catch the time.

She said without turning towards me, 'That must be the north, mustn't it?' She meant across the park beneath us, the rash of rain-trees and casuarinas far too intensely green, to my eye anyway, to be attractive as we're supposed to think, as the hotel management obviously thought them too with its postcards of white towering comfort above hectic colour.

I stepped from the bed and stood beside her. I supposed her hand might touch my leg, her head incline towards me. But I might merely have been a tour guide, or one of the hotel staff, as she asked me again, 'Isn't that the north?'

The sky was a dull greyish wash, the big office blocks harder and firmer chunks of the same drabness. It was hard to imagine that behind this slow leaching of the night the sun might be rising.

'Isn't it?'

'I've no idea,' I said.

'I think it must be,' she said. Her cigarette glowed as she drew on it.

I went to the bathroom, a flash of chrome plating and marble surfaces as I touched the light and turned on the shower.

Whether I'm in the room with her or not, I thought, it's much the same to her.

After coffee in the 'Carousel' cafeteria on the first floor we walked the stretch of park beside the hotel. She snapped a creamy clump of frangipani from one of the trees and held it against her cheek.

'You know what this flower is,' she said, 'for the Chinese?'

I told her, 'I haven't the least idea.'

So I asked Kavanagh that, the closest he came in fact to whatever it was between Karen and myself, between Lucy, Fay, Rachel, Irene, and myself. I said, 'On the last morning she asked me about frangipani before she shot through. She said did I know what that flower was for the Chinese.'

'The last morning?' Kavanagh repeated.

I told him, 'Just before she left.'

'It's the death flower, old cock,' he said. 'It's what you use for the dead.' For four hundred miles away in Penang, almost to the hour.